THE *Regency* COLLECTION

VOLUME

—5—

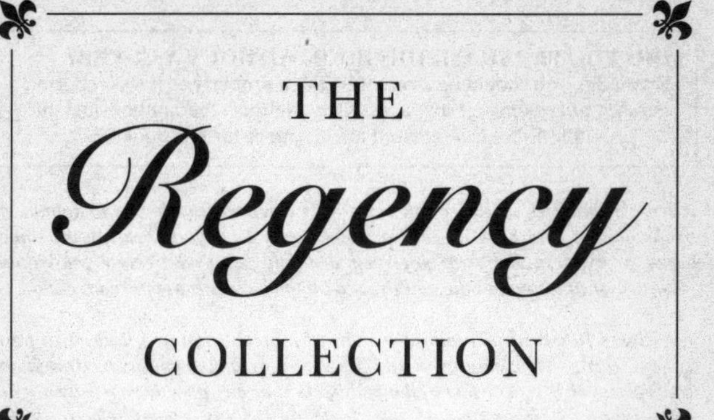

VOLUME
—5—

My Lady Love

by

Paula Marshall

Four in Hand

by

Stephanie Laurens

All the characters in this book have no existence outside the imagination of the author, and have no relation whatsoever to anyone bearing the same name or names. They are not even distantly inspired by any individual known or unknown to the author, and all the incidents are pure invention.

First published in Great Britain 1999 by
Harlequin Mills & Boon Limited,
Eton House, 18–24 Paradise Road,
Richmond, Surrey, TW9 1SR.

ISBN 0 263 81711 3
106-9909

Printed and bound in Spain
by Litografia Rosés S.A., Barcelona

MY LADY LOVE

by

Paula Marshall

Dear Reader

When I began to write historical romances for Mills & Boon®, I chose the Regency period for several reasons. I had always enjoyed Georgette Heyer's novels – still among the best – and had spent part of my youth working at Newstead Abbey, the home of Lord Byron, one of the Regency's most colourful characters. It involved me in reading many of the original letters and papers of a dynamic era in English history.

Later on when I researched even further into the period I discovered that nothing I could invent was more exciting – or outrageous – than what had actually happened! What more natural, then, than to write a Regency romance and send it to Mills & Boon – who accepted it and started me on a new career.

Like Georgette Heyer I try to create fiction out of and around fact for the enjoyment and entertainment of myself and my readers. It is often forgotten that the Regency men had equally powerful wives, mothers and sisters – even if they had no public role – so I make my heroines able to match my heroes in their wit and courage.

Paula Marshall

Paula Marshall, married with three children, has had a varied and interesting life. She began her career in a large library and ended it as a senior academic in charge of history teaching in a polytechnic. She has travelled widely, has been a swimming coach, embroiders, paints pictures and has appeared on *University Challenge* and *Mastermind*. She has always wanted to write, and likes her novels to be full of adventure and humour.

Other titles by the same author:

Cousin Harry
An Improper Duenna
The Falcon and the Dove
Wild Justice*
An American Princess*
An Unexpected Passion
The Cyprian's Sister
The Captain's Lady**
Touch the Fire**
The Moon Shines Bright**
Reasons of the Heart+
The Astrologer's Daughter
Dear Lady Disdain
Not Quite a Gentleman
The Lost Princess
A Biddable Girl?
Emma and the Earl
An Affair of Honour**
Lady Clairval's Marriage+
The Youngest Miss Ashe
The Beckoning Dream
The Deserted Bride
Rebecca's Rogue
The Wayward Heart**
The Devil and Drusilla
The Wolfe's Mate++
Miss Jesmond's Heir++

* linked
** Schuyler Family saga
+ linked
++ linked

CHAPTER ONE

'WHAT can have possessed you, Shad, to behave as you did? So unlike yourself! Last night's excesses at Watier's were the outside of enough. And in front of Cousin Trenchard, too. Shad! Are you listening to me, Shad? You can't still be drunk at four in the afternoon!'

Charles Augustus Shadwell, Viscount Halstead, heir to the third Earl Clermont, always known as Shad since he had been a captain in the cavalry in Wellington's Army—now, in 1818, five years out of it—tried to sit up. He failed. His head, and the room, were still spinning round. His mouth tasted like the bottom of a parrot's cage, and his stomach. . .!

'Do you have to make so much noise?' he groaned at his younger brother Guy.

'Noise!' said Guy indignantly. 'And I thought you never drank, not since the army anyway. What on earth possessed you?' he repeated. 'It's all round the town this morning, and Cousin Trenchard, trust him, has already been to Faa and spun him the yarn.'

'What yarn?' ground out Shad, who had sat up on the bed, to discover that he had fallen into a drunken stupor, still clad in last night's clothes. 'And why are you ringing such a peal over me? And, for God's sake, Guy, as you love me, don't draw the curtains. I feel bad enough in the dark, but the light——'

'Oh, damn that,' roared Guy, and pulled the curtains violently open, to reveal the elder brother whom he had always worshipped, haggard and drawn, his clothes disgustingly soiled, sitting on the edge of the bed, his head in his hands.

Guy's disillusionment was complete. He said so.

Shad tried to remember what he had said or done the night before to cause Guy to behave in such an uncharacteristic fashion—he was usually respectful to his brother. The last thing that he remembered was flinging out of Julia Merton's home in Albemarle Street, yesterday afternoon, head on fire, anger and disgust choking him to such a degree that he was almost outside of himself.

And then he must have got blind drunk, and done something appalling to justify the brouhaha which Guy said that he had created. Only. . .he could not remember anything. All that had passed since he had banged Julia's drawing-room door behind him had vanished from his memory as though it had never happened.

Guy, his frank young face drawn with grief and disappointment, was still ranting on, 'And Faa wants to see you immediately. Good God, Shad, why did you have to do this, just as you and the old man had started to get on reasonably well together? And what about Julia? What will she think when the news reaches her?'

'I don't give a good Goddam what Julia thinks about anything,' said Shad inelegantly, rising to his feet and staggering towards the long pier-glass which stood in the corner of his bedroom.

He shuddered at the figure which he saw there. His face was a harsh one, strong and craggy, but it was not normally tinged principally with yellow and purple. His jet-black hair fell in wildly disarranged ringlets, and his deep blue eyes were red-rimmed and blood-shot. A face to frighten women and children.

Well, the more women he frightened the better. He

had attracted too many of them over the years, and all of them whores at heart—Julia, God help him, being the latest.

Guy was still reproaching him. 'Oh, do give over,' he said at last, and reeled to the washstand, plunging his head into the bowl of cold water which stood there—it might help—and with his head under water he could avoid hearing Guy.

He surfaced, water dripping from him, and turned to face his brother.

'At least have the goodness to tell me what it is I did, or am said to have done.'

'Oh, you said it, no doubt of that,' announced Guy bitterly. 'I was there. Who was it who hauled you home, do you think, and stopped Nell Tallboys's cousin from killing you on the spot?'

'Well, thank you for that,' ground out Shad, and, face wicked, he launched his full thirteen and a half stone, six-foot-one frame at Guy, and seized him by the throat. 'Now, will you tell me what I did? Or do I have to beat it out of you? If I am to be so madly abused, at least let me know what for.'

'You mean you really don't know?' gasped Guy, as Shad released him. 'Oh, pax, pax,' he began hurriedly. 'You came into Watier's, half-foxed already, barely on your feet, began to gamble like a madman, and then. . .'

'Oh, God,' groaned Shad, collapsing on to the bed. 'Enough, Guy. I remember everything. Would that I didn't.'

'Well, that's a relief,' said Guy sturdily. He walked over to the jug on the washstand, poured water into a glass and handed it to his brother. 'Here, drink this. It will make you feel better.'

'Nothing will ever make me feel better,' muttered Shad, looking up at Guy, and feeling sorry for causing his brother's evident distress. Guy at nineteen was eleven years younger than Shad and had always hero-worshipped him. Perhaps, Shad had often thought, because they were so different, Guy being blond, slim and rather diffident; he took after his dead mother, and Shad after their father.

'Here, let me ring for Carter,' said Guy. 'If you're going to visit Faa, you'd better spruce yourself up. You look like an unmade bed at the minute.'

Shad let Guy order him about. It seemed the least that he could do for the brother who, whatever else, had always loved him and stood up for him.

Later, he waited outside his father's suite of rooms in Clermont House, the Shadwell family's London home. Colquhoun, his father's secretary, had told him, a grieving look on his old face, 'My lord will see you shortly; he is at his business at the moment.'

The business of making Viscount Halstead wait, no doubt, thought Shad bitterly. Well, closing his eyes, and remembering yesterday, he thought it was no less than he deserved. Nor was he surprised, when Mr Colquhoun finally summoned him in, to discover his father, standing stern and tall before his desk, over which hung Romney's famous portrait of Shad's dead mother.

'So, you are at last up, Halstead. Is this true, what Cousin Trenchard tells me?'

'Seeing that I don't know what Cousin Trenchard told you, sir, it is difficult to say.'

'Come, Halstead, don't chop logic with me—this scene at Watier's. Making shameful bets and brawling with the cousin of the subject of them is hardly the conduct of the man who is my heir.'

Shad's control, insecure since yesterday, broke. He made no effort to defend himself—he could not—merely replied bitterly, 'I have never ceased to regret, sir, the day that I became your heir. Oh, I have tried, God knows how hard, to fill Frederick's place for you, but in your eyes I shall never be Frederick's equal. He was your. . .nonpareil.'

'Which you, sir, are most definitely not!'

'Yes,' said Shad, feeling that he must defend himself a little, after all. 'His untimely death deprived me not only of a brother whom I had no wish to succeed, but also of a career in the army, which I not only loved, but in which I was beginning to excel. Remember that.'

'Come, come, sir,' snapped the Earl. 'My heir could not remain in the army, and, in any case, the wars are over now. You were needed to learn to run the estate, to take over from Frederick in every way.'

'Which I have tried to do,' retorted Shad steadily. 'You can have no grounds for complaint on that score. Green has told you not only of my application, but of my innovations at Pinfold. Only I can never be Frederick, and that is the true ground of the division between us. The only time, sir, when we were not at odds was when I was away at the wars.'

If the Earl thought that there was any truth in this bitter statement, he gave no sign of it. His dislike for his second son was plain on his face.

'You were always a wild boy, Halstead, and became a wild man. Your marriage to Isabella French, against all my wishes—and look what that led to! Your——'

'Spare me,' said Shad, his face white beneath the jaundiced shadow of his last night's debauch, 'I paid for that, God knows, and in the five years since Frederick's death I have lived an exemplary life, and done your bidding faithfully. Why should last night's work, which I regret more than you can ever do, cause you to cut me up so severely? One failure after so long. . .'

'Because, sir, I have been in the country discussing with her uncle, Chesney Beaumont, her mother's brother, an alliance with the very lady, Elinor Tallboys, Countess of Malplaquet, whose name you soiled last night in your drunken folly. We had reached terms. He is to broach your marriage with her today, in her Yorkshire fastness, and I was to speak to you this very morning, when, instead, you lay in your drunken stupor.'

Shad, composure gone for once, gaped at him. 'Do I hear you aright, sir? You were arranging for me to offer for Nell Tallboys—Nell Tallboys!—without so much as a word to me beforehand. You expected me to marry *her*, at your simple word of command!'

'My mistake,' replied his father coldly. 'I had thought you almost Frederick, who saw my wishes as his command. I cannot imagine him refusing such a noble prize, so suitable an alliance. You would be... would have been...the richest man in England.'

Shad's laugh was almost a shriek, or a curse. 'And that's it, sir? That is to be my end? No arguing, agree, or cut line, is it? You knew that I was involved with Julia Merton, intended to marry her...until yesterday, that is,' he amended with a shudder.

'Oh, that was never on, sir, never on,' shrugged his father. 'One more proof that you have not yet rid yourself of your youthful follies. A steady marriage with a steady woman is what you require to settle you, but now... I wonder what the Countess of Malplaquet would think of a proposal from a man who threw her name about in a gaming house? Why did you choose that woman to slight, sir, why?'

What could he say that would not make matters worse than they already were? Only, in his chagrin and, yes, shame, at his conduct yesterday, the more because he had always prided himself on his iron self-control, he muttered stiffly, 'But Nell Tallboys, a plain bluestocking, past her last prayers, with a face to frighten horses, they say, and a virtue so rigid that any man is rendered ice by it, and her very reputation caused me to lose mine last night.'

He stopped at last; his mixed anger and shame had caused him to make matters worse, not better.

'Yes,' said his father glacially. 'Cousin Trenchard said that you bet an enormous sum—twenty thousand pounds, was it not?—that no woman was virtuous, and that even that paragon would succumb to your wishes without marriage, should you care to try her.'

Oh, God forgive him that he had said any such thing. Was it her cousin Bobus Beaumont's high-minded praise of her which, while he was smarting from his second cruel betrayal by a woman whom he thought had loved him, had caused his drunken self to behave so badly?

'Lightskirts all,' he remembered roaring. 'Damned mermaids, even the best of them.'

'You may well look ashamed, Halstead.' His father's voice was so distant, so cold, the dislike which he had always felt for this second son, unworthy successor—as he saw it—to his beloved Frederick, was so plain in his voice that Shad's shuddering, brought on partly by last night's drinking after years of abstinence, increased.

'And now you have the task of trying to mend matters. All may not be lost. Before this news reaches her, I shall use my influence to suppress this latest folly, while you, sir, must go north, to offer for her. An honourable proposal must wipe out what was said. Idle and jealous gossip will explain all.'

Shad stared dumbly at his father. 'Are you light in the head, sir? What can wipe that out? And besides I have no wish to marry Nell Tallboys, would never offer for her, would never have her if she was handed me on a plate. Nor do I wish to marry again, ever.'

'You will do your duty by me, Halstead,' was his father's only reply to that. 'Or I shall disinherit you. The estate is not entailed, as you well know. I was minded to pass you over and put Guy in your place when poor Frederick died. But my honour would not allow it. If you refuse me now, I shall——'

'You shall, and need do nothing,' flashed Shad. 'I have worked for five years like the trooper I once was to clear up the mess which Frederick made of running your estates. No, do not shake your head; Green will confirm the truth of what I say. Yes, Father, I tell you that now, what I would not tell you before, and my reward is to be disposed of in marriage, without my consent, and be insulted into the bargain, and what's more. . .' He stopped on seeing his father's stricken expression—he could not tell him the truth about Frederick; it would break him—and said instead, 'You may have your way. I shall leave for my mother's small estate in Scotland, and live there. You cannot take that away from me and you may do as you please with the Clermont lands.'

'Glen Ruadh will not finance a luxurious life in London for you,' snarled his father.

'Nor do I want it,' said Shad wearily. 'You do not know me, sir. I shall consider returning to the army. At least I was happy there. I should never have left it.'

'Leave this room, sir, without obliging me over the Countess of Malplaquet, and you may go to the devil for all I care,' was his father's only reply to that.

'Willingly, sir, willingly. And since Nell Tallboys enchants you so much, may I recommend that you marry the lady yourself?' ground out his son, and almost reeled from the room. He had thought that five years of hard work and dedication had reconciled his father to the loss of Frederick and his own succession, but the secretly arranged marriage, and his father's response to one night's folly after such devotion, had shown him his error, for nothing had changed.

His only regret was the loss of Guy, who met him at the bottom of the great staircase, and stood back in dismay at the sight of his brother's face, his own white.

'Oh, no, Shad! You are hopelessly at outs with him still, I see.'

'So hopelessly that he has disinherited me. He wants me to marry Nell Tallboys, God help me. Has arranged the marriage behind my back, without so much as a by-your-leave. I'm off to Scotland, immediately. For good. I'll keep in touch, Guy. Do what you can for him; he does not live in the world as it is, but as he thinks it is. Frederick's shadow hangs over me still.'

'Then I shall tell him the truth about Frederick, Shad, seeing that you will not.'

Shad caught his brother by the shoulders. 'Indeed, you won't—it would break him. Be a mortal blow.'

'And he is not giving you one?' riposted Guy. 'Do you still love him, Shad, after thirty years of curses and dislike—still hope that he may care for you a little? To hand you Nell Tallboys!'

'No,' said Shad steadily. 'I have long surrendered any hope on that score. I should never have left the army, but I thought... Oh, to the devil with what I thought. It's over at last, and I'm not sorry.'

But, as he left the room, and shouted for Vinnie, his late sergeant and now his groom, valet and man of all work, to be ready to accompany him north, on the double, he was. For so long he had hoped to be reconciled with his father, and now all was ashes.

* * *

'No,' said Elinor Tallboys, Countess of Malplaquet, Viscountess Wroxton, Baroness Sheveborough, all in her own right, mistress of all she surveyed here in Yorkshire, châtelaine of so many properties that even she could not remember them all, wealthy beyond the dreams of man, and woman, too. 'No, no, not at all, never. That is my first and last word, Uncle.'

'But only consider, my dear,' said her uncle, Sir Chesney Beaumont, her mother's brother, closing his eyes against her obstinacy, 'only consider.'

They were standing in the Turkish parlour at Campions, the Malplaquets' great house on the edge of the Yorkshire moors, a house over three hundred years old, huge, dominating the landscape and the lives of all those who lived near it. The Turkish room was so called because it was filled with rare *objets d'art* from that country, brought home by a former earl of Malplaquet who had been ambassador there. bOver the fireplace, carved on a ribbon of stone, was the family's motto, 'As the beginning, so the end'.

Nell Tallboys sometimes thought that she was the only thing in the whole house which could not by any judgement be considered a work of art. She was plainly dressed in a prim grey gown, high-waisted, a small pie frill around its neck being her only concession to any form of decoration. She wore no jewellery, and her hair was tied in a simple knot at the back of her head.

'No,' she said, firm again. 'I will not consider—nor reconsider, either. I have no wish to marry—let alone consider a proposal from the father of a man whom I have never met and do not wish to meet.'

'But you must marry, my dear Elinor——' This was met again with his niece's smiling refusal, laced with a touch of the steel which made her the resolute character she was.

'"Must. . .must. . .?" as good Queen Bess said of a similar suggestion. Not a word to use to me, Uncle, I think.' Her smile and her gentle tones took away the sting of her words a little, but her steadfastness, her determination always shone through even her lightest utterances.

He smiled, a little painfully. 'No "must"s then, my dear. But you are already twenty-seven years old; you need a husband and the estate and the title need an heir. You do not wish all this——' and he waved a hand to encompass the sumptuous room and the landscape outside '—to go to your cousin Ulric.'

'God forbid!' exclaimed Nell, shuddering, thinking of Ulric's debauchery, his wasting-away of his own good estate, and what he would do if he got his hands on the Malplaquet fortune.

'Well, Elinor,' said her uncle eagerly. 'What constrains you?' And then he added unluckily, 'The land needs a master.'

'It does?' said Nell, suddenly savagely satiric. 'Tell me, Uncle, have you asked Henson how we are faring here since I took over, compared with what we did before I inherited from Grandfather? If his running of Malplaquet's lands is typical of what a master might do, then I am content to remain merely its mistress!'

There was nothing Chesney Beaumont could say to that. He knew only too well that since Nell had inherited at barely twenty-one, and had taken control of the management of her lands, with the help of Henson, whom she had appointed, the Malplaquet estates had multiplied their returns and their efficiency tenfold.

'Nevertheless, I ask you to consider most carefully this offer from Lord Clermont on behalf of his son Charles, Viscount Halstead. A most noble offer, nobly made.'

'Nobly made to acquire Malplaquet's lands,' said Nell drily. 'What I know of Halstead does not attract. One disastrous marriage, after which he killed his wife's lover in a duel, at outs with his father——'

'You are behind the times, Elinor—he is now at ins, is learning to manage his father's affairs.'

'Then he does not need to practise on mine,' said Nell swiftly. 'An arrogant, ill-tempered man such as Halstead is reported to be is the last husband I could wish for. Thank you for attempting to take care of me, Uncle, but the answer is no.'

'At least see him,' returned her uncle desperately. 'Clermont proposes that you meet with Halstead, either here, or elsewhere, wherever you please, to see if you might suit.'

'Nowhere is where I please,' responded Nell, finality in her voice, 'and that must be that. Halstead is the last man I should wish to marry. I would not have him if he brought me a dukedom—nay, if he were a royal prince, on his knees before me,' and, as her uncle groaned and shook his head at her implacability, she added, 'Come, Uncle, admit it. Even you are acknowledging by what you say that the only reason why any man would wish to marry me is Malplaquet's fortune. What man of sense could wish for a plain woman past her last prayers otherwise? Never once, in all our talks on this subject, have you ever suggested that I should marry other than to secure the estate and the succession.'

'Now that is unfair, my dear,' he said quickly.

'Unfair?' Nell's eyebrows rose. She could see herself reflected in the beautiful Venetian glass above the hearth. A plain woman, plainly dressed, too tall, her features too harsh, too definite, she thought; only the glossy dark chestnut of her hair, and her large grey eyes, softened the severity of her appearance.

That she wronged herself she was not aware. But in a society which preferred pink and white prettiness, Nell's face, full of strength and character, was not the sort to be enshrined in a *Book of Beauty*, and, because she had long since resigned herself to that, she dressed for practical use, not to attract.

'Come, Uncle,' she said gently, 'I have long known that any marriage I make will be one of convenience, but at least allow me to choose the man I make it with.'

'And how will you ever do that, madam, tell me,' said her uncle, at last angry with her obduracy, 'when you never meet a man other than estate servants, old Challenor, your librarian, even older Payne, your secretary, middle-aged Henson, and assorted stablehands and flunkeys, led by that ageing warrior Aisgill, of whom you are so fond?'

He snorted, and then was off again, hallooing himself on, thought Nell with wry amusement, as though he were out with the Quorn Hunt and racing for the kill. 'You are grown a hermit, if a female can be such. How can you choose a man to marry you, unless you consent to go out into the world, or allow them to visit you here? At least let Halstead come to Campions. Talk to him. You might deal well with him. My information is that he is a man of sense, who was a good soldier, undervalued by the world and his father.'

'I am content as I am,' said Nell, turning away, tears springing unwanted to her eyes. 'And I do not wish for visitors, male or female. You forget that I have Aunt Conybeare, and all the care of the estate to keep me busy.'

She remembered her one dreadful season in town, nine years ago, when she was eighteen, and the muttered laughs and comments which had followed her tall, gauche person. 'Such a great gawk,' Emily Cowper had drawled in her spiteful way, 'that, were she not to be Malplaquet's Countess, the season would be a waste. But, be sure, whatever she looks like, she will have offers aplenty.'

Nell was sure that the comment had been meant to be overheard—as were others, equally mocking. Nothing, but nothing, could comfort her after hearing that, and social disaster seemed to follow social disaster.

She had grown more clumsy by the moment, felt everything about her to be too big, too raw, and, once the season was over, and half a dozen suitors repelled, their insincerity so patent that it hurt, she had retired to Yorkshire and happiness in seclusion, and refused to return.

Her grandfather's long illness, and then his death—her father and mother had died in a boating accident years before—had assisted her wish never to visit London again, and, once she was her own mistress, Yorkshire had sufficed.

That the years had greatly improved her looks, given her a poise and command that came from dealing competently with those around her, she had never found out—nor had society—for there was none to see, or tell her, and she would not have believed them if they had.

Her companion, gentle Aunt Conybeare, also hated town, and the two women lived comfortably in their isolation.

'You will regret this, Elinor, my dear,' said her uncle as he took his leave. 'I do believe it might have been better for you to have accepted Ulric, rather than live like this.'

'And there's no amen to that,' said Nell lightly, 'and you know that you don't mean it, Uncle. I shall see Halstead if he arrives here, but I warn you, he won't like what I have to say.'

And that was that. Only to her horror, this time Aunt Conybeare hemmed and hesitated, and finally said in her gentle voice, 'I think that your uncle has a point, my dear Nell, and, if you cannot bring yourself to accept Halstead, perhaps we ought to try the season again.'

'Well, you may,' said Nell, harsh, for once, to her aunt. 'But I shan't and that's flat. I shall marry when I'm nearly thirty, someone old and feeble, just able to give me my heir, and too fond of comfort to want to interfere with my life.'

And then, when she saw her aunt's face crumple a little at her severity, she went quickly over to her, fell on to her knees by her chair, and embraced her.

'No, my dear Aunt Honey-bear——' which had long been Nell's pet name for her '—I must not tease you, who have been so good to me, but you, of all people, know how I feel about men and women and marriage.'

'And I,' said her aunt, a little reproving for once, 'know what a good marriage can mean to a woman, and can do for her. I have never ceased to regret that poor George was taken from me before his time. No, Nell, do not make faces at me. I know what you must endure, which I never did, but believe, as I do, that one day you will meet someone whom you can love and care for, and who will love and care for you.'

Nell grimaced. 'Oh, I thank you for that, Aunt, but it is Cloud-cuckoo-land of which you speak. For I am not you, and Malplaquet stands in everyone's way, and blinds them to me, and what I am.'

Now what could Aunt Conybeare say to that? And the look which followed Nell, as she walked away, tall and graceful, was a sad one, for where would Nell find a man to whom Malplaquet meant nothing, and Nell everything?

CHAPTER TWO

SHAD drove himself and Vinnie hard on the way to Scotland. The weather was poor, but that meant nothing to him. He had begun to see Glen Ruadh as sanctuary, and could hardly wait to be there. Behind him lay his old life and his old self, which he was beginning to dislike.

The nights were the worst, the worst since Isabella, and he had Julia Merton to thank for them.

How could he have been so blind to fall again into the same trap, and this time with, as he had wrongly thought, his eyes open, and himself armoured against betraying women?

Julia had been so lovely and so clever, quite different from Isabella and her dusky charms. Oh, he had thought that, at last, he had found the one woman. From the moment he had met her he had been in a dream of love. He could see now that he had been as infatuated as a green boy.

For she had sought him out, and day by day had bound him with her magics, and he had worshipped the unattainable and hoped to attain her by marriage. He had laughed at those who had suggested that Julia Merton, still unmarried at twenty-four, might be so for reasons not altogether respectable—not that there were any blots on her reputation, simply the lack of response to the many who had offered for her.

'I was waiting for the right man,' she had whispered once, in a scented ballroom, when he had gently posed that very question. And then she had looked at him, wide-eyed. 'And—do you know?—I think I've found him.'

Oh, she had, she had! Her modesty, her gentle wit, the way in which she drew back from him if she thought him over-bold. And then, when he had proposed, on his knees, as though the ten years since Isabella had never happened, she had, ever modest, drawn back, said, 'All must be proper. I know you are of age, but speak to your father, and then, Halstead, then——' for she refused to call him Shad; that was for his old, rowdy army life '—I will accept you.'

Unknowing of his father's other plans for him, he had thought that the asking would be easy, and on that happy morning he had promised her that he would see his father on the next day, when he arrived from the country—where he now knew that he had been conferring with Chesney Beaumont about Nell Tallboys.

She had told him that she would be resting in the afternoon, but he had been to Bond Street, and seen a ring there, an exquisite thing, as delicate as she was, diamonds and sapphires to enhance her blonde loveliness, and he had rushed to Albemarle Street, his head on fire, to give it to her—surely she would see him.

He burned, he absolutely burned, when he thought of how her maid had tried to put him off, of how he had said so complacently, 'Oh, tell her I am here; she will rise for me, I am sure of it,' and he had pushed his way so confidently into the little private sitting-room where she usually received him.

He remembered the maid, pulling at him, babbling, 'No, my lord, wait in the French drawing-room, rather,' but he had hardly heard her, heard anything until he had thrown the door open, and seen the reason for her dismay.

For Julia, his Julia, lay naked beneath Jack

Broughton, that noted lecher, married—but his marriage had never stopped that—and a thousand things, half-heard, half-seen, came together, and when she pushed Jack off, and stared at Shad, face white, whispering, 'No,' as her world collapsed, too, he saw something else which told him why she had pursued him, netted him in her toils.

By her breasts and body she was pregnant, and how she could have hoped to deceive him after marriage, he could not think. Except, of course, once safely married, there would have been nothing he could do without making himself a laughing-stock.

Jack pulled away, and laughed at him, and at the woman both.

'What's this?' he remembered saying in a hoarse voice, and Jack shrugged, even as the woman on the sofa improbably tried to protest innocence.

'Why, Shad, truth will out, I see. She has been my whore these five years, since after I married Nancy. Oh, quiet, Julia,' he drawled. 'Too late to pretend now. And Shad won't talk, you know. Too full of honour—to say nothing of his pride. He won't tell the world what he so nearly did!'

Shad was not proud of what he did do next. For he seized Broughton and beat him nearly senseless, and then had the privilege of watching Julia wail over his battered form.

'You devil,' she spat at him. 'Do you think that I could have borne your ugly face, if it weren't that I needed you, or any man, to hide the proof of my love for him?'

'Love?' he said. 'What's that?' and walked from the room, but not before throwing the ring at her. 'And here's your payment from me,' he said. 'Sell it to buy baby clothes for your bastard.'

And then he had drunk himself stupid and gone to

Watier's and attacked another woman's good name and ended, possibly forever, the fragile *rapprochement* he had achieved with his father.

So much for that. And it was to exorcise these demons that he drove himself and Vinnie on through the bad weather of that dismal autumn.

At what point he was sure that they were being tracked he did not know. They had stopped overnight at a dirty inn, and after a bad night and a poor breakfast, Vinnie grumbling over his flat ale that it was worse than campaigning, they had set out across the moors, north of Bradford on a poor road which grew worse.

The feeling of being watched grew stronger in him, and Vinnie felt it too. But mile after mile as he drove the carriage north, wishing that he had not brought it, but had travelled on horseback, however hard the journey, nothing untoward happened, so that he began to think that his imagination, fevered with the memory of Julia's betrayal was working overtime, was deceiving him.

They stopped at midday to eat bread, cheese and apples and to drink the bottle of ale which Vinnie had brought with him from the inn, and then water from the spring by the roadside.

He remembered that Nell Tallboys's great house stood near by, and he wondered briefly what she might think if told that her uncle's choice of a husband was passing her by without as much as a how do you do.

Well, judging by reports, she probably wanted him as little as he wanted her. He grimaced, wiped his mouth, and they set off again into the teeth of a wind more suited to November than late September.

And then, just after they had reached the moor's highest point, and the road, now little more than a track along which the carraige lurched, descended before them, all his forebodings came true. His instincts for danger, honed by his army career, had not played him false.

Two bullets whined at them. One missed him, the other took poor Vinnie, riding by the carriage, in the chest, and dropped him dead from his horse. The French had not been able to kill him, but a group of Yorkshire banditti had done for him.

Shad never did know who or what they were, whether common footpads or poor devils without work, perhaps even old soldiers lost without a war to fight, but whoever they were they knew their business. They came across the moor at him, on horseback, rode over poor dead Vinnie, and, firing a second shot at him, demanded his valuables on pain of his life.

'You'll have to fight me for them, then,' he yelled in feeble defiance, and, another shot catching him across the shoulder, he lost control of the horses, and one of the cut-throats launched himself at him, and struck him such a blow with a bludgeon that he was felled—to lie half in the carriage, and half out of it.

Stunned, but still with some shreds of consciousness, he felt rather than saw them drag his bags out and begin to plunder them. They were particularly excited by his fine pistols, and the Baker rifle which he had bought from a friend in the Rifle Brigade who had later died at Waterloo.

Then they pulled him from the carriage, he struggling, weakly and futilely, consciousness coming and going. Once they had him stretched on the ground, blood from his gashed shoulder staining his fine coat, they stripped him of his clothing and his possessions, so that he lay naked and shivering on the hard earth.

The leader, a grimy ginger-headed bravo, a man as big as himself, discarded his own filthy rags, put on Shad's, including his top hat, and then, half in malice, half in jest, told his fellows to dress Shad in his discarded clothing.

He struggled with them, was struck again, hard, for his pains, and knew no more until they mounted their own horses, with one of them driving his carriage, with dead Vinnie propped up by his own half-concious self, bumping and rattling across the moor towards a quarry, earlier glimpsed in the distance.

Shad's last thoughts as they pushed the carriage over the quarry's edge—they had kept his horses as plunder—was that perhaps it was fitting that everything should end here so ignominiously, after he had survived a dozen battles, guerrilla war, and his father's dislike. He'll never know what happened to me—nor will he care, was his last conscious thought.

'And that's the end of my fine gentleman,' grinned the man who was now wearing Shad's clothes, watching the carriage break into pieces as it fell towards the water in the quarry's bottom. What he did not know was that Shad, thrown out almost immediately, was caught, a third of the way down, in some bushes, unconscious, but still breathing, and still blindly, instinctively determined somehow to survive.

For Nell Tallboys that day began like any other. There was little to show that, after it, nothing was ever going to be the same again. She had spent the morning going over her correspondence with old Payne, and she had been compelled to admit that her uncle's criticism of him had been just. He was past his best, and she would need to pension him off soon and find someone younger, which would be a nuisance, for she would have to train him—with Henson's help.

She had then gone over accounts with Henson; he had told her of some discontent, not Luddite—that seemed dead, these days—but something similar, over towards Bradford. He hoped that it would not affect Nell's people, but thought not.

The day was fine and sunny, and after luncheon—cold meat and fruit—she had decided on a ride to blow the cobwebs away, and, instead of sending one of the footmen to the stables, she had decided to walk there herself, once she had changed into her riding habit. She liked to come upon the men unawares, see how they behaved when their betters were not about.

Again, she was later to ponder on the might-have-beens, if Nell, Countess of Malplaquet, had not walked into the altercation going on in the stable yard.

The stables themselves were beautiful buildings, large, in the Renaissance style, fine things, with better homes for horses than most men had, she sometimes thought, and the yard was reached by a triumphal arch, with a centaur—half-man, half-horse—galloping across its top.

Beneath, the human centaurs were all gathered, arguing. Aisgill's voice, its broad Yorkshire even broader than usual, was the loudest.

He was railing at Henson, who stood civilised and stolid in his fine black suit, his thin, clever face at odds with the craggy ones around him.

Aisgill stopping to draw breath, Henson began to speak in cold measured tones. Originally a countryman himself, he had adopted the manners and dress of those whom he served.

'Campions cannot,' he said, 'be the refuge for every wandering derelict plucked from the highway or the moors.'

Aisgill began again, 'Common humanity——' to be addressed by Nell.

'What is it,' she asked, seeing that all the stable lads, the grooms and gardeners, together with some of the house's indoor servants, were clustered around one of the doorways to the stable lads' quarters, 'that is worth all this brouhaha?'

Henson and Aisgill began to talk together, and for once Nell spoke with some of the hauteur of the great lady she was.

'One at a time, if you please, and some of you stand back a little. I wish to see what exercises you so.' For she had become aware that the cause of the argument was half sitting, half lying on the steps before them.

'To your work, lads,' roared Aisgill, suddenly aware of the crowd that had gathered while he disputed with Henson, and then on Nell beckoning him, rather than Henson, to speak, said, 'This poor creature was brought in today by Gilbert Outhwaite from Overbeck. He found him wandering on the moor on the way of here. By the looks of him, he had been crawling on his hands and knees,' and he indicated the figure on the steps, visible now that all the servants had reluctantly dispersed, leaving their betters to argue.

'Outhwaite knew that you, Lady Elinor——' for Nell was still Lady Elinor to them, as she had been for many years seeing that she had been merely heir presumptive to Malplaquet until her grandfather died, and disliked being called m'lady, or Lady Malplaquet '—were giving charity to such unfortunates, in exchange for casual labour, and thought that we might help this one.'

Nell looked at the man on the steps. He was bigger, much bigger than all the stocky moors men who had surrounded him. He had a heavy growth of black stubble on his face, and his hair was a mass of shaggy black ringlets. His clothing was so torn and exiguous that Outhwaite had thrown an old blanket from his cart around his broad shoulders. He was shivering beneath it, his feet were bare and bleeding, and his eyes, suddenly raised to stare at Nell, were a brilliant, feverish blue. They held hers almost challengingly.

'Henson will be after telling me that we cannot take in every vagrant in the Riding,' said Aisgill grimly, 'but we cannot turn such a poor thing away. He's starving, ate one of the turnips in Aisgill's cart as though he were a wolf, is perhaps simple, for he hardly knows his own name.'

'Not true,' muttered the man suddenly, his eyes still on Nell. 'It's, it's. . .' He seemed to struggle a moment with himself, then growled something which sounded like 'Chad'.

'Is that all?' said Nell. 'Chad? Ask him what his other name is.'

Aisgill spoke to the vagrant, who shook his head, looked puzzled; then, as he stared again at Nell, his face seemed to lighten.

'That he doesn't know,' said Aisgill ruefully. 'Only that he's Chad. Nor does he know where he comes from, Outhwaite said, nor even where he is. That is why Mr Henson here wishes to turn him away. Says he'll only be a belly to feed, won't bring hands to work with him.'

'That is so, Lady Elinor,' said Henson severely. 'Charity is well enough, but Campions cannot support every useless half-wit who roams the countryside. Either the parish supports him, or he finds work on some farm—but who would employ a simpleton?'

Nell looked doubtfully at the man. Beneath his growth of curling black hair she thought she saw a harsh and craggy face, and his body, what she could see of it, seemed a strong one, well made.

'He does not look a simpleton,' and then, decisively, 'Show me his hands.'

The man looked at her again, held out his hands with a smile which showed excellent white teeth, said,

'Will they do?' in a tone which was almost provocative, sharp and sure, quite unlike his confusion of a moment before—and then doubt and puzzlement crossed his face again, and he hung his head.

His big hands were torn and bleeding, bruised, the nails broken, the hands of a manual worker, Nell thought, although his speech, what there was of it, hinted that he was more than that. Nell caught his brilliant blue stare again, and something there, something powerful, almost feral, had a strange effect on her. She shivered, and as she did so he dropped his gaze, and when he looked at her again his face was dull, expressionless.

'He's had a blow on the head recently, or a fall,' announced Aisgill suddenly. 'There's a half-healed gash on his shoulder. He's been sleeping rough, by the state of him. But he doesn't look a regular idiot to me.'

'An irregular one, then,' snorted Henson. 'He stinks like one. Begging your pardon, Lady Elinor.'

'Be quiet, both of you,' said Nell sharply, seeing Aisgill bridle and prepare to answer Henson angrily. Both men stared at her; she rarely came the fine lady with them. 'We can at least give him a trial, find out what work he can do. Take him in, Aisgill. Feed him, see he's washed, give him some clean clothes. If you think that he might not be well, let Dr Ramsden look at him, and then, when he's fit again, try him as a stable hand. You were saying you had not enough lads only yesterday.'

Henson opened his mouth, saw Nell's expression, said wearily, 'Begging your pardon, *my lady*,' and he stressed the title. 'If he don't suit, and won't work, as many simpletons won't, then he may go to the parish when he's had his chance.'

'He doesn't look a simpleton,' said Nell again, but

best to make concessions to them both, seeming to favour neither the one nor the other. 'But yes. A fair trial with Aisgill first, and, if that fails, as you say.'

The man of whom they were speaking had fallen into a daze, his eyes on the horizon, apparently unaware of Nell, Aisgill and Henson, and that they were concerned with him.

'Chad,' said Nell sharply. 'You heard what I said—that you are to be given a trial here?'

He nodded, looked up at Nell, his eyes clearing again. He took her in, standing tall and graceful before him, in her bottle-green habit, elegant boots, and her tiny top hat, a very Diana. Elusive memory, running before him, stirred in Chad. He spoke without thinking, and the words were almost a command.

'Who are you?' he said, blunt.

'Respect due from you,' snapped Henson, annoyed, but Nell said,

'No, he means nothing by it. Natural for him to wish to know—especially if his memory has gone. You may call me Lady Elinor, as the rest of my people do here,' she told him gently. 'But you must do as Mr Aisgill here bids you, or be turned away. You understand?'

The man nodded. His puzzled look, so different from the one of a moment ago, had returned. 'Do as Mr Aisgill bids me. I understand,' and then, almost as an afterthought, with a slight bow in her direction, 'Lady Elinor.'

Once more those strange blue eyes were on her, and were doing their work, holding her, trying to tell her something, causing her to be patient with him, affecting her in the oddest fashion. And then he turned to look at Aisgill, for instructions, presumably.

Henson sighed noisily, turned away himself. 'Good,' said Nell, 'then we all understand one another. Now, Aisgill, tell one of the grooms to attend me; I wish to ride on the moor this afternoon,' and then as Aisgill nodded, and the man, helped up by one of the hands, for, despite his size, he seemed weak—probably from hunger—was led away, she said, 'His voice is educated, Aisgill, I wonder how he came to be a vagrant, wandering the moor half clothed, his memory gone?'

Henson, still standing there, and now suddenly a little ashamed of his harshness before the hands' gentleness with the derelict, said, 'Many a man ruined these days, Lady Elinor, with the wars over and business failing. Soldiers ruined, too, their occupation gone.'

All three of them watched their new acquisition walk into the men's quarters.

'Well, I don't like us getting a reputation for saving half the riff-raff in Yorkshire, but perhaps one more won't do us harm—if he is willing and able to work, that is, which seems unlikely. Another worthless mouth to feed, no doubt, and throw out after a few weeks.'

Later, Henson's words came back, if not to haunt him, but to remind him that even the cleverest of us could make the grossest of misjudgements.

CHAPTER THREE

'I WONDER how the vagabond Aisgill rescued is getting on?' said Nell idly to Aunt Conybeare, who sat stitching at her canvas work before a roaring fire. Early October was colder than usual that autumn.

Nell had been poring over a thick book, not a lady's mindless and agreeable novel, but a report from the Board of Agriculture on hill farming. All her reading seemed to be functional these days, and Lord Byron's latest—and naughty—work, *Manfred: a Drama*, discreetly hidden from public view by the *Quarterly Review* on the occasional table by her chair, sat waiting for her to find time to pick it up.

Nell knew it was naughty because Aunt Conybeare, sighing and deploring it as she did so, had eagerly read every word, before telling Nell that, as an unmarried girl, she really ought not to open it.

Nell privately wondered whether an unmarried girl who ran England's biggest and most successful stud could be unaware of anything to do with reproduction, human or otherwise, but discreetly said nothing.

For no good reason, ever since she had seen the vagabond on the steps, and he had raised those amazing eyes to look into hers, the derelict she had taken in had haunted Nell's memory.

Really, this is absurd, she told herself. Whatever had she thought that she had seen there? It had disturbed her so much that she had privately determined to avoid meeting him again, and apart from asking Aisgill once if he was still at Campions, to which Aisgill had said, Yes, and he was putting him to work in the yard, she had not spoken of him again, and had avoided the stables.

Restlessness gripped her, a feeling that life was passing her by—probably the result of Chesney Beaumont's doomings about her unmarried condition. She rose, put down her book, said, 'I need air. I think I will go for a walk. No, Aunt,' as her aunt raised agonised eyes to her, for the air was keen outside, 'I shall take John with me, for protection, if not company, and you may enjoy the fire in peace.'

Did her feet take her stablewards consciously or unconsciously? She was interested in the horses, of course. She was a skilful horsewoman, and the Campions stables were nationally famous, particularly the stud, where horses bred by the Malplaquets constantly won the great classic races.

John, the footman, walking behind her, carrying a large green umbrella—although how he was to keep it up in the wind should he need to open it, Nell could not think—she passed through the great arch to stand in the yard.

She was wearing a heavy mannish coat over her light dress, and had put on little black boots against the mud of what appeared to be an early winter.

One of the stable hands stopped currycombing a horse, came up respectfully to take her orders. 'Lady Elinor?'

'Where is Aisgill?' she said. 'I wish to speak with him.'

About what? she thought. What odd compulsion has brought me here?

She looked around the busy scene, at the blacksmith in his forge at the end of the row, the lads mending tack, another lad forking feed into a barrow. She could not see Chad anywhere.

'Maister Aisgill's in the riding school, Lady Elinor. Shall I fetch him for you?'

'Thank you, no.' Nell was always polite to those who served her. 'I'll go there myself,' and she set off towards it.

The riding school had been built by the second Earl, a noted horseman, after he had seen the famous one in Vienna on his Grand Tour. Designed to school horses, not only in the elaborate ritual of dressage, but also in their general management, it had fallen into disrepair until Nell, early in her running of the estate, had had it renovated, and had encouraged Aisgill, who needed no encouragement, to bring it into use again.

In the round building, open at the sides, beneath a slightly domed roof, the work of the stable was going on briskly.

Aisgill, suddenly seeing her, came over, his ruddy face welcoming. Dismayed at first by the thought of a woman taking charge, he had found that Nell was his closest ally in restoring Malplaquet's racing pride, and he was now her most fervent supporter.

'Good to see you here, Lady Elinor. We've missed you lately. You wanted me?'

Nell made a vague motion with her hands, her eyes were busy. 'Nothing, really. Just to see that all's going well,' and then, offered as an afterthought, 'What have you been doing with the vagabond you rescued a fortnight gone?'

'What have *I* done?' he said, with an odd grin. 'You might well ask what *he's* done and doing. He's on Rajah, as you see,' and he pointed at the rider and horse completing a neat trotting circle, and coming to rest not far from them.

In the gloom of the arena Nell had not seen him, but she saw him now. He was straight-backed, in perfect control of the giant stallion. She saw his head turn, and the blue gaze fell on her again.

'On Rajah! You mean you have let him ride Rajah! And he can control him like that?'

'Oh, he's amazing with the horses, Lady Elinor. He says he can remember nothing, but even on his first day at work when Rajah broke loose he stopped him and quieted him when no one else could.'

Aware that the man on the horse was watching them, some delicacy made Aisgill bend his head to speak low to his mistress.

'It's my belief, madam, that he's been in the army, a trooper, possibly. He rides like a trained cavalryman, and he has the scar of a great wound on his chest. Some poor devil turned away because of the peace, fallen on hard times since. He asked to ride Rajah, and, seeing how he gentled him, I gave him permission, and look at him now. It was a good day when we took him in.'

So it was, thought Nell, for Rajah, a great black, the most beautiful horse in the stud, had always possessed a vile, unmanageable temper, and most were frightened to lead him, let alone ride him.

Chad, for so she must think of him now, for he was one of her people, had trotted the horse into the centre of the circle and was teaching him to walk on the spot. Rajah was showing his dislike of the restraint put upon him, but his rider was using his voice, as well as his body, to force his will on him. Nell watched him, fascinated by such power, such control.

'And such patience,' she said at last to Aisgill.

'Yes,' he replied; he was a little surprised, for Nell, although usually interested in the work of the stable, was seldom so particularly interested. Her whole body had gone quite still, her attention given completely to what she was seeing.

'But it's time he stopped. Rajah is growing impatient.'

As though Chad had heard him, he turned the horse towards Nell and Aisgill. He trotted him over, the strength of both horse and rider plainly visible as he controlled the only half-willing beast. Slipping from his back, to hold Rajah firm where he stood, he touched his forehead to Nell, as he had been taught, said briefly to Aisgill, 'He's had enough, sir. Best let him rest.'

The words and the actions were servile, those of a good, obedient servant, but despite that there was nothing servile about him, Nell thought.

Now that she could see him plain, it appeared that the vagabond had been tamed and groomed. His crisp black hair had been trimmed, so that it clustered in loose ringlets about his harsh and craggy face, which was now clean-shaven, although a dark shadow shaded his mouth and jaw.

The face was strong, and there was nothing handsome in it, but it was strangely compelling, and not that of a wastrel. His eyes shone bluer than she had remembered them, and they were surveying her, not insolently, but coolly, as though they were simply man and woman together—a strange experience for Nell.

The rest of him, clad in the smart but serviceable green uniform of the stable hand not engaged in dirty work, with his once bleeding and naked feet in bright black boots, was remarkable as well, broad-shouldered, beautifully proportioned, and looking at him Nell felt the strangest stirrings rising in her, stirrings which she had never felt before.

He was so large that he dwarfed her, another pleasant sensation for Nell, who was usually as tall as, if not taller than, many of the men around her.

Allied to all these odd stirrings and throbbings,

which grew stronger not weaker the longer she looked at him, Nell was experiencing a strange breathlessness which she had never felt before, and her heart began to beat wildly. She mentally shook her head, reprimanded herself. In God's name, what was coming over her that the sight of a strong stable hand who had been plucked half-naked from the moors should cause her to behave like a green girl confronted by her first lover?

For, inexperienced though she was, Nell had no doubt about what was the cause of these strange and involuntary reactions. Desperately she tried to compose herself, for now he was speaking to her in that deep, almost gravel voice, which added to her inward confusion.

'I have to thank you, Lady Elinor, for taking me in. I think I should have died else, my wits were so addled.'

Nell inclined her head, fought for control, was surprised how calm and measured her voice was. 'If you can tame Rajah,' she managed, 'it was a good day for Campions, as well as for you.'

He smiled, showing his strong white teeth again. Whatever and whoever he was, he had been well fed, and decently educated, and Aisgill's guess that he had been a soldier was probably a good one.

'Oh, no one will tame Rajah,' he said confidently. 'Only if you show him who's master, he might choose to do your bidding occasionally.'

And you too, thought Nell, looking at him. For like Rajah, there was something wild about him, something which, like it or not, called to Nell, who, if not wild, seldom did what was expected of her.

'Aisgill tells me that you might have been a soldier. Have you no memories which might help you to recall who you are, or where you came from?'

His eyes were suddenly shadowed. 'No, madam,' he said, almost painfully. 'But I bear a scar of what I think must be a wartime wound and I have. . .bad dreams.'

'Bad dreams?' Nell was aware that she was spending far too much time talking to one poor stable hand, but he intrigued her. 'What sort of bad dreams?'

'Of noise, and fighting, and men dying,' he said simply. 'So yes, I was probably a trooper. I remember riding a horse.' He thought a moment. 'He was white and splendid. . .and then he fell beneath me. . .'

He paused. 'And then?' said Nell encouragingly.

'And then, nothing. The other lads say I wake up shouting, but they cannot tell me what I say.'

'You may remember in time, I hope,' said Nell, only to hear him reply strangely,

'I may not like what I remember, madam.'

She let him go, turned to Aisgill, who had been listening to them, wondering at Lady Nell's interest—but then, she had always been unpredictable.

'Chad,' she said slowly. 'What name do you use for him on the books?'

'Young Peel said that he should be called Newcome, because that is what he is—new come among us,' replied Aisgill with a smile, 'and he agreed, so that is how he is styled.'

Nell was still watching Chad walk Rajah away, watched him until he left the arena, drawn by she knew not what.

'A corporal or a sergeant, you think,' she hazarded. 'By the way he speaks, his sureness, he has given orders in the past—and taken them, too. He has had some education—he knew how to speak to me.'

'Oh, aye,' said Aisgill, who had been a cavalryman when he was a boy, before injury had sent him back to civil life with a permanent limp. 'It's passing strange. He cannot remember who he is, nor anything about himself, but he knows how to school a horse, and a dozen other things. He told Seth Hutton off for being careless with a fowling piece. Said that it was no way to treat a weapon!'

'A useful man, then,' commented Nell. 'And the mare you had in foal—Bluebell—how does she do, these days?' For she thought that it was time that she stopped showing an interest in Chad Newcome, or Aisgill would be wondering what was coming over her—not that she did not make a point of showing an interest in all her people!

Chad Newcome sat on the same steps where Nell Tallboys had first seen him, mending tack. The October day was grey and gloomy, and, to some extent, so were his thoughts.

And yet, in an odd way, he was strangely content. He began to whistle an old song—and where did that come from? he wondered, and how remarkable that he, who could remember nothing about himself, could remember that, and how to school a horse, load and use a gun, and perform a hundred other tasks. Day by day he recovered a little more of what he knew, but, of himself, nothing.

The words of the song ran through his head, and when he came to the phrase, 'One is one and all alone,' there came the unbidden thought, And shall I always be alone, as I have been in the past?

He frowned, and stopped working, busy hands still. Now, how do I know that? Had he no chick nor child, wife nor father and mother to love and care for him? Had he always been a vagrant wanderer?

No, that could not be true. His good body, and the growing realisation, as his powers slowly returned, that he had been an educated man, told him that once he must have had a settled life, and he knew beyond a doubt that he had had women, and more than one, although how he knew he could not say.

To think of women was to think of Lady Elinor, or Lady Nell, or even 'Our Nell', as the men affectionately called her behind her back.

'God send she never marries,' he had heard Aisgill say once, 'for we should never get a master as good as she is, and I never thought to say that of any woman.'

Perhaps it was because his first conscious memory in this new strange life was of her, standing straight and tall before him, that she haunted him a little. He remembered how foolishly pleased he had been that day at the riding school when he had first seen her again, and she had spoken to him kindly about his schooling of Rajah.

It had been difficult not to keep his eyes hard on her the whole time he was with her, and he had frequently looked away because he had not wished to seem insolent, but she drew him in some fashion he could not define.

Or was it, after all, simply that before he had seen her everything had been blurred, a fog through which he had walked unknowing of himself, or his circumstances, uncaring almost, as though he was at one with the few animals which roved the moors?

He shrugged as the song in his head reached the betraying phrase again, and then, as the word 'alone' rang out, she was before him, in his mind's eye, and this time he inspected her closely, as he could not inspect the living and breathing woman, the Countess who held all their lives in the hollow of her hand.

She was tall for a woman, but beautifully proportioned, moving with an easy athletic grace. A grace confirmed when he had seen her ride off on horseback, in perfect control of her mount.

And her face! It was neither pretty nor beautiful, but somehow better than either. Beneath the glossy wealth of her dark chestnut hair, it was as strong and powerful as the face of Diana in an old painting. The high-bridged nose, the full and generous mouth with its humorous set, the grey eyes beneath high-arched black brows, the whole poised on the proud column of a shapely neck.

But best of all was the compassion he had seen there when she had bent that proud head to examine the poor wretch who had been decanted on her very doorstep.

Well, a cat might look at a king, so surely a homeless vagrant, for vagrant he must have been, from his clothes and his condition, might look at a queen—for Nell Tallboys was a queen in Yorkshire.

He rose and stretched. There was a growing pride in him as his faculties returned which Aisgill had noticed, a pride in his ability to control Rajah and to do the menial tasks around the yard well. 'He's been a man under orders,' Aisgill said to Henson when the agent had enquired how Newcome was faring, 'and he's given orders as well. I'd bet my life on his being a sergeant in the army, and a good one. Wonder why they let him go?'

Henson had shrugged. Newcome might be a bit of a mystery, but not one on which he cared to spend time.

Aisgill came towards Chad now, said briefly, 'Lady Elinor needs a groom to escort her on her daily ride this afternoon. You know the lie of the land now, Newcome. Saddle Vulcan, the big gelding, for her, and you may take Rajah, if you think he will behave himself. Without his daily run, he'll be a devil to handle.'

So, later, smartly dressed, wearing a jockey cap with a green and silver cockade at the side—Malplaquet's colours—he helped his Countess into the saddle, wordless, and then mounted an impatient Rajah, to ride with her across the moors, already clad in their winter colours.

Nell thought that Newcome, riding by her side, looked better than he had done since he had arrived at Campions. The drawn, rather haunted look he had worn in the early days had vanished, and like Aisgill she recognised the pride he was displaying in his work.

And his control over Rajah was greater than ever. That proud beast was suddenly willing to serve an even prouder master. What a strange thought, that one of her stable hands could be proud! She took a covert look at Newcome's harsh profile, and when they reached the usual end of her ride, for she always took the same route—safer so, Aisgill said, if they always knew exactly where she went—a pile of stones known as the Cairn, and they dismounted, she signalled for him to sit by her, on one of the large boulders scattered about the Cairn.

Chad hesitated; he had been prepared to stand by Rajah whom he had tethered to a broken tree, and he knew what the proper place of a groom was, and it was not sitting by his mistress. But orders were orders, and Nell, amused, watched him struggle with his sense of what was fitting, and her command.

She had dressed herself more carefully than usual; indeed, for the last week she had chosen to wear turn-outs far more *à la mode* than she usually did, so that when she was about to leave for her ride Aunt Conybeare had stared at her, and said, 'Gracious, Nell, we are fine these days!'

Nell had blushed. She had put on a deep blue riding habit, adorned with silver buttons, and had wound a fine white linen cravat, edged with lace, around her throat and had secured it with a silver and sapphire pin.

Her boots had a polish on them so high that Aunt Conybeare had asked if they had been prepared with champagne; she had heard that the great London dandies did that! And her deep blue top hat had ribbons of pale blue silk wreathed around it, falling in long streamers down her back. Even her whip was a fine thing, decorated with silver trimmings; it had belonged to the third Earl, a noted fop in his time.

As a final concession to vanity, she had had her maid, Annie Thorpe, brush and brush her dark chestnut hair, and then Annie had dressed it for her, far more elaborately and carefully than usual, so that the top hat sat proudly on it.

'A pity you're not going to meet your lover—dressed like that,' had been Aunt Conybeare's final contribution, and one that had had her going hot all over. Because she had asked Aisgill to assign Newcome to her for the ride, and it was Newcome she was dressing like this for, if she told the truth.

And what would Aunt Conybeare say to that? Or Aisgill, or Henson, or. . .? Well, to the devil with them all!

But she was not thinking of this when Newcome finally sat down, and she said in the most bored, Countess-like voice she could assume, 'Tell me, Newcome, have you recovered your memory yet?'

Chad looked at her, and thought that he had never seen anything so superb. Not, of course, that his conscious memory was more than a month old! But Nell Tallboys, who usually walked round the yard looking more like one of the stable lad's girls, shabby clothing pulled on any-old-how, and her hair falling down and blowing in the wind, was truly Lady

Malplaquet this afternoon, and he hardly knew how to address her.

Except that his tongue did it for him. 'No, Lady Elinor. I still know nothing of myself, and Maister Aisgill——' he pronounced the name as the tykes did; his own speech was accentless '—tells me that Blackwell, your tenant on the Home Farm, found me sleeping by the haystack two nights before Outhwaite brought me to Campions, refused to feed me—apparently I begged for food, although I have no memory of doing so—and moved me on.'

'Blackwell is a good tenant but a mean man,' said Nell reflectively. 'He should have sent you to Campions, but he doesn't approve of Campions charity.'

'Well, I approve of it,' said Chad sturdily. 'Or I should likely be dead on the moor by now.'

Nell's laugh at that was not one that any past Countess of Malplaquet would have approved of. 'Well, that is true enough,' she said appreciatively. 'Aisgill tells me that you are a good worker and not only with the horses.'

'But I like working with the horses best,' said Chad, seeing that Lady Elinor was determined to talk to him. 'I have a strange feeling that, while I have often worked with horses, it was not as a groom or a stable lad.'

'Which would support Aisgill's belief that you were a trooper. But you don't object to doing the hard work round the yard?'

'It would be a mean soul who would not work for those who had given him his life back, and who were prepared to take him on without knowing of his past.'

Seeing Nell look a little puzzled, he added, somewhat stiffly, 'A man without a past must be a suspect man, Lady Elinor. Who knows what I have done, or may be fleeing from? It sometimes worries me at night, when I cannot sleep.'

Nell looked at Chad's strong face, the face which she hardly dared inspect too closely, it had such an effect on her.

'You do not look like a criminal, Newcome, nor do you behave like one.'

Chad shrugged. He did not tell lady Elinor that in the long night watches his efforts to recall who and what he was often served only to confuse him. Once, when he had been unable to rest at all, and had finally fallen asleep from very exhuastion, he had had a nightmare in which she had figured.

Something about her and himself which had made him cry out so strongly, and throw himself from his bed. His behaviour had been so violent that he had awoken several of the lads and they had been compelled to restrain him because he was not properly awake and he had tried to fight them off. When he had woken up he could not remember what in the dream had distressed him so.

Seeing that he could never have met her before the day on which she had ordered him taken in, and had shown him nothing but kindness, it seemed a strange dream to have.

To take his mind away from unhappy things he did something he knew no good servant should do; he initiated a topic of conversation with his mistress, for the pleasure of seeing her lively face turned towards him, and hearing her beautiful voice.

'These stones, Lady Elinor. Were they put here of a purpose, or did Nature simply pile them up at random?'

Nell looked sharply at him. More and more Newcome was beginning to demonstrate that he had been given a good education.

'The people round here believe that the gods threw them down in play, the old Norse gods, that is. This part of the North was never properly Christianised, they say, until long after the South. There is a book in the library—Challenor showed it to me—which says that people lived in the Cairn long ago, although I find that hard to believe. Think how cold they must have been in winter!'

Unconsciously she had spoken to him as an equal, and he answered her in kind. 'If that were true, there must be an entrance.'

'And so there is,' said Nell. 'Look, I will show you.' She rose and walked to the side away from the one where they had been sitting, and, pointing to a gap in the stones, said, 'Follow me,' turned sideways and wriggled through.

With difficulty, Chad followed her, to find himself in a small low chamber, so low that Nell, as well as he, had to bow herself to stand in it.

'They must have been dwarfs!' he exclaimed.

'So Challenor believes,' answered Nell, turning to go, but as she did so her foot slipped and she felt Chad catch her, to break her fall.

Nell was suddenly hard against him, could feel the heat from his body, his male strength, and was held there, face to face, her head level with his chin, tall man and tall woman, bowed—then he tried to avoid standing up, so as not to bang their heads, lost his footing as well, and they were on the ground.

It was the first time that he had touched her, other than to hold her foot as she mounted Vulcan, and the sensations Nell experienced were extraordinary. She remembered being in a man's arms, dancing a waltz, being lifted by a boatman, Aisgill picking her up once, when she had been thrown from her horse, and in not one of these encounters had she felt what she now did when Chad Newcome touched and held her.

I am going mad, running a fever, loneliness is making me prey to a disgraceful lust; I should never have brought him in here; whatever would Aunt Conybeare—Aisgill, Uncle Beaumont, Henson—think if they knew how wanton I am grown? ran through Nell's head, before he released her, and they crouched, face to face, in the gloom of the confined space.

Chad was suffering, if suffering was the right word, the same experience as Nell. Loss of memory, he was finding, was leading to some loss of control. He had a mad desire to kiss the woman half kneeling before him. He repressed it, the refrain 'And lose your place to be thrown out to starve' running through his mind and stopping him from following his natural inclinations.

Whatever would she think if he assaulted her so? Worst of all, his strongest instinct was to do much more than that to her; it was to bear her to the ground and take his pleasure with her.

Still half crouched, he turned, and pushed his way into the open again, to lean on the biggest stone, fighting for self-control before she came after him.

Once outside, Nell was Countess of Malplaquet again; she said in a voice so false that it frightened her, 'I think, Newcome, it's time we went home. I feel strangely tired.' She was pleased to see that Newcome appeared his usual stern self, that he merely bowed his head silently, and silently helped her back on to Vulcan before mounting Rajah and waiting for her to lead them home.

Still silent, they rode back to Campions. What neither of them understood was that both of them had reacted in the same way to the other, and each thought that he or she was the only one to experience such savagely strong feelings that rank, decorum, climate, and rules of conduct had meant nothing to them. Had they followed their natural inclinations they would have mated inside the Cairn as though they were at one with the birds and the beasts around them!

CHAPTER FOUR

'NELL,' said Aunt Conybeare reprovingly—they were sitting in Nell's private room, overlooking the park, 'your wits are wandering today. This is the second time that I have asked you the same question, and you have not answered me on either occasion. Most unlike you. What can you be thinking of?'

Nell flushed. In her wild and wicked thoughts she had been on the moors again, with Newcome, and then in the Cairn, on her knees before him. How to inform her aunt that she was trying to tell herself that she must have dreamed her reactions to him? An elderly female of twenty-seven, untouched and past her last prayers, could not possibly have felt as she did about a stable hand, a nobody who had arrived at Campions half-naked—and why did she have to think of him in that state? Her whole body flushed hot at the thought.

Of course she had imagined the whole thing, including the way in which Newcome had looked at her when they had been crouched in the Cairn together, as though he wanted to eat her, whole. On the ride home, and afterwards, he had been stiffly proper, had helped her down without so much as looking at her, and had led Vulcan and Rajah away, still with his eyes averted. Which, now she came to think about it, told its own story!

Well, she would not look at him, and would try to avoid his company—but, on the other hand, not too much so; unfair to him, to let Aisgill think that he had offended her, when the offence was hers, not his. He had done nothing.

Nell was almost too distracted to read her private correspondence—sorted for her by old Payne, who had looked more decrepit than ever this morning. One badly scrawled missive was from Cousin Ulric Tallboys, informing her that he intended to visit her on his way north to the Borders, and would arrive some time in the next fortnight, he did not know when. He was staying with the Staffords at Trentham.

'Who probably wanted him as little as I do,' said Nell drily to Aunt Conybeare, 'but are too polite to say so. I'll tell Mrs Orgreave to make a suite of rooms ready for him—he is the heir, after all.'

Work seemed a way to drive out improper thoughts about Newcome. She also considered a visit to High Harrogate. Perhaps more company was what she needed, to meet some young and sleek gentlemen whose smooth and civilised charms would compare well with Newcome's austere, straightforward manner.

Newcome again! Nell rose smartly to her feet, said abruptly, 'I'm going to work in the library. Challenor said that he'd found some old folios, stuffed away in a cupboard, and I ought to look at them.'

'Yes, do, dear,' said Aunt Conybeare comfortably. 'It might settle you. Your bibliomania is nearly as bad as his, although the stables seem to have seen more of you lately than the library.'

That did it! Nell almost bolted from the room. Oh, dear, is it as bad as that, that Aunt Conybeare is noticing something? Humour touched the corner of her mouth at the thought. Well, some fusty old books, dry as dust, perhaps containing woodcuts of men and women who looked more like Mr and Mrs Noah in a child's version of the ark which her grandfather had once given her than the people she saw around her, might cool her down and drive away these feverish fantasies which were filling her errant mind.

Pushing open the library door, registering old Challenor's pleasure at the sight of her, she said firmly to herself, I will forgo my usual afternoon ride for a time, come here instead. Say I don't feel quite the thing—God forgive me for the lie, I feel too much the thing—and then I needn't go to the stables at all, and shan't see. . .him.

She did not even want to think of his name, for that seemed to have nearly as strong an effect on her as seeing him.

These splendid resolutions lasted exactly forty-eight hours. . .

Nell awoke early, restless. She could not remember her dreams, only that her sleep had been disturbed and that they were vaguely disgraceful. She remembered crying out once, then sitting up, sweat streaming from her, although the air in the room was cold once she had pushed back the bedding.

Indoors seemed oppressive. She did not ring for Annie, but did what she often did, although Aunt Conybeare as well as Annie disapproved of the habit; she pulled on her clothes rapidly, finishing with her old grey woollen thing, which she wore to work with Challenor, and then a shabby overcoat over that—it had been worn by a young male Tallboys in the last century, and she had rescued it from the bottom of an old press to wear when she visited the stables.

She would, she told herself firmly, go for a walk in the grounds immediately round the house, so she would not need John or Annie to accompany her.

The day was grey and cold, but dry, and the walk exhilarated her. She made a circuit of the house, quite alone; it was so early that the house still slept, all the windows close-curtained, and, at the end, instead of going in again, her wandering feet led her to the stables as though they were leading her home.

Well, Aunt Conybeare, she thought afterwards, wryly, always did say that if I wandered into the stable yard without warning I should end up regretting it, and at last I did.

But did I? Regret it, that was.

As she walked through the arch the place seemed, at first, deserted. And then she turned the corner, into the flat paved area before the stable hands' quarters, a place she rarely visited, but which seemed safe at this hour.

And there, in the morning's half-light, standing in front of the pump, a bucket of water at his feet, and water all about him, was Chad.

He had evidently, despite the cold, taken an impromptu outdoor bath, and his face was hidden by the towel with which he was drying his hair, so that he could neither see nor hear her coming.

But that was not it at all, not at all. What was *it*, was that he was stark naked, and facing her. Nell was paralysed, except that at the sight of him her body was suddenly prey to the strangest feelings.

The worst was in the pit of her stomach—no, be honest, Nell, lower down altogether—where a most strange ache, exacerbated by throbbing and tickling, suddenly began, and her breasts, also, had begun to ache, and feel sensitive, and it was exactly as though she, too, were stark naked before him!

For he had lowered the towel to reveal those brilliant and disturbing bright blue eyes, and he was staring at her, as she, dreadfully, was staring at him.

Nell had never seen a naked man before, but she knew at once, without being told, that she had in front of her just about the most superb specimen of the male sex that she could hope to encounter. Almost against her will her eyes drank him in, from the powerful column of his neck, his broad and splendid shoulders, deep chest, covered in fine, curling black hair, a triangle which narrowed into an arrow, and then into another inverted triangular fleece above his . . .sex. . .which hung proud and magnificent before her, so that she hurriedly transferred her gaze to his long and splendid legs, muscular thighs, calves and feet, all perfectly proportioned, as though the giant statue of Mars, god of war, in the entrance hall of Campions had come to sudden and inconvenient life.

She also took in the great scar below his shoulder of which Aisgill had spoken, but most shaming of all was that she registered that he had seen her fascinated interest in the figure he presented, and was staring back at her, before he slowly dropped the towel to cover his loins, and began to turn away.

But not before saying in that deep, gravelly voice which so matched his harsh and powerful face, 'My apologies, Lady Elinor, I did not know that you were here.'

'Not—not at all,' she stammered inanely, as though she was addressing a fellow aristocrat, fully dressed in a polite drawing-room. 'My fault; I know that I should not have come here without warning.'

He half turned back, to speak again, she thought, except that he did not, merely gave her his rare and brilliant white smile, the smile that softened his face, and which, although Nell did not know it, had already won the heart of every female servant at Campions—only Chad had not cared to do anything with or to them, despite its power to seduce.

The paralysis that had gripped Nell left her as suddenly as it had come. She walked briskly away, still dreadfully aware of her own body and its primitive reactions. She had never experienced such a thing before when with any man.

It was a sensation so strong that it frightened her. For she knew, beyond a doubt, that if Chad Newcome had walked over, taken her into his arms and begun to. . .to. . .she would have been unable to stop him; nay, more, would have collaborated with him, stable hand though he was, and Countess in her own right though she was!

The primitive call of man to woman which she had always denied had any meaning for her—had denied, indeed, her very sex, and even that a man could ever rouse her—had her in its thrall.

Nell was compelled to face the fact that it had merely been sufficient for her to see him naked, for the pull of him which she had improbably felt the very first time on which she had seen him, which she had felt again in the Cairn, to be revealed in its purest and most passionate form, to tell her that merely to see him thus was enough to rouse her completely.

Pure! What a word to describe the sensations that coursed through her, and which gripped her still. Nell, unbelieving, shook herself as she walked blindly back through the arch.

It is being on my own so much, and seeing so little of anyone but old Challenor and Aunt Conybeare and the rest, old and middle-aged men, all of them. I really must order my mind a little. It cannot be him, it cannot!

But she could not forget what she had seen, and for the rest of the day, every time her mind strayed, Nell saw before her the form and physique of the perfect athlete that Chad Newcome had revealed to her, accidentally, that morning.

* * *

Aisgill was working in his little office when Chad came in for his day's orders. He was struggling with his paperwork, the stud book, the accounts of the hands' wages, the expenditure on the stud, everything connected with the stables, and for which he was responsible.

He waved an irritated quill at Newcombe, 'Wait, man, wait. I'll deal with you in a moment,' for the details of his work were refusing to sort themselves out on paper, however clear they were in his head.

He was aware of Newcome, standing there, quiet, and when his pen dropped ink on the paper for the second time, so that he screwed it up and flung it across the room, he saw Chad begin to speak, and then stop, hesitant.

'Yes, man, spit it out, what is it?'

Chad looked at Aisgill, who had been consistently kind to him, if stern, as he was with all the lads; he reminded Chad of someone—who? A vague figure in the mists of lost memory who had given Chad orders which he felt, rather than knew, he wanted to carry out efficiently. He also wanted to be of use.

He decided to speak; after all, Aisgill could always rebuff him.

'Maister Aisgill, sir. I have recovered a little more of my memory, not much, but it might be useful to you...' He stopped. Something told him that in his old life, whatever that was, he had given orders, and men had jumped to them, but here he was a menial, and must know his place.

'If you have something to say,' barked Aisgill, 'then say it. Time is valuable.'

Chad threw caution to the winds. 'I remember that I know how to keep books, write letters, and, if you wish, I could be your clerk; I know...' he hesitated again, but in for a penny, in for a pound '...that

Henson chases you about the paperwork, and if you used me, he could not.'

Aisgill was minded to roar at him, but something in Newcome's humility, a humility which he sensed was not natural to the man, but which told him that his servant did not wish to offend, but to help, stopped him. Stupid not to use a man's talents. More and more it was becoming plain to him that Newcome was other than a feckless fool who had ended up walking the roads because of his folly. Bad luck had probably done for him, as for others. What he actually had been was difficult to gauge.

'I took you in,' he said slowly, 'at my and Lady Elinor's wish, because we thought that you might be of service. You have proved yourself a hard worker, and, more than that, your skill with horses and around the stables is exceptional. If you think that you could be helpful to me in other ways, then why not? A man would be a fool not to take up such an offer.'

He rose, said with a wry smile, 'If you can write without blots, do so. Do you think you can copy out in fair what I have writ there in rough?'

Chad picked up the quill and sat in Aisgill's chair, looked at the pile of odd and grimy pieces of paper and scrap on which Aisgill kept his daily records, said cheerfully, 'I think I have a memory of working with worse than this,' and he let Aisgill instruct him in what was needful, before beginning to transcribe, in a fair copper-plate hand, and swiftly, what was before him.

'I was not,' he said, raising his head, to see Aisgill watching him intently, 'used to doing much figuring, I think.' He frowned; he could not tell Aisgill, for it appeared improbable, that he seemed to remember that other men had done that for him, and that he had inspected their work. 'But I do have a little grasp of the matter, enough to keep these simple accounts.'

When he had gone, the work done, and some letters written, still in the same fair hand, with a number of suggestions, diffidently made, which improved their sense, Aisgill walked over to the table which served as his desk, picked up the papers, and frowned.

The work before him was meticulous, and he laughed a little to himself at Henson's probable reaction. There'll be no grumbling this week, that's for sure, about my careless undecipherable hand, for he meant to go on using Newcome as his clerk—and then he frowned again. Every new talent which Newcome uncovered only served to demonstrate that he had been a man of more than common affairs.

Which made his arrival here at Campions, a nameless, memoryless vagabond, more than passing strange.

Aisgill was not the only person Chad Newcome troubled. His mistress hardly knew what to do with herself for thinking about him. She had always prided herself on her downright stability—what the late Dr Johnson had robustly called bottom. That, she knew, was a quality which denied fiddle-faddle, hemmings and hawings, acknowledged the truth of what was, as another philosopher, Hume, had said, and not what ought to be.

Men—and women—were naked, forked animals, she knew that well enough, and she should not have been so shocked to be reminded of what he, and she, so essentially were.

Be truthful, Nell, she said to herself, severely. You know perfectly well that what is shocking you is not having seen him, but what the sight of him did to you! You can no longer pretend complete indifference to the opposite sex, which you have done since you were nineteen. That is gone forever, along with your innocence. For what happened in the Garden of Eden to Adam and Eve has just happened to you. Be truthful again; you desired him, your stable hand and groom, a nameless nobody, and nothing that you can say or do will alter that one simple and undeniable fact.

And his own cool acceptance of what had happened, there in the yard, no mark of shame about him, at having been so found—what did that tell her about him?

Restlessly, Nell put down the book which she was reading in the library. One of the giant folios which Challenor had found—her predecessors, apart from the fourth Earl, had been careless of their books.

They had been careless of everything, and she had seen it as her duty to put matters in order, and since her succession six years ago order was what she brought to her great possessions.

And inside them her own life had been the most orderly thing of all—but no longer. Outwardly, all was the same, but inwardly—oh, inwardly, was a different matter, and cool Nell Tallboys had gone forever.

CHAPTER FIVE

'WELL,' said Henson, 'here's a turn-up!' It was a week later, and the Countess of Malplaquet and her advisers, Henson, Aisgill, Challenor and old Payne, her secretary, whom she had privately nicknamed her Privy Council, were having their Friday meeting in her study.

It was a vast room, with windows running from the floor to the ceiling, looking towards the park, which sloped away before them, and then across to the moors, a view so splendid that Nell was thinking of commissioning Turner to come and paint it. One wall was covered with bookshelves containing everything which Nell had thought it necessary to read in order to run Campions and her other properties correctly.

Over the hearth was a portrait of her grandfather, Patricius Tallboys, in all the glory of his youth, painted by Gainsborough, a lovely feathery thing, with the blue of his Garter ribbon glowing like a jewel across his white court dress. Two Canalettos, depicting views of London, were mounted on each side of the hearth above cabinets full of precious porcelain from China, Japan and Germany.

Nell's desk was a work of art, walnut, with inlays showing elaborate flowers, and had a little gilt rail at its back. But its use was practical, not decorative, and she and her cohorts had been doing their weekly examination of the estate's books.

Henson's exclamation had been provoked by the sight of Aisgill's books, which usually evoked either derision or criticism from him. 'You've been learning,' he accused. 'Who taught you?'

The two men had a running battle, half friendly, half not, for Nell's favour. Aisgill, hesitant, decided to tell the truth. Better so.

'Not me,' he offered. 'Newcome. He offered to be my clerk; and it is his work you are admiring.'

Payne picked up the letter written out for him to approve, amend and send out in Aisgill's name. 'I need make no alterations or additions to this,' he said in his cracked old voice. 'I take it that he did not copy it, but wrote it for you.'

'Wrong to deny it.' Aisgill was brief. 'Credit where credit is due. Yes, I told him what to say, and he did the rest.'

'A man of parts,' commented Henson, the comment grudging. They were all a little surprised by these further revelations of Newcome's abilities, including Nell. She did not let them see how much this news pleased her.

At the end of the meeting Nell made a decision. 'Stay behind, Aisgill. I would have a word with you.'

Henson looked sharply at them as he left. Nell walked over to the windows, looked out, spoke to Aisgill, uncharacteristically, without turning her head. 'I have not taken my daily ride lately. Pray see that Vulcan is saddled for me at two of the clock.'

She turned as she finished, to see Aisgill bob his head. 'It shall be done,' and then, for no conscious reason he could think of, he said, 'Will Newcome do as your groom, Lady Elinor?'

'If you can spare him from his clerkly duties, yes,' replied Nell lightly, and then, as though idly, 'I take it that he has recovered more of his memory—but still has no idea of who he is, or where he came from?'

'That is true, Lady Elinor.' Aisgill was hesitant. 'It

is strange, is it not, how much has come back to him, and yet he does not know himself? I am an ignorant old man, but I sometimes wonder——' And he paused again.

'Yes,' said Nell encouragingly. 'What do you wonder, Aisgill? You know that I value your opinion.' Which was true, she thought. He might not be educated, like Henson and Payne, but he had an earthy and unsentimental shrewdness which was sometimes better than book learning.

'I wonder, which is stupid, I know, whether he does not wish to remember himself. He has such bad dreams, madam.'

'You think that he may have done something dreadful, perhaps,' said Nell, a little anxious.

'No, not that. I think he may have been unhappy, but is happy now, except when he sleeps.'

Nell was glad that she had said and done nothing—such as asking for another escort—to make Aisgill suspicious of Newcome; he seemed to trust him, not only to do his work well, but to protect her. Originally, when he had assigned him to ride wth her, he had said, 'What better than an old soldier to look after you? If he cannot protect you, no one can.'

She was thinking of that, and what had passed in the morning, when she waited that afternoon for Newcome to bring her horse round to the steps before the grand entrance, and when he appeared, leading Rajah, young Peel behind him with Vulcan, there was nothing in the behaviour of either of them to suggest that anything untoward might have happened on their last two meetings.

Nell mounted Vulcan, and they rode off together, Peel watching, in silence, my lady and her respectful groom, riding slightly behind her as though nothing had ever passed between them.

What nonsense! Of course nothing had happened. A couple of mischances, that was all. She had stumbled, and he had saved her, and then they had met... somewhat unfortunately... And not a word of that was true. She had been strongly affected, and, trying to look behind at him without him realising it and failing, she could sense without knowing how that he, too, had been affected, but how, she could not tell.

If Chad had told her the truth, which he had no intention of doing, he wondered how shocked Lady Elinor Tallboys would be. Would she recoil from him, have him thrown back on to the moor from which he had emerged? For what he had felt when she had come upon him, naked, and had felt so strongly that his body had almost betrayed him before her, was a desire for her that, although he did not know it, was no stronger than Nell's for him.

No difference of rank or circumstance had meant anything. Simply, he was a man, and she was a woman, and the accident of their meeting thus, even more than the encounter at the Cairn, had finally told him that what he felt for Elinor Tallboys, Countess of Malplaquet, Viscountess Wroxton, Baroness Sheveborough, all in her own right, was more than simple lust. It was a longing for her as his partner as well as his love!

Which, look at it how you would, was preposterous. For how should he, poor Chad, nobody from nowhere, lucky to have a coat on his back, dare to raise his eyes to that?

No, he must go carefully. Give no hint of his true feelings, be surly, even, and his dour expression made his harsh face so much harsher that Nell, looking at him, felt her heart sink. Was he annoyed with her that she had disturbed his privacy that morning?

Before they left Aisgill, as usual, had seen that they

were properly equipped to protect themselves. There were dangerous men about, he had said, and, although he doubted that there might be any on Lady Elinor's land, the moor must not be considered perfectly safe. So each rider had a horse pistol in a holster on their saddle, and Chad had orders to guard his mistress with his life.

Nell always refused to ride with more than one escort, 'For who would attack me?' she had said. 'And I do not wish to ride out in a procession, and besides I never go far.'

But that afternoon, instead of turning for home at the usual point, fairly low on the moor by the Cairn, restlessness overcame her. She swung off her horse, and, turning, said to Newcome, 'Tell me, have you ever ridden to the Throne of God?'

To her amusement, the strong face broke up a little as he replied. 'No, Lady Elinor. I have not had that privilege.'

Nell laughed; she could not prevent herself. With one light sentence he had diffused the tense atmosphere between them.

'Not the real one,' she said. 'I mean the great pile of rocks there.' And she pointed with her whip to the far distance, where a massive cluster of giant rocks and boulders reared, high on the moor. 'That is what we Yorkshire tykes call the Throne of God, and, being good Yorkshiremen, we think it natural that God should have made his home on the moors.'

It was Chad's turn to laugh even as, standing, he tried to hold the impatient Rajah.

'You surely don't intend to ride there this afternoon, madam,' he ventured. 'It is hardly wise. The hour is late, and by the looks of it the journey is not a short one.'

For whatever reasons, Nell suddenly became skittish, she who was always so full of common sense—and, yes, bottom.

'Are you giving the orders, Newcome? Or is it your Countess's commands that you must, and should, obey? I wish to ride there now, immediately, and you shall accompany me, unless, of course, you prefer to return on your own, and explain to Aisgill why I am not with you!'

Afterwards, she was to curse her light-headed folly, and the behaviour that was so out of character for her. Perhaps it was being with Newcome; perhaps, in some fashion, she wished to tease, to provoke him. She never knew.

Chad was uneasy. While they were standing there, talking, he had been overcome by the oddest feeling. A feeling of being watched, secretly observed. It was a feeling which he knew that he had experienced before, but of the where and when he had no notion. Only that it might be unwise to ignore it.

He tried again. 'I cannot,' he said, voice grave, 'advise your ladyship,' and he used her correct title deliberately, 'to do any such thing. I have a. . .bad feeling about such a journey.'

'Well, I have not,' averred Nell gaily, feeling delightfully irresponsible for once in her oh, so serious life. 'So spurs to horse, Newcome, and take *my ladyship*——' and she trod on her title comically '—where she commands you to go.'

No help for it; against all his instincts and the raised hair on the back of his neck, there was nothing for it but to obey, and they set out again, riding through the withered heather and bracken, dull after the flaming reds, golds and mauves of autumn.

And now, he thought, the dark was threatening to be on them early, well before they saw Campions again, and the other threat was Aisgill's anger with him if anything happened to the suddenly wilful woman who was now riding alongside him, and if he fell back as a good groom should she reined back so that alongside he was compelled to remain, unless they were to lose even more time.

The feeling of danger grew stronger and stronger as they approached the Throne itself. Nearer to, he saw that several piles of rock were heaped together, some at quite a distance from the main grouping of stones and boulders which stood in the middle, and which with a little imagination could be seen as a throne of sorts.

Nell, having got her way, was a little ashamed, but not so ashamed that she was above playing games with Chad over riding level with him. But, like Chad, she was beginning to realise that an early dusk would be on them before their return, that they were in a lonely and isolated spot, and she had no business undertaking this mad expedition, just to contradict her groom, and to impress on him who was master—or, rather, mistress!

Master, she thought was better; mistress had unfortunate associations!

They had reached the Throne itself, and were on level ground. She was preparing to dismount, and Chad was dismounting before her—she had difficulty in thinking of him as Newcome—when disaster struck. There was the whine of a bullet coming from the direction of the far group of rocks, and Nell's horse dropped wounded, and probably dying, beneath her.

Fortunately she was thrown clear, to land, stunned and shocked, on the bare earth. Chad, who was still in the act of dismounting, holding Rajah only loosely, was also thrown down, as Rajah, on hearing the shot, flung back his head with a great whinny, and bolted, running at speed across the moor.

Chad rolled away in the direction of the Throne, instinctively protecting himself from a possible further shot, if more than one man was firing at them—he had no doubt that the bullet had been meant for Nell.

Silence had fallen; with both on the ground there was no target for a sniper—if sniper it were—for him to aim at. Chad, memories stirring in him, crawled over to Nell, to find her living and apparently unharmed, only winded by her fall, but shocked, her face grey. On seeing him, apparently unharmed, she gave a little cry and tried to rise.

'No,' he said urgently, pushing her down again. 'Not yet. Do not make yourself a target.' Words, ideas, memories were roaring through his head.

Being shot at from ambush was not a new experience, and he knew how to deal with it. Words of command unthinkingly streamed from him.

'Come,' said Nell, a little fiercely, 'you cannot believe that the bullet was meant for me. A sportsman's accident, surely.'

'At this hour, on the moor, with little on it, from someone who I am sure has been tracking us all afternoon, staying to windward, out of sight,' rasped Chad. 'Best take no chances. Crawl with me to the Throne, or, even better, wriggle like a snake. Now!'

Nell took one look at his face, hard and set. His tone had been so authoritative, that of a man ordering other men, and expecting to be obeyed.

She shivered. Supposing that the bullet had been meant for her! Prudence dictated that she obey him, and she wriggled away from the screams of her horse on her hands and knees. She reached the shelter of the Throne, turned, to find that Chad had not immediately followed her, had detoured to poor Vulcan, and was pulling her pistol from its holster.

Foolishly, her first thought was that he meant to put

Vulcan out of his misery, but no such thing. The pistol once in his possession, he was crawling after her, to push her further beneath the seat of the great Throne, so that she could not be easily seen, or even shot at.

'That's my brave girl,' he whispered, as though she were a wench from the village, and not his Countess. 'Do as I say, and you may yet be safe.'

'And what do you say?' Nell asked of this new man, who seemed to know what to do in a tight corner.

'I say that you will stay here, hidden, and I shall leave you to smoke out who shot at us and why. It may be that I am imagining ghosts, that you were right, a sportsman's accident, that he took himself off when he saw what he had done, but I think not.'

'You would leave me?' panted Nell.

'What else to do?' answered Chad, with indisputable logic; a habit of his she and others were to find in the coming months. 'If we stay here, we are his sitting targets sooner or later, for we cannot stay hidden forever. I assume that he is better armed than we are. If I track him—and he will not be expecting me to do that—I might. . .dispose of him. . .otherwise, he will surely do for us.'

He did not add and nobody knows where we are, as you, in your wilfulness, have decreed, but the thought was there, unexpressed, and Nell swallowed at it.

'I'm sorry,' she said ruefully. 'I broke all Aisgill's rules. . .'

'No,' he said, and then, perhaps not strictly truthfully, for he wanted her to maintain her brave spirit, and not repine at her folly, 'If he meant to shoot you, and God knows why, he might have done it at any time, and there are more dangerous places to be than this—at least we have cover. Enough of talking. I must go.'

'And if you do not return?' she asked steadily,

although her heart was hammering, for his danger as well as her own.

'You are still in no worse case than you are now—for at least if I go there is the chance of my scotching the snake,' he replied, 'and that is the best I can offer you, for our case, yours and mine, is desperate. Stay here, do not come out, and if I am lost, pray, lady, pray, for only your god can save you.'

Nell had to be content with that for he was impatient to be off. She pushed herself further under the seat, nothing of her to be seen, and he was gone, silently, like the snake of which he had spoken. She remembered what Aisgill had said of him, that he thought that Chad had been a soldier, and almost certainly a good one. She thought by his manner, and what he had said, that he had stalked men like this before, and that after all the outcome might not be too terrible.

Oh, she must hold on to that while she lay hidden beneath God's seat, and time passed with infinite slowness. She prayed a little that he might be safe, and, shocked, realised that she had prayed for him before she had prayed for herself.

Dear God, he must not suffer for my folly. I could not bear that. I might deserve to pay for a moment's light-mindedness, but Chad does not.

And then suddenly, shockingly, there was the sound of two shots, and, after that, silence.

CHAPTER SIX

CHAD remembered that he had, as Nell suspected, done this before: that was, stalked a sniper who was ambushing him and his men—although when and where this had happened he had no idea, only knowing that he had done it.

Warily, like a serpent, belly to the ground, he worked his way forward as silently as he could, making a wide detour through the bracken to a point slightly below that from which the shot had come, and where there had been no movement, no action, since.

Above him, he suspected, was a man with a rifle, who had carefully stalked himself and Nell, raising Chad's own hackles in the process. He should have listened harder to what his instincts told him, and, if necessary, have thrown her wilful ladyship over Rajah's saddle, and hauled her home, before he had ignored what some kind god was trying to tell him.

And now, with one ball in a horse pistol, he must try to overcome a man armed with a rifle, and probably a pair of loaded pistols as well.

Suddenly, there was the man himself, and his horse, loosely tethered to a dead tree, ready for a quick getaway. He could not have moved since he had loosed his shot at Nell, and yes, he had a rifle, like the ones he had seen in. . .in. . . His tortured mind gave up the useless struggle. Suffice it that he knew what he was seeing.

Chad worked his way silently, silently as a guerrilla—what guerrilla? Where?—towards his enemy, who was lying prone, his rifle propped on a stone, to hold it steady. He had evidently done this kind of thing before. There was a brace of pistols by him, on the same stone. He was waiting for him and Nell to emerge from their fastness, as sooner or later they must.

He could not shoot the man from where he was, as there was no target to aim at—the prone position protected him—as it was meant to. If he could get nearer. . .he wriggled another few yards, and then, his hand closing around one of the small stones which littered the ground, he threw it, to hit the man on the back.

Cursing, the man above him rose, turned, snatching up a pistol to fire at where the stone had come from, probably judging that to raise the rifle and sight would take too long. He was sharp against the skyline, a perfect target, even in the gathering gloom, and Chad, who had leapt to his own feet the moment the stone had left his hand, ran forward, and shot him at point-blank range, in the chest—nothing for it; it was kill, or be killed.

As he fell forward, dying, the assassin's finger clenched on the trigger. The second shot, which Nell heard, rang out, and at its sound the dead man's horse broke from the rope which held him, and, like Rajah, bolted across the moor.

Chad waited. His adversary might not be quite dead, might be shamming, might even have accomplices close by, although Chad thought not, but best take no chances.

And then, when nothing stirred, he went over, rolled the man into a position where he could see his shattered chest and grimy face, fringed with a ginger beard.

Something about him and his clothes was almost familiar. Chad shrugged, damned his lost memory, and examined the rifle on the stone with a professional eye.

It was a beauty, a fine thing, delicately engraved, its cost, he would have thought, far beyond what the dead ruffian could have paid for it. Something odd about the rifle, too. He shook his head again to clear it. Trying to remember always troubled him.

Thoughtfully, he put it down, and, no need to be cautious now, he ran back to where he had left Nell, as he had begun to think of her. She would be imagining him dead, and wondering when her turn would come.

Nell, hearing the sound of a man running towards her, cringed a little, and then, when Chad's voice came, 'Do not be frightened, Lady Nell, there is no one left to do you harm,' she gave a little cry of relief.

'And you are safe?' she called.

'Quite safe. You may come out of hiding now.'

Nell, clothes filthy, her whole body one ache from the combined effects of her fall and lying cramped for so long, crawled out, tried to stand, needed Chad to steady her.

For a moment they stood, locked together, for her to feel the strength of him, to murmur fervently, 'Thank God you are unharmed. My fault, my fault.'

Even in this last desperate strait, for they were now abandoned on the moor, their mortal enemy dead, but left to the night and the elements, with none knowing where they were, Chad could not help registering what a vital armful he held.

And then he loosed her from him.

'What happened?' she asked. 'I heard two shots. You are not wounded, and he? Where is he?' And she made as if to go look for him.

Nell felt him restrain her. 'No,' he said. 'Best not. He's dead, I fear.'

'Dead,' she half moaned, and then fiercely, 'He meant to kill you, so you shot him.'

'No alternative,' said this new grave Chad, who had killed to save her, and oh, she honoured him for it. 'And a pity, Lady Nell, a great pity.'

'Oh, your wish to have spared him honours you.'

'No,' said Chad, his face hard. 'Not that. Dead, we cannot question him, you see, discover why he did it, perhaps who paid him.'

'But some Luddite malcontent, surely,' said Nell, 'who shot at me because he sees me as his enemy.'

'Perhaps.' Chad was grave. The devious mind which he had recently discovered he possessed was working hard. He thought of the splendid rifle again, and wondered why it troubled him. He also wondered what enemies Lady Elinor might possess. Who, for instance, stood to benefit by her death? He shivered at the thought, and said no more. He did not wish to disturb her.

For they were not yet out of the wood, or, more properly, off the moor!

Aisgill was beginning to grow anxious. Lady Elinor and Newcome should have returned long since. He was debating what to do when he saw Henson coming across the yard, struggling against the bitter wind which had sprung up.

'What's this?' Henson said, almost angry. 'I was due to meet her ladyship an hour ago, and Mrs Conybeare tell me that she is not yet back from her ride, and it is almost dark. Where has she gone, and who rode with her?'

He was determined to prove to Aisgill, whom he thought Lady Nell gave far too long a rope, that in the last analysis he, the agent, was master here.

Aisgill regarded him sourly. 'You cannot be more

worried than I am,' he announced. 'Yes, she should be back, but Newcome is with her. She should be safe enough.'

'Newcome with her!' ejaculated Henson. 'You've gone light in the attic, man, to send her out with him. You know nothing of him, and that loss of memory could be all a pretence. Ten to one, he's made off with her.'

'That I do not believe,' said Aisgill, although he was beginning to have qualms himself about letting the mistress go off in the company of one so dubious, when all was said and done. 'I am about to be sending search parties to look for them. Lady Elinor usually rides only to the Cairn.'

'And if that were where she has gone,' said Henson sharply, 'she would have been back long since, and I should not be troubling you.'

It was while Aisgill was drawing up and instructing search parties, every face worried, for Lady Nell was loved, and Newcome was beginning to be liked, that one of the lads ran up, face alarmed.

'It's Rajah,' he blurted. 'He's running on the moor, riderless, and none can get near him to bring him in.'

'And Vulcan?' said Aisgill, desperately, sure now that something was badly wrong.

'No sign of Vulcan, nor either of their riders. Rajah's in a fair old lather, looks to have come a long way.'

It took some time to corner Rajah, his weariness letting them catch him rather than any acts of theirs, and while this was going on the first party of lads, carrying lanterns, and with orders to halloo when they reached Lady Nell's usual turning-point, had set off on their mission.

Foam flying about him, Rajah, who bucked and snorted at every hand laid on him, was inspected.

'No sign of hurt,' reported Aisgill to the worried Henson, 'the pistol still in its holster. No reins broken. All his lines intact. Nothing to explain why he lost his rider, and was parted from Vulcan.'

Rajah continued to show his dislike of everyone who was not Chad Newcome before he was finally wrestled into his stall. Both of Nell's senior servants were beginning to be seriously worried, and Aunt Conybeare finally appeared in the yard, shawl about her shoulders, to voice her distress that her darling was missing. Nell was a daughter to her, the daughter she had never borne.

'More search parties,' ordered Aisgill, and then, decisively, 'and I shall lead one to the Throne of God.'

'The Throne of God,' snorted Henson, 'why there? It's miles away.'

'Because Lady Nell loves the place, and think, she might have wanted Newcome to see it. He's never been so far afield to my certain knowledge.'

Henson stared at Aisgill. Something odd there. Something both men instinctively felt.

'Lady Nell to take Newcome to see something! *Newcome*! The vagabond hauled half-naked off the moor. Why should she do that?'

'They deal well together,' said Aisgill, almost uncomfortably.

Henson stared again. 'What are you saying, man?'

'Nothing,' growled Aisgill angrily. 'What are you saying? Lady Nell is kind. The man is good with her horses. She might think the Throne of God a good place to show him—and why am I gossiping here with you? The more I think of it, the more likely it seems. The night is drawing on, and if they are unprotected out there in the open. . .' And he ran off, shouting to round up the horses, to order yet another group of Nell's people on to the moor, himself leading it.

Behind him, Henson stared at nothing. 'Rainbows,' he said finally to himself. 'Whimwhams, and dammit, since that man arrived here, nothing has been the same.'

That man sat with his mistress in the lee of the rocks around the Throne of God. The night was bitterly cold, and a fine rain had succeeded a strong wind. Beside him, Nell, wrapped in the warm green coat from his livery, shivered, and tried to prevent herself from shivering further. Shock as well as the bitter night held her prisoner.

And, to keep her warm, Chad had stripped to his shirt, and must be feeling the cold dreadfully. What was worst of all was that it was her silly irresponsible fault. Without the journey to the Throne, they would have been home and dry hours ago.

She said as much to Chad, who grunted, 'Nonsense,' at her. 'He could as well have tried to shoot you on the journey back from the Cairn, as he did later, when we pressed on.'

Nell had suggested that they try to walk towards Campions, but he had said, 'Nonsense,' to that as well. Since the attempt on her life, and his killing of the would-be assassin, ladyships and stable hands seemed to have flown away; they were man and woman together, struggling for survival.

'There's no shelter on the way should we need it,' Chad said, 'and its cloudy tonight, with little moon to help us. God knows where we should end up. Rest here, and we may try to walk at first light. Aisgill will surely be sending search parties after us, and with luck Rajah might have run in, to warn them that something is very wrong.'

Nell thought of poor dead Vulcan, whose screams had stopped long ago, and of the other body, lost among the rocks where Chad had left it, beside all the incriminating evidence of guilt and murder.

'Newcome. . .' she said suddenly—she really must not be thinking of him as Chad.

'Lady Nell?' For Chad had begun to call her by the affectionate name the hands always used of her in her absence.

'You might as well have your coat back,' she said, teeth chattering. 'It might warm you. I think that nothing is going to warm me.'

Chad became quite still, turned towards her where she sat by him, took her small frozen hand in his large one.

'I have been remiss,' he said abruptly, memory stirring in him again, for his hand, although he wore less than she, was warmer than hers. 'We must do something to warm you. . .or. . .'

Nell knew what the 'or' meant. Men and women had died of exposure on the moors in temperatures similar to this. There was, fortunately, no frost, but the wind and rain were working against her instead.

'Come,' he said, slipping his coat from her shoulders. 'There's no help for it. Forgive me, my lady,' he said, all formality, which was ironic enough in the face of what he was about to do.

For he wrapped his coat closely about the two of them, but not before he had drawn Nell into his arms, against his broad chest, to hold her in order to warm her, and then he began to chafe her cold hands, to restore them to life.

Oh, thought Nell dreamily, how comfortable this is, to be sure. She could feel the living warmth of him, the clean male scent of Chad and stables mixed, the latter a smell Nell had known and loved all her life. She could feel the steady beat of his heart, and she turned her head further into his chest, so that its rhythm began to affect her strongly, and as heat passed from him to her another heat began, slowly and stealthily, not outside her, but inside, as though flames were being ignited in her.

What was happening to her? For this new feeling was not only powerful, but was making strange demands of her. For she wanted to burrow further and further into Chad, to put her arms about him, to. . .

Chad knew quite well what was happening to Nell—and to him. He felt her breathing change, took a deep breath, and began to speak, to take both their minds off their errant bodies.

'A strange thing happened out there, Lady Elinor,' he said, speaking with exquisite formality to keep his voice steady and his own breathing easy.

'Oh, Chad, what was that?' murmured Nell drowsily, forgetting her resolution to address him as Newcome, the strongest sense of well-being beginning to take her over, repressing a little her desire to seize hold of Chad and stroke him as he was stroking her hands and arms.

'I recovered a little of my memory,' he answered. . . and paused for her to say warmly,

'Oh, how splendid. You know who you are?'

He shook his head, as much to clear it as to deny what she had said. The woman in his arms, so warm and soft. . . He started to speak again. 'Not that, but I had glimpses of my past, which tell me that Aisgill's guess that I was once a trooper is correct. Flashes only, but I know that I was once in Spain, with the guerrillas there. I must have been cut off from the army and my officer, because I was giving orders, so Aisgill was right that I was a sergeant.'

He stopped again. 'Which would explain my clerkly abilities a little, except. . .' How to say that somehow none of these deductions seemed correct to him, there was something missing, but what, he did not know?

And in the meantime, however much he tried to distract himself, Nell's proximity was beginning to affect him so powerfully that it was all that he could do not to begin to make love to her on the spot.

And what he felt for her was not simple lust. The woman he held was not just any woman, she was... she was...the one woman, the woman the memoryless wanderer had wanted all his life—and never found, until now. And how did he know that? But he did.

It was the Countess Nell, hard-working, proud, compassionate, careful of those who served her, whom he held and wished to pleasure. Countess Nell of the strong, sweet face, whose presence lit up every corner of Campions. Countess Nell who had taken pity on him, and, Oh, God, I want to make love to her, not fiercely, but slowly and gently, to see her fulfilled beneath me, her pleasure more to me than mine, for Countess Nell gives, never takes, and I must give, to her.

And temptation was too much, at last, for he was only a man, and not a saint, and he bent his head, to cup her chin in his hand, and tip her face towards him. To do—what?

Nell, lost in a dream of happiness, hardly aware of where she was, obediently turned her head to help him as she felt his big hand cup her face so gently, and as he tipped it up towards him, before she knew what she was doing, she kissed the palm that cherished her.

For Chad as for Nell, time stood still. Propinquity, the growing warmth spreading between them, was doing its work. After she had kissed him, he returned her kiss, gently, on the cheek, and then, since she showed no sign of distress at what he was doing, kissed her again, on the other, turning her head slightly, and her response was to make a little noise, almost like a cat purring. For, thought Nell light-headedly, he saved my life at the risk of his, and he surely deserves some reward.

Besides, I like what he is doing!

She was now fully in his arms, body as well as face offered to him, and Chad was desperate. Honour said that he must not take advantage of her, reason said that he would suffer for it if he seduced her, as he now so easily might, but something deep and strong was telling him that what he wanted she wanted too, and that was all that mattered.

His right hand now cupped her breast, stroking it through the cloth, and she purred again, said indistinctly, 'Oh, thank you, Chad, thank you,' and her right hand stole up around his neck to stroke him in return.

He kissed her again, and this time not on the cheek, for as he bent to do so she turned her own head hungrily towards him, and the kiss found her mouth, and they were suddenly drowning in passion.

From the depths of the memory he no longer possessed, something called, No! so loudly that Chad pulled away for very honour, for it was honour that was calling, and said in a voice husky with desire, 'No.'

And then still holding her, to keep her warm against him, he said, even more formally than before, 'Lady Elinor, it is no uncommon thing, when men and women have been in danger together that. . .' And he gulped; how to say this delicately, without offending, or hurting her?

Nell, cradled in Chad's arms, had never felt so mindlessly happy in her whole life. He was big enough to make her feel small and delicate—no mean feat—and not since she had been a little girl could she remember being held so lovingly, being treated with such careful kindness. She was light-headed enough with shock, excitement, exhaustion, and yes, true love, not to want him to stop caressing her.

At the back of her mind a little voice was telling her where this might end, but in her delirium of mingled love and desire she thought, If Rajah can pleasure White Princess, why should not Chad pleasure me? And she saw no lack of logic in this disgraceful notion; rather it was as though she, Chad, Rajah and the Princess were all partners in a dance of nature, where titles, social conformity and duties to God and King meant nothing.

'Yes?' she said dreamily, aware not only that he had stopped speaking, but he had ceased making love to her, and she did not wish him to do that. 'You were saying, and then you stopped. What was that about men and women?'

'That when they have been in danger together they frequently. . .desire one another afterwards.'

'And that, you think,' said Nell, wishing all this would end and that Chad would get down to the true business of loving again, 'is why we are behaving like this now?'

'Yes,' Chad said briefly, and, as far as he was concerned, although he was not so sure of Nell, he was lying in his teeth.

By now, Nell was far gone, already on the edge of sleep, a sleep induced by his gentle lovemaking on top of her exhaustion and shock.

'You're wrong, you know,' she said confidentially and sleepily, and how good it was to sleep in one's lover's arms, 'I felt like this about you long before tonight,' and, so saying, she finally drifted into a warm slumber, her changed breathing telling the man who held her not only that he had warmed his Countess into life, but in return she had frankly and freely offered him her love.

And what, he thought, still holding her carefully, and giving her one last, chaste kiss on her forehead, would she think when daylight claimed her, and she was the Lady Malplaquet again, and he was Chad, her groom and stable hand? Would she even remember what she had said and he had done?

The moon, long missing, came from behind a cloud, and threw strange shadows on the moor which lay all about them. Chad could not sleep. First his roused body prevented him, and then when desire faded, and it was enough to hold her in his arms and study her sleeping face, the necessity to stay awake, to guard and protect his woman remained.

Even stranger shadows, quite unlike those on the moor, ran through his head. How did he know that he had never felt like this for a woman before, that the other women he had known had always taken, never given? He did not remember their names or their faces, nor how and why they had loved, and why it had not been satisfactory, as it had been tonight—even though nothing had been consummated.

Chad sighed, and Nell stirred in his arms. In her dreams she was in a ballroom, full of people wearing court dress, orders and decorations. She was looking for someone, and then she found him. He had his back to her, was wearing an officer's splendid dress uniform, the uniform of an aide; even from the back she could see the bullion on his broad shoulders.

And then he turned and walked towards her and she saw his face plain, and it was Chad! But as she touched him wonder and delight rising her, his arms enfolding her, the dream faded, and she fell into the deep sleep of oblivion, safe in Chad's arms beneath the Throne of God.

CHAPTER SEVEN

TOWARDS midnight, as he later discovered, for he did not sleep, but remained awake to protect his lady from any further danger which might befall, Chad heard the noise of Aisgill's party, heading towards them, across the moor.

Nell lay in his arms, face trustfully turned up towards him; once or twice she stirred, and a small smile crossed her dreaming face, his warmth and hers mingling.

All passion, all desire, had leached from him. All he felt was an enormous protectiveness. He had killed for her once, and knew that he would do so again, if necessary. He was at one with Rajah, or the lion who protected his pride, the falcon who stooped to destroy his enemy. What he felt for Nell had been sealed in blood.

The spilling of blood had not been necessary for him to love her—that had come of itself, born from the gratitude for her saving of him from starvation, nurtured by all that he had seen of her since, come to full-blown maturity when he had taken her in his arms to warm her.

But the bond which had been created by what he had done for her was there, a living thing between them, and the instinctive man he was, who needed no memory to guide him, knew that she, being the woman she was, would acknowledge that bond, as she had already acknowledged her love, before she had fallen asleep in his arms.

The noise below told Chad that the everyday world,

the world where peeress and lowly servant could not meet as equals, was upon them. He heard the sound of horses and men, voices calling, saw the light of lanterns, knew that rescue was near, and he feared that, despite all, once the bright day was on them again what Nell Tallboys had said would be denied or forgotten—but he could neither deny, nor forget.

They must not be found like this, and he slipped out of the coat which they had shared, wrapped it around her lovingly, and, while she protested in her sleep at losing him, he propped her against one of the pillars of the Throne, and left her—to walk, shouting, towards Aisgill and the men with him.

'Praise be to God,' cried Aisgill fervently. 'Lady Nell is safe?' And then, 'I knew it, I knew it, she took you to the Throne—and what,' he demanded fiercely, 'happened to your horses, Newcome, that Rajah should come home without you? Where is Vulcan? Never say you let that mild beast get away from you both!'

'A private word with you, Maister Aisgill,' said Chad, face grim, after he had taken Aisgill's hand, and pointed to the sleeping Nell, half hidden under the Throne's seat, 'before you tell the rest.' For the search party was now upon them.

'As to Vulcan,' he began, leading Aisgill over to the spot where the poor beast lay dead, 'it is as you see,' and he poured the whole story of the attack and its consequences into Aisgill's disbelieving ear as carefully and lucidly as though he were reporting to his senior officer.

Aisgill's early disbelief did not survive the evidence of the bullet which had killed Vulcan, nor the sight of the body and rifle lying among the rocks parallel with the Throne.

'I was sorry to kill him,' said Chad, 'for could I have

taken him alive we might have learned something of why he attacked Lady Elinor, but I had no choice.'

'No,' agreed Aisgill. 'You did your duty, Newcome, and protected your mistress as a good servant—and a good soldier— should.'

Nell had been awakened by the noise of the search party and she walked unsteadily towards them, Chad's jacket still around her shoulders, and for the first time Aisgill saw that Chad was shivering in the night air.

'Come,' he said roughly, to one of the lads, 'give Newcome a blanket for his shoulders, and you, Lady Elinor,' he said reprovingly to her, as though she were the child she had once been, whom he had taught and reprimanded, 'may explain to me tomorrow why you should bring Newcome here, so late in the day.'

Nell coloured, and put out a hand in Chad's direction. 'I was wrong,' she said, and then, to Aisgill, 'but he saved me. . .'

Aisgill saw that, despite the sleep she had enjoyed since the ambush, his mistress was exhausted and shocked. He dared to interrrupt her. 'Enough for now, my lady. In the morning you may both tell the whole tale, although Newcome's bravery is plain to see, and fortunate for us all, the day we took him in.'

As they left, beginning the long journey back to Campions, Chad riding one of the horses, Nell's side-saddle transferred from Vulcan to one of the lads' mounts so that she might travel home between Aisgill and himself, he turned once to look at the place of the stones where his Countess had first kissed him in love and gratitude.

Nell sat up in bed the next morning, being petted by everybody. A great fire roared in the bedroom hearth, and Aunt Conybeare was in a chair by her bed, a magnificent four-poster, its crimson curtains looped into a gilt earl's coronet high above it.

Her aunt was worrying over her, exhorting her not to overdo things, then said, almost reprovingly, 'You look very well, my dear, for one who has had such an unfortunate experience. Half a night in the open, a man and your horse killed in earshot, a long ride back, and you look blooming, positively blooming. Lately you have looked a trifle. . .wan. . .to say the least.'

Nell snuggled into her pillows, drank hot chocolate laced with cream, ate new-made white rolls, with delicious strawberry jam and butter, and tried not to let the dreadful thoughts she was having show on her face. But oh, dear, from her aunt's comments, they obviously did!

Had she really kissed Chad Newcome last night, before he had kissed her, and virtually invited him to make love to her? Worse, had she actually told him, quite wantonly, that she had been wanting him to make love to her from the moment she had first seen him?

No, surely not. She could not have done *that*. Not she, Nell Tallboys, whose reputation had frightened every suitor away, who could by her cold stare reduce strong men to mumbling inanity when they had tried to court her. Icy Nell Tallboys had lain in the arms of her giant stable hand and had invited him to make love to her, in so many words—no, a very few words, and all of them plain.

But if she had not behaved like a lady, let alone a noblewoman, Chad Newcome had behaved like a gentleman. No, revise that Nell, *better* than most gentlemen. He must have distanced himself from her before Aisgill and the other lads had arrived, to stifle any suggestion of improper behaviour, although how

Aisgill thought that she had managed to keep warm she could not imagine.

And what should she say when she next saw him—and what would he say to her? What etiquette governed what she had done? Well, he had saved her life, and she had already heard from Aunt Conybeare, so late had she slept, that Henson, Aisgill, Payne and old Challenor the librarian had met in conclave, talked to Newcome, stared at the body which had been brought in, sent for a constable from Keighley, the nearest village, and had discussed putting up bills to try to find out who Nell's would-be murderer was.

All in all, Aunt Conybeare had told her, interest and excitement between Newcome's astonishing resourcefulness and the mystery of who might want to kill her, seeing that no one, rightly, thought that the shot was meant for Newcome.

'And no more riding on the moors with only one groom, my dear,' said Aunt Conybeare tenderly. Nell had only just been able to prevent her spooning bread and milk into her unwilling mouth.

'Oh, no,' she had said determinedly when Aunt Conybeare had processed in with a great china bowl of the wretched stuff, 'you can take that away,' and then, mischievously, quoting from *Macbeth*, which she had been told one ought never to do,' "Throw physic to the dogs; I'll none of it".'

'What in the world has come over you this last week or so, Nell?' sighed her aunt. 'You have always been so prim and proper. And now, suddenly, you are a positive hoyden—no, that is not the word; I cannot think of one which fits your goings-on. Why in the world, for example, should you drag poor Newcome to the Throne of God, the last thing a stable lad would be interested in, I dare swear?'

'On the contrary, Aunt,' said Nell, looking at her

from under her eyelashes, 'he seemed so interested in the Cairn when we rode there that I thought that the Throne of God would entertain him even more, and so it did, until that murdering wretch arrived. And, besides, he said that it was a good thing we did go there.'

Her mouth was now so disgracefully full of buttered roll and strawberry jam that she had difficulty in getting the next bit out. 'He said that we were better off in the shelter of the Throne than on the moor. We were not so good a target for a sniper.'

'Aisgill said that you owe your life to his courage,' remarked her aunt.

'So I do, and I want to see him, as soon as possible, to thank him,' said Nell, mouth free again, 'because I didn't thank him properly last night.'

'But not in your bedroom, my dear,' said her aunt, reprovingly again. Really, what *was* getting into Nell lately?

'Well, the queens of France used to receive their subjects in their bedrooms,' said Nell rebelliously, thinking at the same time, What on earth is making me so frivolous and light-minded? Is this what kissing Newcome has done to me?

'But you are not the Queen of France, my dear,' said Aunt Conybeare, uncontrovertibly.

'A pity, that,' said Nell naughtily, watching her aunt's mouth frame a dismayed circle of surprise. 'No, I will see Newcome in my study, with my face so,' and she pulled her features into a parody of Nell Tallboys at her coldest.

Her aunt looked helplessly at her. 'You will thank him properly or not at all, my girl. But you know he was only doing his duty.'

'His duty, Aunt?' Nell was fascinated. 'Was it his duty to risk his life for me, and then compound that by giving me his coat? No, Newcome went beyond his duty last night, I think.' In more ways than one, Nell, in more ways than one! said the devil which seemed to have taken up residence in her mind.

'Gratitude, no doubt,' offered her aunt. 'For you did save his for him, when you took him in, after all.'

'So I did,' said Nell. 'That makes us quits, you think? I shall tell him so. No, Newcome, I cannot thank you for what you did for me. It was merely tit for tat, although you risked your life for me when you went after my assassin, and I risked nothing when I gave you shelter.'

Except my reputation, said the devil inside her, for I fear that what I so inconveniently feel for him will soon be going to show on my face, or on his!

But there was nothing on either of their faces when she met him in her study after luncheon. She had, for some unknown reason, dressed herself carefully again. Flyaway Nell Tallboys seemed to have disappeared for good!

She was wearing green, a deep green high-waisted wool dress, trimmed with saffron lace, and she had wound round her head a turban which Aunt Conybeare had presented to her, and which she had always refused to wear. It was a flaming thing in vermilions, deep oranges, blues and greens, and she pinned an antique jewel set with rubies to its side, to hold it steady.

Even Henson's opaque stare shivered a little when he saw her unaccustomed magnificence. They were all here, all the Privy Council, old Payne looking frailer than ever—and Newcome, of course.

He looked quite splendid, a figure to match her own. As a reward, no doubt, for faithful service, Aisgill had ordered him dressed to perfection in the

Malplaquet royal livery, only worn when Malplaquets entertained kings and courts.

His stock was so white, his boots so shiny, his hands so beautiful in their kid gloves, his body so well set off by the splendid green and gold of his bullion-trimmed coat that he made Nell feel quite weak at the knees—nearly as weak as she had been in her dream.

He held, of all things, a shako in those hands, with the most giant Malplaquet cockade pinned to it that she had ever seen.

And Nell was nervous, as she had never been in her whole life. Her voice nearly came out in a squeak, until she managed to control it, so that his eyes, previously fixed on the floor, or his boots, suddenly lifted, and she saw mirth in them, and yes, an understanding of her predicament—how to speak normally to him after their intimate moment of the previous night?

'I have to thank you, Newcome,' she said primly. 'I was too overset last night through fright, shock and weariness——' oh, dear, what lies '—to make you properly aware of my gratitude for your devotion. . .' What a word, devotion, and what a lie to say that he was not aware of her gratitude, so aware of it had she been that she had virtually offered herself to him.

And by now Nell was in full flow, one part of her saying all the proper things, and the other part having the most improper thoughts at the sight of him, glorious in full fig—whatever was Aisgill thinking of? Had he no more sense than to turn Newcome out so completely *à point* that now it was she who wanted to eat *him*?

'I understand that Aisgill has proposed that you be offered a bonus on your wages for the gallantry which you displayed in defending me at the risk of your own life.' There, she had said it, without falling on her knees before him, before them all, and saying, 'Take me, Newcome, I'm yours,' like a mad maidservant in a bad French farce, by an inferior imitator of Marivaux!

She practised it, in French, in her head, while Aisgill, speaking before Newcome could, said, 'He has refused to accept anything, Lady Elinor. He says that he merely did his duty and wants neither money nor favour.'

'Is this true, Newcome?' asked Nell, willing him to look at her.

'Yes, Lady Elinor,' he replied, looking her full in the eyes, so that they met there, if nowhere else.

Nell was suddenly frantic. She felt that she was on the edge of a cliff, about to slide over, and nothing and no one there to save her.

Unwittingly, old Payne did. 'An illuminated address,' he said in his cracked voice, saving her from speaking. 'I think I may still be able to limn one, recording the thanks of the House of Malplaquet for saving its jewel.' And he bowed to Nell.

'Perhaps a little premature,' said Newcome, standing stiff and straight before his superiors. 'With respect, I hope that you have considered that whoever planned this might strike again.'

For a moment there was silence, then noise, as all spoke together, only Nell and Newcome silent, gazing into one another's eyes.

'Planned this?' said Henson, incredulous. 'A malcontent, a Luddite surely, like the man who shot Cartwright.'

'Do Luddites own or have access to rifles of such precision and quality that a sharpshooter in the Rifle Brigade might be proud to possess it?'

And how do I know all that? thought Chad. Yes, I was in the army, but in the cavalry, and suddenly another series of questions shot into his head, which, in the mental stasis produced by his amnesia, he had never thought to ask himself before. When did I leave the army, and why? I know—how do I know?—that I was happy there.

Aisgill was regarding him steadily. Newcome had told him of his suspicions about the attack the previous evening, but, like the others, he could not bring himself to believe the murder attempt to be by other than a dissident, a Jacobin.

He said so, adding, 'The rifle was doubtless stolen,' only for him to meet Newcome's hard stare. Chad kept his body still, his voice submissive, but he differed from them and was not afraid to say so.

'The man had been a soldier once, had some grasp of how a guerrilla would strike from ambush. Did you inspect his back? I had not time last night. Lady Elinor's safety was my prime concern.'

'His back?' Henson stared at Newcome, puzzled, but Aisgill took the point.

'The marks of the lash, you think, saving your presence, Lady Elinor. The body is still here, awaiting burial. It shall be inspected.'

'Not that their presence would prove anything,' remarked Henson, annoyed that, once again, Newcome appeared to be instructing his betters.

'No,' agreed Aisgill. 'But, if there, they would prove he was a soldier, and, perhaps, explain the rifle and his stalking skills. And would add weight to the notion that he was hired.'

The room was suddenly so quiet that the ticking of the small French clock over the hearth was loud in it. Nell shivered. She did not like to think herself a target. The face she showed Newcome was now as grave as his.

'My lady should be guarded at all times,' he said, 'if

I may say so. We had a saying in the army: better safe than sorry.'

'I shall arrange it,' said Aisgill quickly, before Henson could speak. 'The house shall be protected, too. Best, in future, that Lady Elinor does not leave the park to ride.'

'And I,' said Henson, 'with Lady Elinor's permission, shall write to the Bow Street Runners, asking them to send me some of their best men to investigate this whole murky business.'

He had hardly finished speaking when Payne, whom Nell had given permission to sit, half rose, uttered a strangled cry, and fell forward on to the carpet.

All of them, paralysed a moment, by surprise, stood staring at him, and it was Newcome, flinging down his shako, who fell on to his knees on the carpet, to take the old man in his arms, revealing a livid and distorted face, the eyes rolled up.

'He has had a fit, he may be dying,' he said, and, rising to his feet, the old man in his arms, Chad carried him to the giant oak table in the centre of the room, and swept what was on it to one side to lay Payne down and begin to chafe his wrists and then his poor distorted face.

'The doctor, quickly,' commanded Henson, annoyed at Newcome's speed of reaction and the almost unconscious arrogance with which he had taken charge, and begun to give orders.

Of them all, only Aisgill was not surprised. He had seen Newcome behave like this before, when he was not conscious of himself.

Water was fetched, and the doctor and the footmen came to carry him to his room at the doctor's insistence. One thing was plain to them all—if old Payne had not exactly died in harness his useful life was almost certainly over.

'Poor Payne,' said Nell, tears in her eyes. 'My fault, I should have made him retire.'

'No,' said Henson, 'he would not have been happy to go. He told me so.'

'And now my lady has no secretary,' said Challenor, suddenly conscious of the weight of his own years. 'For Payne has always refused an assistant.'

'May Newcome leave us, Lady Elinor?' said Aisgill. 'He has duties to perform. Rajah needs gentling after yesterday. Leave off your finery, Newcome, and put him through his paces in the riding school. He needs to be reminded who is master.'

'Yes,' said Nell, not wishing to lose Chad but, after all, he had his work to do. She watched the door close behind him.

Aisgill turned towards her, Henson and Challenor.

'Now, Lady Elinor, you may think my wits are wandering. But I sent Newcome away so that he would not hear what I am about to say. You need not look far for a secretary; Newcome would do admirably, I dare swear. I should hesitate to lose him, but perhaps you could release him in the afternoons to school Rajah and some of the better horses.'

Henson began to argue, only to hear Challenor say, 'What an excellent suggestion, if I may say so. The work he has done for you, Aisgill, is exemplary. And he could guard Lady Elinor at the same time. What could be better?'

Nell realised that they were all looking at her, including Henson, who could make no further protests in the light of the other two men's recommendations.

Did she want Newcome as a secretary? Of course she did! Outrageously, proud Nell Tallboys knew that of all things in the world she wanted Chad Newcome to be her secretary, to be by her side. . . She must be careful in what she said.

Slowly and deliberately she lowered her head, looked at the papers on her desk. 'On probation,' she said at last, trying to make her voice sound grudging.

'Oh, of course,' said Henson, eagerly. 'A stop-gap, perhaps.'

'Indeed,' said Nell. 'He might not suit. He seems an outdoors person. Being indoors might be a trial for him.'

'True,' said Aisgill, watching his lady carefully. Still something odd there, where Newcome was concerned. But even Aisgill could not have imagined the truth of the matter. 'But Newcome seems adaptable, and as his memory had recovered, although he has still lost himself, he shows that he has a rare range of skills. Best of all is his application. The army lost a good man when it turned him out.'

'That is that, then,' said Henson briskly. He disliked these eulogies of Newcome, a man rescued from ruin, after all. 'He cannot have been so remarkable, to end up as he did, wandering the moors, memoryless. Best I keep an eye on him, Lady Elinor.'

'A good idea,' said Nell, making her face as serious as she could. The person who most meant to keep an eye on Newcome was herself—and what an eye she would keep!

'Speak to him, then, Aisgill. Send him to Henson for his first instructions.'

'He'll need some clothes,' offered Henson, who disliked the whole idea, but did not care to say so. 'He cannot bring the stables in here with him, begging your pardon, Aisgill.'

'The tailor can make some for him,' said Aisgill, 'and in the meantime, if Lady Elinor does not disapprove, he can wear one of her grandfather's old black suits. He has much the same size as Newcome.'

'So he was,' said Nell, struck. 'You are full of invention today, Aisgill.'

She could almost feel Henson bridle, added gently, 'You can see to that, Henson, I am sure. And my grandfather's old shirts. You could check Newcome's boot and shoe size, as well. Nothing must be wasted at Campions.'

After they had gone, Aisgill with instructions to speak to Newcome when he had finished schooling Rajah, and Henson grudgingly off to check her late grandfather's wardrobe, Nell sat herself down at her desk.

Before he had left the room, Aisgill having gone first, Henson had fixed Nell with a stern eye, and said, 'The world has turned upside-down since that man came here. Aisgill has made such a pet of him as I have never seen. Best watch him carefully, Lady Elinor. After all, we know nothing of him.'

'I know that he saved my life from an assassin, and from the cold after that,' said Nell gently.

'And he is a young man,' said Henson doggedly. 'Not like having Payne in the room with you.'

'Then poor Aunt Conybeare shall sit with me,' said Nell, exasperated. 'She will not like it, but there it is. Have you any more instructions for me, Henson?'

'I have only your best interests at heart,' replied Henson stiffly.

'Yes, I know that,' said Nell, and thought, and you are right to worry a little, but bonnets over the windmill, Nell, my girl. You may have your giant stable hand by you at all times, and your own Privy Council suggested it!

CHAPTER EIGHT

'BEGGING your pardon, Lady Elinor,' said Chad Newcome respectfully, 'but I should like to re-organise Payne's records for you. He seems to have fallen into a muddle of recent years—his age doubtless.'

Payne was in bed, recovering. He had not died immediately from his fit, but would always be semi-paralysed, and Chad had been her secretary for just under a week.

True to her promise to Henson, Aunt Conybeare sat in a corner of her study, placidly tatting, so that having Newcome with her was not quite the delight Nell had thought it might be.

Besides, he was being most stupidly proper. It was just as though their magic night together, for so Nell thought of it, had never happened.

Perhaps she had imagined it. Except that whenever their fingers touched when he handed letters and papers to her it was almost as though she had been subjected to one of Signor Galvani's shocks. She jumped just like one of his poor frogs was reported to have done. And she was sure that Newcome felt the same. His blue eyes took on a smoky look, exactly as they had done in the Cairn, and that night at the Throne of God.

So it was no use pretending that he was indifferent to her, but what with Henson popping in and out, and Aunt Conybeare sitting there, they might as well be living in a goldfish bowl, and there were times when Nell thought of dragging him off again to see the mere over to Slaitherbeck, and hope that a regiment of

Luddites might attack them, so that they could snatch a few more forbidden moments together.

Her study opened into the library—or was it the other way round?—and when he had written the morning's letters he had gone there to do some work for Challenor, that being part of her secretary's duties.

She rose, said loudly, 'I wish to check a quotation from Madame de Sévigné,' to excuse her leaving the room. 'You need not come with me, Aunt. Challenor may play duenna.'

Chad was standing at the big map table, with one of the folios Challenor had found lying on it open before him.

Nell had crept in very quietly, to surprise him, and Challenor was nowhere to be seen. But Chad must have had an extra eye, in the back of his head, perhaps, for he said to her, 'Yes, what is it, Lady Elinor? May I be of assistance, or do you require Mr Challenor?'

'No, Newcome,' she said severely, 'I do not require Challenor, I require you. Pray what are you doing?'

'Mr Challenor has taught me how to collate books, and I am recording the details of this book for him,' he replied, ignoring the challenging note in her voice. 'You know, I have the oddest feeling that I have seen the book before,' and he indicated the map in it.

'Impossible,' said Nell, firmly, taking him literally. 'Challenor only found it by accident, some three weeks ago.'

'Oh, not this book,' said Chad, frowning. 'Another copy. If I am correct in so thinking, there should be a plate showing Terra Australis near the end,' and he turned the pages rapidly, to discover that the last map in the treatise was, indeed, of Terra Australis.

'Yes, you have seen a copy of it before,' said Nell slowly. 'I wonder where?'

'And so do I,' replied Newcome, looking her straight in the eye for the first time since their adventure, and she noticed that his own eyes had gone smoky again. 'But you wanted something of me?'

'Yes,' said Nell, 'I wonder if you would accompany me to the annexe? There is an edition of Madame de Sévigné's *Lettres* there, on a high shelf, and you could hand it down to me, if you would.'

The annexe was a smallish, book-lined store-room, where works not in good repair were kept, and Nell had purposely chosen one on such a high shelf to have the excuse to take Newcome in with her.

'You would wish to remain here while I collect it?' he enquired.

'Indeed, not,' said Nell rapidly; that would not do at all. 'I like the annexe——' another lie; Newcome seemed to provoke them '—and I shall certainly accompany you. I may—check what is there,' she said wildly, trying to think of a convincing excuse to be alone with him.

So there they were in the annexe, and she made sure that the door was closed behind them before she hissed at him, as he lifted the little library steps over to mount them, to reach her book, 'Newcome, pay attention to me and not to Madame de Sévigné. She is not your mistress. Why are you avoiding me?'

Chad put the steps down, and turned to look at her.

'Avoiding you, Lady Elinor? I was not aware that I was avoiding you. We have been constantly together ever since I became your secretary.'

'You know perfectly well what I mean. Do not prevaricate, Newcome,' said Nell, exasperated.

'Prevaricate, Lady Elinor?'

'And do not repeat every word I say, Newcome. Yes, avoiding me, dodging me. Listen to me,

Newcome. I am giving you an order; you are not to avoid me in future. You understand me?'

'Perfectly. I am not to avoid you in future. But I have not been doing so in the present, nor in the past.'

'Newcome!' said Nell in an awful voice. 'Were it not that I have no evidence to support what I say I should suppose you to have spent a year in a Jesuit's seminary being instructed in the art of Machiavellian dialogue. You do know what I mean, Newcome. You are the most devious creature I have ever met with. Why are you laughing, Newcome?'

For not only were his eyes smokier than ever, but his expression was so full of honest amusement that she wanted to. . .wanted to. . . 'Quickly, Newcome, speak, or else Aunt Conybeare or Challenor will be upon us.'

'My very dear,' he said tenderly, taking her by the hand, and bowing his splendid head; he looked so handsome in proper clothing. 'You know I must not behave to you as I did that night we spent together. I am your humble secretary——'

'And I am your Countess, Newcome,' she said impatiently. 'Why do you keep telling me things I know, Newcome?'

'Because, if I speak to you as I wish, it would not only be improper, but it would also be unfair.'

'To whom unfair, Newcome? Tell me that, you or me?'

'Both of us. There can be nothing between us, Lady Elinor. You must see that in all conscience. You are a good woman, and to consort with me could only ruin you.'

'Suppose I command you to ruin me, Newcome, what then?'

'I don't think you know what you are saying.'

'Of course I know what I am saying. I want you to

make love to me, Newcome. Is that plain enough for you, Newcome? Would you like me to draw you a diagram, Newcome?'

Her expression as she said this, and the low tones in which they were conversing, had him laughing again, but he said, almost roughly, 'Nothing I would like to do better in the whole world, Lady Elinor, than oblige you, but I must not.'

How he was able to restrain himself Chad did not know. Her eager face was alight with passion and impudent mockery, a woman enjoying herself in the lists of love for the first time, jousting with him with her tongue, trying to provoke him into action.

By God, if it were action she wanted, she should have it!

He was upon her, all his restraint gone, conquered by her nearness, his own passion for her, she was in his arms, saying breathlessly, before he stopped her mouth with his, 'Oh, no, Newcome, you do not need diagrams,' and he was kissing her, before common sense ruled, and he released her.

He turned away. 'Sévigné, you said,' and oh, God, it was torment to know that she was there, but duty and honour, newly returned to his memory, must rule him. He could not throw Countess Nell to the ground to love her, however much she wished him to, and however much he wished to make her his.

Nell tried to hold on to him. The passion which ran through her every time they touched one another had her in its grip, stronger than any duty to her name or to Campions. Ever since her mother and father had died she had lived only for both of them. Her grandfather had seen the steel in her and cultivated it. Careless himself, he knew that Nell was not.

The lonely child she had been had grown into a lonely woman. The education he had given her, intellectually sounder than that of any boy, allied to her natural gifts would have made her senior wrangler had she been a boy. She rode as well as any man, and from seventeen had begun to manage the stud for him, creating it again, making it what it had been in the second Earl's time.

And through it all she had remained proud and cool Nell Tallboys, who at some time in the future would coldly choose a husband, give him a child, but keep her inner self intact. No man should move her, make Countess Nell his toy, his thing, in the end his nothing, as she had seen other women were to their husbands.

Love, what was that? A joke, a myth, something of which poets sang. It had nothing to do with what Nell understood of life. Love was Rajah and the mares he covered, that was all. A name to romanticise lust.

Campions was all she had loved—and all Malplaquet's possessions.

Until she had seen Chad.

Reason had fled, and poetry made sense. The passion previously reserved for Campions was now for him

Conscience, he had said. Now what was that? Conscience withered and died when she was with him. Was it because he was nameless, and she was the queen who stooped, because to stoop was better than to be equal, that she had come to love him?

No, that was not true, because she gloried in him—all of him. Covertly watched him, walking across the room, driving his quill across paper, schooling Rajah. And what she felt for him was of the mind, as well as of the body, no mere condescension of a great lady, but a woman consorting—his word—with her equal in the sight of God, if not of man.

Joy ran through her. The humour she had never expressed before, hardly knew she possessed, welled up in her, to tease him, to play with words, to watch his face light up—I grow maudlin, she thought, and when he mounted the steps to find her book, and she heard Challenor approaching, she said loudly, in her best Countess Nell voice, 'Oh, dear, Newcome, I could have found that book a dozen times were I tall enough. How long you have taken!'

He looked down at her, the book in his hand, said, 'Madam, you are pleased to be wilful. You're sure you really need the book at all?' and her own laughter rang in the air, as Challenor put his head round the door, said,

'There you both are,' and, being innocent himself, saw innocence in them. 'You have visitors, Lady Elinor. Henson has sent your uncle Beaumont to your study and asked your cousin Ulric to await you in the Turkish room.'

'Visitors!' exclaimed Nell. 'We grow strangely frivolous these days. More new faces in Campions in the last few weeks than are usually seen in a twelvemonth. You may come down now, Newcome, with or without your book. My secretary must meet my uncle, I will not say for him to approve of you; he never approves of anyone.'

And then she added, with such a look on her as Challenor had never seen, so that he gazed after her in puzzlement, 'Do you think that he has come to see me with yet another proposal from some nobleman who would like to take Campions from me to waste it away on the turf or the gaming tables or women?'

Chad would have stayed behind in the library, but she would have none of it.

'No, you must come with me. Old Payne would have done, so why not you?'

* * *

Sir Chesney Beaumont, Nell's dead mother's brother, was a fine-looking man, with a strong urbane face, and was busy discussing the day's news with Aunt Conybeare. He had already admired her tatting, and they were well into the affairs of the Princess of Wales, as the Regent's wife was always called.

'My dear,' he said to Nell, as she walked in, Newcome behind her, 'you look positively blooming. So much better than when I last saw you. You looked a trifle peaky then, not at all yourself. Mrs Conybeare has told me the sad news about Payne, and that Henson has rightly sent for the Runners to investigate this strange attack on you. Luddites, I am sure. Luddites.'

'None of my people thinks so, uncle,' said Nell, adding conciliatorily, 'But you may be right.'

'And this is your new secretary.' Sir Chesney's eyes took in Chad, who thought it best to stand submissive. For some reason, Chesney Beaumont made him feel uneasy, and he could not think why. His very name drew odd resonances from the air.

'Yes,' said Nell, walking to kiss him on his florid cheek. 'I hope you have not come to tease me about marriage, my dear uncle, for I am more set against it than ever.'

Sir Chesney was still exercised by Chad. 'I had not thought him to be such a young man,' he said doubtfully, 'and no, I have not come to talk to you about marriage, least of all with Charles Halstead. Particularly not with Charles Halstead.'

He stared at Chad, made waving motions at him, 'We could perhaps talk alone, my dear.'

'Why?' said Nell coolly. 'You would not have sent Payne away. I prefer Newcome to stay. I have no secrets from him,' she added, and threw Newcome a killing look, which had Chad coughing, and looking desperately anywhere but at Nell, or Sir Chesney.

'Well, that must be your choice, my dear,' he remarked, a trifle miffed. 'These matters are delicate.'

'From what I have heard of Charles Halstead, delicate is not the word I would have used,' said Nell, 'but then, fortunately, I have never met him.'

'Nor I, my dear,' said Sir Chesney, 'and now I am glad I never shall, and I am sorry I ever spoke with his father of a match between you. His conduct has been abominable, as you shall hear.'

'Never met him,' said Nell, seating herself, with Chad standing at her elbow, a little behind, as befitted a good secretary, 'and yet you recommended him to me in marriage.'

'Oh, I know his father well—Clermont, a sterling fellow. But Halstead—*there* is a horse of a different colour. He, I regret to say, visited Watier's in a drunken fit, railed against all women, and when your cousin Bobus was foolish enough to exempt you from his strictures, as an example of strict virtue, you understand, made a dreadful bet that he would, he would. . .' Sir Chesney ran down, finding it difficult to say exactly what Charles Halstead had roared in his drunken misogyny.

'Would what?' said Nell impatiently, and then, 'Oh, you do not like to say. Come, Uncle, Aunt Conybeare has been married, I run a great establishment, and I am sure Newcome will not be shocked by what you have to tell us.'

She was wrong. Newcome, if not exactly shocked, was, for some strange reason, distressed at Sir Chesney's news. And as Sir Chesney elaborated a strange red rage seized him.

'Oh, very well, Nell, if you must. He said that no woman was virtuous and bet that, if he cared to try, he might have you, as he pleased, without benefit of marriage, you understand. What's worse, he bet twenty thousand pounds on it.'

Nell rose, paced to the hearth, stared into the fire, face averted, and said in a muffled voice, 'Charles Halstead said that! Before or after you had arranged with his father to offer for me?'

'Oh, before, I assure you. When his father knew what his son had done, he forbade him the house, and withdrew his sponsorship of your marriage to him.'

'Kind of him,' said Nell, satiric. 'I have never wished more that I were a man. Were I so I would have shot Halstead dead for the insult,' and then, a desperate humour in her voice, 'But, of course, if I had been a man, you and his father would not have arranged the match with him. What nonsense I am talking.' She turned towards Chad, whose rage was now so black and strong that he was shaking with it, had bent over the desk, feeling light-headed with a curious mix of—what was it? Shame, surely not—unless it was for all men who lightly spoke of women thus.

'Newcome,' said Nell sharply, 'are you ill, that you look so?' and Aunt Conybeare looked up, equally sharply, struck by the note in her niece's voice.

'Nothing,' gasped Chad, 'a passing malaise. I have had such, once or twice, since I arrived here.'

Which was true. He had thought that it was perhaps his lost memory struggling to revive itself, but why Sir Chesney's story should have such an effect on him was a mystery.

Sir Chesney stared at Nell's concern for her secretary, said indifferently, 'I understand from Henson that your cousin Ulric is here. I hope his presence does not mean that you are thinking of marrying him. Most unwise.'

Since Chad appeared to be recovering, Nell looked

over at Sir Chesney, said coldly, 'I don't think you listened to what I was saying, Uncle. I repeat, I have no intention of marrying anyone, least of all Cousin Ulric. And now I must see him. Disliking him, and his proposal, does not absolve me from practising the common courtesies. Newcome, if you are quite well, you may spend the afternoon in the riding school. Aisgill was asking for you this morning.'

She bowed to her uncle, and left him wailing at Aunt Conybeare over Nell's intransigence where marriage was concerned, and glared suspiciously at Newcome when he took his leave. Nell's secretary to work in the riding school—what next?

'Really, Nell,' said Ulric Tallboys petulantly, 'it is too bad that I was consigned here alone, while Chesney Beaumont was admitted immediately to you. You should have a word with that butler of yours, and your man, Henson. After all, I am your heir.'

'Sir Chesney arrived first,' replied Nell briskly. She disliked her cousin, an overweight man, pasty-faced, in his early thirties, and disliked him even more when he continued, still petulant, 'Well, I have come here on business, too. It is high time that you made up your mind to marry me, Nell. That way we keep the Tallboys name in existence, and before you come out with some havey-cavey that you do not love me, let me remind you that you have made it quite plain that you do not wish to marry for love.'

'I don't intend to marry for dislike, either,' retorted Nell, goaded into unwisdom. 'And the Tallboys name will live on without you, for I intend to have anyone I marry assume it. It will be a condition of my marriage—the lawyers can deal with it when they draw up the settlement.'

'But you should marry me,' pursued Ulric blindly.

'Safer so. It is all about the North that you were shot at by Luddites, and that you have nothing better to do than make some stable lad your personal secretary. You would be better advised if I were here to look after you.'

His expression was made the sulkier by the thought that if the first Earl had not insisted on the reversion of his title to the female line, because his only child was a daughter, and a sovereign grateful for his victories in the early eighteenth-century wars had not agreed, he, Ulric Tallboys, and not Nell, would now be the proud possessor of Campions and all the lands and title that went with it—a fact of which he never ceased to remind himself almost daily.

'Oh,' said Nell dangerously. 'And how do you know all that? I never thought that Campion affairs had already become the talk of Staffordshire and Trentham.'

'I heard of your goings-on when I stayed at Habersham Hall with the Gascoynes before I came on here. You are the talk of the Riding, Nell.'

'But then, I always was, wasn't I, Ulric? And I always shall be, because I have no concern in joining Ridings or any other society for that matter.'

'But Nell——'

'Do not "But Nell" me,' said Nell, feeling more like a reincarnation of good Queen Bess than usual, 'or I shall have second thoughts about continuing your allowance.'

'You would not do that?' cried Ulric, aghast. Ever since some eight years ago, after he had squandered his own inheritance, first Nell's grandfather, and then Nell, had made him, as heir presumptive, a generous allowance, on condition that he did not ever go to London where he had once been involved in a scandal so enormous that Nell's grandfather had almost cut him off forever. Nell had continued to support him on the same terms, and he roved round provincial society, tolerated, if not welcomed, because of his Malplaquet connections.

'And what about this secretary of yours, Nell?'

'What about him?' Nell had never sounded so dangerous, but, unobservant, Ulric galloped on.

'I tell you what, Nell, it is not at all the thing for you to make some yokel your private secretary, particularly when he is a young man——'

'I tell *you* what, Ulric,' said Nell savagely, 'if I cared to make a one-eyed dwarf, with a hunch back, my private secretary, it is no business of yours. And if you feel so strongly about my doings, why, to save yourself pain, you may leave within the hour. Out of my kind consideration for your own feelings, I would not stop you.'

She had never spoken to him so before, had always been courteous and patient, and he stood there with his mouth open. 'I say, Nell,' he began, only for her to reply, as she strode to the door,

'And I say, Ulric, that if you do not care to remain for luncheon I shall quite understand, and now I must leave you. I have work to do. My days are not spent in fiddle-faddle and gossip.'

'Have a heart, Nell,' he protested as she swept through the door, 'I've only just got here, and dammit, I'm your heir.'

'So you keep saying,' were Nell's last words, 'and a great pity for Campions that it should be so,' and she was gone, leaving him gasping, but determined to stay.

After all, he had his own fish to fry at Campions.

Luncheon was a somewhat constrained meal. Ulric sat there with an aggrieved expression on his face, and Sir Chesney felt a strange annoyance with Nell, stronger, perhaps, than her mere refusal to marry deserved. Something odd going on at Campions, but what he could not decide.

As was usual since Nell had taken over, the place ran like clockwork. The food was good, the service perfect, the whole estate was in splendid order, and he looked forward to a visit to the stables and riding school in the afternoon, although he could have done without Ulric's company.

To prevent Nell's sending him away, Ulric stuck like glue to Sir Chesney, whom he disliked as much as Sir Chesney disliked him. He thought that Nell would not be so deuced rude to him before her uncle, and he was right about that, if little else.

The stable and the stud were in splendid fig, too, thought Sir Chesney crossly. It would be nice to have something to complain about, so as to put Nell down a little, but, dammit, with Aisgill there to give his usual friendly meeting, there was little he could say, and like Ulric he was surprised to see the supposedly unmanageable Rajah being given a dressage work-out.

'Who's on Rajah, hey?' he said, to nobody in particular, to hear Ulric grind out,

'I thought Nell said that she never had suitors here, so who the devil's he?'

Chad was up on Rajah, dressed in one of the late Earl's country suits, charcoal-coloured jacket, modest cravat, grey breeches, beautiful boots—his feet, Nell had been pleased to discover, were the same size as her grandfather's—and he was wearing a dated bicorne hat, which made him look particularly dashing.

Swinging Rajah around the circle, keeping him under tight control, for he had been wild ever since the attempt on Nell's life, he was suddenly aware that he had an audience, and that Nell, dressed more smartly than he had ever seen her, had added herself to the group.

Some mischievous devil made him sweep off his bicorne to her as he passed them, and when Rajah, annoyed, reared, he treated the group to the spectacle of a superb piece of horsemanship, which culminated in Rajah performing a splendid caracole—an extravagant sideways leap, which had him apparently standing in the air—much against his lordly will.

'Oh, bravo,' cried Nell.

Ulric asked again, 'Who the devil's *that*, Nell?' to hear Sir Chesney say, in a hollow voice,

'Good God, it's the secretary! Damme if it ain't.'

'You mean that's the yokel?' gasped Ulric, looking from Rajah's rider to Nell, and back again.

Nell's pride in Chad was almost visible, she suddenly realised, and quelled it.

'Yes,' she said, in her most bored Countess Nell voice. 'I understand he was a trooper once, which I suppose was where he learned to do that.'

Sir Chesney looked down his nose. 'A trooper who has visited Vienna,' he muttered. 'Damned difficult trick, that. You've a jewel there, Nell. Wasted as a pen-pusher, if I may say so.'

'Well, I need a pen-pusher more than I need a circus turn at Astley's, so a pen-pusher he'll have to stay,' said Nell, not wishing to have Sir Chesney begin to make all kind of suggestions about Chad Newcome's future, and pleased to appear to put him down a little. It would not do for her uncle to begin . . .suspecting things. . . And surely, she thought, amused at herself, females must possess a natural talent for intrigue, for no one has taught me to be so devious.

She was thinking this later that afternoon, when she met Chad on the stairs, about to return to his quarters on the top floor, to change out of his riding clothes into his secretary's drab uniform.

'Lady Elinor,' he said, staring at her a little. She had already changed for dinner, and was magnificent, simply magnificent. He had heard Aisgill say that the gentry thought Nell plain, but to him she was the most stunning thing he had ever seen.

She was dressed in white and silver satin, high-waisted, with an over-dress of gauze and net floating about her tall person. Around her throat, her wrists and on her fingers, and finally as a crown in her gleaming chestnut hair, were the famous Malplaquet diamonds which she rarely wore. And tonight she wore them like the glorious Diana she was.

They shimmered and sparkled in the light of the chandeliers, fully lit because Sir Chesney and Ulric Tallboys were dining with her.

'You will attend me tonight, Newcome,' she said, all arrogance, like her stance, the tilt of her neck, which the diamonds adorned, a monarch to her humble subject.

But Chad, standing straight and tall, was equal to her. If desire roared through him at the sight of her, he quelled it as well as he could. 'I think not, Lady Elinor. Unwise perhaps.'

'A command, Newcome, you hear me? A command.'

'Sir Chesney will not like it, nor, forgive me, will your cousin.'

'Servants'-hall talk, Newcome. Henson will be there, and Challenor, too. Old Payne would have sat with us.'

'I am not old Payne.'

'Very true, and to both our advantages. You will attend me. I will brook no denial.'

'You are as wilful as Rajah, my lady, and far less manageable.'

'A compliment, Newcome, a compliment. You grow more courtier-like by the instant.'

Face to face they stood, and any watcher could not have failed to see the tension which crackled between them.

'Not meant as such, but if you choose——' and she interrupted him, like lightning.

'Oh, I choose, Newcome, to take it as one, and I choose to have you sit at my table, which I would never ask Rajah to do.'

As so often, Chad could have taken her, there on the spot, as she was almost defying him to do, for whenever they met the battle of words between them was merely a symbol of the sexual heat which passed between them.

Nell saw his face change, his eyes begin to smoke, and whispered, face wicked, 'Confess, Newcome, confess. You wish to call me your lady in every way, Newcome, in every way, and this very moment, too. And if I am your lady you will wear my favour, do my bidding,' and she took the scrap of lace which was her pocket handkerchief from where it hung from the fortune in diamonds on her wrist, and leaned forwards to wipe his sweating brow, sweating as much from frustrated desire as from his exertions in the riding school.

He could not deny her further. He took the lace scrap from her, and put it to his lips, but before he could speak a door on the landing opened, and Sir Chesney emerged.

Chad stood back, bowed, said submissively, 'As you will, Lady Elinor,' and made his way up the stairs, bowing, equally submissively, to Sir Chesney, who looked after him, a worried look on his honest old face.

But Nell, sweeping an arm into his, as he exclaimed, 'My dear, you look radiant, radiant! Why you will not come to London and conquer society I shall never understand,' laughed and replied,

'But Uncle, dear, I have everything I could want, or desire, here in Yorkshire; what could London offer me better than that?'

And if she was speaking of Chad Newcome, neither Sir Chesney nor her cousin Ulric could yet have an inkling of that.

CHAPTER NINE

For Chad and Nell it was heaven, and it was hell. To be so near, and yet to be now so hedged about by others that they could only enjoy snatched moments, two-edged conversations and the touching of hands, was to suffer the torments of Tantalus in the old Greek legend.

Not that any yet suspected them. Only as Countess Nell, and still unmarried, she was rarely ever alone. When Chad had only been her stable hand they could go on the moors, mistress and man, but now that he was her secretary they could not even do that. He could school Rajah and her other prime horses occasionally, but that was in public, too, and then she could only yearn at him, in the riding school, on the excuse of seeing her horses being properly trained.

Yes, there was an atmosphere, something in the air, for Nell was now so volatile, after so many years of being sober. Her laugh rang out, her happiness was plain for all to see, but her people were glad merely to see her happy.

The Runner and his assistant arrived. Cully Jackson was a big, raw-boned, red-headed man who questioned them all, made something of Chad's newness, until he heard the full story. Of them all, as he first sniffed about Campions before disappearing into the Riding, he saw what existed between the Countess and her secretary—but said nothing. *That* was not his business.

The year ran towards Christmas, and Newcome was no longer new. The women servants still followed him with their eyes, but he made nothing of them. He burned for Nell; his body, not his memory told him that he had been long continent, and that made the burning worse, but he would not betray the mistress to whom he had never made love.

Sir Chesney left the day after he had arrived; Ulric stayed a little longer, leaving shortly before the Runner was due. The Runner was told of him, the dissolute heir, nodded at the news, but said nothing about that. The dead murderer had borne the marks of the lash on his back as Chad had suspected, but the rifle he carried remained a mystery. 'A gentleman's piece,' Jackson said to Chad, holding it in his big hands. 'You must have seen such in the army, perhaps?' and he watched his man as Chad shook his head ruefully.

Jackson knew of Chad's lost memory, and tried, Chad was sure, to trip him up, to test him, but left Campions on his journey of enquiry certain that Newcome was not lying about himself.

'And now, Newcome,' Nell said teasingly to Chad one morning, shortly after Sir Chesney had left, and Ulric was packing to go, 'you know exactly what my worth is, do you not?'

Chad looked up at her. He was writing at his desk, placed near to hers, Aunt Conybeare dozing gently in her corner by the fire. 'How so?' he said, abstracted. He was checking accounts for Henson, for though he claimed no special talent for figuring Henson had found him useful with figures, too.

'Why, Charles Halstead set my price,' she said gaily, 'at twenty thousand pounds, no less. A high price for him, perhaps, but small, is it not, for Campions's owner, and Malplaquet's lady? Would you kill him for his insolence to me, Newcome? He wished to murder my reputation, not my body. I wonder which crime God considered the worse of the two?'

For some reason to hear of Charles Halstead's bet always disturbed Chad. He looked up at his lady, as usual turned out *à point* these days, her cheeks flushed, and the look in her eyes which was for no one but Chad Newcome.

'I would gladly kill such a cur for you, my lady,' he offered, 'should you wish it, and should he arrive here to try to win his bet.'

'No, I do not wish it, Newcome,' she said. 'He may stay in exile for me. My uncle said that he has gone to live in Scotland, and that his father talks of transferring the estate to his younger brother, leaving him only his title.'

Chad cursed beneath his breath. His hand had shaken unaccountably as she spoke and ink splattered over the virgin page.

Greatly daring, there being no one to see her, Aunt Conybeare's snores growing louder, Nell placed her small hand over Chad's large one.

'Does it trouble you so much to hear me traduced, Newcome?'

'Yes,' growled Chad. 'I'd like to break his damned neck, begging your pardon, my dearest. The sound of his name is enough to distress me.'

He stroked the hand which had been so lovingly offered, and then, as Nell bent her head, Aunt Conybeare growing noisier, and kissed him on the cheek, he lifted the hand to kiss her palm.

Nell felt him shiver, said gently, 'Oh, you burn as fierce as I. Is there nothing we can do, nothing?'

He looked squarely at her. 'Nothing. And there is nothing we should do. I have told you that, my love, my own, and you must believe it.'

Aunt Conybeare's noise stopped, and she gave a great sigh, said 'Where are you, Nell? And where am I?'

The lovers pulled away. 'In the study, dear Aunt,' replied Nell gently. 'Playing chaperon.'

'Oh, yes,' said her aunt vaguely. 'So I am. Not that you need one,' and she went back to sleep.

'You heard that?' said Nell softly to Chad, her face so amused that he leaned forward and kissed her absently on the corner of the mouth, and, pulling away, muttered thickly,

'You almost destroy my resolution with your humour, but mere passion would not answer for us.'

'My passion is not mere,' she riposted, 'nor, I think, is yours. Tell me, Newcome, if my aunt, wise monkey that she is, the one who places his hands over his eyes, and says, "I see nothing", has no suspicion of us, why, then, are we not innocent? And being innocent, may we not do as we please? What the world does not know cannot exist.'

Chad put a hand to his forehead, said hoarsely, 'And you accuse *me* of logic-chopping.'

'Oh, I learned it from you,' said Nell sweetly. 'My servant, who will not obey me in the only thing which matters to me in the whole wide world,' and she held him with her eyes.

'Lady Elinor——' he began.

'Why, who is that?' she interrupted him.

'The lady whom Mrs Conybeare chaperons,' was his eager answer to her. 'My mistress—who can never be my mistress.'

'Never, Newcome, never?' She saw his hands rise, to twist together, agonised. The hands which could not hold her. 'Is the man who is not afraid of Rajah afraid of me?'

'Shall I be no better than Charles Halstead?' he muttered. 'For he betrayed you with his talk, where I shall betray you with my body. Your reputation, your honour, what of them?'

'My spotless reputation did not prevent Charles Halstead from staining it. You see, Newcome, you cannot defeat me in the combat of words; defeat me in the combat of love instead. I wish to die in your arms. You may kill me in that contest; I shall not allow you to win in any other.'

Their eyes met, and oh, his smoked, were smouldering into flames. She was winning! She knew it!

There was a knock on the door, and the spell was broken. She called, 'Come in,' and Chad turned away, was at his desk in a trice, head down, quill driving, and she was at her own, as Henson entered. Nothing there to see, although Nell felt that her recent passion was written in letters of fire in the air.

Henson could only read words on paper. Fire was beyond him. 'Ah, Lady Elinor,' he intoned. 'A dispatch from Jackson. He has traced your murderer,' he said, placing a budget of letters on her desk. 'I have read what he has to say—do you wish to read yourself, or shall I save you the trouble?'

Nell thought that reading was beyond her. 'Tell me,' she said.

'Newcome was correct in his suppositions. The man was an ex-soldier, turned off in the peace. He lived at Bradford for a time, turned footpad, had a small gang of men. The rifle was stolen, they say, and some weeks before he shot at you he left his gang and his usual haunts, none knows why. It was supposed by his associates that he was hired.'

'Hired!' said Nell. She saw that Chad had stopped writing, was alert. 'By whom?'

'Jackson does not know. He will endeavour to find out. Meantime he asks what others beside your cousin stand to gain by your death.'

Nell shivered, rose impulsively, walked by Chad, placed a hand on his shoulder as she passed him.

'Ulric! He surely cannot think that Ulric would stoop to that.'

She remembered his anger when she had last refused him. 'I know he envies me—all this.' And she waved a hand at the splendour around her. 'But murder, that is quite another thing.'

'Desperate men seek desperate remedies,' said Henson slowly. 'Jackson accuses no one. In the meantime, he says, you should go carefully.' He turned to Chad. 'You will guard my lady with your life, will you not?'

'Willingly,' said Chad, 'with my life, seeing that she gave me mine.'

He spoke quite levelly, but perhaps Henson could read letters of fire, after all. Something in the quiet intensity of Newcome's speech reached him.

'See that you do,' he said roughly. 'You will not go out, ever, madam, without Newcome, and a footman, or a groom with you until this snake is scotched.'

Nell could not protest. With a sinking heart she faced a future in which few opportunities would be given her to. . .deal with Chad as she wished.

'I hear you,' she said in a hollow voice, staring out of the window at the magnificent view. 'But you cannot really believe that it is Ulric who wishes to kill me.'

Chad spoke. 'With respect, Lady Elinor, you would be foolish to ignore Jackson, and Mr Henson's advice.'

'You hear him,' said Henson, face impassive. 'We are of a like mind, and I'm sure that Aisgill and Challenor would tell you the same. Your advisers are agreed—you must take no risks, whether it be your cousin, or another, who threatens you.'

The bright day had grown dark, even though the November sun shone across the moor. Nell shivered, wrapped her arms round herself, turned to face the two men, Chad standing now.

'I must obey you,' she said, 'in all things,' and that message was for Chad, a two-edged one. 'Until——' and she hesitated '—my judgement tells me otherwise. You all advise me; you do not rule. I will not be wilful, but I will be mistress.'

Henson bowed his head. 'You are my Countess, madam, and you have never been unreasonable, have always consented to listen, and to understand.' He looked hard at her. 'For that reason your people serve you with love as well as loyalty. I know you will take heed for yourself, and of yourself.'

Nell looked at the two men. Henson, after his fashion, loved her, too. He did not merely serve her for his pay. And, for the first time, she understood Chad's reluctance to take her without thought.

But I love him, ran through her mind, truly love him, and I know, because he holds off, that he truly loves me, and they say love finds a way, and I must clutch that thought to me—for it is all I have.

Thus, thought Nell, exasperated, was how it always went. Snatched moments when, at the crucial point, they were always interrupted. And now it was worse than ever, with men guarding her all the time from any possible threat.

Her mind went round and round, a whirligig, she thought, pondering possibilities. If Rajah wanted Princess, the whole of Campions arranged for his pleasure, but if Campions's owner wanted her lover, all of Campions—were they to know—would conspire to keep her from him.

Why could she not have fallen in love with one of the sleek young men whom Uncle Beaumont had paraded before her? They would have handed her over to Charles Halstead without a thought, wretched though he was, but Chad, whom she loved, would be almost whipped from the grounds were it known what she and he felt for one another.

For everyone would assume that it was he who was seducing her, when, ever since the night of the attack, it was *she* who had been pursuing *him*. He thought only of her honour; she thought only of him.

If I were a man, hissed Nell furiously to herself, making angry faces in her mirror, I could have as many lovers as I pleased, and no one would think anything; they would admire me, rather, for my virility. Even well-bred young women would snigger knowingly when I walked in a room, 'Look, there is Malplaquet, a devil with the women—won't marry unless he meets one of whom *he* approves and not his advisers. And when he does marry, why, he will *still* go on his merry way.'

And I, I can have no merry way. Why was I not a boy, or the Empress Catherine of Russia, who had all the men she pleased in her bed? I only want Chad, none other, and, damn them all, I *will* have him.

She rose, walked downstairs, busy brain scheming. The last time that they had been able to meet privately was when she had pursued him into the annexe. Well, she could take him there again, could she not?

But when she reached the library they were all present, the whole Privy Council, Newcome with them, wearing the new suit which the tailor had made for him, which fitted him perfectly, showing off the length of his legs, and the strength of his thighs. His cravat was so white that it looked like a fall of snow. His whole appearance did nothing for her equanimity.

Nell stared at them. 'What's to do? I had not thought we were to meet today.'

They must have agreed that Chad should speak for

them all, for he bowed, and said, 'The Runner, Jackson, is here, Lady Elinor, and wishes to speak to you. He will not trust what he has to say to the post.'

'He is here?' Nell looked around.

'In the ante-room,' Henson spoke. 'I thought, we all thought, that he ought to speak to you with your council present. It is our duty to guard you, and we must know everything, if we are to do that.'

Nell could not argue with them, so inclined her head, said briefly, 'Admit him, then.'

It was Chad who went to do her bidding, and Jackson followed him in, a rough figure in the splendid room, only Aisgill, sturdy in his country clothes, having any common ground with him.

'My lady. . .' Jackson made an awkward reverence. 'There has been a strange development, of which I must tell you, and your people here. It is about the rifle which Mr Newcome here thought must have been an army man's. I have traced it, and an odd turn-up indeed.' He paused.

Strangely, of them all, it was Henson who was impatient. 'Spit it out, man. Why stand havering?'

'I took it with me, as you know. Returned to London, and showed it to a gunsmith who has his shop in the Strand. I asked him if he had ever seen it before; the piece bore signs of a cunning repair. He recognised it at once, although it was nigh three years since he had last seen it. He would not say who had brought it in until he found its details in his books.

'And there it was, repaired shortly after Waterloo; he identified it by the roses engraved on its steel, and by the coronet he placed upon it for its owner——'

'A coronet?' interrupted Nell. 'Not Ulric Tallboys, then?'

'No, indeed,' said Jackson, 'and here is the puzzle, for Viscount Halstead, old Clermont's heir, bought it off a friend of his, and took it in to be overhauled and repaired, and there is no doubt that it is he who owns the rifle which was used to fire at you, my lady.'

There was a babble of voices. 'Charles Halstead?' said Nell, incredulously. 'You are telling me that *Charles Halstead* owned the rifle? Are you saying that it was he who organised the attempt on me?' She hardly paused before adding, 'To prevent the need to pay out twenty thousand pounds when he lost his disgraceful bet? What did he say when you spoke to him of this?'

'He is not to be found, my lady. I went to his father's home. His father refused to see me. I saw only his secretary who said that Lord Halstead was in Scotland. He knows nothing of him, said that Lord Clermont wished to know nothing. I showed him the rifle—although I did not tell him why I needed to know whether it was Halstead's—but the secretary knew nothing of it, merely that it bore Halstead's initials and arms—which I already knew. He added that Lord Halstead had left for Scotland in September. And that is that. A dead end.'

'And we are almost at December,' said Nell reflectively. 'Well, I agree, a strange turn-up. What's to do?' she added, turning to the men about her. 'Can we seriously believe that it was Halstead hired a man to kill me?'

Jackson spoke again. 'If I might advise, I also investigated the affairs of your cousin, Ulric Tallboys, who has the most to gain by your death. It is not commonly known that he is at *point non plus* where money is concerned. He has unpaid bills in every town he frequents. At York, they are for having him consigned to a debtor's prison. There is a lien on the small property he still owns, and his affairs are desperate. His reputation. . .' He hesitated, said bluntly, 'He has no reputation, whereas Lord Halstead, there's a different matter.'

'In what way?' It was Chad speaking, his voice hoarse. Whenever Charles Halstead was the subject of discussion, with or without his dreadful bet over Nell, he always felt quite ill.

'This,' said Jackson. 'He has always been at outs with his father, I gathered, but the rest of the world tells a different tale. The servants at Clermont House think the world of him, as do his friends—I made the most discreet enquiries, as you would wish. His reputation as a soldier shows him a nonpareil for courage and ability. The Duke himself commended him, and was sorry when his elder brother died, and he was ordered by his father to leave the army and take his place. He is reputed to be generous to a fault, unfortunate only with women——'

'He made a disgraceful bet concerning myself,' said Nell frostily, 'this nonpareil of yours.'

'Indeed,' bowed Jackson, 'and I would not seek to deny that, but I do not think that he is your man, whereas—and I speak with caution, no proof you understand—I think that Mr Ulric Tallboys should be watched. As for the rifle, I propose we write to Glen Ruadh in Scotland where I understand from the secretary that Lord Halstead has gone, to ask him what he knows of it. It was almost certainly stolen from him.'

'So,' said Nell, 'we are a little forward. Newcome here shall write to Glen Ruadh, and you may arrange for my cousin to be watched. You will continue your enquiries, will you not?'

'Indeed, and I shall remain in touch with you, and you must guard yourself at all times, my lady.'

He hesitated. 'I must say this. Mr Tallboys is not nice in his conversation where you are concerned. He hates you, madam, and is foolish enough to let the world know that he does. Which, of course, might mean that he is not our man, but my instincts tell me that he is.'

Henson said slowly, after Jackson had gone, 'Either way, Lady Elinor, a dreadful thought that he or Lord Halstead should wish to murder you.'

Nell shivered. 'Do not speak of it. Newcome, write that letter today. At least, with luck, we may clear that puzzle up.'

'At once,' Chad replied, but she thought that Newcome looked perturbed, and when the others had gone, old Challenor taking himself to his own desk by the library's fire, she signed to Chad to return with her to her study.

'Come, Newcome, what ails you?' she said, for she had developed an extra sense where he was concerned.

'I don't know,' said Chad honestly. 'There are times when I feel that something of my true past is trying to break through, and just then, in there, while Jackson was speaking, I had the strangest sensation. I felt on the brink of I know not what, I had a sensation of dizziness, a feeling of disaster.'

'Disaster,' said Nell thoughtfully, 'that's an odd word, Newcome.'

For the moment her personal feelings were in abeyance. He looked so ill that rather than make love to him she wanted to mother him, feed him gruel, hold his head—these were, of course, different ways of making love to him.

'You wish to be relieved of your duties, to rest a little?' offered Nell tenderly.

Chad looked at her ruefully. 'No, indeed. The malaise is merely a passing thing.'

'Like Aunt Conybeare struggling to stay awake in

here,' said Nell, trying to lighten the situation a little. She seemed to have gone from a state of mad desire for Newcome to be in her bed to an equally mad desire for him to be in his own bed—with her as his nurse.

She fantasised him needing to be returned to his room, where she would put on her brown holland apron, feed him soothing drinks, sit on his bed, stroke his brow, stroke his. . . She blinked.

'I trust you to tell me if you are not well. Campions needs you to be in the finest fettle, Newcome, and so do I.' She could hear the note of love in her voice and looked across at Aunt Conybeare, in case that lady had heard it too.

But Aunt Conybeare was sitting there lax, her canvas work forgotten on her knees, dreaming of summer, perhaps, or her coming good dinner.

Impulsively she put her hand on Chad's brow, found it cool; he took the hand, kissed the palm, returned it to her. 'You are too kind, my love.' For he also had seen that Aunt Conybeare had effectively left them alone again.

'Well or ill, Newcome, I need to see you alone, and soon. You understand me?'

'Too well,' said Chad.

'Then we must arrange it,' said Nell firmly, ignoring his answer. 'Tomorrow, I shall require you to be in the annexe, to solve a matter of grave intellectual import. I am concerned about what Kant actually meant when he spoke of the Moral Imperative. Judging by the answers you have been giving me when I have been trying to seduce you, it would seem that you know a great deal about it.

'Instruct me, I command you, on that topic, Newcome. You are so very moral that perhaps you do not need Kant, whereas I, I need not only Kant, but a whole library of philosophers to make me behave properly. On second thoughts, perhaps I ought to instruct you on Immoral Imperatives! At two-thirty tomorrow, then, on the stroke. Aisgill and Rajah require you this afternoon, and I would not wish to disappoint them.'

Chad's expression as he looked at his wilful mistress told its own tale.

'Why are you not making a note of my appointment with you, Newcome? Do so immediately; I want no excuses for your absence. None at all. I need succouring after this afternoon's revelations, and you are large enough to succour anyone. Now, I must go to Henson's office to sign papers, and give silver coins to deserving servants.'

She turned at the door, blew him a kiss as Aunt Conybeare slept on. 'Tell me, Newcome, what present shall I give to my most deserving servant of all?'

CHAPTER TEN

THE annexe hardly seemed the most romantic of places: no windows, narrow, lined with bookshelves, a glass window in its ceiling the only light, but to Nell and Chad it was a haven, the one place where they might catch a few moments together—if their luck held, that was.

Luck was with them. Challenor was unwell; he had retired to his room, leaving Chad alone there, collating at the map table, for Nell to find him, and Aunt Conybeare was gone to her sitting-room, after her morning's stint in the study overlooking Nell with her secretary.

Nell, aware of Challenor's absence, burning with impatient desire, controlled herself, and as Aunt Conybeare made off said, 'A moment; I must consult with Henson, Aunt. I will join you later.'

Amorous conspiracy had made such a liar of her that now her voice carried no false overtones, and without the slightest trace of guilt she pushed the library door open to see him standing there, broad back to her.

She did not even need to speak, put up her hand, and he followed her into the annexe where she closed and locked the door behind them and they stood face to face.

But oh, dear, *his* face! He had yet another noble fit of conscience on him, that was plain.

Nell drew a ragged breath, said wearily, 'Yes, Newcome, what is it this time? A sudden religious conversion, or another inconvenient attack of honour?'

'Neither,' said Chad, face grim. 'My wits recover slowly, but they do recover. Two things struck me this morning: first of all, if I accede to your wishes, and my own love and yes, desire for you, the chances of you falling with child are great,' and before he could continue she was there before him.

'Oh, Newcome, what of that? Are you fearful that I shall not make an honest man of you, somehow?'

Despite himself his face lightened, even if, as Nell was pleased to see, his eyes began to smoulder. 'No, it won't do,' he said, blunt with her for once. 'Consider—and I must truly have lost my wits as well as my memory not to think of this before—I may have a family, children, somewhere, and, if so, what of them?'

'What indeed?' said Nell, who wondered what her own wits had been doing—struck down by mad desire, she supposed. 'You do not seem a married man to me,' she offered, 'a derelict wandering the moors. Had you deserted them, Newcome? Or have you remembered your family, and this is a kind way of telling me of them?'

Chad closed his eyes, and as so often tried to conjure up his past. Nothing—vague clouds passing over the sun, blackness with lights in it, a dying horse squealing, soldiers shouting, an old man's angry face, despising him, a sensation of falling, sorrow, regret and pain felt—for what?

'Nothing,' he said at last, 'nothing. The harder I try to remember, the less I can recall. Flashes come when I am not attending to my condition. I do not feel that I was married; on the contrary, my deepest self tells me I was not, but——'

'Oh, what a but that is,' said Nell sorrowfully. 'Let us think of what you are, and what it tells us. You had an education, a good one. You speak like a gentleman, but you were not in the condition of one when you were found. Aisgill says you were undoubtedly a cavalryman. "He knows the brand", he says. A gentleman fallen on hard times, penniless perhaps, enlisted in the army as a private, one supposes, turned off in the peace with nowhere to go—does all this seen reasonable to you, Newcome?'

Chad nodded. Reasonable but wrong, something beyond reason told him, but he followed Nell's line of logic. 'Such hard times that I could find no occupation, began a-wandering, somehow ended up attacked and my memory gone. I do not sound married, and such instincts as I possess tell me I was not, but oh, my dearest lady, that may be my wishes, my love speaking, not the truth.'

'What is the truth?' said Nell softly. 'The present truth is that you are here at Campions, my secretary who saved my life, and whom, God forgive me, for reasons which are no reasons, I love beyond reason. I do not care if you are married, and have twenty children, Newcome, do you understand me? I do not care. I am Nell Tallboys who has lost her wits, and about whom Charles Halstead was right—when we love, all women are the same. Light-skirts, everyone of us! He has won his bet—and will never know it. Forget your conscience, Newcome, as I am forgetting mine. What price my being a Countess and owning half Yorkshire, and a quarter of England, if I cannot have the man I love?'

'You love the wrong man,' said Chad hoarsely. Proximity was fuelling desire; the sight of her, the scent of her, was working in him. Oh, yes, he might have twenty children, but what of that?

In the here and now there was only Nell, and she was offering herself to him, and if what they snatched together would be brief, at least he would have that to set against the dark, which was all that he possessed of himself.

Conscience, honour, reason worked against them both, but '*Amor vincit omnia*' flashed though his mind; love conquers all, and against love nothing could stand, nothing.

He moved forward. So did she. Nell saw on his face the message that she had won. What she offered him he could not refuse. They were so close together now, in the narrow room, that no man or woman could be closer, outside of the act of love itself.

Nell trembled as Chad's hands rose to cup her face, and then he brought down his face to kiss her. And the kiss was not like any of his previous ones. It was fierce. It almost bruised her mouth, which opened beneath his to take him in, his tongue and hers meeting and touching, as though all the words which had passed between them had been made flesh, killing the need for speech.

His tongue was the first of him to enter her. She exulted in the sensation, wound her arms around his neck to draw him even closer, to feel the long length of him against her, his arms around her, equally demanding, as though they could sink into one another, become an entity which, being both, was neither, but something new.

How long they stood like that Nell did not know. Only, suddenly, his busy hands were at work about her. He was pulling her dress down from her shoulders so that her breasts sprang free, and he was caressing them, first with his hands and then with his mouth, so that her head fell back, and she gave long shuddering gasps, gasps which were in rhythm with the shuddering ecstasy which ran through her body.

The sensations which Nell was experiencing made

her knees weak, her head swim, and she gave an inarticulate cry, steadied herself against him, and then her wanton hands did something quite disgraceful, something she had never dreamed of doing.

For she undid his breeches flap and it was his turn to spring, hard, into her hand, which grasped and stroked him, so that he groaned beneath her loving hands, and now his hands peeled her dress up, up.

Nell was on fire, lost to everything but the fact that they were at last on the verge of doing what she had hardly dared to dream was possible, and when his hands transferred themselves to her buttocks, to clasp her to him, ready for the final act, she said thickly, 'Oh, yes, Chad, yes.'

Her voice broke the spell which bound him. He shuddered, put a hand down to take her hand from him, said hoarsely, pulling away a little, 'No, Nell, no.'

'No?' babbled Nell, who by now had only one idea in her head—to impale herself on him. . .on what her hand held. 'What do you mean by no, Newcome? I say yes. Your Countess orders you, Newcome. Yes, immediately. Now.'

'No, not like this,' was all that he could say, trying to detach himself from her and Nell resisting.

'What do mean, not like this, Newcome? I thought that this was how one did it. Is there another way? If so, pray show me, at once, Newcome, at once!'

She felt him, rather than heard him, give a half-laugh, half-sob. 'Oh, by God, Nell, you tempt me sorely with tongue and body. This way, any way you please, but not here, not now, hugger-mugger. I don't want to take you like a drab in an alley, I want to love you, slowly, properly.'

'Oh,' she wailed, 'I want you now, properly or improperly, my love, or I shall die. Here on the spot I shall die, and how will you explain that, my darling, when Challenor finds me stark and cold, slain by your Moral Imperative, an unwilling sacrifice to virtue?'

'No, never cold,' he said, free of her, facing her, trembling with unfulfilled desire, his body reproaching him as much as she. 'In life, in death, Nell, never cold. But not now...not here... It should be a sacrament...'

'But where, Newcome, Chad, my own love, where?' Nell was frantic. 'No private place for me or you. Oh, here and now is heaven and hell,' and she put out her hand to stroke him again, so that he rose on tiptoe, said roughly, chokingly,

'For God's sake, Nell, would you have me pleasured without my knowing you? I can only stand so much...'

Nell was on the brink of she knew not what. The excitement she felt was so powerful that it sought release. If he would not pleasure himself within her, then she would give him release without her, for she had brought him to this with her wilfulness, and at least she could give him that.

'I would give you fulfilment,' she said, 'this way, if not the other.'

His grip was suddenly on her wrist, stilling her hand. 'No,' he said. 'No. Without you, nothing.'

'For you,' she whispered, 'for you. For I have done this to you.'

'My love, my life, my dearest lady...' he was articulate *in extremis* '...it is *you* I want. Our pleasure together. Oh, Nell, you must take, as well as give. Take my unfulfilled flame of love, it is all I have to give you, against what you wish to give me. I will contrive, somehow, that we meet in a place more fitting, that we may make a ceremony of it. Please, Nell, please.'

Nell stopped, her head drooping on his chest. They

panted together, self-denial more exhausting than fulfillment.

'If that is what you want, then I want it too. Oh, I am greedy, I know, but I want all of you, not just your hands and mouth.' She hardly knew what she was saying, and for a moment they stayed there thus, unmoving, content to hold one another. Except that at the end Chad turned to face the wall, leaned against it, his whole body shaking, and Nell dropped to her knees, shuddering, her forehead on a low cupboard's top, passion contained, not destroyed.

And then they turned towards one another. He straightened her dress for her, and gently, gently, she restored him, refastened the cravat she had pulled undone in her passion to get at him, rebuttoned him, still without speech between them. They had gone beyond words.

But once outside, in the library, the clock ticked above the fire in the hearth, the busts of the Roman Emperors looked down on them, blind, and the books stood in their rows behind their lattices as though nothing had happened, as though in their precincts two lovers had not suffered and inwardly bled, torn by their forbidden passion.

Nell walked to the door, turned there before she left, to say but one word. 'Soon!'

The word was easily said, the doing difficult. The guard kept on Nell, the duties which bound him, the presence of her aunt, servants, Aisgill, Henson, Challenor, her duties, all contrived to keep them apart. The annexe they avoided.

Christmas, its pleasures and further duties, was upon them. Nell entertained the Riding. Men and women arrived for a great feast. They stared at her. Despite sexual denial, she was radiant, for was *he* not always by her side, to sustain her, if he could not physically love her?

'I never thought Nell Tallboys beautiful before,' said one bluff squire to his wife, as Nell moved among them, magnificent in toffee-coloured silk, wearing her rarely seen diamonds, the knowledge of being cherished plain upon her face for the perceptive to see, 'but, by God, she's a marvel tonight.'

Chad was there, sporting a new silk suit, especially made for him, black, with knee breeches and stockings also of silk, standing in the background with the rest of Nell's council, one or two staring at the size of him.

Memory still lost, he had bad dreams. The night after the scene in the annexe he had shouted so loud in his sleep that he had woken up Sandby, Henson's assistant, who had a room next to Chad's small suite on the top floor, and Sandby had gone in to find him tangled in the bedclothes, sweating and shaken.

He could remember little of what had disturbed him so. Only a feeling of desolation, and of falling, of clawing himself up a steep slope, and then losing himself. Nell had been there, but the sight of her had distressed him so badly that he was suddenly beside himself with pain and shock, after the first joyful sight of her.

He had had such dreams when he had first arrived at Campions, but of late they had disappeared. Perhaps the encounter in the annexe had brought them back. One thing did surprise him, and that was that just before Sandby shook him awake he had seen in his hands, quite plain, the rifle he had taken from the would-be assassin. But the hands that were holding it were wearing white gloves, and he was talking to an officer in full regimentals in terms of cheerful equality, almost of authority, and then the scene vanished into the dark.

Like all dreams, it ran away from him in the day, and little was left of it. He had learned to accept his condition, to accept that perhaps he would never find himself again, and to live with that knowledge. The dogged dedication with which he worked owed a little to his determination to forget himself in his duties, and a great deal to his love for Nell, which he tried, for her sake, not to betray to those around him.

But the big event of the Yuletide season for those at Campions was the party that Nell always gave for her staff, the day when the state dining hall was given over to those who created and maintained the estate, and not to those who simply lived off it.

Chad, with the rest of Nell's council, dressed again in his black silk suit, walked in that evening. The hall was decked with boughs of holly, every chandelier was aflame with light, fires blazed in the two hearths, and Nell was even more stately than she had been on the night she had entertained the Riding.

She had dressed herself like a bride in white and cream; she wore not the diamonds but the emeralds which Catherine the Great of Russia had given to the third Earl, when he had been ambassador in St Petersburg, after she had taken him to bed as her lover.

It was a suite of even more splendour than her diamonds, consisting of a tiara, earrings, necklace, bracelets, rings, and a belt of gold, set with pearls as well as emeralds, cinched under her breasts. Her fan matched the suite, huge, decorated with parrots of green and scarlet. Annie had dressed her hair high beneath the tiara, and if she took Chad's breath away she had the same effect on everyone else. Even mild Aunt Conybeare was a little stunned.

The boar's head had been carried in, the plum pudding served, drink of all kinds handed around, and at a signal Nell rose, and the company adjourned to the long gallery, where there was a small collection of musicians, brought especially from York to play for Nell's people, and a group of waits who broke into 'God rest you merry, gentlemen' at the sight of Nell.

Chad knew one thing. He had never before been present on such an occasion—he needed no memory to tell him that. Old Challenor, her senior council member, led his mistress out for the first minuet, for court dancing alternated with the country dances put on for her staff.

'And you,' Nell murmured to Chad, after Challenor had returned her to her place on the small dais set up before the great window which ran for a third of the length of the wall, 'will take me out for my fourth dance after Henson and Aisgill. We follow strict precedence here, you see. After you, the butler!' and her eyes shone with mirth.

Strangely, they had been easy together since their last powerful encounter in the annexe. It was as though they knew who they were and how they stood with one another; that they could be patient, hold off, and work together in a comfortable amity, even though a cauldron of passion might lie below the smooth surface of their lives.

'Biding our time,' murmured Nell, when he stood up to lead her out. 'What good creatures we are, to be sure.' The Yule log roared in the hearth, Nell's people clapped their hands each time she took the floor, and many clapped louder when it was Newcome who took her hand. He was liked—and not only by the women, who yearned over his size and his rugged charm; the men respected him, too, a pen-pusher who could match them at many of their outdoor pursuits, and beat them in some.

He was Rajah's master, and recently had been

discovered to have a punishing blow in the ring. He had stopped one day to watch young Seth training—he was a useful fighter at little bouts in the Riding—had offered him some advice, and then been challenged to put his fists where his mouth was, a challenge he had taken up with some success.

He had arrived in Nell's study with a black eye, but he had managed to put Seth down twice before Seth put him down, and Aunt Conybeare had clucked and fussed over him, to Nell's amusement. She thought that all Campions was falling in love with Chad, not merely its mistress!

They moved through the pattern of the dance, meeting, parting, symbolic of life itself, Nell thought, and thinking so she arrived back at him again, and unselfconsciously, naturally as she met him, there in the centre of the floor, for a fleeting moment all that she felt for him, and he for her, was written plain on their faces.

In the hurly-burly of the dance it might have gone completely unnoticed, the spark which betrayed them both. One man, and one man only, saw it.

Aisgill, whom all such occasion as this bored, found his entertainment not in taking part but watching others. He was leaning against one of the pillars of the fireplace, half-cut, but even so the shrewdness and knowledge of man and beast which made him so successful as Nell's lieutenant were still with him. His lazy eye was on the dancers; he saw Nell turn, saw her and Chad meet, and it was as though lightning flashed in front of him to illuminate a landscape he had never seen before.

He had no doubt of what he had seen; his only doubt was how far the lovers had gone. He knew his Countess, and the lightning illuminated something else—the change in her, and what had provoked it.

Nell watched Chad move away from her, turn, to greet her again, and joyfully, she curtsied before him as the dance ended, and he bowed, to lift her, to take her hand, to escort her to the dais, passing Aisgill on the way, his shrewd, sad old eyes on them both, his mistress and the man he and she had rescued, half-naked, from the moor.

CHAPTER ELEVEN

IT WAS six weeks since they had broken off their lovemaking in the annexe. Snow covered the moors; Nell thought that her heart was frozen too, and wondered at Chad's. She had not thought it possible that they could be so cool with each other.

They met, worked together, spoke as in a dream. Had she dreamed it, their passion? Had he dreamed it? No, of course they had not, for if they were foolish enough to let their hands touch, ever so slightly, the fever sprang up between them again. Nell felt her body grow lax, saw his eyes begin to smoulder with desire, and then for the rest of the day she needed to control herself.

And how, and when, had he learned to exercise such iron control? For Nell had come to recognise that he did. How fortunate, she thought bitterly, they they were so strong, for none watching them could see what they meant to each other, she was sure of that.

She walked towards the stables in the dim light of early morning. White Princess, her mare, always known as Princess, was in foal, due to bear Rajah's progeny any day. She fantasised herself as Princess, and Chad as Rajah. How simple it was for the members of her stud, and how difficult for her, Nell Tallboys, who had everything, but who had nothing.

Aisgill met her in the yard. 'Lady Elinor?'

'I have come to learn of Princess, Aisgill,' she said, pulling her coat tighter about her, against the cold. 'You said that she was about to foal at any time now.'

She paused, went on, 'You will think me stupid, but I awoke, worrying about her.'

'Not stupid, my lady,' he answered. 'Sometimes I think that where your horses are concerned you have an extra sense. I am worried, too. She has begun to have her foal, but things are going ill. I had hoped that they would go better before I needed to tell you of her.'

'I may see her?' asked Nell. She had assisted at births before, insisting that she needed to know all of the work of the stud, not just the pleasant, easy bits.

'Yes,' he replied curtly. Nell thought that for some reason Aisgill was short with her, and she wondered why.

He led her to where Princess lay, and there, kneeling by her beautiful mare, now *in extremis*, was Chad, wearing not his fine black suit but the rough clothing he had been given when he first arrived at Campions.

Aisgill saw her eyes on Newcome, sighed. He had thought, after the Christmas dance, when the tenants and the servants had gone, that perhaps he had been wrong, deceived by the drink he had taken; and the impassive masks his mistress and her lover had worn in the days after Christmas reinforced his belief that he had been mistaken. But here, in the gloom, the look which Nell gave to Chad, assisting at the primal moment of birth, told him that after all he had been right.

Nell moved over to Chad, fell on her knees beside him. He had looked up on seeing her enter, and looked away again, fearful that he might betray himself.

Aisgill, behind them, spoke. 'I thought that Newcome,' he spoke the name roughly, as though Chad were still only one of his hands, not the almost-gentleman he was in the house, 'would be of most use here. He helped me when Lady Luck had her foal and things went ill. You owed that foal to him, Lady Elinor. He has good hands for birth, as well as for controlling Rajah.'

'Yes,' said Nell, almost absently. 'What is wrong, Newcome?'

'Her foal is wrongly positioned,' said Chad. 'Not like Lady Luck's was. Worse, I fear. Her chances are not good.'

There were several other stable hands present, all with grave faces. To lose Princess and her foal would be a blow to them all. For no good reason that Nell could think of, it suddenly seemed desperately important that Princess lived. It was almost as though the beautiful beast, lying there helpless, was Nell herself, about to die—or, rather, that Princess symbolised the love she felt for Chad, and could not express.

She rose to her feet, said, 'No!' and walked over to the wall, to stand there facing it, leaving them all surprised that she, usually so cool, who had seen all this before and had not flinched, could show such emotion.

Chad could not stop himself. Something of what she was experiencing passed from her to him. He rose, regardless of etiquette, and what Aisgill might think, and he walked over to her, and touched her arm. 'Lady Elinor,' he said, and the sound of his voice eased Nell's torment a little, 'Lady Elinor, we shall do our best to save her, and the foal as well.'

Nell turned towards him, showing him a face of such grief that he retreated a little.

'Poor Princess,' she said. 'There are times when I feel——' and her voice thickened '—that running the stud is more than I can endure.'

'It is the way of life, Lady Elinor,' he said gravely, fighting the wish to take her in his arms and comfort her. 'With or without the stud, mares would be in foal, and occasionally their lives would be at risk because of it.'

It was as though they were alone, and the frustration which Nell felt that she could not be Princess, lying there, having *his* foal, even at the risk of her life, was in her voice and manner.

'Where did you learn such wisdom, Newcome? Or have you forgotten that, along with everything else?'

Oh, she was being unfair to him, she knew, and saw that he understood why she spoke as she did, that the rapport between them was now so strong that it went beyond words.

Aisgill spoke sharply. 'The mare needs you, Newcome, more than Lady Elinor does.'

Both lovers were so engrossed that the full import of what he was saying did not strike them. Chad heard only the command to action, Nell hardly heard him at all.

Until Aisgill added, 'This is going to be difficult, Lady Elinor. I think that you should leave us to it. Not a fit place for you.'

'My mare,' said Nell, proud, 'my stud. You would not say that to me if I were the sixth Earl, instead of your Countess. I shall stay.'

Aisgill bowed his head. He could not deny her. He knew that she had been present at births before, but in some fashion, and why he did not know, he felt that she should not be present now. But he could not gainsay her, and for the next hour of blood and pain and noise Nell stayed, carrying buckets of water for them, until Princess's foal was pulled into the world, and Princess, though sorely hurt, and beside herself with pain, still lived.

Nell had willed the mare's survival, that Chad and Aisgill should succeed, wanting an omen for herself that she thought to be good, and once all was over her legs turned to water, not with desire, as they had done in the annexe, but for sheer blessed relief.

'And now will you go, madam?' said Aisgill, surlily mutinous for once, Chad washing Princess's blood from his hands and arms in the pail which Nell had carried to him, the foal—which Aisgill had announced was to be called Lightning, in a voice which brooked of no argument—staggering about, and Princess trying to rise.

'I will escort Lady Elinor back to the house,' announced Chad; he was towelling his face now.

'No,' said Aisgill sharply. 'Go and eat with the lads; you need to rest. I shall see Lady Elinor back.'

'I need no escort in Campions's grounds in sight of both house and stables,' said Nell, equally sharply, wondering what had got into Aisgill that he should be so surly. 'You need your own breakfast. No, I will brook no denial,' and she walked off, head high, Countess Nell at her most icy cold, almost as she had been before Chad's arrival at Campions.

Chad ate his breakfast hungrily, although sorry that he was denied Nell's companionship on the way back to the house. The hands' fare was simple, but good, and he was grateful for the plain food after all the kickshaws at Nell's table. What did that tell him of his old life? he wondered.

Aisgill came late to breakfast, and when Chad rose to return to the house, to dress himself to be Nell's secretary again, said to Chad, still harsh, 'A word with you, Newcome, before you leave.'

Like Nell, Chad was a little puzzled by Aisgill's manner, the more so when Aisgill led him to the stable yard, away from any overhearing of what he was about to say.

'Do not misunderstand me, Newcome,' began

Aisgill, his colour high, even for him. 'You are a good worker, the best, and I understand from Henson that you have made a good clerk. But remember, the Lady Elinor is your Countess as she is mine, and I do not want to see any hurt come to her, especially from those to whom she has shown kindness. You understand me, Newcome. I should find means to turn you away tomorrow, if I thought that your presence here was a threat to Campions.'

The thunderbolt had hit Chad. Aisgill knew! But how? He was certain that he, and she, had done nothing to betray themselves. But Aisgill knew men and animals. Could he scent them, then? And if he could, could not others?

'I would do nothing to bring harm to Lady Elinor, or Campions,' he said, 'seeing that they have given me life. Without her, I should be cold on the moor.'

'Then see that you remember that, man,' said Aisgill, showing his teeth. 'You are her secretary, who was her stable lad, and before that you were nothing, scum, starving, naked, plucked from the ditch. Keep that well in mind, and you cannot go far wrong.'

What could he say? God help me, I love her, and she loves me, and that stands before everything, even my honour, and hers.

Instead, he bowed his head stiffly before her faithful servant who wished only to protect her, while he, what did he wish to do but dishonour her? And Aisgill's words were one more barrier between himself and his love.

Nell, newly dressed for the day, elegant in tan, was expecting to find Chad in her study, at his desk. But only Aunt Conybeare was there, placid, her sewing on her knee.

'Where's Newcome?' she said, abrupt.

'He came in, went out again.' Aunt Conybeare was unruffled. The weeks of sitting in on Nell and Chad and nothing happening had left her used to his presence. The undercurrents between the two escaped her. Gifted at reading novels, Aunt Conybeare could not read life.

Nell sat down at her own desk. There was an envelope on it, her name written there, in Chad's hand.

She opened it, read the short sentence inside.

'Lady Elinor. I must leave Campions. With, or without, your permission,' and then his signature, bold, firm, like himself. Chad Newcome, plain, no flourishes.

Nell's heart clenched inside her. She could have screamed, thrown herself about. Of all the things which she could have imagined—never this, never this! To lose him. No, no, it was not to be borne. To be alone again, and this time to know what she was missing. She could never be uninvolved Nell Tallboys again.

Where was he? He must be in the library, if he was not with her, or in Henson's office. She must see him, speak to him. What had brought this on?

He was in the library. He was sitting on the book-steps, a book in his hand. Challenor was nowhere in sight.

Chad saw Nell advancing on him, the letter in her hand, an avenging fury.

She walked to where he sat, waved the letter at him, and, careless of whether Challenor was about or not, said, 'What is the meaning of this, Newcome? Tell me at once.'

Chad made no effort to leap to his feet, to pay her his due respects, but said, from his sitting position, 'I thought the meaning of what I have written quite plain, Lady Elinor.'

'Did you, indeed, Newcome? Get down, at once, pay me the respect due to my rank from yours. I am your Countess, Newcome! Remember that!'

Chad rose, stood before her, head bowed, deferential, said, 'I am remembering that, Lady Elinor. And *that* is why I have written you my letter.'

'Oh!' Nell's desire to scream was almost not to be denied. 'Stop it at once, Newcome. You are back in the Jesuit seminary again. Answer a plain question plainly.'

He could temporise no longer. The anguish which tore at Nell tore at him.

'It is not right that I should stay. For your honour, I must go. We are. . .remarked upon.'

At last something to give Nell pause. To have her staring at him, face white.

'We are. . .' and then the intuitive leap. 'Aisgill! I knew it, somehow, this morning. He was odd, strange. But how in the world could he guess at such a thing? For guess it must be.'

'Does it matter?' said Chad wearily. 'He knows. That is enough.'

'He knows nothing, Newcome, for there is nothing to know.'

'Now you are enrolled with the Jesuits, Lady Elinor,' said Chad. 'For there is everything to know. I must go, and soon. To save us. . .' And then since Challenor seemed absent, and for a moment they were safe, 'Nell, I would not have written the letter else. I *must* go.'

'Go! Where will you go, Newcome, my love, my own? To starve again? To die on the moor this time? You have no home, no haven, not even a name. I will not let you go to. . .nothing.'

She but echoed what Aisgill had said earlier.

'What am I,' he said, and, since Aisgill had spoken to him that morning he had dredged his mind for memories, something to tell him who he was, but nothing, nothing, 'but a piece of scum, found and cared for, betraying those who cared for him, by seeking to dishonour their lady?'

'No dishonour, Newcome, when your lady commands. Was Princess dishonoured by Rajah?'

Chad closed his eyes, that he might not see her face. He would carry the memory of her to his death. His gallant lady.

She took his silence for consent, pressed home her advantage, as she thought. 'Besides,' she said feverishly, 'you are now my secretary. I shall demand three months' notice, you hear me, Newcome? Three months' notice, before you leave. And you are not to try to run away; I shall set the dogs on you, to haul you back.'

The tears were rolling down her face; she was frantic. No thought for those who might find them, her only thought was not to lose him.

'Hush,' he said, pulling out his handkerchief, and leaning forward to mop her face with it. 'You are brave, my Countess. Remember your ancestor on the field of battle. "The day is lost, surrender", his enemies told him, and his answer, "I scorn to surrender my living body; you may take it only in death". And saying so he fought on, but not to lose his battle, to win it against all odds, in the end.'

'Fine words,' she said, through her tears, 'from one who is running away.'

'Oh, it is you who carry the banner, not I,' he said, his mouth twisted. 'I am only your slave, whose duty is to die for you, or sacrifice himself to save your honour.'

'But you sacrifice me, too,' she wailed, 'for what is left for me but a loveless marriage, and an empty life? I have no battle to win, unlike the man whose name I bear. I would be a cottager's daughter and have the man I love rather than be what I am. You must not leave me.'

Chad saw that she was distraught, which moved him, and he knew also that what she said and did came from her heart. But he saw Aisgill again, and the contempt in his face for a man who would do what he thought he saw Chad doing.

Again, it was as though she had picked up his very thoughts.

'Am I, are we, to do what Aisgill tells us? Is Aisgill master here——?'

But Chad came back at her, 'He thinks of Campions, as well as you.'

'Campions!' Nell almost choked on the word. 'Do you, does he, love Campions more than you love me? If every great lady who loved where she should not were to be punished as I am, the nobility would be decimated.'

'But you are not every great lady. You are Nell Tallboys, brave and true.'

'Words, Newcome, words. I cannot compel you, I know. Whatever you were, you are a strong man; I could not love a weak one. No,' she said, eyes blazing. 'If I give you leave to go, it will not be yet. Give me but a little longer, before my life closes in on me for good. Only that! I ask only that.'

What could he say or do? What was his honour, or hers, before such suffering?

He hesitated. Nell knew that she had won. 'You will stay a little longer, and we shall be careful. Just to have you near me will be enough.'

But even as he assented, saying, 'The usual notice, three months, and it must be known that I am going,' Chad knew that it would not be enough, for what lay between them was too strong for that.

CHAPTER TWELVE

FRUSTRATION and desire were one word for Nell—and that word was Chad.

The self-control which had ruled her life for twenty-seven years, which had created the icy Countess Elinor, noted for her stoic uprightness, her austere virtue, the woman who had turned away suitors until suitors had ceased to come, had disappeared when she had met Chad.

The woman who had proclaimed so confidently that love was not for her, that she would marry someone, anyone, when she chose, merely to secure the succession, and, that done, her partner could go hang—she treating him as a man might treat a woman he had married for her money and lands—that woman no longer existed.

She had discovered in herself a well of passion... no, not well, that word was too placid for what she felt for Chad. It was a cataract, or a fire, a raging fire, the flame of which the poets sang, which consumed her.

When she read Lord Byron now, it was not with superior amusement; she knew only too well of what he wrote, and she forgave him for what he was, and what he did, because, knowing what love had done to her, she knew what it had done to him.

How could Chad be so strong? She could almost feel the iron control which he maintained over his emotions, and in the face of the temptation which she knew that she presented to him. For the first time, she truly asked herself what he had been in his lost past.

Where and how had he learned to deny himself? And what toll had it taken of him, was taking of him? She knew, because nothing that happened at Campions was unknown to her, that he never touched the women servants who yearned after him, being quite unlike most of the men servants in that respect.

Nell had said to him, and to herself, that she could only love a strong man, and had told true. Otherwise she would have taken Ulric as a husband, and, she now knew, contrary to her earlier beliefs, that she could never have married the weak man whom she thought she could have used to serve Campions.

She had fallen in love with a man whose will and control matched her own—so how had he managed to arrive on the moor and at Campions, abandoned and derelict? And now she must know, somehow, what she thought had never mattered—Chad himself having been all that she had previously wanted—what the man she loved had been before his memory had gone.

Sitting at her desk that afternoon, his resignation formally written out now, lying before her, she made her resolutions. She had three months in which to keep him, to change his mind, to try to bend him to her will.

Chad was at the riding school when Henson came in to her, carrying the account books relating to the estate, and a further budget of letters. Before she opened them in Chad's absence, she showed him the letter of resignation.

Surprisingly, Henson was annoyed and offended. 'What maggot's in his brain?' he almost grunted. 'Where will he find work to equal what he has achieved here?'

'I thought you disapproved of him,' commented Nell mildly.

'I did.' Henson was brief. 'But the man has compelled me to admit both his competence and his honesty—to say nothing of his courage in saving you. Besides, his devotion to his duty is exemplary. I had not thought him ungrateful to wish to leave what has saved him.'

Nell began to close her eyes in pain, said, 'I don't think it's ingratitude, Henson.'

'Then what the devil is it? Has he recovered his memory?'

'No, it's not that. I. . .taxed him with that. He says——' and Nell invented wildly, and reminded herself to tell Chad of the excuse which she had found for him, for *something* must be said to Henson '—that he wishes to leave to try to discover who he is.'

'I suppose that makes some sort of sense—so long as he does not end up as a vagabond again,' replied Henson grudgingly. 'In the meantime, we must try to persuade him to stay. Campions must not lose good servants. To lose first Payne and then Newcome would be too bad.'

Payne still lay in his bedroom in the attic, and would never rise from it again, another old servant dying in harness and cared for by the family.

Nell opened the first letter, read it, handed it to Henson, who had taken a seat at Chad's desk. The letter was from Scotland, and its message was simple. The writer, factor to Charles, Viscount Halstead, had received the letter from Campions asking for information about my lord's rifle, but no answer could be given: the Viscount Halstead was not at Glen Ruadh, and no word had been received of his arriving there. Campions was advised to write to Clermont House in London.

Henson handed the letter back to Nell. 'Another dead end,' he commented bitterly, 'and where the devil is the man? Saving your presence, Lady Elinor. And isn't it time that Jackson reported back to us?'

'Yes.' Nell had opened, and was reading, another letter. 'He hopes to be back with us tomorrow. He say he has little to report, but would like to confer with us.'

Henson shrugged his shoulders at that. 'Nothing satisfactory for us today,' he snorted. 'First Newcome off, then Halstead missing, and now Jackson at *point non plus* by the sound of it.'

'I know,' said Nell, and then naughtily—cheerfulness would break in, even in her misery, 'I know, Henson, the world is going to the dogs. But it always has done, and it always will.' And if that doesn't comfort Henson, she thought sadly, why should it comfort me?

'So there it is,' said Cully Jackson to Nell and her council, all in Nell's study the next afternoon. He had arrived, as he had said he would, and his news was that apart from the rifle, which he had asked to keep, he had nothing tangible with which to work.

'I am certain, beyond a doubt, from all I have learned since I last saw you, that Mr Ulric Tallboys was behind the attempt on you. But I have no proof, no proof at all. One of the dead man's associates awaits hanging in Bradford gaol, and I am to see him there soon. He might, facing his end, tell me a little more of his dead leader; throw light on where Halstead's rifle came from. A slim chance, I fear. And I shall make more enquiries there. I have set up a nice little ring of informers in these parts, who may be of use to me in the future, if not now. . .'

'And that's all,' Henson almost snarled. Of them all he hated the attack on Nell most. A civilised, orderly man, he saw it as a giant crack in his world, as well as an attack on his mistress.

'After that,' said Jackson, mildly, ignoring Henson's bile, for he had met such before, 'I shall hie me to London again, to try to find a clue to Halstead's whereabouts. He has certainly been in these parts once, but must have left. None here knows of him. Clermont House might have some information on his whereabouts now. And after that, if I fail there, you must save your money; the trail is dead.'

'You will stay here tonight,' said Nell. 'I insist. The housekeeper will find you a room, and the butler will see that you are properly fed.'

Jackson bowed. 'Before that I should like to speak to Mr Newcome again, if I may.'

They all, Newcome as well, stared at him.

'Oh, I do not suspect Mr Newcome of any wrong-doing,' said Jackson, 'but he may know more than he thinks he does. Witnesses often do, and he is our only witness.'

Nell rose. 'Pray accept my thanks for your efforts so far, and Jackson, I would wish to speak to you alone before you leave. Tomorrow morning, after breakfast, here.'

If Nell's council was surprised by this, none indicated that he thought so. Jackson looked across at Chad, said, 'I should like to see you in the riding school, Mr Newcome. I understand that this is the afternoon you work out there. My interest in horses has previously been with the money I have put on their backs, but I have a mind to see a stable in action.'

'So you shall.' Aisgill was jovial. 'You shall see Newcome on Rajah—that is a sight.' He felt that he could be generous towards Newcome, seeing that he was doing the decent thing by taking himself and his temptations from Campions.

So, that afternoon, a good lunch inside him, Jackson stood in the riding school watching Chad on Rajah, as Aisgill had promised. Both horse and rider had come on since their early days together. Rajah still hated all men, including Chad, except that with Chad he did strange and wonderful things, and, which, although he did not want to do them, there was an odd magnificence in the doing.

First Jackson watched horse and rider go through a series of tricks which Jackson had seen previously, in simpler forms, at Astley's Circus in London. The caracoles and airs above the ground entranced him, as did the obvious control which Newcome was exercising over the unwilling stallion.

And then the lads put out fences around the arena, and Chad took Rajah over them, snorting, blowing and foaming, hating his rider and the admiring spectators, but compelled to do as he was bid.

And when the show was over two lads warily led Rajah away, and Chad walked to where Jackson was standing. 'You wanted to speak to me?'

Jackson was fascinated by Newcome. There was something so ineffably haughty and commanding about him when he was unselfconscious. He had his own theories about what Newcome might have been, and they were not those which obtained at Campions.

'Yes,' he said. 'As I said earlier, I wanted to ask you some questions about your finding of the rifle.'

For some reason Chad did not believe him. His intuition, which he knew—how?—had been powerful in dangerous situations, but not in emotional ones, was working in him. He answered Jackson's innocuous questions calmly; he had no desire to make an enemy of the man. They were now quite alone. It was cold, and the lads had drifted indoors, and Aisgill had gone to his little office.

'And that is all?' asked Jackson. 'You have no conscious memory of having seen the man before?'

Chad's expression grew dangerous, his whole body quite still; he said softly, 'Are you suggesting that I was in some way connected with the attack on Lady Elinor, that I was a Trojan horse planted here to lead her into danger?'

'No,' said Jackson, recognising that the man who had tamed Rajah so easily might not hesitate to tame him. 'I have no doubts about your honesty. It was Lady Elinor's decision that you rode to the Throne; she was adamant that you tried to dissuade her to the point of mutiny. But I have the strangest feeling about the rifle every time I hold it, and I have not learned not to ignore such feelings——'

'And that is?' prompted Chad, his voice still dangerous.

'That you, Chad Newcome, and the rifle are somehow connected. It is what makes me a good thief taker. Feeling, not reasoning connections.'

'I would not argue with you,' said Chad, easing a little, the aura of danger about him dispersing. 'Because, not from memory but from my own instincts, I know such things may be true.'

'And you are leaving Campions, when your notice is up?'

'Yes,' said Chad.

'And you will let me know where you are going, when you go. You may do so through Lady Elinor,' and then, daring danger, 'You are leaving because of Lady Elinor, are you not, Mr Chad Newcome?'

Jackson was on his knees gasping, Chad Newcome's hands were about his throat. Old campaigner that he was, he had not seen Chad move, only knew that he had done so when he was overwhelmed.

'Say that again, to anyone but myself, and I shall not hesitate to kill you, Mr Jackson,' said Chad, almost conversationally. 'It is no business of yours, nor your investigation, why I am leaving. Mention her name to me again and I shall step on you and crush you as I would a beetle.'

He released Jackson, who began to laugh, although his throat pained him. 'Oh, my fine gentleman,' he choked, 'I have properly smoked you out. A trooper, were you? Someone's servant? I think not.'

He had the satisfaction of seeing Newcome's face change, lose its colour.

'And what the devil do you mean by that?' Chad grated.

'You may work it out for yourself, sir. In the night watches. It might help you to recover your memory, tell you why you chose to lose it. No, do not attack me again, I know you are not faking. But you might try asking yourself why you do not wish to know yourself, a man of honour, such as you most plainly are.'

The Runner strolled off, laughing to himself. He had not needed to bait Newcome to find out that he and Lady Elinor were involved, he had seen that for himself, but he had discovered to his own satisfaction that Newcome was rather more than the poor ex-trooper that Campions thought him to be. What exactly he had been was quite another matter. He took that knowledge with him to his meeting with Lady Elinor.

Nell had spent her time wondering what to say to Jackson. When he came in with his ill-made, dangerous body and face, the thief taker *par excellence*, she decided that the simple truth might be the safest.

'I have another task for you, Jackson,' she said, without preamble, 'and it is this. You know that Mr Newcome has lost his memory, that he is shortly to leave Campions. I am disturbed that he may leave us without being able to sustain himself properly. Consequently, I'm asking you, without his knowledge, to try to discover where he came from, how he arrived, injured and starving, on the moor. It seems to me that you could make your enquiries at the same time that you pursue the mission for which Campions has employed you.'

Jackson kept his face straight. He did not fear that Lady Elinor might attack him, as Newcome had done, but it would not be safe to be on the wrong side of such a powerful woman.

'Yes, my lady,' he said. 'I can do what you wish, and, of course, I shall say nothing to him.'

'And I will tell you all I know of his arrival here,' began Nell, and proceeded to do so, so lucidly that at the end Jackson said respectfully,

'If I may say so, Lady Elinor, I could do with you as my assistant. Few of the ones I possess are as clear as you in the reports they make to me.'

Nell laughed at that. 'When I am no longer Countess Nell,' she said gaily, 'I shall come to Bow Street and ask you for work.'

It was not difficult for Jackson to understand why Chad Newcome, and all her people, for that matter, loved her. He determined that if it were possible he would try to find out who was plotting to kill her, and would nail him.

Nell watched him leave the room, dour and honest. She felt as though she was betraying Chad by setting Jackson on his trail, for who knew what he might find?

Jackson turned at the door before he left, and said, 'Whatever I discover, of both good and ill about him, you will hear of it from me, will you not?' and his tone was almost a challenge.

'Yes,' she said, 'yes,' and then thought, as he left the room, All's fair in love and war, and only myself and my God know how much I love you, Chad.

CHAPTER THIRTEEN

'NEWCOME!'

Chad was in the library; his time when he was not acting as Nell's secretary was divided between the stables and the library, which Campions did not find strange since their Countess's time was similarly shared.

He was standing at the lectern, working, when Nell came in, his back to the door from her study by which she had entered. The few occasions on which they had been alone together were either in the library proper, or in the annexe. A little earlier Nell had seen Challenor walk by her window, away from the house, knew that Chad would likely be working there, and had immediately seized her opportunity to speak with him unchaperoned.

Chad turned, gave her his smile, the smile which wrenched her heart. Dressed as he was, he was virtually indistinguishable in appearance from the aristocrats and gentry who had once besieged her, except that he was Chad, and none of them had stolen her heart from her bosom.

Nell treasured the smile for it was all that he gave her these days—they had reached the stage where they dared not touch.

'Lady Elinor?'

He was suddenly so grave, so proper, so all that he should be that the devil whispered in Nell's ear. Oh, to destroy his hard-won composure. She spoke, eyes glinting, dark brows lifting, her whole aspect one of such innocent wickedness that the man before her clutched at the shreds of his reason.

'I have not given up, you know, Newcome. I shall never give up!'

'I know,' said Chad, his eyes smoking, Nell noted happily; Not so composed after all, my love, she thought. Let us see if I can shake that nobly intransigent front of yours. 'I know, Lady Elinor. You take after your ancestor in that.'

'Oh, no,' said Nell, still naughty. 'It was his body he refused to surrender, whereas the body I refuse to surrender. . .' and she paused, her eyes hard on his face '. . .is yours.'

Chad could not prevent his smile from broadening at her impudent wit.

'Do not smile, Newcome,' commanded Nell severely. 'You are not to smile when my heart is breaking.'

'If I do not smile, Nell,' replied Chad softly, 'I shall shriek to the heavens for what they deny me.'

'Oh, you feel as I do, then,' she said. 'How can you be so strong, to deny yourself and me so calmly?'

'As strong as you, Nell,' he said, still standing aloof from her. 'As strong as you.'

'No, I am weak,' she returned. 'Touch me, Newcome; you will see how weak I am.'

Chad put his hands behind his back. They now stood face to face, but apart, neither moving towards the other.

'Infinity,' said Nell, pointing at the eighteen inches of parquet floor which separated them.

'An eternity,' said Chad. 'Two names for the same thing.'

'And what name is there for love denied?' asked Nell.

'Honour,' Chad returned, as quick as she.

'Honour?' Nell repeated sadly. 'I think it a word for men to use.'

'Ah, but you play a man's part, Lady Elinor,' said Chad. 'For you are Countess as a man is an earl. No husband gives you that title. It is yours by birth and by right. So, men's words are your words.'

It was as though an arrow pierced Nell's heart, as though a bell had tolled, or a sentence had burned itself in letters of fire before her in the air. She almost staggered and fell. For he had unlocked the door, found the heart of the maze in which they stood, liberated them both from the bonds which bound them.

'Why, so I am,' she said. 'And their deeds are my deeds, their rights mine. I am blessed among women, for whatever a man can do, so may I do. Oh, Chad,' and she laughed joyously. 'You have played with words as other men play with dice, and this time your throw is so true that I, your Countess, salute you,' and she dipped into a great curtsy before him, as though he were her monarch, chestnut head bent. 'And now I must leave you, to think on what you have said—and to act!'

Why, what have I said to affect her so? thought Chad, puzzled, watching her face, glowing as it had not done since they parted, love refused, in the annexe all those miserable weeks ago.

Nell turned at the door, to find that he had not moved, had followed her going with his eyes alone.

'You do not ask me where I am bound, Newcome,' she said, her eyes sparkling, her whole mien changed from the stoic one of the recent past.

'To your room, I suppose.' For once he was at a loss for words.

'You suppose wrongly, Newcome. I am bound for the long gallery, to where my painted forebears hang, for I think that they have a message for me. You have reminded me of what I am, and what they are, and love may yet conquer all. It is *au revoir* I bid you, Newcome, not goodbye.'

Eyes still shining, Nell paced the long gallery, staring up at the family portraits, at the first Earl, godlike in his early eighteenth-century battle dress, banners and plumes, cannon smoking behind him. At the second Earl, Hanoverian George's minister, sardonic in dark blue court dress, the man who had founded the Campions stud, at the third Earl, who had combed Europe for the treasures which filled the house, and had refused office because he disliked his monarch, at the fourth Earl, who had died young, but not before he had created the library which was Challenor's treasure, and at her grandfather, his brother, painted in his old age by Sir Thomas Lawrence.

Their word had been law, they had defied kings, princes, done as they pleased, as the male Tallboyses had always done. She looked at the first Earl again; she had thought him the founder of the House of Tallboys until her grandfather had told her otherwise.

'Oh, no,' he had said, one rainy evening, as she sat at his feet, looking at the first Earl. 'He simply acquired for us the Malplaquet title. We go further back than that. Not him, my dear; he was already noble. Never forget that we are sprung from nothing, or so the legend says.'

Strange that she had forgotten this, and that it should come back to her now.

'What does the legend say?' she had asked him, as he fell silent.

'Why, that one day in the mists of time, long ago, in King John's reign, the unmarried lady of Barthwaite rode from her manor, and, being tired, stopped at a cottage where a tall woodcutter rested on his axe. Ivo of the Woods was all the name he had.

'"You may give me a drink," she said to him, "for I have a great thirst."

'"I would give you more than that, lady," he said, bold eyes on her, leaving no doubt as to what he meant.

'"Why, so you may," she said, looking at the size and strength of him, "and in exchange I will give you myself and Barthwaite, too," for she knew that here was the only man who could match and master her, and she would have him, for was not she the lady and he the serf?

'"I have no name to give you, lady," he said.

'"Then I will give you one, woodcutter, and a good French one it shall be, and then you may give it to me when the priest weds us. You shall be Taillebois, the man who cuts wood, and so shall all be to whom we give life."

'And so it was, and Taillebois—Tallboys—we are to this day, for we are all their descendants, and you, barring Ulric, are the last of the line, my dear.'

'And is the story true, Grandfather?' she had asked him.

'I would like it to be so,' he said, 'if only to show that, noble or simple, we are all the same beneath our clothes. I am at one with the Radicals in that, if in nothing else.'

Remembering this, Nell struck her hands together fiercely. She was the last lady of the line, and, through the first Earl's doing, she also stood as the last man, with all of a man's rights and privileges. She knew what she had to do, and, being practical Nell Tallboys, who organised her life so well, she decided to organise it further—and at once.

'I shall go to York tomorrow,' she said aloud, and

she almost ran from the gallery, calling on Annie, her aunt Conybeare, and the butler, all of whom she would take with her to her house in York, which stood in the lee of the great cathedral.

'I have a mind to play, to shop, for a week,' she lied to a puzzled Aunt Conybeare, 'and my council shall rule Campions for me in my absence, for I shall take none of them with me. They may work while I dally, for the house there needs to shelter its owner a little.'

Exactly when Guy Shadwell first began to worry that he had heard nothing from his brother since he had left for Scotland he could not say.

All Guy's life his elder brother had loved and protected him. His relationship with his other brother Frederick had always been a cold one. But Shad had taught him to swim, to shoot and to ride—not as Shad rode, for Shad was a marvel with horses—and he had always encouraged him to study hard as well, the eleven years between them making Shad more of an uncle than a brother.

And when Shad was away at the wars he had written constantly to Guy. A little reserved in speech, on paper he was a witty and informative correspondent, and Guy had always looked eagerly for the post to bring him Shad's latest letter. He had tried to show them to his father, for Shad's letters to the Earl were stiff, dutiful things, the constraint between them operating on him, but his father had always pushed them away pleading, 'No time.'

Shad's last words to Guy as he had left for Glen Ruadh had been quite clear. 'I shall write to you, Guy—but not immediately.'

Time passed, and no letters came. At first, Guy thought nothing of it. He knew that Shad had been mortally hurt by the final breach with his father, but surely, he thought, he must have recovered sufficiently to write to the brother who he knew had always loved him? Unless, of course, he had cut himself off from everything that was related to Clermont, and that included Guy, too, which Guy found difficult to believe.

Shortly before Christmas, growing troubled, Guy wrote to Glen Ruadh, but nothing came back. He wrote again, still nothing, until one day, after his third despairing letter begging Shad to remember that he, Guy, still loved him, on a blustery day in early March, a letter came from Shad's factor at Glen Ruadh.

He wrote that correspondence had arrived so constantly for Lord Halstead that the factor, in my lord's continued absence, had opened it, and was further writing to say that if my lord had set out for Scotland he had certainly never reached there. What was worse was that this first letter had been two months on the way; a second from the factor, written within the last fortnight, was delivered only a few days later and said that my lord had still not arrived and asked for guidance.

Guy stared at the paper before him, face going slowly white. It was now nearly six months since Shad had flung out of Clermont House, announcing that he was off to Glen Ruadh, and no one had seen or heard from him since. Guy had thought him in his Highland fastness, refusing to acknowledge the rest of the world, which was bad enough, but to learn that he had dropped off the edge of the world. . . Guy had spoken to several of Shad's friends in London, none of whom had heard from him, and were themselves troubled by his disappearance from his old haunts, and lack of any news from him.

Carrying the letters, Guy went to his father's study,

put them on the desk before him, and poured out the tale of Shad's disappearance.

'I would have a search made for him, Father,' he finished. 'But better that such an initiative came from you. Your name is a powerful one.'

The Earl, who had stared, face hard, at Guy while he spoke, looked down at his work again, said coldly, 'Most convenient if he has disappeared. You may, after due formalities, be Halstead and my heir. A more satisfactory eventuality than I could have hoped for.'

The obedience which Guy had always shown to his father broke on that.

'No!' he said violently. 'You shall not speak so. No! You wrong him, Father. You have always wronged him. Shad is good, brave and true, as the whole world knows, aside from yourself. What maggot works in your brain, sir, that you have never given him his due? The Duke himself——'

His father interrupted him. 'Do not bore me, Guy,' he began.

'Bore you, sir! Bore you! It is time that you knew the truth about Shad—and about Frederick, too. Shad forbade me to tell that truth, but if by bad chance he is dead his death absolves me from my promise to him. It is time you knew what Frederick really was, and what Shad did to save the family honour and to spare you pain.'

He had his father's attention now. The Earl rose, face stern.

'Explain yourself, sir—or I will deal with you as I did with Halstead.'

'Oh, you may cut me off, too,' said Guy furiously, quite unlike his usual mild and charming self. 'But you *shall* know the truth. Frederick's death was no accident as you and the world thought. Frederick shot himself, committed suicide. He. . .' Guy choked on the words, could hardly say them. He ignored his father's suddenly ashen face, began again.

'Frederick loved boys; he always did. He could not live without his. . .vice. He frequented special houses. . . Shad knew, he always knew; I didn't know until just before his death when I heard Shad and him talking.

'He was being blackmailed, had been blackmailed for years, was threatened with exposure if he didn't pay large sums of money over. He was bleeding the estate dry to pay the swine off. And when ruin and exposure finally stared him in the face, because their demands became impossible, he. . .shot himself, leaving a letter for you, to tell you what had happened, and why he did it.

'Shad found the letter, and Frederick, dead in the gunroom at Pinfold—it was when he was recovering from that dreadful wound he got in Spain. He knew what it would do to you, and to the Clermont name, but particularly to you, who loved him so, if you knew the truth. He fetched me, I was there that weekend—you were over at Broadlands at the time—and together we secretly arranged it to look like an accident. No one ever guessed the truth.'

The Earl's face was livid, ghastly. 'And how do I know that this remarkable story is the truth?'

'Oh, the agent knew that Frederick was robbing the estate; he may even have guessed why—but there's more than that. Shad thought that he had destroyed the letter, but I—and I don't know why I did it, I was only fourteen at the time—but perhaps I felt that the truth should not be completely destroyed. I substituted blank paper for it, and Shad burned that. I have the letter still, and you shall see it. He never knew what I had done.'

The Earl sat down, all his beliefs in ruins about him. He could not speak. Guy, uncharacteristically voluble, continued. 'And that, sir, should tell you how Shad loved you and protected you and the family name both, for he dealt with the blackmailers as well—how I never knew—and put straight the estate which Frederick had nearly ruined. That should tell you how unworthy you have been to prefer Frederick to him, and now he is likely dead, taking your unfounded dislike to the grave with him.'

Guy saw that he had broken his father, and, even though it was for Shad that he had done it, it gave him no pleasure.

'I believe you, sir,' said the Earl, at last. 'But I would like to see the letter,' and he sank his face into his hands, a man suddenly grown old before his time. Which son he was grieving for he could not have said, the one whom he had wrongly valued, or the one he had never valued—and both lost.

Finally, he raised his head, said, 'You are saying that Halstead set out for Scotland, but never reached there, and has not been heard from since he left here?'

'That is so, sir.' Guy's throat had closed, his revelations over; he could hardly speak. He had always thought that one day he might tell his father the truth about his two older brothers, but had never thought to do so in such tragic circumstances.

'Then I shall institute enquiries, and also I must. . . order my thoughts. Come to terms with what you have told me. You say that he did what he did to save me pain?'

'Yes,' said Guy sturdily, 'and to save Clermont's honour. Think of the scandal if anyone other than Shad had found him.' He did not add that Frederick had been careless of that as well as of everything else—he did not need to. 'Shad is what I said he was, good and true, but you were always fixed on Frederick. He understood that, although it grieved him.'

The Earl looked sadly at his youngest son, said, 'It seems that I have never known any of you. I think that I have never properly valued you either, sir. You showed a shrewdness beyond your years when you saved the letter. When you have given it to me, you will leave me alone with it, and we must both pray that somehow, somewhere, Halstead still lives. My greatest punishment would be never to see him again, to rectify the lost years.'

CHAPTER FOURTEEN

NELL had arrived back from York late in the evening. She retired to her room without ceremony, without seeing her council; she pleaded tiredness, but sent a message to Henson that they should all meet in her study on the following morning, no exceptions.

She sat in her bed that evening eating buttered rolls and drinking hot chocolate, feeling one moment like the cat that had stolen the cream, and the next moment like the cat turned out into the rain at midnight. What would they say when she threw her bombshell on the carpet before them all in the morning? What would Chad say? Would he kiss her, or kill her? She had no idea how he would react.

She thought she knew how the others would, and she was inwardly bracing herself to face them. She could not sleep for excitement. The lawyer whom she had brought back with her from York was given a room on his own—and told to talk to no one. His cynical old face was even more cynical than usual as he ate his excellent food, and drank his good wine.

Morning broke, the sun was up, and the scents of an early spring were everywhere. Nell dressed with uncommon care in a deep green wool, cut on classic lines, belted high under her waist, and which emphasised the depth of her magnificent bosom, and although the neck was high with a tiny man's cravat the whole effect was voluptuous. She looked a far cry from the icy Nell Tallboys of the past.

She could not eat her breakfast, the food stuck in her throat, and she could hardly wait to reach her study, Aunt Conybeare consigned to the drawing-room; this was not an occasion at which she ought to be present. The lawyer Nell had banished to an anteroom, to be sent for, if required, and Nell had a stack of legal documents on the desk before her. I am armed at all points, she thought. A military metaphor seemed suitable, seeing that she was about to deal with an ex-trooper.

Promptly at ten, the appointed hour, her Privy Council arrived. Almost as though they knew that this was a solemn occasion they were all dressed *à point*. Henson and Challenor were grave in charcoal-grey, Henson was wearing cream riding breeches tucked into shining riding boots; later in the day he was to tour the tenant farms in the Riding around Campions.

Even Aisgill was smart in his country clothing, and Chad was wearing his best black silk suit, and he had, in Nell's honour, although she did not know this, tied his cravat in a waterfall favoured by the late leader of London society, George Brummell.

Standing before his mirror that morning, Chad had had a flash of memory. He had seen himself standing before another mirror with a splendid frame of eagles soaring high above its top. And he was tying his cravat, and talking to someone behind him, whom he could not see, 'And this is a waterfall,' he had said, and tied the cravat *so*, and then everything disappeared again.

The flashes were disturbing because they were inconsequential, had no beginning, and no end, came from nowhere, and disappeared into nowhere. This one was particularly disturbing because he had felt that his surroundings were luxurious, and how could that be?

All in all, he looked severely magnificent, but then he always did. Severe was a good word to describe him. Well, thought Nell, mischievously, we shall see if severe is a good word for him in another hour. She begged leave to doubt it.

'Lady Elinor,' said Henson, almost reproachfully, 'this is not our usual day to meet you.'

Nell smiled at him. 'I agree, but this is not going to be a usual day for anyone.'

Henson, she saw, frowned. He did not like surprises; he wanted life to be orderly. Chad, Nell was amused to see, looked wary, as though a sniper were hidden behind the boulle cabinet in the corner. What intuitive message was passing between them that of the four of them he seemed to be the only one to have some inkling that she was about to commit a most outrageous act?

'I have called you in. . .' she said, quite cool; she was, indeed, astonished at how level her voice was. She could see herself in the Venetian glass over the hearth, and she looked quite calm, the portrait of a lady totally in command of herself, not one about to breach every canon of etiquette which controlled the actions of ladies.

She began again, almost absently, 'I have called you all in to tell you that I am about to follow the advice which you have so frequently given me.' She paused dramatically; some devil inside her was drawing this out, so that what she was about to say would be all the more devastating to them all when they heard it.

It was Henson who broke when she did not continue. 'And that is, Lady Elinor?'

'Oh,' said Nell, 'there is only one piece of advice on which you have all agreed, ever since I inherited, and I am about to take it. I have decided to marry.'

Nell saw Chad's face change. He undoubtedly thought that he had lost her, that she had done the honourable thing, gone to York to arrange a loveless marriage which would remove them both from temptation. She smiled inwardly.

As usual, Henson constituted himself spokesman, forestalling Aisgill. 'I think that I speak for us all,' he said, 'in offering you my felicitations, Lady Elinor. Your decision is welcome, if a little overdue. I take it that we may expect suitors to be arriving here at Campions.'

'No, you may not,' said Nell, smiling sweetly; she was beginning to enjoy herself, even if Chad wasn't. 'I have already decided whom I will marry.'

There was uproar. All but Chad began to speak as one, her Countess-ship quite forgotten, she was amused to note. Chad was silent, his face more severe than ever. Oh, how he was suffering, her darling, her poor love; her heart bled for him.

'Not Ulric Tallboys, after all, Lady Elinor,' began Aisgill, red in the face. 'Not after what Jackson has told us of him. You could not be so unwise.'

'No, not Cousin Ulric——' said Nell, to be interrupted, almost rudely, by Henson.

'And not, I hope, to someone whom you met only last week in York, and hardly know, I trust.'

'Oh, no,' said Nell, 'I would not inflict Cousin Ulric on you and Campions. Nor is it someone I met last week in York; that is not my way, either. But it is perfectly true that I went to York to arrange this marriage.'

She paused, held them all in turn with her eyes, finally arriving at Chad, almost compelled him to look at her, which he did, so that for a moment it seemed to Nell that there was no one in the room but the pair of them.

'I am,' she said, 'entitled to arrange my own marriage, for am I not Countess of Malplaquet with exactly the same rights and powers as though I were the Earl? I am, in short, in the same case as a man, and as a man I need no one to arrange a marriage for me and I may propose to my future partner as a man would. I therefore propose a marriage which will please me and benefit Campions.

'I have decided that in view of my. . .inclination for him, and the talents and devotion to duty which he has shown since he arrived here, I can do no better than to ask Mr Chad Newcome to marry me, and for you all to support me as I do so. Accordingly, I formally ask you, Mr Newcome, to take my hand, and Malplaquet, and all that goes with Malplaquet's name with it.'

Chad, who had gone quite white, so that Nell's stunned Privy Council could see at once that this was as great a surprise to him as to them, said something inarticulate, strode to the window, and stood with his back to the room and to Nell, staring out at the wild and beautiful view over the moors. It was plain to them all that he was the prey to strong emotion, was struggling to control himself.

The stunned silence gave way to uproar, Henson, Aisgill, Challenor all talking at once. Nell ignored them, and in the moment of silence which followed as the three of them endeavoured to collect themselves and their scattered wits she said steadily, face white, coming from behind her desk, to pass her Privy Council, addressing Chad's straight back, 'You reminded me, Mr Newcome, sir, that I stand in the place of the Earl. I ask you to recognise that fact, turn to face your Countess, and give her your considered answer.'

Behind her, her Privy Council muttered as Chad slowly restored his self-control. He now knew why she had reacted as she did that day in the library, when he had so idly said that she stood in the Earl's place, and he could guess why she had gone to York. He refused to turn, for Nell had placed him at a disadvantage by the manner of her proposal, and he was seeking to restore the balance between them.

Henson spoke. 'May I advise, madam?'

'No, you may not,' said Nell again. 'I am Earl and Countess here. I await Mr Newcome's answer.'

Chad stood, unmoving. And Nell, suddenly nervous, for oh, he was strong, stronger even than she might have thought, would give her neither yea nor nay easily, would make her bleed her heart dry, to test how true this proposal was, said, 'I may advise *you*, Mr Newcome, as you have no lawyer, no family to help you. The special licence for our marriage, given at York, should you wish to accept my offer, stands on the desk here. The marriage settlement between us, which is the same as I would offer any man, gentle or simple, is also there for you to sign. My grandfather's ring is ready for your finger; as the Earl would give his pledge to the partner he chose, I will give you mine. So do I honour you, Mr Newcome,' and as she had done that last day in the library she sank down before his turned back in her most elaborate curtsy.

At last, Chad turned, and the man they saw, although neither he, nor they, knew it, was the man he had been before memory deserted him.

His soldiers in Spain would have known his manner, as his fellow officers and the Duke had done. As Jackson had shrewdly noted, when unselfconscious, as he now was, he reverted to the haughty aristocrat birth and military training had made him. Cold, hard and imperious, it was the face of a man who gave orders, and expected them to be obeyed.

'Madam,' he said, 'though the manner is not one I would have chosen, you do me the greatest honour a woman could do a man. You offer me, a landless nobody, taken naked from the moors, the noblest prize in England. You are sure that you wish to do this thing? That you understand what you are offering me?'

'None better,' answered Nell, quaking internally, for all her brave front, for here was a Chad she had never seen, nor her Privy Council either. 'I offer you myself, and the guardianship of Malplaquet, for guardians are what we shall be. We shall jointly hold it in trust. It owns us. We do not own it. Those are the terms of the settlement.'

Aisgill spoke, breaking the paralysis which had seized the three of them at Nell's monstrous proposal. 'Madam, I cannot remain silent in the face of this.'

'But you will, Aisgill, you will,' said Nell, not turning her head. 'For I am Earl here, and you would not so have spoken to my grandfather, without he asked you to. I do not ask you.'

Aisgill would not be quiet. 'The man may have wife and children, he has no name, he is nobody. . .'

'As to the first,' said Nell, 'I think not. As for a name, I shall give him that. As with the first of the line, so with the last. Should he so wish, he shall be Tallboys.'

Chad had remained silent. If anything, his hauteur had grown.

'No,' he said. 'If I accept, madam, you will take *my* name. I will not take yours. You may be Countess, and Earl, I grant you that, but you will still be my wife, and I shall not be your servant. I shall be your partner—or nothing. And, should I accept, they——' and he waved a hand with the utmost arrogance at the Privy Council '—they must accept me, and accept, too, that I had no part in your decision to do this thing, that you made it freely and without my knowledge, that I shall be master here, as you will be mistress, but they will still advise.'

Henson had said nothing so far, only now, before Chad made his final decision, spoke.

'You have still not given a straight answer, man, and what the world will say if your answer is yes will be a scandal and a year's wonder, and I will advise you now. If Campions needs a master, and Malplaquet an heir, and you are her choice, and I would not have chosen you, yet your answer must be yes.'

Of them all he was the one whom Nell and Chad would have thought the most adamant against such a marriage.

'You may offer me your advice, as I said——' and Chad's face was closed and cold '—I did not say that I would take it.'

'So you refuse me,' said Nell, white to the lips, head high, bleeding internally; her gamble had failed, after all.

'Oh, no,' said Chad, and smiled at her for the first time, his brilliant white smile. 'In honour, I could not accept you in less than marriage, in honour, I accept your offer of marriage, and now, in honour, I must offer for you. Lady Elinor, will you marry me? I can give you nothing but my signature on a piece of paper, and my love and reverence for you, ever and always.'

And he bowed his proud head in answer to her earlier curtsy, while Aisgill hissed, and old Challenor looked bemused, and Henson's face was a sardonic mask.

Nell murmured a whispered, 'Yes,' suddenly shy, 'yes, with all my heart,' and curtsied again. He put out his hand to lift her, kissed her hand, and then she pulled from her thumb, where she had placed it before she came into the meeting, her grandfather's ring, the ring which the first Earl had been given by Prince Eugene of Savoy after the battle of Malplaquet.

'I seal our betrothal with this,' she said, handing it to him, for him to slip on his finger, and then he pulled from his pocket the lace handkerchief which she had given him at the time of Sir Chesney's visit.

'My lady, I have little to give you, so you would honour me by receiving back the favour which you gave me. I have carried it ever since.'

Nell took the handkerchief, after he had kissed it, and she too kissed it, before tying it to her belt.

The ice which had enfolded them both throughout the whole passage broke as Chad finished speaking. The face which he had shown them lost its sternness, Nell's lost her air of cool command, and for a moment the look which passed between them was unguarded, and of the fiercest passion. The Privy Council could have no doubt but that this was a marriage for love.

'And now we must fetch the lawyer who has been patiently waiting in the ante-room, settlement papers shall be signed, the parson brought from Keighley, and the marriage shall be solemnised in Campions chapel tomorrow, with Campions people around us.'

'So soon,' said Henson.

'No delay.' Nell was firm. 'Neither he nor I wish to wait, I am sure. And I have no wish for outsiders here.'

'Sir Chesney...' began Henson, to fall silent at Nell's raised eyebrows. 'No,' he said resignedly. 'This is enough of a turn-up, without having Sir Chesney's bellowings about it, begging your pardon for my disrespect, Lady Elinor, Mr Newcome,' and his sardonic eye took in Chad. Like the others, he had noticed his changed demeanour during the proposal ceremony, and that Chad had now reverted to the pleasant man he had been since he had first recovered from the confusion which had gripped him on his arrival at Campions.

He was not to know that Chad's own soldiers had always noticed the difference between Chad in a tight corner, the commander on the battlefield, and the courteous man he was in daily life.

Aisgill had the last word when all the legal business was over, and Chad and Nell had retired to the long gallery, where Nell had said that he must be properly introduced to those who had preceded him.

'It might be worse,' he said to Henson and Challenor. 'He is young, personable, has many talents, has obviously been a soldier, and a gentleman, but who and what he is God knows; we probably never shall.' He hesitated. 'The thief taker Jackson said a thing I thought was strange at the time when he last left us. He said—and God knows how he knew what even I was not sure of—that passion lay between them—that I was not to worry about the turn events might take, that Lady Elinor and Campions would be safe with Newcome. God grant it may be so. She has leapt into the dark today, and taken Campions with her.'

Challenor spoke for the first time. 'There was never any stopping Lady Nell. She is a true Tallboys, and the first Earl would have been proud of her. As for the man, I think him honest, but as you say, Aisgill, only time will tell.' He paused. 'He is a good book-man, and that says much for him.'

CHAPTER FIFTEEN

NEITHER of them spoke until they reached the long gallery. Once inside, now alone, permitted—nay, encouraged for the first time to be alone, Chad turned to her.

'It is not too late to change your mind——' he began.

Nell interrupted him, her expression dangerous. 'You regret your proposal to me, then?'

'No, not that,' he said. 'Never that. But you, are you sure that you know what awaits you? You rule Campions, but what of the rest of the world? It can be harsh, unfeeling, to those who break the code which binds us.'

Chad said 'us' without thinking, making himself one of the great ones of the world, part of the cousinry, the network of nobility which owned and ruled England.

Nell was so troubled by his questions that she did not notice this unconscious assumption, and nor did he.

'Oh,' she said, lip curling, 'they have always disapproved of me. I have simply given them a real reason for their dislike. And you, are you afraid to marry me? Or is your honour troubling you again? It need not; we are to be married, and honourably. I have no fear that you will do other than deal well with me and Campions—which is more than I could have said had I chosen to marry Ulric, or another of his kind.'

He took her hand, and kissed it. He could wait now, to love her as he wished to, for when they finally met together in her great bed their union would be blessed, not something illicit, love celebrated hugger-mugger in a corner, but nobly, in the open, Nell's people about her at the wedding ceremony.

'I hope,' he said simply, 'that I shall prove worthy of what you have given me.'

'No fears for me on that score,' said Nell, 'and now I must show you your inheritance, the painted images of those who have gone before you,' and she waved a hand at the Tallboyses who lined the walls, their wives beside them. 'Bravery and beauty combined,' she said with a smile, 'until they reach me. For bravery,' and her smile at him was a mischievous one, 'I showed today, but as to beauty—I have no illusions about that.'

Chad knew that she was not saying this simply for him to deny it indignantly. He took her by the shoulders and turned her towards him, gently held her chin in his big hands, and tipped her head back slightly. 'I do not think,' he said softly, 'that you do yourself justice. Beauty without character is not worth having, and character is beauty, and so you are the most rare of Tallboys ladies, since you possess both.'

'Oh, my love,' and Nell's smile was dazzling, 'you play with words again. Were you a lawyer, after all, and not a soldier? Challenor says that you are a man who should have been a scholar, but I have seldom seen a scholar who looked as though he could go into the ring with the Game Chicken and acquit himself respectably!'

Chad laughed at that, and released her so that they paced the gallery together, and before she introduced her recent ancestors to him she told him the story of the lady of Barthwaite and Ivo of the Woods.

He listened to her in silence, and thought of the gulf which she had leapt in order to offer him herself, and thought that in the shock which had followed that offer, against all common sense and urgings of the head, he had followed his heart and now on the morrow, like the lady and her serf, she was to be his.

His bright blue eyes hard on her, the eyes with which he had done such execution, he said, 'And you are the lady and I am Ivo?'

'If you like,' she answered him. 'As the beginning, so the end. I wonder what my grandfather would have said, were he to have known of this day. But he told me once that all men and women are the same under their clothes, so we are not Countess and secretary, but simply Chad and Nell, man and woman.'

'Chad and Nell.' His voice was grave. 'So be it, then. And you have no regrets?'

'None, and that is an end of that. I know that you and I will serve Campions well, and love one another in the doing, and that is all I need to know. The omens are good, Chad.'

Chad nodded his head, and let her tell him of the pictured men and women, long dead, who had sprung from that meeting in the woods. He thought of the dark behind him, and the brightness before him, and paradoxically, now that his future was secure, was settled, he suddenly needed to know his past. He had thought himself reconciled to his loss of memory; indeed, in the days when he had first come to full consciousness of himself and his surroundings, it had been enough for him to know that he existed.

He knew that Henson and the others had made enquiries about him, but everything had led nowhere. He had appeared on the moor as though he had been dropped from heaven, and none had known nor seen him before he had been found lost and wandering.

Short of his memory returning to him, his past was gone, not to be recovered, it seemed, with no clue to lead him to his origins. And then, as Campions claimed him and he became part of it, first in the stables and later as Nell's secretary, that had come to seem enough. The brief flashes of memory annoyed him, and his attempts to remember distressed him so much by their uselessness that he abandoned them altogether.

Except that now he was to marry Nell he had a sudden passionate wish to know himself.

'Perhaps,' he said, when her tale was done, and they were to return to the others, 'when we have been married for a little, we might try to find where I came from, how I arrived on the moor.'

'We must have no secrets between us,' said Nell. 'When Jackson left us last month I asked him to try to trace your past. He wrote privately to me, two days ago, that all his efforts so far had ended in failure. He had scoured the Riding, and you had not been seen before you were discovered begging by the farmer. He also said something I thought strange; that he connected the rifle with you, and that when his search in the North was ended he would visit London to try again to speak to Charles Halstead, to discover whether he had sold, lost, or even had the rifle stolen from him. His answer might give us some lead to the assassin, or even, unlikely as it sounds, to the mystery of your origins.'

'He told me that, too,' Chad said, and frowned. Somehow Charles Halstead's name always had the power to disturb him. 'But I cannot think what the rifle has to do with me, except that I found it by the man who tried to kill you.'

'Chad, my love,' said Nell quietly, taking his hand, distressed by the unhappiness on his face. 'Let us not talk of this now. I am marrying you, not your past, and what I know of you, as all Campions knows, and Henson and Aisgill admit, is good and true.

'The future is all that matters to me. I cannot think your past disgraceful. Unfortunate, perhaps. . .and now I fear we must return to the others. Tonight we dine with the Privy Council, and after we must retire separately; the conventions must be honoured. We shall not meet again until we meet in the chapel. I must go to Aunt Conybeare tomorrow morning, and you will be attended before the wedding by Challenor. Henson shall give the bride away, and Aisgill, as is fitting since he first rescued you, shall stand at your side as your best man.'

Her face was full of mischief. 'I am only sorry that Rajah cannot be present. He shall have a new set of plumes, and we shall both visit him after the ceremony so that he may know that we have not forgotten him!'

Chad bowed solemnly. 'It is, as you said to me when we last parted, *au revoir*, and not goodbye. I trust and pray that you may never regret today's work, my gracious lady.'

'Not I,' said Nell, 'and now Aunt Conybeare and Campions must be told that their mistress has found her master.'

After dinner, a formal occasion, all the participants splendidly dressed and the best dinner service—the china from the present given to the third Earl by Catherine the Great of Russia after he had taken her to bed, the silver given him by a Bavarian princess for similar favours, and the great epergne in the centre of the table showing Hercules killing the Hydra, brought home in triumph after a conquest so noble that he never even named the lady—fetched out in honour of Nell Tallboys's marriage to her servant.

Afterwards Nell and Chad, equally formal, bowed and parted to their own quarters, Nell to her splendid suite of rooms, Chad to his small and humble pair in the attic under the roof.

Before he went there, he returned to the study, to pick up his copy of the settlement, to study what he had let himself in for by marrying Nell.

The door to his rooms was ajar, and someone had lit the candles there. He raised his eyebrows, walked in, to discover Henson waiting for him, leaning against a chest of drawers, the book from Chad's nightstand open in his hand. It was a copy of *Les Liaisons Dangereuses* in the original French.

He raised his eyes from it as Chad entered, made no apology for his presence, merely said coolly, 'So you read French, too. When did you discover that?'

'Early on,' said Chad. 'It hardly seemed worth mentioning.'

'Difficult to plumb all your talents,' drawled Henson, and Chad did not know whether it was praise or criticism which he was being offered. 'But the one talent which might benefit you, your personal memory, is still missing.'

'Yes,' said Chad briefly, 'I am not fooling you, though the expression on your face suggests you do not necessarily believe me.'

'Oh, I believe you,' returned Henson, his face expressionless. 'Your choice of reading is interesting—in the circumstances.'

Chad chose to ignore any inference which he might draw from Henson's suggestion that a novel which dwelt so constantly on human wickedness and sexual intrigue might have some point, some connection with Chad's own astonishing rise to fortune. He said instead, 'To what do I owe your visit?'

Henson closed the book, put it carefully down. He was particularly finely dressed, at all points one with the mighty whom he so faithfully served.

'I came to warn you,' he drawled.

'Ah,' said Chad, face watchful. 'I thought your acquiescence in Lady Elinor's wishes odd, in view of your care for her and her interests. Of you all, I would have expected opposition to such a marriage to come from you.'

Henson shrugged his beautifully tailored shoulders. 'And what, my fine young man, would the lady have cared for my opposition? Nothing. She was determined to have you. No, I could only lose by gainsaying her. I have watched you since you came into the house as her secretary, and——' He paused.

'And?' said Chad, giving him nothing.

'And—and nothing. From the moment you began to recover yourself you revealed a man of education, a man who has undoubtedly been a soldier. There is also no doubt that at great risk to yourself you saved my Countess's life, and for that I am grateful. Nell Tallboys is a remarkable woman; it is a pleasure to serve her. But, on the other hand, who the devil are you? And have *you*, despite what my Countess believes, angled for this match, used the attraction you undoubtedly possess for her to make yourself master of Campions?'

'Guardian, guardian only,' was Chad's answer to that.

'Words,' said Henson. 'You may or may not be as honest as you seem, but if you are not, beware. My duty is to her, and only to you through her. She is Countess, you but her consort, and, if you prove false, why, God help you, for Campions will deal with you, sir, and hardly.'

Rage stirred in Chad. The temper which he usually kept in firm control, the temper which he knew must have played its part in his old life—perhaps, unwisely used, he had sometimes thought, might have brought him to destitution and beggary—rose and filled his throat. His hands clenched.

He mastered himself. His true inclination would have been to seize Henson by the throat, force him to his knees, make him retract the unspoken accusation. Reason told him that the man was a good servant, the best, who sought to protect his mistress from harm.

The calmness of his voice did not deceive Henson; the man who could control Rajah, charm Nell, and charm also the men and women about him, was no tame tiger. The hint of wildness behind the self-control was always there. He shivered a little despite himself as Chad spoke, 'Rest easy, Mr Henson, sir. I shall guard Campions, as I would Lady Elinor, with my life. Do you be careful that you are as honest with both as I intend to be.'

'Bravely spoken,' replied Henson, giving not an inch himself. 'Enough; we know where we stand.' He walked to the door. 'I bid you goodnight, Mr Newcome. From now on I serve you, not you me. I must tell you that the staff of Campions, indoor and out, have been informed of tomorrow's ceremony. Representatives of all parts of the house and estate will be at the chapel; the rest will attend you later, and you will be expected to show yourself and your lady to them, in due form.

'Tomorrow morning Challenor will escort you to the guest suite, and will help you to dress, with the assistance of old Wilson, the late Earl's valet, brought from his retirement to be of service to the late Earl's successor. From what I have seen of you, you will play your part properly. I bid you goodnight, and I hope that your dreams are more pleasant than I hear they usually are.'

He bowed. Chad returned the compliment, saying coolly, 'I know, Mr Henson, that anything you arrange will be both correct and apropos. You need have no fears that I will let my lady and Campions down.'

He was gone, and Chad sat down on the bed, his hands sweating, his whole body racked from the necessity to hold himself in. But, in all honesty, he thought wryly, what could he expect? He had told Nell earlier of the commotion which this strange marriage would cause, and he could not fault Henson for seeking to protect his mistress's interests.

He slept at last, for sleep, not surprisingly, was long in coming, but he did not dream until daybreak, and then his dreams were confused, but not painful, until the last one. He was in a hot and crowded room. He thought that he was drunk. The men around him were laughing and staring; one pulled at his arm, saying, 'Quiet, Chad, quiet,' but he would not be quiet, he would have his say, and improbably, as he started from sleep, it was Nell's name that he was crying out, and where and to whom he said it he did not know.

Nell also could not sleep. First there had been Aunt Conybeare to tell, to ask her to be Nell's matron of honour, to hold her bouquet when the ring was placed on her finger. As she had expected, even Aunt Conybeare's usual placidity was shaken by such momentous news. 'But Newcome,' she had said, bewildered. 'I knew that you liked him, of course, and he saved you. But to marry him!'

'I love him, Aunt,' she had said simply. 'And I had never thought to love anyone.' She did not say that she loved him beyond reason; she did not need to, for even innocent old Aunt Conybeare knew that she would not have married her servant, of unknown origin, unless her passion for him was so strong that it transcended common sense, and the conventions that governed the class to which Nell belonged.

The servant's hall thought the same. 'Wants a man in her bed, a real man, don't she?' being the most common comment, and said admiringly, not sniggeringly. 'Better than Maister Ulric and them pretty boys what have come up here from London. One of us now, you might say.' For Chad, although not a seeker after popularity, was popular. From the moment he had tamed Rajah, he had been accepted, and there were many who connected that event and the marriage. 'Our Nell's a grand lass, and needs a real man to hold her,' being another remark. 'Besides, he's almost a gentleman himself, for all he was taken starving off the moor. You might say that Campions is all he's ever known, seeing that he remembers nothing before he came here.'

The last was the butler's comment, and served as Campions's opinion of the match. The only thing lacking in him being, as young Seth said, 'Pity he's not really a Yorkshireman, but he's a tyke by adoption.'

And so, as a fine March day dawned, Campions prepared for the event which many had feared might never happen—the marriage of its Countess, and the settlement of Malplaquet's lands.

CHAPTER SIXTEEN

NELL had awoken that morning with such a feeling of well-being as she had never experienced before. She stretched herself, lifting her arms above her head, so that her toes almost touched the bottom of the great bed.

She did not wait for Annie to come, but leaped from it, ran to the window, pulled back the curtains, and looked out across the lawns, beyond the giant fountain, where sea-nymphs and dolphins, the latter spouting water to the heavens, frolicked in the kind of joy she was feeling, beyond the grove of trees planted by the third Earl, the giant obelisk commemorating the first Earl's glory, to the moors above them, rising grand and glorious, until they reached the Throne of God itself, far, far beyond her sight—but not her memory.

Oh, she had defeated them all, Chad included! She thought of his dear face when she had finally cornered him, how it had changed from the stern severity it normally wore to the joy and delight he had shown her as they parted in the long gallery, secure in the knowledge that their love was outrageous, but that they were about to fulfil it in honourable marriage.

Yes, Nell Tallboys was about to defy them all. Charles Halstead, when he heard of this, could make further disgraceful bets, tongues would buzz wherever she went—but what of that? She was the lady of Barthwaite, who had married whom she pleased, or the first Earl, who had made his own rules on the battlefield and in life. Tallboyses all, living up to the house's motto, emblazoned on the ribbon which ran below the arms: 'As the beginning, so the end'.

And the arms themselves, the shield which bore three tree stumps, in honour of Ivo. She hugged herself. I shall petition the College of Heralds; I shall have the shield divided, the trees on one side, Rajah rearing on the other, for Rajah is Chad, the strong man who tamed the strong horse—and his Countess. Unknowingly, she echoed the comments of her staff.

Yes, she was the lady of Campions, and today would marry her choice, the first time both parties to a marriage had proposed to one another, she dared swear.

Annie came in, Aunt Conybeare behind her. Annie was carrying a breakfast tray. Aunt Conybeare carried nothing but a grave face. She said what Chad had. 'It is not too late to change your mind, Nell.'

'Change my mind!' Nell had jumped into bed again, was stuffing hot rolls into her mouth, drinking coffee this morning. 'Why should I do that, when I am marrying my heart's desire?'

Aunt Conybeare sighed. Nell had never looked before as she now did. It was almost, outrageously, as though her lover had already pleasured her, and, had not Aunt Conybeare known for sure that both partners to this mismatch had spent the night chastely apart, she would have thought the opposite. There would be no shy bride in Campions chapel today, that was for sure!

Nell's joy continued, through the bath, its water full of scents, and through the dressing for the ceremony. The parson had arrived shortly after dawn, sent for by Henson, and after she was dressed she went into her drawing-room, so that the bed could be stripped, new linen put on it, herbs strewn between the sheets, a new fire lit in the grate, all to celebrate Campions's proudest day for many years.

Annie had put a little bag under the pillow. 'And what is *that* for?' Nell had said.

Annie blushed. 'It is to bless the bed,' she said shyly. 'Granny Goodman says that the Mother will give you a son, after this night's work, if a virgin places it there, and the bride goes virgin to her man.'

'A son!' Nell was enraptured. She, who had scorned men and marriage, could hardly bear to wait for her true love's child. She knew that when Annie and old Granny Goodman spoke of the Mother they meant the Earth Mother of the old religion which had never really died out in these parts. A century earlier and Granny Goodman might have been in danger of being burned as a witch. Now, she prescribed her herbs and simples to the suffering, and blessed marriages, high and low.

The thought of a child changed Nell's mood. She became girlish and trembling, not the madcap who had risen with the dawn. Aunt Conybeare, who had left to eat her own breakfast, returned to find her niece as modest as a bride might be, except that every now and then a fit of such delight passed over her that her face took on the shining aspect of her early morning ecstasy.

Finally, carrying a spray of early spring flowers, brought from the hothouse, Aunt Conybeare, resplendent in deep blue satin, with Nell herself in cream, a pearl circlet in her hair, a small string of pearls around her neck, Chad's handkerchief tucked into the lemon silk sash at her waist, walked downstairs to the great salon where Henson, Challenor, the butler and the senior servants of the house, including her housekeeper, magnificent in black satin, awaited her.

They bowed as low when she walked in as they would have done had she been marrying Britain's premier Duke, instead of her former stable hand.

Henson, who seemed to have constituted himself as a kind of benevolent grand vizier, despite his private thoughts, said, 'Madam, I am to tell you that, if you are prepared, everything is in train. The groom awaits you in the chapel, the priest is at the altar. The ring and the book are ready. If you will take my arm, I shall escort you there.'

He bowed low, low, and when he straightened up his eyes were hard on her, and the message was Aunt Conybeare's, 'It is not too late,' but Nell knew what she wanted, and, shy and trembling although she now was, all her bold hardihood quite gone, she was a girl again, the girl Henson remembered from his first day at Campions when he had walked into the Earl's study to see her standing by old Malplaquet's side.

'You know the way, Henson,' she said. 'And today it is your privilege to give away your Countess and... revive Malplaquet's line, which otherwise would die with me.' For she had no faith that Ulric would do anything but waste himself and the estate.

Together, they walked through the great house, past everything which Nell had known all her life, her staff behind her, past lines of her other servants, the occasional, 'God bless you, my lady,' offered by the bolder spirit.

And there, before her, was the paved forecourt to the chapel, where another group of servants was set, waiting for those behind her to take their places, and there at the altar *he* stood, Aisgill beside him, magnificent in his livery as master of the horse, a livery worn only on great occasions such as this. Nothing, nothing, was to be omitted from this wedding, all was to be done in proper form, until finally, on Henson's arm,

Aunt Conybeare behind her, she walked towards Chad, and they were there together, the wondering parson before them, Challenor now at the pianoforte to play for them.

Joy contained, her face as white as his, bride and groom suddenly nervous, bold spirits though they normally were, faced one another, for life, as it were, he tall, his black curls clustering about his head, wearing a fine suit once worn by Nell's grandfather, possessing neither name nor fortune, only the manifold talents of which Henson had spoken.

Nell, for her part, had been granted a strange beauty, which came from knowing that she was loved, that she had found a mate for whom she could feel respect, as well as passion, who had held off when he could have taken her on the library floor as though she had been a poor girl from the village, but who had preferred to leave her, so that she and he might keep their honour intact.

The service began, and when the priest issued his challenge to any who might gainsay the match there was silence, and then they were man and wife, neither voice faltering, and when Chad pushed on Nell's finger the marriage ring of the Tallboyses the expression on his face and his smouldering blue eyes told Nell all that she wanted to know.

And then they processed out of the chapel. Tables had been spread with food and drink in the long gallery, and the only guests were Nell's people—the marriage was a marriage for Campions and no one else. Bride and groom and the Privy Council ate nothing, but drank a toast proposed by the butler, and enthusiastically seconded by every voice.

Nell thought that the long day would never end; her face ached from smiling. Later, as she had promised, they visited the stables, and Nell's small bouquet was hung over Rajah's stable door.

The day was fine, and hand in hand they walked the length of the gardens to stare together at the moor where Chad had been found, a barely conscious derelict, and now it and Campions were his, as much as they could be anybody's.

But still they were not private. Tenant farmers came in, to see their lady and her chosen husband, until at last evening arrived, and now they were to dine alone for the first time, in the great state dining hall, in the same splendour as the night before, but now as the Countess and her husband.

For a moment, they were alone, and Chad embraced her, kissed her cheek, saying softly, 'A pledge for tonight, Mrs Newcome,' and then the door opened, and the servants entered with the food, and facing one another, absurdly, at each end of the table, they ate the fine fare set before them, more to honour the staff who had prepared it than to satisfy their non-existent hunger. The true hunger they felt was for one another.

At the meal's end, the double doors were thrown open by the butler, and Henson entered, the Privy Council at his heels, carrying bottles of wine, for yet another toast.

'It has long been the custom in this part of the world,' he announced, his eyes for once merry, 'for bride and groom to be publicly put to bed before their servants and dependants. But these, I think, are more civilised times. We shall not demand that of you, my lady Countess. Instead, you shall have Campions to light your way to bed.'

He put down his glass, beckoned to them both, said, 'Come,' and Nell, wondering what she was about to see, walked from the dining-room into the great hall from which the stairs rose for full two storeys of the house.

Before her, to the stairs, was an alleyway of servants, each carrying a candle. On every step two servants stood, also holding candles, and along the landing, and all the way to the state bedroom where Nell and Chad were to sleep, Nell's lonely days being over, servants lined the way, candles in their hands, smiling and lighting them, as Henson had said, to their bed.

Nell felt tears pricking her eyes, and each man or woman said as she passed, 'God bless you both, and Campions, too,' until finally they stood at the great oak doors, which Henson threw open, bowing—and, at last, they were alone.

Nell sank on to the bed, eyes alight, as though the flames through which she had passed had found their home there.

'You see, my love, you are accepted; Campions welcomes you. Let the rest of the world think what it will—here we are at home.'

Chad stood for a moment, looking down at her. The day seemed unreal. Any moment he expected to open his eyes to find himself—where? At this point of fulfilled love and triumph his lack of a name and past seemed the doubly cruel; he felt that he had nothing to offer his mistress, and he said so.

'No,' said Nell, passionately, opening her arms to him. 'You offer me yourself, and what is better than that? Oh, I am unmaidenly, I should be shrinking. Perhaps,' and she coloured, 'that will come later.'

Nell knew that she was not being strictly truthful. Whether it was the effect of the long day, or the many eyes upon them which knew exactly what they were going to do on the great bed, once she and Chad were alone together—just as though the pair of them were Princess and Rajah, performing for Campions—she did not know. She only knew that the maidenly reserve which she had felt for so long and which had flown away from the moment in which she had first met Chad had returned some time during the wedding ceremony and was with her again.

She looked up at him almost fearfully. She felt her legs weak beneath her, sank on to the bed, and everything about her alerted the man before her to what had happened.

His viking, his valkyrie had gone; the passionate woman passionately demanding fulfilment from her mate had disappeared. Nell Newcome was what Nell Tallboys had never been with him, the shy virgin, who loved her new husband, but was suddenly aware of what that love meant.

Chad went down on one knee, reined in his own pent-up passion, the desire to take her immediately into his arms and begin to make love to her at last, took her hand, said gently, 'Do not be afraid, Nell,' and for once she did not spark back at him as she would have done in the past, but looked at him, her great eyes full of a loving demand for his consideration.

'I love you, and I would do nothing to distress you.' He hesitated, then added, 'Suppose I go to the dressing-room and change there, while you ready yourself for me here?' He saw, in retrospect, that it might have been better if Annie had stayed, to help her to prepare for him, and he had come to her later, but the ceremony which had preceded their entry into the room had pre-empted that.

Nell looked up at him, grateful for his consideration, his understanding that what had happened today had temporarily quenched the fire within her.

'Yes,' she answered him, and then almost with a

sob, 'Oh, you will think me a fool, after all I have said and done, to behave to you like this, but. . .' and she shook her head.

'No,' he said, 'no,' and, as he reached the door to the dressing-room, 'Oh, Nell, you are as precious to me in your modesty as you were in your pride, and I hope to prove that to you, if not tonight, then another.'

He was gone, and Nell was alone with what she had done. Oh, she had no regrets, and the way in which he had reacted to her untoward fit of the vapours, once they were alone together, told her that her choice of him had been no mistake, so considerate was he of her.

She rose, slowly began to take off her beautiful dress, until she stood naked before the roaring fire, which cast its rosy glow on her, so that she was not a marble woman, but a glowing nymph whose image she saw briefly in the long mirror before she took her night-rail from the bed, to hide away what she would so soon share with him.

Nell debated anxiously whether to enter the bed, or sit on its side, and laughed at herself a little—what matter, either way? But to enter the bed might look as though she were trying to hide from him, and Nell Newcome must not be more fearful than Nell Tallboys had been.

He knocked on the door, another concession to her new-found shyness, and she called, 'Come in,' to see him enter, dressed in an overgown which had belonged to her grandfather, a magnificent brocaded thing, and the familiar sight of it reassured her, and when, after extinguishing several of the candles which stood about the room, so that they were bathed in a dim red-gold glow from candle and firelight combined, he came and sat by her, she said, with something of her old fire, 'Oh, I sometimes think that I fell in love with you because you so resemble Grandfather, not in looks and manner, but in body and carriage, the man he must have been in youth.'

Chad took her face in his hands, but gently, 'I see that my fiery lady is back with me again.'

Nell blushed beneath his gaze, the touch of his hands having its usual effect on her. 'Not entirely,' she said, shyness still with her. 'I am stupid with love for you, cannot really believe in what I, we, have done.'

'Believe it,' he said, 'believe it,' and then, 'Nell, my darling, I may have no memory, but I do know this. I am a man who has not made love to a woman for a long time, and I will try to be kind to you, but I desire you so passionately that the body may subdue the mind. I will try not to hurt you too much, or frighten you by the fierceness of my passion for you, but. . .' And at the look she gave him, passion and innocence combined, he said thickly, before bending to kiss her, 'Oh, you do understand me, I am sure, and will forgive me if. . .'

'Hush,' said Nell, beginning to drown in sensation as his kisses awoke her sleeping senses. 'There will be nothing to forgive, nothing.'

'At last,' he said, and she echoed the words, but he was so gentle and so slow with her that his very holding back excited her, as first his kisses were light, innocent things, ranging around her face, her neck, before he found her mouth, and even then the first of them were like a child's, so gentle, until suddenly, giving a harsh sob, he forced her mouth open below his, and they kissed as they had done in the annexe, his tongue meeting hers, and hers welcoming it, so that, as then, fire ran through Nell, and she grasped him by his thick black curls, pulling his head closer to her, to force him even further into her mouth, as though they might consummate themselves there.

By now, his hands were busy about her, unbuttoning her nightgown, to find the treasures of her bosom, his hands on her breasts, stroking, his mouth following, and her hands were a reflection of his, loosening and untying the bedgown, and even in her passion her wit returned to her, and she muttered as she found his bare chest, the black curls thick on it there, too, 'So far, so good, my darling,' to hear his choking laugh, as her hands grasped and stroked him there, finding his nipples, like hers, already erect.

'Oh, Nell, you witch, my witch.' His voice was hoarse and shaking, his hands now ranging around her naked body, his mouth on her breasts, her own hands wildly stroking him, finding his sex, holding it hot and throbbing in her hand, so that as his hands found her buttocks he stopped, body shaking, to say, 'Oh, God, Nell, no, not there; it's difficult enough for me not to take you before you're ready as it is.'

Nell hardly knew herself; the need for him, contained over the weeks since they had denied themselves in the annexe, the daily necessity to renounce such thoughts of him, had taken their toll. She was more than ready to receive him, on fire all over, her body an aching void to be filled.

'Oh, no, Chad, I cannot wait, either, no need to deny yourself,' and, her mouth now on his, he having turned her above him for a moment, he swung her beneath him, stroking her inward thighs, until he pulled his mouth away to gasp,

'Be a soldier, my dearest girl, bite the bullet, for a quick hurt is kinder than a slow one,' and with one hard thrust he was in her, and they were one.

And being one was so satisfactory that the pain was worth it, even though she cried out at the shock, so that he began to draw back, until she clutched at him, crying, 'No, you are mine now, Chad, we are one, not two, and that is all I want.'

After that, for both of them, sensation took over; thought and coherent speech flew away. Countess and secretary disappeared, and the great bed consecrated their love as they reached fulfilment together, Chad Newcome pleasuring his Countess so thoroughly that, climax achieved in a great wave of pleasure, Nell was near to fainting from it.

Chad's own pleasure was so strong that his memory, long dormant, almost revived, so that in the aftermath of calling Nell's name he knew that, although he had made love to other women, never before had he felt the satisfaction he had just achieved with this one.

Beneath him, Nell, who had been laughing for sheer joy, now, in the final transports of all, long and slow, was suddenly weeping, her tears—born not of sorrow but of joy run beyond its bounds—slowly falling.

Her sobbings alarmed Chad, who tightened his grip on her, raining tender kisses on her tear-stained cheeks, pausing only to say, 'Oh, my love, my darling, what a brute I am, I have hurt you. Forgive me.'

'No, no,' said Nell, stroking the anguished face he bent over her. 'A little pain at first, but, later, what I felt, what you made me feel, was beyond anything.'

She kissed him back, and, reassured, he cradled her in his arms as though she were a child, kissing and stroking her gently, until she put a finger on his mouth to stop him, saying mischievously, 'I liked it so much, pray tell me, is it possible that we can do it again soon, and often?'

Chad's shout of laughter was spontaneous. 'If you look at me like that, and say such things, you will rouse me to such efforts as Hercules might envy! Give me but leave to hold you like this a little, and your pleasure shall be mine. You are as generous in love as you are in life, my own.' For she had given herself to him, and to helping him to secure his pleasure, as she had given herself to Campions and its people.

They had both given and taken, they had shared their love in mind and body both, and their mutual pleasure had been so strong because, although Nell and Chad had disappeared when they became one, they still gave and shared, and when they were separate again the knowledge of the one thing remained with them.

Spirit had been involved as well, and, because of that, although their first pleasure was over, he had the impulse to stroke and soothe his partner as he had never done before, so that gradually their sweating, panting selves, for two athletic bodies had celebrated their strength, were slowly brought back to peace and harmony.

'The calm before a new storm,' he whispered in her ear. 'That was merely the first of many such delights.'

'Oh,' said Nell, laying her head on his shoulder. 'That was even better than I might have hoped. Such joy, such bliss, I wonder anyone is ever out of bed.'

'If every man had the pleasure of loving such a beautiful body as yours,' was his answer to that, 'then I would agree with you.'

Shyly, her old fears about her lack of looks reviving again, she said, 'Unlike my face, then,' only for him to cover her mouth with his big hand.

'You are the most beautiful woman in the world to me, Nell, and, have no fear, few look more strong and true. I have had enough of empty prettiness.' And where did *that* come from? he wondered, for the thought to disappear in the glory which his words had evoked on her face.

And later, when they had made love again, this time

slowly, so that she had screamed her pleasure at the end, clutching him so fiercely that her nails scored his back, and she lay, half-asleep, a satisfied houri in his arms, she whispered to him, 'No regrets, then?' to hear him say,

'For me, Nell, none, but for you? Even in my pleasure I know that gossip will follow you everywhere, the Countess who married her stable hand. Only the thought of what we have shared tonight, and what I hope we share in the future, life and love both, comforts me.'

Nell was suddenly all proud fury. She sat up, magnificent in her nakedness, rosy in the fire's ebbing glow. 'Gossip!' she said fiercely. 'How can you be so foolish? It is not like you. I have done nothing, nothing until I fell in love with you, and yet gossip has always followed me everywhere. You know as well as I do that Charles Halstead made his shameless bet about me when I was still virgin, unawakened and untouched. What could be worse than that?'

For no good reason that he could think of, Chad's breathing became short and painful when Nell repeated this tale, first heard several months ago. It had affected him badly then, and did so again.

'Oh, Nell,' he said hoarsely, 'how can you trouble yourself about what such a brute as he must be says about you——?' only to be interrupted by Nell's kiss on his mouth, and her drawing away to say,

'Oh, come, my love, only a moment ago you were worried about people blowing on my reputation, and now you tell me not to worry about Halstead's bet. Where is the logic which you so often show? Of which Henson so often complains?'

'He does?' asked Chad, suddenly sidetracked.

Nell rolled on top of him, kissing him whenever she reached a comma or full stop in what she was saying, her whole face and body amused, provocative again. 'Oh, yes. He once said that you must have been a divinity student gone to the bad, you were so able to rout him with such pitiless and carefully reasoned arguments based on such undeniable premises.'

'Now, now,' said Chad, imitating her, but giving her two kisses at each stop, 'not only are you funning, my darling, but of one thing I am sure. I was never a divinity student, even one gone to the bad.'

'Well, all I can say is that if,' remarked Nell, 'a divinity student gone to the bad is as good at pleasing a woman as you are we shall have to arrange special examinations in which the prize will be failing, not succeeding!'

'For that suggestion, Mrs Newcome, you shall be properly punished,' said her husband, 'and the victim shall choose its manner.'

'When, and if, you fully recover,' said Nell thoughtfully, stroking his broad chest, running her fingers again through the black curls there, 'such a *satisfactory* body you have, my darling, a regular work of art——'

'As you saw in the stable yard,' interrupted her spouse, equally naughtily.

'Oh, yes,' said Nell, not at all ashamed, 'I'm sure that from that moment on I was determined to have you in bed with me so that I could do—this,' and she tweaked a vital portion of his anatomy. 'Why, I do believe, Mr Newcome, you are almost ready to begin to administer punishment! Which of us deserves the praise? You for your virility or me for my powers of temptation——? Oh! Chad!' For he had rolled her beneath him, and the whole delightful business had started again.

'And I was wicked in the stable yard,' he said hoarsely, before all speech stopped once more, 'for I was so entranced by you and your delighted face—

yes, it was delighted, do not deny it—that all my decent modesty flew away, and I was slow to cover myself!'

Later, much later in the night, when, after that final bout, sleep had claimed them both, Chad slowly surfaced for a moment, to find his body lax after loving, Nell in his arms, sleeping quiet against him, body and tongue still at last. He had been dreaming, and dreams of happiness and fulfilment, not the fear and horror which sometimes came to him of a night. How satisfactory it was to make love to a woman who matched him physically, And why, he thought drowsily, did I always believe I liked little, clinging women? Isabella and Julia were both little, and they were similar in their ways, quite unlike Nell, both flutteringly modest and submissive on the outside, but whores inside, whereas Nell—Nell is the opposite, frank and fearless in manner, but at heart a truly modest, good woman.

He sat up suddenly, wide awake, his heart thudding, but instinctively careful, even so, to try not to disturb his sleeping wife. Isabella and Julia! Who were they? He had for a moment remembered them, and then they were gone, into the dark, and, strive as he might, he could not bring them back.

Chad lay down again. Nell turned in his arms, said, half-awake herself, 'Chad?' questioningly.

'Nothing, my love. Nothing. Rest easy,' for whatever else he had forgotten he knew that he had never felt like this before for any woman, and not simply in the business of sex and bed, but for the whole of living, and that his lost memory had surfaced to tell him so.

Nell's warmth against him, her love freely and frankly expressed, his own sense of having met, at last, his other half, was so strong that the memory could not disturb him, and he slept with Nell in his arms, and both their dreaming was of love crowned, love fulfilled.

CHAPTER SEVENTEEN

EVERYTHING had changed—and nothing had changed. Chad's desk still stood by Nell's, and he worked there daily, but not as her secretary, as her partner. The Privy Council met each week, and Chad, as Nell, was one of them—but the one to whom Nell listened the most. His judgement, as Henson grudgingly admitted, was sound. He proposed some changes, and all were useful, and needed. They involved not only the running of the stud, but the manner in which the estates were administered. He did not put them forward all at once, but was tactful, so that Henson, who had been fearful that, once married, Nell's upstart husband might show himself in colours far removed from those he had worn as stable hand and secretary, was reassured: Campions looked to be in safe hands.

More, Chad suggested to Nell that she lived at Campions too much; that Malplaquet's other lands and homes needed to see more of their mistress, but although she argued with him a little she at last agreed.

'For,' he said, after examining the accounts which had come in from Wroxton and Sheveborough, and the Welsh estates, 'I think that not all may be well there. Agents left to their own devices may grow careless—and greedy.'

Henson was compelled to echo this advice, and was ruefully pleased to see that Nell intended to take it—because Chad had put it forward.

'Grandfather spent most of his time at Campions,' she said, a trifle defiantly, one evening, as they sat alone before the fire, the Privy Council, who now dined with them twice-weekly, having left. Aunt Conybeare had taken her leave shortly after the wedding to visit her sister, she said, adding,

'You no longer need me now, as chaperon or companion. You have your husband to guard you.'

She had never criticised the marriage, was unfailingly polite and kind to Chad, but Nell was not sure what she truly thought.

'You will come back, dear Aunt Honey-bear,' she had said.

'Perhaps,' said Aunt Conybeare. 'When the children arrive, you may need an old woman then.'

Chad, who was setting out the backgammon board, looked up at her and smiled. 'You have said yourself that your grandfather was not always wise in his rule.'

'Sophistry,' Nell flung at him playfully, 'to turn what one says against the sayer.'

He laughed at that, and put out a hand to her. 'Come, your turn to win.'

'And that,' said Nell, 'will be a day to run up the union flag, unless you are chivalrous enough to let me win—which I do not want.'

'Brave girl,' replied her husband affectionately. 'For that sentiment you will be suitably rewarded.'

Their marriage was, of course, a scandal. The Riding visited, to stare at him, his size and strength, his good manners, and his equally good speech. 'A gentleman, down on his luck,' was the usual verdict. 'But to marry him!'

Chad, and Nell too, bore it patiently. It was inevitable. Sir Chesney did not come immediately; he was away, and the news was late in reaching both him and Ulric. Ulric had left the Riding to visit his mother's family in Ireland, he had said in an ill-scrawled letter, and did not know how long he would be gone.

He would return soon enough, was Nell's wry reaction—when he heard the bad news. Sir Chesney's visit came when they had been married for a fortnight, and were still the wonder of the North, as Nell frequently joked.

Chad was at the stables, working out Rajah, a Rajah who was pleased because they so often took him out on the moors, Nell and Chad riding together, unsupervised these days, doing everything together, and, if the world disapproved of them, Campions did not.

Nell, working in her room, heard the noise of his arrival, and sighed when the butler told her that Sir Chesney was in the Turkish room.

She put off her brown holland apron, to reveal beneath it the modish dress which she now always wore, her hair carefully coiffed, feet perfectly shod, face soft, the very picture of a satisfied woman, and went to join him; she hardly dared think that he would welcome her, any more than she welcomed him.

He turned as she entered. 'Nell! I ask you to tell me that this story is not true. You cannot have married your stable hand!'

She kissed his warm cheek as though this were a normal visit. 'Not my stable hand, my secretary,' she said calmly.

He dismissed her chopped logic. 'Piff-paff, Nell. It's all one, and you know it. How could you do such a thing? What would your grandfather have said? Do you know what the world is saying? Such a marriage cannot stand.'

'Come, Uncle,' replied Nell, still calm. 'The deed is done and I am happy with it. He is a good man, and even Henson approves of him, and you know what Henson is.'

'Oh, by God, damn Henson; who's he to decide

who Malplaquet marries? You are wanton, my girl, seduced by a strong body and——'

'Do not say handsome face,' responded Nell incorrigibly. 'My husband has many attributes, but he is not handsome.'

'You have taken leave of your senses and your modesty both,' shouted her uncle, now thoroughly roused to anger. 'A pity that we are no longer allowed to thrash our womenfolk. A good beating twice a week would soon restore you to your senses.'

Before Nell, eyes furious, could respond, a cold voice spoke from the door. Chad had returned, to be told of Sir Chesney's arrival, to hear him shouting even before he opened the door, to be in time to register his displeasure by threatening Nell.

He walked over to his embattled Countess, slipped an arm around her. True, he could never be called conventionally handsome, but even Sir Chesney had to recognise his physical power and the air of effortless authority which had returned to him permanently on the day he married Nell.

'I allow no man to speak to my wife in such a fashion,' he said, his voice ice and fire, the voice his men had heard in the Spanish mountains, and on the night before battle. 'Unless you are civil to her both in and out of her presence, you are not welcome in this house, sir.'

'Why, you. . .' Words failed Sir Chesney, faced with the man himself, standing there so cold and sure. 'Who are you to tell me whether I may or may not visit Campions, see my niece?'

'My husband, Uncle.' Nell was as cool as Chad, and, to Sir Chesney, equally infuriating. 'I do not wish to lose you, Uncle. I have few relatives, God knows, but if you wish to see me you must respect the fact that I freely chose the man by my side to be my partner, to run my lands with me, to father my children, and nothing you can say or do will alter that. Your choice, Uncle. Go or stay, as you please, but I will not allow *my* choice or my husband to be traduced.'

'You are shameless, madam, shameless,' almost gobbled her uncle. 'I shall have this piece of trash you have chosen to elevate from the gutter investigated. Better for you to have married Ulric than for you to do this.'

'I give you leave to go, Uncle.' Nell was still calm, but shaking a little. 'You will not, I am sure, wish to remain here longer, and, much though it pains me to see you go, I cannot have my husband miscalled. As he protects me, I will protect him.'

'Protects you!' was Sir Chesney's answer to that. 'Pillage you more like. Mark my words, my girl. You will rue the day you married him.'

'I am not your girl, Uncle, I never was, and my judgement tells me I have done aright. But right or wrong, done is done, as we say here, and I joy in the doing. I am sorry that you have had an unnecessary journey. Should you wish to eat before you travel home, I will arrange for you to dine alone, so that we do not disturb you by our presence.'

He saw that there was no shaming her, no shaking her.

'God damn it, madam, the food would choke me. What a work you have made of this. What can have possessed you, I ask myself?'

Nell could not resist the opportunity offered. 'Why, Uncle,' she whispered sweetly, 'I did but follow the Tallboys motto: "As the beginning, so the end". What was good enough for the lady of Barthwaite is good enough for me.'

'You were like to have given him a fit,' said Chad,

a little ruefully, when he had stamped out, 'but I could not allow him to speak to you so in your own home.'

'Nor I hear you miscalled,' sighed Nell. 'You were right, of course, when you foresaw trouble. But I cannot allow it to affect me. I am sorry to have made an enemy of him, yet Ulric troubles me even more. I cannot think what he will say or do when he finally hears that I am married—and to whom.'

'Nothing useful,' said Guy Shadwell dispiritedly to his father, 'and really, after all this time, not surprising. Only an innkeeper in South Nottinghamshire who thought that Shad "might" have passed through last autumn. He seemed to remember Vinnie—made them all laugh, trust Vinnie—and if Shad's missing, where's Vinnie? He was always watching Shad, guarding him—that was quite a joke, only it ain't one now.'

'What I expected,' sighed his father. 'So it seems that he disappeared somewhere between South Nottinghamshire and Glen Ruadh, which leaves a lot of country to cover after nearly seven months. And the carriage and horses—what happened to them?'

'Attacked by footpads somewhere lonely,' hazarded Guy bitterly. 'After all he went through in the war, surviving that dreadful wound, to disappear somewhere in England—or Scotland—and be lost without a trace.'

'I'll not give up.' The Earl rose, his face distraught. 'I cannot believe that I shall never be able to see him again, ask his forgiveness for thirty lost years. I cannot refrain from thinking of him. I ask myself why it was I disliked him so much for so long. Perhaps it was because he was always so much his own man, whereas I now think Frederick always consciously sought to please me. The Duke asked after him yesterday, said he was sorry that he was lost to the army. I nearly told him that Shad——' the first time that Guy had heard his father use the affectionate nickname '—was lost to life, but I will not give up hope. The search must go on. See to it, Guy.'

It was Guy who was despondent now; he thought his father's hope was based on a desperate desire to make up to Shad for the cruel indifference he had shown to him all his life. He left, to prepare to visit again the old ex-Runner whom he had employed in the attempt to trace his lost brother.

The Earl sat at his desk after Guy had gone, his head in his hands. Despite his brave words to Guy, who he knew mourned his brother sincerely, he had no real hope that Shad might be found after all this time.

His secretary put his head around the door. 'My lord?'

'Yes.' The Earl lifted his head—life must go on. 'Yes, what is it?'

'The Runner is back, my lord; says he needs to speak to you urgently.'

'The Runner? What Runner? Guy is dealing with him.'

'Not that one, my lord. The one who came before Christmas about Lord Halstead's rifle. The man you refused to see then—I spoke to him. He insists that he needs to speak to you personally, no one else will do.'

How wrong he had been to refuse to see the Runner. Halstead's rifle might offer some clue to his disappearance. Anything to do with Halstead must be investigated, my lord thought. 'Send him in,' he said curtly.

Cully Jackson, who had been waiting in the anteroom, carrying the mysterious rifle in its leather case, was not abashed at the prospect of meeting such a great man as Lord Clermont. On the contrary, he stared about him, taking in the splendid room with the trained eye of a man used to summing up his surroundings for his professional purposes.

The study was superb, bookshelves in the bays on each side of a hearth elaborate in white marble, nymphs holding up its mantelshelf. Above the hearth was a giant painting, which he offered only a cursory inspection—neither the books nor the painting were of real interest to him; the man standing behind the desk was. He drew in a long breath, let it out again. He knew that he had seen this man before, or someone younger, very like him. One mystery, he was sure, would have been solved by the time that he left the room. But he was wary, was Cully; he had to make sure.

'My lord,' he began, 'I am sorry to trouble you and your office about this matter again.'

The Earl put up his hand. 'You are right to do so. I should have made it my business to see you before. Is that my son's rifle you carry?'

Jackson lifted the rifle from its leather case, handed it to my lord. 'With respect, you may tell me, sir.'

The man opposite took the rifle, inspected it carefully, said slowly, 'This rifle belonged to my son. His initials are there, engraved beneath his Viscount's coronet. I remember it.' He looked up, his face ravaged. 'He showed it to me once when. . .when we were on good terms. It almost certainly went with him on his journey north last autumn. He bought it from his best friend who was later killed at Waterloo, and treasured it because of that. He would not lightly have parted with it. And now he is lost, almost certainly dead, I fear, and how the rifle came into your possession is something which you must explain to me.'

My lord's face disturbed Jackson. He thought that he knew why. He had not been on the best of his terms with his heir, but now that he thought that his son was likely dead... He looked away from naked grief to stare more closely at the painting over the fireplace.

His stare held. He knew at once that his search was over, and that my lord's grief was misplaced. But why, and how, the rifle had come into the possession of the dead thief and would-be murderer, and my lord's son was—what he was, Jackson did not know, but was sure that he could find out.

'Forgive me,' he said. 'The question may seem strange to you. But is that painting there,' and he indicated the portrait over the hearth, 'your son, who is missing?'

The Earl was surprised; it was his turn to stare a little at Jackson. 'Indeed,' he said, 'that is my son Charles, Viscount Halstead, done after he came home from the wars, when he had recovered from his wounds. Yes, that is my worthy son,' he said painfully, 'whom I spent years neglecting for my unworthy son. I am rightly served that I lost him before I found him.'

'A cavalryman?' asked Jackson, still staring at the painting.

'Indeed,' said the Earl, turning to look at the portrait, which hurt him every time he passed it. 'A good one, they tell me. A wonder with horses and at commanding men. Not so fortunate with women.'

'Oh, I wouldn't say that, my lord,' offered Jackson with a sly grin, referring to the last part of my lord's judgement on his son, 'but, I agree, a wonder with horses.' He thought of Chad Newcome, the man without a memory, last seen controlling the uncontrollable Rajah in the riding school at Campions.

For the sumptuous painting by Sir Thomas Lawrence, flaming in its glory above the hearth, was of Chad Newcome, but a Chad Newcome whom Campions had never known.

He was standing, straight-backed and tall, face stern, magnificent in full regimentals, black curls blowing in the breeze, his left hand on his sabre, his right hand holding a superb white horse. His breast blazed with decorations, including a giant star. The bright blue eyes gazing down at Jackson he had last seen some weeks ago, and like Chad Newcome's were those of a man of pride, will and astonishing self-control.

The Earl's voice broke into his reverie. 'You admire the painting, I see.'

Jackson turned, said coolly, London in his speech, 'Yes, but I admire the man more.'

'You have met my son?' The Earl's voice carried incredulity.

'Yes,' returned Jackson, suddenly man to man; Earls and thief takers had no place here. This man was grieving for what he thought was lost—but how would he take the truth? 'I beg pardon, my lord, for my effrontery, as you will see it, if I ask you to sit down before I speak to you of your son and where he may be found, although the finding may be painful to you, and what it will be to him I cannot even guess.'

He held the Earl with the eyes which had frightened thieves into confession, and consigned murderers to the gallows, so that the Earl slowly sank into his chair, and began to listen, in mounting shock, to what Jackson had to tell him.

Guy had been sent for, caught as he was about to leave to initiate further search for Shad.

'And Shad—Halstead—is alone, you say,' said Guy, 'and does not know who he is, only that he was Shad, which, of course, they translated into Chad, and he did not know enough to correct them? And where, then, is Vinnie, his faithful shadow and protector?'

'Shad?' said Jackson, for up to now the Earl and his son had spoken only of Halstead.

'Yes,' said Guy, 'he was so nicknamed from a boy, Charles Shadwell, you see—Shad.'

'And Vinnie, you said. Who and what was he?'

'Shad's factotum, old sergeant, valet, groom, man of all work. They'd saved one another's lives in the war. He would never, living, desert Shad.'

'You're sure that he was with him?' asked Jackson—everything must be double-checked in his line of work.

'Quite sure,' replied Guy. 'I saw them drive off, and it was Vinnie who was remembered in the last trace we have of them.'

'All I know,' said Jackson, 'is that Chad, Lord Halstead, as I believe him, was found alone, starving, half-naked, mind and memory gone, wandering on the moors. It's my guess that they were set on, robbed, Vinnie killed, Lord Halstead not quite finished off, horses and possessions, including the rifle, stolen by a gang led by the thief who later tried to kill Lady Malplaquet.'

Even in his relief that Shad still lived, Guy could not help laughing. 'And what a turn-up that is,' he exclaimed, 'to be saved and employed by Nell Tallboys, of all people!'

'Oh,' said Jackson with a grin, 'there's more to it than that. He became her secretary, and, begging your pardon, sir——' he turned to the Earl, who had sat silent, listening '—he and the lady are sweet on one another. So sweet that he gave his notice, and is due to leave any day—doing the honourable thing, you see. We'd best hurry north, the young gentleman and I, to catch him before he disappears again.'

Jackson had no knowledge of what had happened at Campions since he left—the proposal and the marriage.

'Sweet on Nell Tallboys!' Guy was incredulous. 'Even more of a turn-up. And you're sure he has no knowledge of who he is?'

'Quite sure,' said Jackson.

'Poor Shad,' said Guy obscurely, thinking of the scene at Watier's the night before Shad left, and his oft-repeated statements that the last person he would ever marry would be Nell Tallboys!

The Earl rose. 'We owe you our thanks, Mr Jackson. You have given us hope. And this Chad, you say, who you think is my son, saved Lady Malplaquet from an assassin, worked as a stable hand, and then as her secretary—and that they. . .favoured one another?'

'Indeed, my lord,' said Jackson with a grin. 'I taxed him with it, and got half killed for my pains. A man of honour, your son, for so I believe Mr Chad Newcome to be.'

'Well, Guy shall go north with you,' said the Earl, ringing the bell for his secretary, 'to check whether your belief is correct, but what he will do if Charles's memory is still gone he will have to decide when he meets him.' He paused and for the first time his stern old face cracked into a smile, albeit a grim one. 'I can tell you one thing, Mr Jackson; if my son does recover his memory to discover that he is. . .sweet on Nell Tallboys, that shock will be a profound one, too!'

CHAPTER EIGHTEEN

NELL found that each day as a new wife brought its own pleasures. She and Chad, who had now been married for a month, an anniversary which they had happily celebrated during the previous night, were due to visit one of Nell's properties situated in north Nottinghamshire, an old hunting lodge-cum-country house known as Penny's Hall. Word had been sent ahead that my lady and her new husband would be expected to arrive on the Friday afternoon, that their baggage would come by coach and cart, and they would ride there, suitably attended by grooms and outriders.

Nell had protested at the state in which she was to travel, but Chad had agreed with Henson and Aisgill that she should not only be protected—the outriders would be armed—but also that the people at Penny's Hall would be flattered by their Countess honouring them so, after all these years without a visit from the family.

'Depend upon it,' Nell said ruefully, 'the place will be shabby and damp.'

'And when did such things trouble you, Nell Newcome?' said Chad, giving her an absent kiss; they were dressing for the journey. Chad was to ride Rajah, Aisgill having given his reluctant consent, but, as Chad had said, the beast deserved some reward for having been so patient in his dressage exercises, and for having also given them four new foals, one of which looked likely to rival his father in beauty, wickedness and power.

'You'll be careful with him,' Aisgill had said the previous day.

'As with my life,' Chad had replied truthfully.

Aisgill had given him a queer look. 'I thought that the lady had run mad when she decided to marry you,' he said bluntly, 'but now. . .' And he shrugged his shoulders. 'Now I think she could have done worse. Much worse,' he added as an afterthought, watching Chad's face change when Nell came into the yard, dressed as magnificently as she always was these days; flyaway Nell Tallboys had vanished for good. Mrs Newcome was a fashion-plate.

Breakfast over, and both dressed for the journey, the coach and other baggage gone the previous day, the train they were taking with them assembled on the sweep before the beautiful façade, Vulcan's successor, Pluto, was brought round for Nell, and two lads escorted Rajah, who would still only behave himself for Chad.

Nell felt quite sentimental. It was the first time that she had gone out into the great world as a married woman. They had all decided that the stay at Penny's Hall must be done in style, Nottinghamshire society entertained, Nottingham itself visited for a few days, a boat trip to be taken up the Trent, Colwick Hall and the Musters visited, and all to be done in the intervals of looking at the coal pits there, examining the books and quizzing the obviously lax agent, before deciding whether to keep him.

'Time to go,' Chad announced, taking Nell's arm, and they walked out of the front door, through lines of servants assembled to see them off; impossible to do anything these days, thought Nell, amused, without Henson making a pantomime of it, as though determined to show that although Nell Tallboys had married a nobody she was still the greatest lady in the North.

And finally they were on the steps, more of her people assembled, the Privy Council standing in the doorway, the train, all on horseback, patiently awaiting her—at least the men were patient, their mounts less so.

Nell was already up when the first intimation of trouble occurred. A horse and rider, foam flying in all directions from the mad speed of travel, flew through the great arch at the end of the sweep, and came to a stop before them all.

It was Ulric Tallboys. His face was alternately ashen and scarlet, his expression wild in the extreme. He advanced on Nell and on Chad, who was holding Rajah, a lad controlling the stallion on his other side.

His voice was high, furious, and he had a pistol in his hand, pulled from the holster on his saddle as he dismounted. 'So, it's true, then. You've done for me, married this piece of scum,' and he waved the pistol dangerously at Chad.

Nell, controlling her fright and unease, tried to stare him down. 'What the devil do you think you're doing, Ulric? Put that pistol away, at once. And yes, I've married Mr Newcome, as I suppose you've just heard. You received my letter?'

'Received your letter?' raved Ulric, waving the pistol at Chad, who had moved towards him. 'Keep back, I tell you, or I'll drop you where you stand. Yes, I read your letter, and you've ruined me, you bitch. I only went to Ireland to avoid a debtor's prison. The Jews and the bailiffs were after me already when it looked as though we were not to marry, and now that you have married this piece of dirt I'm like to be in a debtor's prison all my life, thanks to you. Well, I'm not having it, Nell, be damned to all of you.'

He waved the pistol again, and those around Nell, fearful for her, were afraid to do anything that might cause him to shoot her.

'Damn you,' he shrieked, 'it was only that clod you've married who saved you from death when he killed my man. Be damned to him, what have I to lose now? He shall have his reward.' And to Nell's horror he finally stopped waving the pistol, brought it up and fired at Chad, as Chad, careless of what Rajah might do if he loosed him, made for Ulric's throat, fearful that it was Nell for whom the bullet was intended.

This diversionary tactic almost certainly saved his life, since the bullet creased his skull as he lowered his head to charge, instead of taking him in the breast, but it dropped him to the ground, and Ulric, realising that he had failed, and that Nemesis was on him in the shape of Nell's people, suddenly horrified into sense by what he had done, made for Rajah in the hope of mounting him, and escaping on him.

Nell's scream of shock and horror as she saw Chad fall was lost in Rajah's snortings and whinnyings at the sight of Chad brought low, and the feel of Ulric's clumsy hands as he tried to climb into his saddle—he had already broken free from the lad.

Rajah tossed Ulric from him, and, turning, rearing, trampled him beneath his iron hoofs, transforming him into bloody rags on the ground, before flinging back his head, narrowly missing the prostrate Chad, to bolt down the drive, disappearing through the archway at the end.

Nell had already dismounted from a disturbed Pluto—all the horses present were distressed by the sudden shot—to fall on her hands and knees beside Chad, who she feared had been killed by the man whose maimed body lay a few yards away from that of his victim. Aisgill dropped down on Chad's other side, Henson began giving frantic orders. The sudden nature of the tragedy had shocked them all, but action now followed paralysis.

She was sobbing, wailing, all her normal stoicism gone, cradling Chad's head, regardless of the blood running down his face and covering her hands, regardless of Aisgill saying, 'Come, Nell,' all ladyships forgotten, 'you must let us examine him,' for she knew only one thing: Chad might be dead, and what then did life hold for her, the reason for it being gone?

Guy and Jackson had kept up a good pace on the way north, for Jackson was fearful that Chad might already have left. He had no clear idea when exactly Chad was to go from Campions, only knew that he was working out his notice.

Guy was quite unlike his brother, in looks as well as manner, but Jackson found him a congenial companion, although a little *distrait*; his thoughts were with his brother whom he hoped to meet at journey's end.

And what then? He had asked Jackson his opinion of Shad's loss of memory, and how likely he was to regain it. Jackson had shaken his head. He had met such cases before, and they were all different, he said. Some got their memory back after a time, some never. Some, having retrieved it, forgot what had happened in the interval; others didn't. 'And no one knows why, or how,' he said. 'You meet some strange things in my line of work, Mr Guy—I mean Mr Shadwell.'

'Mr Guy,' said Guy, smiling. He liked the man, there was a bluff honesty about him, liked him the more because he seemed to respect Chad—who might be Shad.

And at last they passed into the Riding, where the land was wild and rough, like its people, Jackson said, and they were making for Campions, the great house on the edge of the moors, of which Guy had often heard and never seen, like the legendary Nell Tallboys, Countess of Malplaquet, its eccentric owner.

The the house was suddenly before them, in the distance, glowing in the watery sunlight of a late March day, at the end of a suddenly improved road—the Countess's doing, Jackson said; she had improved everything to do with her estate since she had inherited.

The works of past Earls of Malplaquet were everywhere, follies, stone bridges, triumphal arches leading to nowhere, until they could see the final great arch through which they must drive in order to reach the front of the house.

But a quarter of a mile from the arch their driver, nicknamed Pompey—another of Shad's old soldiers, now working at Clermont House, and brought along to share in the driving—said suddenly, 'Here's a fine to-do,' and tried to pull off the road, as a huge black stallion galloped past them, narrowly missing the carriage, foaming and bounding, so that it almost seemed that fire might be coming from his nostrils, finally leaving the road behind them, and running on to the moor.

'Rajah!' exclaimed Jackson, turning to stare. 'Now what the devil's up? Drive on, man,' and so Pompey did, through the giant arch, and there in front of them on the sweep before the Corinthian columns and the flight of steps up to them was a scene like, as Jackson said later, something in a Drury Lane spectacle.

Groups of people were milling about. A dead man was lying on the ground, broken and bloody, his head at an odd angle. Another man lay on the ground being attended to, a woman was being comforted by a middle-aged man in gamekeeper's clothes, another man in a fine gentleman's suit was shouting orders, before himself bending down to the man on the ground, who was wearing, Guy saw, a fine suit of riding clothes, and beautiful boots.

He had thick black hair in loose ringlets, was big. . . and Guy gave a hoarse shout. 'Stop, Pompey, stop,' and, on Pompey's doing so, hurled himself from the carriage to run to the group about the prostrate man, ignoring shouts and attempts to push him away by the man in the fine suit.

'Who the devil are you, sir?' the gentleman demanded, to have Guy hurl at him,

'Oh, to Hades with you, sir,' and then, 'It's you, Shad, at last,' to the man on the ground who had begun to stir, as though Guy's voice had been some sort of signal, recalling him to his old life.

Nell, Aisgill's arms around her, as though she were a girl again, began to recover herself. Nell Newcome must be as brave as Nell Tallboys had been. She was in the act of moving away from Aisgill to question Henson about Chad's condition, but as he straightened up, shouting for a servant to go fetch Dr Ramsden at once, she saw the new actors, as Jackson would have called them, arrive on the scene.

Astonished, she saw a tall fair young man, shouting something incomprehensible, hurl himself at poor Chad, who, assisted again by Henson, had begun to stir, driving away her first fears that Ulric had killed him immediately.

For Ulric she felt nothing. Later, the horror of his death would strike her, to visit her occasionally in nightmares, even though he had brought his death on himself by attempting to kill Chad, but now her only concern was her husband, and why the strange young man should throw himself at Chad, and how it was that he knew the name which Campions had given him, for Shad, to her ears, had come out as Chad.

To her infinite relief she saw Chad, blood still running down his face, try to rise, said hoarsely to Aisgill, 'Oh, thank God, he's not dead,' to hear Aisgill answer briskly,

'I told you so, my lady.'

And to her astonishment and horror she watched Chad's gaze pass over her unknowingly, and heard him ask the young man in a puzzled voice, 'Guy, where the devil am I? And what are you doing here? I thought myself in Spain when I woke up. Where's Vinnie?'

Nell was suddenly frantic at this non-recognition, the more so as Chad, ignoring her, attempted to stand, the young man, Guy—and who was he?—helping him most lovingly, an expression of acute concern on his face.

And Jackson was there, too, dismounting from the carriage, his sardonic gaze hard on them all, like a sphinx who knew all the answers, and, if he did, she, Nell Newcome, wished he would supply them.

Countess Nell at her proudest, she questioned the young man fiercely, 'Who are you, sir? And how do you know Chad?' while Henson, who had uncharacteristically been struck dumb by this strange turn of events, recovered his self-possession, and also roared at the stranger.

'Come, sir, who the devil are you?' and, pointing at Chad, 'And who the devil's he, since you seem to know him?'

Behind them, Jackson, the only one of all of them to realise that Chad had his memory back, watched and waited.

Chad, now held upright between Aisgill and Guy, stared at Nell, said thickly, and to Nell's consternation,

'Who are you, madam, and how did I get here? I thought——' for as he had recovered consciousness he had been a guerrilla in Spain again '—I thought I was in the mountains, but then how could you be in Spain, Guy? And who are all these people? What am I doing here?' and he looked dazedly about him, wondering who the handsome woman was who stared at him so poignantly, two great tears running down her face, as the truth hit her, to bring her almost to her knees again.

Chad had got his memory back, and did not know her!

'Who am I?' said Guy, loosening his grip on his brother a little—he had been holding him as though he feared to lose him again if he were not careful—and at last answering the questions posed by Henson and the woman, who he had suddenly realised must be Nell Tallboys, and, if so, report had lied cruelly about her looks, for what a magnificent specimen she was, even in her grief. 'Why, I am Guy Shadwell, Lord Clermont's youngest son, and this——' but he was interrupted by his brother.

'Enough, Guy, enough. It must be for me to... confess who I am.'

Even before Guy had begun to speak, the sight of Nell moving towards him, arms outstretched, murmuring his name—for Chad sounded like Shad to him—saying brokenly, 'Oh, Chad, never say that you have forgotten me,' a look of such love and concern on her poor face, had caused something to move in Shad's head, and he remembered everything—would that he could not!

He knew that Vinnie, poor Vinnie, was seven months dead, knew why he had left London, knew of the attack, knew why he had been found wandering on the moor, knew of his service at Campions, knew why the rifle, and the dead man who had carried it, were familiar to him, knew, to his piercing horror, that he truly loved and had married the woman before him, who would not, could not now love him once she knew who he was—Charles Halstead who had defamed her—but he, and not Guy, must speak the unpalatable truth, even though it destroyed him, for the truth was all Shad had ever possessed, and he had lived by it all his life.

His face a mask of agony, he said, 'I have remembered everything. I am—God forgive me, my dearest Nell, for what I said of you, before I knew you—Charles Shadwell, Viscount Halstead; I was set on by footpads, my poor sergeant Vinnie was killed, and I was stripped and left for dead, to be saved by you and become your servant...'

The effort of thought, of speech, was too great for his failing senses. Shad—Chad—welcomed oblivion to give him surcease from pain and shame, and fell gratefully forward into the dark again, unconscious at the feet of the most noble lady, Nell Newcome, Countess of Malplaquet, Viscountess Wroxton, Baroness Sheveborough, all in her own right, whom he had mortally and publicly insulted seven months ago, and who he had loved with a passion beyond reason from the first moment he had seen her, and to whom he was now married.

CHAPTER NINETEEN

'You married him!' Guy's voice was almost incredulous.

'Yes,' said Nell shyly. She and Guy were in her private drawing-room, Chad's and her possessions all about them. The chessboard was set up, the backgammon board waiting to be set up, Nell's canvas work on an upright stand, books everywhere, the Campions stud book among them, the room left as it was for them to return to—everything bearing witness to their happy and useful life together.

Shad had been carried to the great bed, unconscious, their journey postponed. He was not in any danger, Dr Ramsden said, but when he had surfaced for a moment and had spoken it was plain that he was greatly confused and shocked. The strain of discovering who he was, and what had happened over the last seven months, coupled with the wound, even though it was not severe—a gash similar to the one which had helped to cause his loss of memory—had been too much for even the strong man that he was to accept easily.

He had been given laudanum to make him sleep soundly. Nell's doctor was a great believer in sleep, and now Guy was talking to Nell, and finding her quite unlike the lady of legend, in speech as well as appearance.

'Well, I'm not surprised that you did marry him,' he said slowly, 'even if, forgive me, it does seem a trifle odd, for you to marry your secretary, but Shad's such a splendid fellow.'

'Yes, he is, isn't he?' said Nell simply.

Guy hesitated, and Nell looked at him affectionately. If he thought Chad—Shad—a splendid fellow, Nell thought that Guy was a chip off the same block.

'You mustn't take any notice of the bet,' he said finally. Nell saw that Guy knew that he was on dangerous ground, and spoke to reassure him.

Even since Chad had told her that he was Viscount Halstead, who had publicly shamed her, her mind had been in a turmoil. Her first thoughts were angry, for Lord Halstead seemed to have nothing to do with Chad Newcome, her husband whom she loved beyond life, so that when she had thought that he was dead she had understood for a moment why some widows threw themselves on funeral pyres, committed suicide.

But to reconcile Chad Newcome and Charles Halstead, that was difficult. Whenever she thought of Halstead, either now, or in the past, she was consumed with a fierce anger. But what had that to do with Chad? He was so unlike what she had assumed Charles Halstead to be from what she had heard of him. But then, wasn't she quite different from the Nell Tallboys of gossip? Her mind went round and round.

'But why?' she said, at last. 'Why did he—who you say rarely drank, get so blind drunk that he spoke of me as he did? A man who, all the time he was here, was abstemious, respected women, never troubled the female servants—why, I even had to propose to him myself in order. . .' she paused, said defiantly '. . .to get him into my bed—whereas he bet that he could have me without marriage. *That* I do not understand.'

'Well,' said Guy, 'it's like this, you see. When I was a little lad, and Shad was barely twenty—he had just joined the army, not that he wanted to be a soldier at first; he went to Oxford at fifteen, wished to be a scholar there, but Faa. . . Father. . .said no, the second son always went into the army—he met Isabella French, and fell madly in love with her.'

He stopped again, and Nell wondered what was coming, he looked so miserable. She said gently, 'You needn't tell me, if it makes you unhappy.'

'Oh, I have to tell you,' said Guy earnestly. 'He married her, you see, against Father's wishes, and Father was right—not that he knew what Isabella was; it was just that he never liked Shad for some reason, always wanted to thwart him.'

He went on. 'Well, at first the marriage seemed to be happy. She was a pretty little dark thing, not a bit like you. All Shad's women, not that there were that many,' he hastened to reassure her, 'were little. And at first they were very happy. But Shad's duties kept him away a lot, and she. . .couldn't live without him . . .it was a kind of sickness, Shad said, and she. . .well, she gave herself to anyone who would have her when he was away, particularly to Shad's best friend, Harvey Black, who couldn't seem to resist her.

'In the end, Shad found out; he arrived home one day to find her in bed with Harvey, and then it all came out—about him and the other men. What was worse, he fought a duel with Harvey, and then, when Harvey shot at him and missed, Shad deloped, fired into the air—he didn't want to kill him—but Harvey was ashamed of his betrayal of Shad, swore and insisted that the duel be a proper one, Shad must fire at him. They fired again, and Shad wounded him so badly that Harvey died six months later from it. You can imagine what that did to Shad.

'And then, to make it all worse, Isabella was found to be pregnant, and the baby couldn't be Shad's. But he stuck with her, until she died in childbirth. Yes, I know, Nell,' he said gently, on seeing her horrified face, and hearing her murmur,

'Poor Chad.'

'Yes, I know it's a horrid story, couldn't be worse. After that, he barely looked at women seriously, until last year he met Julia Merton, another little thing, and the whole rotten business began again.

'It turned out that Julia was Jack Broughton's mistress, and was marrying Shad for convenience. It all came out when Shad found her with him—you can imagine what *that* did to him after the business with Isabella, and that was why on the day he found out he drank himself stupid, went to Watier's and made that awful bet about you; your cousin Bobus was boasting about your—inaccessibility, and that worked him up. Father was badgering him to marry you, into the bargain. I know he shouldn't have done it, but you can see why.'

Yes, Nell could see why. She walked to the window, looked out over the moors, and thought of a young and chivalrous Shad, his life in ruins—and then for it to happen again!

'Not Shad's fault,' said Guy, 'that he picked wrong 'uns; his misfortune. I suppose they picked him because he was so good and steady at bottom. Everyone envied him Isabella and Julia. It was only afterwards people realised that they were both lightskirts at heart.'

Nell thought of how she had tempted him, and flushed at the memory—and then of how he had held off. He had been good and steady with her, too, and that was partly why, in the end, she had been so wild to marry him.

'He quarrelled with Faa over it,' Guy said, 'and that was when he drove north, to be attacked and lose his memory. Was he happy here?' he asked.

'Yes,' answered Nell, 'very happy. We were both happy.' She thought of their mutual joy, of the badinage which had passed between them, as well as the passion, of their shared pleasure in the horses, in their books, and the running of Campions. 'Yes,' she repeated, 'very happy.'

'I'm glad,' said Guy fervently. 'He's never been really happy, except perhaps when he was in the army, doing his duty—Shad's great on duty—and then he had to give that up when our elder brother Frederick died. And Father wasn't even grateful when Shad cleared up the mess Frederick had made of running the estates.' And then he added thoughtfully, 'Perhaps he was happy because he no longer carried the burden of the memories of Isabella, Julia and Faa's dislike,' unknowingly echoing what Jackson had said to Chad Newcome earlier.

He didn't tell Nell the truth about his eldest brother, but Nell knew from his manner that he had not loved Frederick as he plainly loved Shad.

'One good thing about all this—apart from Shad meeting you, that is—is that Faa's wild to make up to Shad for mistreating him all his life. Wants to be reconciled. I can't wait to tell him. Shad always loved Faa—God knows why, he was never fair to him.'

Nell walked over to Guy, and kissed him on the cheek. 'A present for my new brother,' she said. 'I've never had a brother, and now I've inherited a good one. Welcome to Campions, Guy.'

She was amused and touched at his response. 'Oh, you're a good 'un, Nell. Not a bit like they said you were. And so handsome, too. Whatever was all the gossip about. . .?' He stopped, flushing at what he had almost said.

'That I was plain, you mean?' she said, laughing at him, looking more vital than ever. 'Well, I know I'm no beauty.'

'Nonsense,' said Guy sturdily. 'You're the finest

woman I've ever met, and I really envy Shad. You won't be hard on him when he's himself again, will you?' he said anxiously. 'I know Shad. He'll be worrying himself sick over the bet.'

Talking to Guy, listening to him about Shad, and not only the sad story he had told her, but the way in which his face lit up when he spoke of his brother, his unselfish joy that he was alive, when his death would have meant Guy's advancement, touched Nell, told her that her choice of a husband, made blindly, and against all conventional common sense, was a good one.

'No,' she said. 'No. I won't hate him and reproach him. Why, Guy, let me tell you the sad truth about myself. I believe I told my uncle that nothing in the world would induce me to marry Charles Halstead, and then when I met him I couldn't wait to do so, married him in defiance of the whole world!

'You have *no idea* how relieved Henson, my agent, is that Chad is a nobleman in disguise. He had been repressing his misgivings since the wedding-day, and now he's cock-a-hoop. I told him an hour ago that Chad is still Chad, even though he's Shad, but he'll have none of it.'

'Henson's your grand gentleman ordering everyone about?' asked Guy ingenuously, amusing Nell again.

'Yes, that's Henson. He liked Chad, but not as Malplaquet's master. I can't wait to see him bowing and scraping to Chad—"Yes, my lord, no, my lord". His universe will be an orderly one again.'

She was suddenly happy Nell Newcome again. Yes, she would tease Chad a little about the disgraceful bet, but be sure to let him know very soon that it was only teasing, that nothing he had said and done in his old life could wipe out what they had come to mean to one another since they had first met.

'And I must write to Faa,' said Guy. 'Jackson can take the letter back to London with him. And he's cock-a-hoop, too. All his mysteries solved, and he was right about your cousin Ulric, as well.'

'Poor Ulric,' said Nell. 'I can't grieve too much for him. He did try to have me killed, but he was my cousin, and as a little boy he was a bully, yet he was, apart from Uncle Beaumont, practically the only relative I had.'

She began to giggle. 'Uncle Beaumont! What's he going to say when he learns the truth? Let me tell you of him. What an about-facer that will be!'

'No,' said Shad, bruised and broken though he felt. 'I am not staying in bed for a head wound as mild as this is, and, as for damaged nerves and restoring my system, I am not a fourteen-year-old schoolgirl afflicted with the vapours. If you don't send for my clothes I shall take you by the throat, and throttle you until you give way,' and he glared at poor Ramsden who said, dodging away as his patient looked thunder at him,

'Now, Mr Newcome, my lord, pray do not excite yourself, but you really ought to rest a little.'

'I don't intend to excite myself,' ground out Shad, 'merely give myself the satisfaction of half killing you unless you do as I wish,' and he threw back the bedclothes and made motions at Ramsden, trying to ignore his swimming head. The one thing that he wanted to do was to see Nell and try to convince her of how much he loved her, and how he regretted what he had said of her in his drunken folly, and this fool was keeping him from seeing her. And he was damned if he wanted to talk to her flat on his back in bed like a. . .mollycoddle.

Ramsden, now with his back to the door, said

wearily, 'I see that there is no stopping you, my lord. Perhaps it may be wise on my part to allow you to rise; you will soon discover how shaky you are.'

All Shad's ill-humour, which was partly caused by his fears about where he really stood with Nell—ludicrous to think that as a nobody he had possessed no such fears, but now as Charles Halstead, her equal, he felt as queasy as a green boy every time he thought of her—leached out of him. Shameful so to speak to a man who was, after all, only doing his duty. All his old charming courtesy, so well known to Campions, returned.

'I'm sorry, sir,' he said. 'I should not have spoken so. Do but allow me this, I beg.'

'Only if you allow me my reservations,' said Ramsden stiffly. 'I will send for one of the footmen to bring you your clothing, and help you to dress.'

And where was Nell? Shad thought, as he allowed the footman to tie his cravat, grateful to allow himself to be nannied for once, he felt so weak and worthless. Was she so disgusted that she had married the brute who had bet on her and maligned her that she no longer wished to see him?

Almost he wished that his memory had not returned, that he was still plain Chad Newcome, and then he thought of Guy's face when he had seen him, and of his duty to his father, and the estate to which he had been born. He could not be Chad Newcome, accountable to no one but Nell who had given him life, love, herself and Campions.

He shuddered at the thought of her, at the possibility of losing her, and her love, and, when Ramsden returned to examine the bandage around his head, said abruptly, beneath his ministrations, 'And Lady Elinor, she is well, I trust.'

'I hope so,' said Ramsden drily. 'She spent most of

the night at your bedside after she dined with your brother, and I suspect that she is catching up on her sleep—if she is wiser than you are, begging your pardon, my lord, about her health.'

She had sat by his bed! Perhaps after all she could forgive him. He jerked a little as the doctor's touch became painful, called, 'Come in,' to the knocker at the door.

Henson entered; a cat whose cream had proved satisfactory. 'My lord,' he said—Nell's prophecy had been correct, the world was no longer turned upside-down, and Henson was happy. 'My lord, your brother has suggested that you be asked if you can remember where you might have been attacked, and in what circumstances. It might lead us to where your sergeant's remains may be found. We have assumed that he was killed when you were attacked, as you were found on your own, no sign of a companion.'

Poor Vinnie. Here he was having the blue devils about himself, with no thought for what had happened to the faithful friend with whom he had campaigned both in and out of war.

'I think I remember,' he said slowly. 'You must understand that I was barely conscious at the time, and everything is confused. After they killed Vinnie, they stripped me, and then sat him beside me, and later I remember falling, and after that climbing. They threw the carriage and the pair of us into a quarry, you think? Which would account for the state of my hands when I was found.'

'Most like, my lord, most like,' said Henson, his manner, previously correctly cool to poor Chad, now almost unctuous, or as unctuous as such a dry stick could be. 'There are two near Campions land; a search shall be made at once, my lord. I shall organise it,' and he turned to go.

'Henson,' asked Shad, 'tell me, is Lady Elinor up yet?'

'I heard that she was stirring, my lord, and her maid said that she had eaten a late breakfast. She slept in the guest suite, my lord. Dr Ramsden thought it best that you be left on your own, my lord.' He was gone, and painfully Shad walked out of the room himself, to find Nell, and learn how he stood with her.

Nell, seated in her drawing-room, late up for the first time in years, was debating whether or not to go and see her husband, when the door opened, and, to her astonishment, he walked in.

'Chad!' she said. 'Should you be up? I thought you still asleep. Dr Ramsden refused me entry this morning.' His face was white, with great purple smudges under his eyes, and his head bandaged, giving him the appearance of a rakish Arab, she thought.

'Lady Malplaquet,' he said, bowing, quite formal, and quite unlike his manner as Chad, so that Nell knew at once that Guy had been correct when he had said how troubled his brother would be.

'Not wise, perhaps, but I am not a great one for lying in a bed, and besides, I needed to see you.'

Oh, the poor love, how nervous he was! She longed to go over, hug him, tell him not to worry, but perhaps he deserved to suffer a little for what he had said and done in his drunken folly seven months ago, even if he had got his injury as the result of attacking Ulric when he had thought Ulric might be attacking *her*.

'My lord?' she said, as formal as he, so that suddenly, to her delight, she saw his grim aspect lighten a little.

'Oh, dear, Nell, don't you start. I've already had Henson my-lording me at every second word; you'd think that no one else had ever borne a title.'

Nell gave an un-Countesslike giggle. 'Did he so? I told Guy that he would.'

'Relieved to find me respectable, I suppose,' remarked Shad, a little morosely. 'Nell, I have so much to say to you, so much to ask you to forgive me for, that I hardly know how to begin. Isabella——'

'No need to speak to me of Isabella, or Julia Merton for that matter,' replied Nell briskly. 'I've already heard all about them from Guy, and I really do not wish to hear any more, so you may set your mind at ease over that.'

Shad hardly knew whether he was grateful to Guy or not; on balance, he thought, probably gratitude was in order. 'Now, about the other matter——'

'By other matter,' interrupted Nell sweetly, 'I suppose, Lord Halstead, you mean your bet. Now, that really does exercise me. I am not sure what you exactly wagered, so I cannot decide whether or not you won or lost. Foolish of you to refuse me in the annexe; you would have been richer by twenty thousand pounds had you done so. On the other hand, if the bet was suitably vague—and only you know that, if, of course, you can recall what you actually said; I believe you were dead drunk at the time, most unlike you, but there it is—then perhaps our marriage may be sufficient for you to win it. You see what a quandary I am in. I don't know whether to congratulate you or commiserate with you.'

At the end of this remarkable speech she had the pleasure of seeing her husband look suitably agonised, so added to further disconcert him, 'I understand that we are a sorry pair. I heard that you had said that of all people you would never marry me, while I told my dear uncle Beaumont exactly the same thing in the same somewhat indelicate terms about you. And here we are, tightly joined to the very partner for whom we had previously expressed extreme aversion. Sheridan, were he still alive, would have found it a suitable subject for comedy, I'm sure.'

'Nell, Nell, it is not a joke,' protested Shad. 'Here am I trying to tell you how sorry I am for what I said. . .' He stopped. His head was thundering away, and his heart was doing the same thing. Had he lost her or not? Difficult to tell when she was roasting him so preposterously—but, after all, he deserved it, did he not?

'Well, I don't propose to cry over it,' said Nell robustly, 'and it's hardly grounds for divorce, so we seem to be destined to remain firmly attached to one another, legally, if in no other way. I wonder if the terms of the settlement allow me to pay your bet? If you've lost it, that is. And will that noble conscience of yours allow you to accept my assistance?'

'I'm hardly stumped for twenty thousand,' Shad said, 'little though I shall like paying out such a sum as the consequence of my own folly—why are we going on in this havy-cavy manner, Nell? I came down to apologise to you, and you have done nothing but talk nonsense since I arrived. My head won't stand it,' he said plaintively.

'Well, let me relieve your deserved misery a little,' said Nell, deciding not to push the joke too far. 'Guy tells me that the bet was never properly registered; you were too foxed to sign anything, or whatever gentlemen do on such occasions, and consequently the terms of it are immaterial, and there is no chance of your winning or losing anything, and I shall not need to perjure myself by declaring that we. . .anticipated our wedding vows—you see how delicate becoming a married woman has made me; goodness knows, by the time we have our first child I shall be so proper that a

College of Vestal Virgins would envy me. Why are you laughing, Chad? What are you doing?'

For, thundering head and all, Shad had given a little groan, leaned forward and pulled her from her chair where she had been sitting, looking up at him with the most provoking smile on her face as she teased him beyond endurance.

'I won't have it, Nell,' he muttered distractedly. 'I don't care how badly I behaved, or what you think of me; I love you, dammit, to distraction, and if you continue as you are doing you will be pleasured on the carpet immediately, thereby either finishing me off for good, or allowing Henson to come in and find us at work, and how he would deal with that I should like to find out, but am unlikely to do so.'

And then he had her in his arms and was kissing her wilful mocking face, until they both sank on to the sofa, where for a moment it looked as though they might end up celebrating the fact that they were husband and wife despite the possibility of being interrupted, or doing Shad's head a permanent harm.

Sanity suddenly reigned. They pulled apart, Nell rosy, Shad greyer than ever, but happier than he had thought was possible since he had finally remembered who he was on the previous afternoon.

'So, I am forgiven, Lady Malplaquet, for the wicked things I said before I knew you?'

'And I am forgiven, Lord Halstead,' she answered, suddenly serious, 'for the wicked things I said and thought about you?'

His answer was a kiss, and another saucy look from Nell when lovemaking paused for a moment. 'Well, one thing that's certain,' she said wickedly, 'is that whatever anyone else thinks of our marriage we are sure to please your father and my uncle, and that must be something to cheer about, seeing that neither of them has ever been pleased with us before!'

Shad's shout of laughter at that nearly took his poor head off.

'Oh, Nell,' he groaned, 'you really must stop, or you will have me back on my bed of pain again, and Ramsden will say, "I told you so," and I don't think I could endure that; he's displeased with me enough already.'

'Happy to think that my wishes come second to your physician's,' Nell riposted, and then, when he reached for her again, 'No, Shad, for Shad you will be from now on, I will be serious. We have a great deal to arrange as soon as you are recovered, for, whereas Lady Malplaquet marrying penniless and landless Chad was one thing, I am sure that Lord Halstead marrying the lady will provide the lawyers with work for a twelve-month.'

Shad had already thought that life as his old self was likely to be a great deal more complicated than that which he had lived since he had arrived at Campions. He thought wistfully of unencumbered Chad, who was rapidly disappearing into the past—the Chad who Aisgill had thought *might* have been a corporal, or perhaps even a sergeant, in the cavalry, but who, in reality, had been a captain, and later an aide, and a good one. Landless unknown Chad, actually Charles Shadwell, Viscount Halstead, Clermont's heir, with all that that entailed in duties, responsibilities, as well as rank and privilege.

Campions, and Aisgill, would have to come to terms with Shad, but there were already signs that Campions was happy to discover that the mistress had chosen so truly when she had given poor Chad her heart and her inheritance.

'Not yet,' he said gently, pulling her into the crook

of his arm, where she fitted as though she had been designed for nothing else. 'For the moment, alone here, let us be the Countess and her secretary, duties and responsibilities forgotten.' And then, belying his own words, he started up. 'Rajah, what happened to him?'

Nell pulled him down again. 'He trotted in off the moor late last night, exhausted, like his master, but, like him, he will recover, I hope.'

'I am already recovering,' announced Shad firmly, 'and will continue to do so, provided you do not provoke me too much. A suitable deference to your lord and master would do wonderful things for me. See to it, Mrs Newcome, see to it.'

'Willingly,' murmured Nell, 'willingly, provided always you offer a similar duty to the mistress of Campions.'

They lay there, comfortable and settled for life, Chad Newcome—and his Countess.

FOUR IN HAND

by

Stephanie Laurens

Dear Reader

I've always loved the world of the Regency – a world of wit, of elegance, of drama and romance. The rich tapestry of Regency life, with the balls and glittering entertainments of the London Season, and its frenetic pace, contrasting with the relaxed ambience of country house parties and family life on large country estates, provides a perfect background against which to examine the questions of love and marriage – two subjects that, in the Regency, were not considered necessarily synonymous. The characters, too, lend themselves to romance – the dashing blades, reckless bucks, the ineffably elegant gentlemen, and the innocent misses, the self-willed young ladies not at all sure they wish to cede their independence, and the eccentric damsels intent on tasting adventure, all these contribute to the depth and passions that can be found in Regency romance.

Working within the Regency has always brought me a great deal of pleasure – I hope my Regency romances bring you the same enjoyment, and take you back in time – to when lovers waltzed under the crystal chandeliers.

Enjoy!

Stephanie Laurens

Born in Sri Lanka, **Stephanie Laurens** has lived mostly in Australia. After qualifying as a scientist, she and her husband travelled extensively through the Far and Middle East, as well as throughout Europe and England. Four years in London gave her the settings for her Regency romances. Now settled once more in Australia, she lives in a comfortable suburban house with her husband, two young children, a mindless but lovable dog, and a cat with a crooked leg.

Other titles by the same author:

Tangled Reins*
Impetuous Innocent
Fair Juno*
The Reasons for Marriage**
A Lady of Expectations**
An Unwilling Conquest**
A Comfortable Wife

* linked
** linked

CHAPTER ONE

THE rattle of the curtain rings sounded like thunder. The head of the huge four-poster bed remained wreathed in shadow yet Max was aware that for some mysterious reason Masterton was trying to wake him. Surely it couldn't be noon already?

Lying prone amid his warm sheets, his stubbled cheek cushioned in softest down, Max contemplated faking slumber. But Masterton knew he was awake. And knew that he knew, so to speak. Sometimes, the damned man seemed to know his thoughts before he did. And he certainly wouldn't go away before Max capitulated and acknowledged him.

Raising his head, Max opened one very blue eye. His terrifyingly correct valet was standing, entirely immobile, plumb in his line of vision. Masterton's face was impassive. Max frowned.

In response to this sign of approaching wrath, Masterton made haste to state his business. Not that it was *his* business, exactly. Only the combined vote of the rest of the senior staff of Delmere House had induced him to disturb His Grace's rest at the unheard-of hour of nine o'clock. He had every reason to know just how dangerous such an undertaking could be. He had been in the service of Max Rotherbridge, Viscount Delmere, for nine years. It was highly unlikely his master's recent elevation to the estate of His Grace the Duke of Twyford had in any way altered his temper. In fact, from what Masterton had seen, his master had had more to try his temper in dealing with his unexpected inheritance than in all the rest of his thirty-four years.

'Hillshaw wished me to inform you that there's a young lady to see you, Your Grace.'

It was still a surprise to Max to hear his new title on his servants' lips. He had to curb an automatic reaction to look about him for whomever they were addressing. A lady? His frown deepened. 'No.' He dropped his head back into the soft pillows and closed his eyes.

'*No*, Your Grace?'

The bewilderment in his valet's voice was unmistakable. Max's head ached. He had been up until dawn. The evening had started badly, when he had felt constrained to attend a ball given by his maternal aunt, Lady Maxwell. He rarely attended such functions. They were too tame for his liking; the languishing sighs his appearance provoked among all the sweet young things were enough to throw even the most hardened reprobate entirely off his stride. And while he had every claim to that title, seducing débutantes was no longer his style. Not at thirty-four.

He had left the ball as soon as he could and repaired to the discreet villa wherein resided his latest mistress. But the beautiful Carmelita had been in a petulant mood. Why were such women invariably so grasping? And why did they imagine he was so besotted that he'd stand for it? They had had an almighty row, which had ended with him giving the luscious ladybird her *congé* in no uncertain terms.

From there, he had gone to White's, then Boodles. At that discreet establishment, he had found a group of his cronies and together they had managed to while the night away. And most of the morning, too. He had neither won nor lost. But his head reminded him that he had certainly drunk a lot.

He groaned and raised himself on his elbows, the better to fix Masterton with a gaze which, despite his condition, was remarkably lucid. Speaking in the voice of one instructing a dimwit, he explained. 'If there's a woman here to see me, she can't be a lady. No lady would call here.'

Max thought he was stating the obvious but his henchman stared woodenly at the bedpost. The frown, which had temporarily left his master's handsome face, returned.

Silence.

Max sighed and dropped his head on to his hands. 'Have you seen her, Masterton?'

'I did manage to get a glimpse of the young lady when Hillshaw showed her into the library, Your Grace.'

Max screwed his eyes tightly shut. Masterton's insistence on using the term 'young lady' spoke volumes. All of Max's servants were experienced in telling the difference between ladies and the sort of female who might be expected to call at a bachelor's residence. And if both Masterton and Hillshaw insisted the woman downstairs was a young lady, then a young lady she must be. But it was inconceivable that any young lady would pay a nine o'clock call on the most notorious rake in London.

Taking his master's silence as a sign of commitment to the day, Masterton crossed the large chamber to the wardrobe. 'Hillshaw mentioned that the young lady, a Miss Twinning, Your Grace, was under the impression she had an appointment with you.'

Max had the sudden conviction that this was a nightmare. He rarely made appointments with anyone and certainly not with young ladies for nine o'clock in the morning. And particularly not with unmarried young ladies. 'Miss Twinning?' The name rang no bells. Not even a rattle.

'Yes, Your Grace.' Masterton returned to the bed, various garments draped on his arm, a deep blue coat lovingly displayed for approval. 'The Bath superfine would, I think, be most appropriate?'

Yielding to the inevitable with a groan, Max sat up.

One floor below, Caroline Twinning sat calmly reading His Grace of Twyford's morning paper in an armchair by his library hearth. If she felt any qualms over the propriety of her present position, she hid them well. Her charmingly candid countenance was free of all nervousness and, as she scanned a frankly libellous account of a garden party enlivened by the scandalous propensities of the ageing Duke of Cumberland, an engaging smile curved her generous lips. In truth, she was looking forward to her meeting with the Duke. She and her sisters had spent a most enjoyable eighteen months, the wine of freedom a heady tonic after their previously monastic existence. But it was time and more for them to embark on the serious business of securing their futures. To do that, they needs must enter the *ton*, that glittering arena thus far denied them. And, for them, the Duke of Twyford undeniably held the key to that particular door.

Hearing the tread of a masculine stride approach the library door, Caroline raised her head, then smiled confidently. Thank heavens the Duke was so easy to manage.

By the time he reached the ground floor, Max had exhausted every possible excuse for the existence of the mysterious Miss Twinning. He had taken little time to dress, having no need to employ extravagant embellishments to distract attention from his long and powerful frame. His broad shoulders and muscular thighs perfectly suited the prevailing fashion. His superbly cut coats looked as though they had been moulded on to him and his buckskin breeches showed not a crease. The understated waistcoat, perfectly tied cravat and shining topboots which completed the picture were the envy of many an aspiring exquisite. His hair, black as night, was neatly cropped to frame a dark face on which the years had left nothing more than a trace of worldly cynicism. Disdaining the ornamentation common to the times, His Grace of Twyford wore no ring other than a gold signet on his left hand and displayed no fobs or seals. In spite of this, no one setting eyes on him could imagine he was other than he was—one of the most fashionable and wealthy men in the *ton*.

He entered his library, a slight frown in the depths of his midnight-blue eyes. His attention was drawn by a flash of movement as the young lady who had been calmly reading his copy of the morning's *Gazette* in his favourite armchair by the hearth folded the paper and laid it aside, before rising to face him. Max halted, blue eyes suddenly intent, all trace of displeasure vanishing as he surveyed his unexpected visitor. His nightmare had transmogrified into a dream. The vision before him was unquestionably a houri. For a number of moments he remained frozen in rapturous contemplation. Then, his rational mind reasserted itself. Not a houri. Houris did not read the *Gazette*. At least, not in his library at nine o'clock in the morning. From the unruly copper curls clustering around her face to the tips of her tiny slippers, showing tantalisingly from under the simply cut and outrageously fashionable gown, there was nothing with which he could find fault. She was built on generous lines, a tall Junoesque figure, deep-bosomed and wide-hipped, but all in the most perfect proportions. Her apricot silk gown did justice to her ample charms, clinging suggestively to a figure of Grecian delight. When his eyes returned to her face, he had time to take in the straight nose and full lips and the dimple that peeked irrepressibly from one cheek before his gaze was drawn to the finely arched brows and long lashes which framed her large eyes. It was only when he looked into the cool grey-green orbs that he saw the twinkle of amusement lurking there. Unused to provoking such a response, he frowned.

'Who, exactly, are you?' His voice, he was pleased to find, was even and his diction clear.

The smile which had been hovering at the corners of those inviting lips finally came into being, disclosing a row of small pearly teeth. But instead of answering his question, the vision replied, 'I was waiting for the Duke of Twyford.'

Her voice was low and musical. Mentally engaged in considering how to most rapidly dispense with the formalities, Max answered automatically. 'I am the Duke.'

'You?' For one long moment, utter bewilderment was writ large across her delightful countenance.

For the life of her, Caroline could not hide her surprise. How could this man, of all men, be the Duke? Aside from the fact he was far too young to have been a crony of her father's, the gentleman before her was unquestionably a rake. And a rake of the first order, to boot. Whether the dark-browed, harsh-featured face with its aquiline nose and firm mouth and chin or the lazy assurance with which he had entered the room had contributed to her reading of his character, she could not have said. But the calmly arrogant way his intensely blue eyes had roved from the top of her curls all the way down to her feet, and then just as calmly returned by the same route, as if to make sure he had missed nothing, left her in little doubt of what sort of man she now faced. Secure in the knowledge of being under her guardian's roof, she had allowed the amusement she felt on seeing such decided appreciation glow in the deep blue eyes to show. Now, with those same blue eyes still on her, piercingly perceptive, she felt as if the rug had been pulled from beneath her feet.

Max could hardly miss her stunned look. 'For my sins,' he added in confirmation.

With a growing sense of unease, he waved his visitor to a seat opposite the huge mahogany desk while he moved to take the chair behind it. As he did so, he mentally shook his head to try to clear it of the thoroughly unhelpful thoughts that kept crowding in. Damn Carmelita!

Caroline, rapidly trying to gauge where this latest disconcerting news left her, came forward to sink into the chair indicated.

Outwardly calm, Max watched the unconsciously graceful glide of her walk, the seductive swing of her hips as she sat down. He would have to find a replacement for Carmelita. His gaze rested speculatively on the beauty before him. Hillshaw had been right. She was unquestionably a lady. Still, that had never stopped him before. And, now he came to look more closely, she was not, he thought, that young. Even better. No rings, which was odd. Another twinge of pain from behind his eyes lent a harshness to his voice. 'Who the devil are you?'

The dimple peeped out again. In no way discomposed, she answered, 'My name is Caroline Twinning. And, if you really are the Duke of Twyford, then I'm very much afraid I'm your ward.'

Her announcement was received in perfect silence.

A long pause ensued, during which Max sat unmoving, his sharp blue gaze fixed unwaveringly on his visitor. She bore this scrutiny for some minutes, before letting her brows rise in polite and still amused enquiry.

Max closed his eyes and groaned. 'Oh, God!'

It had only taken a moment to work it out. The only woman he could not seduce was his own ward. And he had already decided he very definitely wanted to seduce Caroline Twinning. With an effort, he dragged his mind back to the matter at hand. He opened his eyes. Hopefully, she would put his reaction down to natural disbelief. Encountering the grey-green eyes, now even more amused, he was not so sure. 'Explain, if you please. Simple language only. I'm not up to unravelling mysteries at the moment.'

Caroline could not help grinning. She had noticed twinges of what she guessed to be pain passing spasmodically through the blue eyes. 'If your head hurts that much, why don't you try an ice-pack? I assure you I won't mind.'

Max threw her a look of loathing. His head felt as if it was splitting, but how dared she be so lost to all propriety as to notice, let alone mention it? Still, she was perfectly right. An ice-pack was exactly what he needed. With a darkling look, he reached for the bell pull.

Hillshaw came in answer to his summons and received the order for an ice-pack without noticeable perturbation. 'Now, Your Grace?'

'Of course now! What use will it be later?' Max winced at the sound of his own voice.

'As Your Grace wishes.' The sepulchral tones left Max in no doubt of his butler's deep disapproval.

As the door closed behind Hillshaw, Max lay back in the chair, his fingers at his temples, and fixed

Caroline with an unwavering stare. 'You may commence.'

She smiled, entirely at her ease once more. 'My father was Sir Thomas Twinning. He was an old friend of the Duke of Twyford—the previous Duke, I imagine.'

Max nodded. 'My uncle. I inherited the title from him. He was killed unexpectedly three months ago, together with his two sons. I never expected to inherit the estate, so am unfamiliar with whatever arrangements your parent may have made with the last Duke.'

Caroline nodded and waited until Hillshaw, delivering the requested ice-pack on a silver salver to his master, withdrew. 'I see. When my father died eighteen months ago, my sisters and I were informed that he had left us to the guardianship of the Duke of Twyford.'

'Eighteen months ago? What have you been doing since then?'

'We stayed on the estate for a time. It passed to a distant cousin and he was prepared to let us remain. But it seemed senseless to stay buried there forever. The Duke wanted us to join his household immediately, but we were in mourning. I persuaded him to let us go to my late stepmother's family in New York. They'd always wanted us to visit and it seemed the perfect opportunity. I wrote to him when we were in New York, telling him we would call on him when we returned to England and giving him the date of our expected arrival. He replied and suggested I call on him today. And so, here I am.'

Max saw it all now. Caroline Twinning was yet another part of his damnably awkward inheritance. Having led a life of unfettered hedonism from his earliest days, a rakehell ever since he came on the town, Max had soon understood that his lifestyle required capital to support it. So he had ensured his estates were all run efficiently and well. The Delmere estates he had inherited from his father were a model of modern estate management. But his uncle Henry had never had much real interest in his far larger holdings. After the tragic boating accident which had unexpectedly foisted on to him the responsibilities of the dukedom of Twyford, Max had found a complete overhaul of all his uncle's numerous estates was essential if they were not to sap the strength from his more prosperous Delmere holdings. The last three months had been spent in constant upheaval, with the old Twyford retainers trying to come to grips with the new Duke and his very different style. For Max, they had been three months of unending work. Only this week, he had finally thought that the end of the worst was in sight. He had packed his long-suffering secretary, Joshua Cummings, off home for a much needed rest. And now, quite clearly, the next chapter in the saga of his Twyford inheritance was about to start.

'You mentioned sisters. How many?'

'My half-sisters, really. There are four of us, altogether.'

The lightness of the answer made Max instantly suspicious. 'How old?'

There was a noticeable hesitation before Caroline answered, 'Twenty, nineteen and eighteen.'

The effect on Max was electric. 'Good lord! They didn't accompany you here, did they?'

Bewildered, Caroline replied, 'No. I left them at the hotel.'

'Thank God for that,' said Max. Encountering Caroline's enquiring gaze, he smiled. 'If anyone had seen them entering here, it would have been around town in a flash that I was setting up a harem.'

The smile made Caroline blink. At his words, her grey eyes widened slightly. She could hardly pretend not to understand. Noticing the peculiar light in the blue eyes as they rested on her, it suddenly seemed a very good thing she was the Duke's ward. From her admittedly small understanding of the morals of his type, she suspected her position would keep her safe as little else might.

Unbeknown to her, Max was thinking precisely the same thing. And resolving to divest himself of this latest inherited responsibility with all possible speed. Aside from having no wish whatever to figure as the guardian of four young ladies of marriageable age, he needed to clear the obstacles from his path to Caroline Twinning. It occurred to him that her explanation of her life history had been curiously glib and decidedly short on detail. 'Start at the beginning. Who was your mother and when did she die?'

Caroline had come unprepared to recite her history, imaging the Duke to be cognisant of the facts. Still, in the circumstances, she could hardly refuse. 'My mother was Caroline Farningham, of the Staffordshire Farninghams.'

Max nodded. An ancient family, well known and well connected.

Caroline's gaze had wandered to the rows of books lining the shelves behind the Duke. 'She died shortly after I was born. I never knew her. After some years, my father married again, this time to the daughter of a local family who were about to leave for the colonies. Eleanor was very good to me and she looked after all of us comfortably, until she died six years ago. Of course, my father was disappointed that he never had a son and he rarely paid any attention to the four of us, so it was all left up to Eleanor.'

The more he heard of him, the more Max was

convinced that Sir Thomas Twinning had had a screw loose. He had clearly been a most unnatural parent. Still, the others were only Miss Twinning's half-sisters. Presumably they were not all as ravishing as she. It occurred to him that he should ask for clarification on this point but, before he could properly phrase the question, another and equally intriguing matter came to mind.

'Why was it none of you was presented before? If your father was sufficiently concerned to organise a guardian for you, surely the easiest solution would have been to have handed you into the care of husbands?'

Caroline saw no reason not to satisfy what was, after all, an entirely understandable curiosity. 'We were never presented because my father disapproved of such. . .oh, frippery pastimes! To be perfectly honest, I sometimes thought he disapproved of women in general.'

Max blinked.

Caroline continued, 'As for marriage, he had organised that after a fashion. I was supposed to have married Edgar Mulhall, our neighbour.' Involuntarily, her face assumed an expression of distaste.

Max was amused. 'Wouldn't he do?'

Caroline's gaze returned to the saturnine face. 'You haven't met him or you wouldn't need to ask. He's. . .' She wrinkled her nose as she sought for an adequate description. 'Righteous,' she finally pronounced.

At that, Max laughed. 'Clearly out of the question.'

Caroline ignored the provocation in the blue eyes. 'Papa had similar plans for my sisters, only, as he never noticed they were of marriageable age and I never chose to bring it to his attention, nothing came of them either.'

Perceiving Miss Twinning's evident satisfaction,

Max made a mental note to beware of her manipulative tendencies. 'Very well. So much for the past. Now to the future. What was your arrangement with my uncle?'

The green-grey gaze was entirely innocent as it rested on his face. Max did not know whether to believe it or not.

'Well, it was really his idea, but it seemed a perfectly sensible one to me. He suggested we should be presented to the *ton*. I suspect he intended us to find suitable husbands and so bring his guardianship to an end.' She paused, thinking. 'I'm not aware of the terms of my father's will, but I assume such arrangements terminate should we marry?'

'Very likely,' agreed Max. The throbbing in his head had eased considerably. His uncle's plan had much to recommend it, but, personally, he would much prefer not to have any wards at all. And he would be damned if he would have Miss Twinning as his ward—that would cramp his style far too much. There were a few things even reprobates such as he held sacred and guardianship was one.

He knew she was watching him but made no further comment, his eyes fixed frowningly on his blotter as he considered his next move. At last, looking up at her, he said, 'I've heard nothing of this until now. I'll have to get my solicitors to sort it out. Which firm handles your affairs?'

'Whitney and White. In Chancery Lane.'

'Well, at least that simplifies matters. They handle the Twyford estates as well as my others.' He laid the ice-pack down and looked at Caroline, a slight frown in his blue eyes. 'Where are you staying?'

'Grillon's. We arrived yesterday.'

Another thought occurred to Max. 'On what have you been living for the last eighteen months?'

'Oh, we all had money left us by our mothers. We arranged to draw on that and leave our patrimony untouched.'

Max nodded slowly. 'But who has you in charge? You can't have travelled halfway around the world alone.'

For the first time during this strange interview, Max saw Miss Twinning blush, ever so slightly. 'Our maid and coachman, who acted as our courier, stayed with us.'

The airiness of the reply did not deceive Max. 'Allow me to comment, Miss Twinning, as your potential guardian, that such an arrangement will not do. Regardless of what may have been acceptable overseas, such a situation will certainly not pass muster in London.' He paused, considering the proprieties for what was surely the first time in his life. 'At least you're at Grillon's for the moment. That's safe enough.'

After another pause, during which his gaze did not leave Caroline's face, he said, 'I'll see Whitney this morning and settle the matter. I'll call on you at two to let you know how things have fallen out.' A vision of himself meeting a beautiful young lady and attempting to converse with her within the portals of fashionable Grillon's, under the fascinated gaze of all the other patrons, flashed before his eyes. 'On second thoughts, I'll take you for a drive in the Park. That way,' he continued in reply to the question in her grey-green eyes, 'we might actually get a chance to talk.'

He tugged the bell pull and Hillshaw appeared. 'Have the carriage brought around. Miss Twinning is returning to Grillon's.'

'Yes, Your Grace.'

'Oh, no! I couldn't put you to so much trouble,' said Caroline.

'My dear child,' drawled Max, 'my wards would certainly not go about London in hacks. See to it, Hillshaw.'

'Yes, Your Grace.' Hillshaw withdrew, for once in perfect agreement with his master.

Caroline found the blue eyes, which had quizzed her throughout this exchange, still regarding her, a gently mocking light in their depths. But she was a lady of no little courage and smiled back serenely, unknowingly sealing her fate.

Never, thought Max, had he met a woman so attractive. One way or another, he would break the ties of guardianship. A short silence fell, punctuated by the steady ticking of the long case clock in the corner. Max took the opportunity afforded by Miss Twinning's apparent fascination with the rows of leather-bound tomes at his back to study her face once more. A fresh face, full of lively humour and a brand of calm self-possession which, in his experience, was rarely found in young women. Undoubtedly a woman of character.

His sharp ears caught the sound of carriage wheels in the street. He rose and Caroline perforce rose too. 'Come, Miss Twinning. Your carriage awaits.'

Max led her to the front door but forbore to go any further, bowing over her hand gracefully before allowing Hillshaw to escort her to the waiting carriage. The less chance there was for anyone to see him with her the better. At least until he had solved this guardianship tangle.

As soon as the carriage door was shut by the majestic Hillshaw, the horses moved forward at a trot. Caroline lay back against the squabs, her gaze fixed unseeingly on the near-side window as the carriage traversed fashionable London. Bemused, she tried to gauge the effect of the unexpected turn their futures had taken. Imagine having a guardian like that!

Although surprised at being redirected from Twyford House to Delmere House, she had still expected to meet the vague and amenable gentleman who had so readily acquiesced, albeit by correspondence, to all her previous suggestions. Her mental picture of His Grace of Twyford had been of a man in late middle age, bewigged as many of her father's generation were, distinctly past his prime and with no real interest in dealing with four lively young women. She spared a small smile as she jettisoned her preconceived image. Instead of a comfortable, fatherly figure, she would now have to deal with a man who, if first impressions were anything to go by, was intelligent, quick-witted and far too perceptive for her liking. To imagine the new Duke would not know to a nicety how to manage four young women was patently absurd. If she had been forced to express an opinion, Caroline would have said that, with the present Duke of Twyford, managing women was a speciality. Furthermore, given his undoubted experience, she strongly suspected he would be highly resistant to feminine cajoling in any form. A frown clouded her grey-green eyes. She was not entirely sure she approved of the twist their fates had taken. Thinking back over the recent interview, she smiled. He had not seemed too pleased with the idea himself.

For a moment, she considered the possibility of coming to some agreement with the Duke, essentially breaking the guardianship clause of her father's will. But only for a moment. It was true she had never been presented to the *ton* but she had cut her social eye-teeth long ago. While the idea of unlimited freedom to do as they pleased might sound tempting, there was the undeniable fact that she and her half-sisters were heiresses of sorts. Her father, having an extremely repressive notion of the degree of knowledge which could be allowed mere females, had never been particularly forthcoming regarding their eventual state. Yet there had never been any shortage of funds in all the years Caroline could remember. She rather thought they would at least be comfortably dowered. Such being the case, the traps and pitfalls of society, without the protection of a guardian, such as the Duke of Twyford, were not experiences to which she would willingly expose her sisters.

As the memory of a certain glint in His Grace of Twyford's eye and the distinctly determined set of his jaw drifted past her mind's eye, the unwelcome possibility that he might repudiate them, for whatever reasons, hove into view. Undoubtedly, if there was any way to overset their guardianship, His Grace would find it. Unaccountably, she was filled with an inexplicable sense of disappointment.

Still, she told herself, straightening in a purposeful way, it was unlikely there was anything he could do about it. And she rather thought they would be perfectly safe with the new Duke of Twyford, as long as they *were* his wards. She allowed her mind to dwell on the question of whether she really wanted to be safe from the Duke of Twyford for several minutes before giving herself a mental shake. Great heavens! She had only just met the man and here she was, mooning over him like a green girl! She tried to frown but the action dissolved into a sheepish grin at her own susceptibility. Settling more comfortably in the corner of the luxurious carriage, she fell to rehearsing her description of what had occurred in anticipation of her sisters' eager questions.

* * *

Within minutes of Caroline Twinning's departure from Delmere House, Max had issued a succession of orders, one of which caused Mr Hubert Whitney, son of Mr Josiah Whitney, the patriarch of the firm Whitney and White, Solicitors, of Chancery Lane, to present himself at Delmere House just before eleven. Mr Whitney was a dry, desiccated man of uncertain age, very correctly attired in dusty black. He was his father's son in every way and, now that his sire was no longer able to leave his bed, he attended to all his father's wealthier clients. As Hillshaw showed him into the well appointed library, he breathed a sigh of relief, not for the first time, that it was Max Rotherbridge who had inherited the difficult Twyford estates. Unknown to Max, Mr Whitney held him in particular esteem, frequently wishing that others among his clients could be equally straightforward and decisive. It really made life so much easier.

Coming face to face with his favourite client, Mr Whitney was immediately informed that His Grace, the Duke of Twyford, was in no way amused to find he was apparently the guardian of four marriageable young ladies. Mr Whitney was momentarily at a loss. Luckily, he had brought with him all the current Twyford papers and the Twinning documents were among these. Finding that his employer did not intend to upbraid him for not having informed him of a circumstance which, he was only too well aware, he should have brought forward long ago, he applied himself to assessing the terms of the late Sir Thomas Twinning's will. Having refreshed his memory on its details, he then turned to the late Duke's will.

Max stood by the fire, idly watching. He liked Whitney. He did not fluster and he knew his business.

Finally, Mr Whitney pulled the gold pince-nez from his face and glanced at his client. 'Sir Thomas

Twinning predeceased your uncle, and, under the terms of your uncle's will, it's quite clear you inherit all his responsibilities.'

Max's black brows had lowered. 'So I'm stuck with this guardianship?'

Mr Whitney pursed his lips. 'I wouldn't go so far as to say that. The guardianship could be broken, I fancy, as it's quite clear Sir Thomas did not intend you, personally, to be his daughters' guardian.' He gazed at the fire and solemnly shook his head. 'No one, I'm sure, could doubt that.'

Max smiled wryly.

'However,' Mr Whitney continued, 'should you succeed in dissolving the guardianship clause, then the young ladies will be left with no protector. Did I understand you correctly in thinking they are presently in London and plan to remain for the Season?'

It did not need a great deal of intelligence to see where Mr Whitney's discourse was heading. Exasperated at having his usually comfortably latent conscience pricked into life, Max stalked to the window and stood looking out at the courtyard beyond, hands clasped behind his straight back. 'Good God, man! You can hardly think I'm a suitable guardian for four sweet young things!'

Mr Whitney, thinking the Duke could manage very well if he chose to do so, persevered. 'There remains the question of who, in your stead, would act for them.'

The certain knowledge of what would occur if he abandoned four inexperienced, gently reared girls to the London scene, to the mercies of the well-bred wolves who roamed its streets, crystallised in Max's unwilling mind. This was closely followed by the uncomfortable thought that he was considered the leader of one such pack, generally held to be the most dangerous. He could hardly refuse to be Caroline Twinning's guardian, only to set her up as his mistress. No. There was a limit to what even he could face down. Resolutely thrusting aside the memory, still vivid, of a pair of grey-green eyes, he turned to Mr Whitney and growled, 'All right, dammit! What do I need to know?'

Mr Whitney smiled benignly and started to fill him in on the Twinning family history, much as Caroline had told it. Max interrupted him. 'Yes, I know all that! Just tell me in round figures—how much is each of them worth?'

Mr Whitney named a figure and Max's brows rose. For a moment, the Duke was entirely bereft of speech. He moved towards his desk and seated himself again. 'Each?'

Mr Whitney merely inclined his head in assent. When the Duke remained lost in thought, he continued, 'Sir Thomas was a very shrewd businessman, Your Grace.'

'So it would appear. So each of these girls is an heiress in her own right?'

This time, Mr Whitney nodded decisively.

Max was frowning.

'Of course,' Mr Whitney went on, consulting the documents on his knee, 'you would only be responsible for the three younger girls.'

Instantly, he had his client's attention, the blue eyes oddly piercing. 'Oh? Why is that?'

'Under the terms of their father's will, the Misses Twinning were given into the care of the Duke of Twyford until they attained the age of twenty-five or married. According to my records, I believe Miss Twinning to be nearing her twenty-sixth birthday. So she could, should she wish, assume responsibility for herself.'

Max's relief was palpable. But hard on its heels came another consideration. Caroline Twinning had recognised his interest in her—hardly surprising as he had taken no pains to hide it. If she knew he was not her guardian, she would keep him at arm's length. Well, try to, at least. But Caroline Twinning was not a green girl. The aura of quiet self-assurance which clung to her suggested she would not be an easy conquest. Obviously, it would be preferable if she continued to believe she was protected from him by his guardianship. That way, he would have no difficulty in approaching her, his reputation notwithstanding. In fact, the more he thought of it, the more merits he could see in the situation. Perhaps, in this case, he could have his cake and eat it too? He eyed Mr Whitney. 'Miss Twinning knows nothing of thc terms of her father's will. At present, she believes herself to be my ward, along with her half-sisters. Is there any pressing need to inform her of her change in status?'

Mr Whitney blinked owlishly, a considering look suffusing his face as he attempted to unravel the Duke's motives for wanting Miss Twinning to remain as his ward. Particularly after wanting to dissolve the guardianship altogether. Max Rotherbridge did not normally vacillate.

Max, perfectly sensible of Mr Whitney's thoughts, put forward the most acceptable excuses he could think of. 'For a start, whether she's twenty-four or twenty-six, she's just as much in need of protection as her sisters. Then, too, there's the question of propriety. If it was generally known she was not my ward, it would be exceedingly difficult for her to be seen in my company. And as I'll still be guardian to her sisters, and as they'll be residing in one of my establishments, the situation could become a trifle delicate, don't you think?'

It was not necessary for him to elaborate. Mr Whitney saw the difficulty clearly enough. It was his turn to frown. 'What you say is quite true.' Hubert Whitney had no opinion whatever of the ability of young ladies to manage their affairs. 'At present, there is nothing I can think of that requires Miss Twinning's agreement. I expect it can do no harm to leave her in ignorance of her status until she weds.'

The mention of marriage brought a sudden check to Max's racing mind but he resolutely put the disturbing notion aside for later examination. He had too much to do today.

Mr Whitney was continuing, 'How do you plan to handle the matter, if I may make so bold as to ask?'

Max had already given the thorny problem of how four young ladies could be presented to the *ton* under his protection, without raising a storm, some thought. 'I propose to open up Twyford House immediately. They can stay there. I intend to ask my aunt, Lady Benborough, to stand as the girls' sponsor. I'm sure she'll be only too thrilled. It'll keep her amused for the Season.'

Mr Whitney was acquainted with Lady Benborough. He rather thought it would. A smile curved his thin lips.

The Duke stood, bringing the interview to a close.

Mr Whitney rose. 'That seems most suitable. If there's anything further in which we can assist Your Grace, we'll be only too delighted.'

Max nodded in response to this formal statement. As Mr Whitney bowed, preparing to depart, Max, a past master of social intrigue, saw one last hole in the wall and moved to block it. 'If there's any matter you wish to discuss with Miss Twinning, I suggest you do it through me, as if I was, in truth, her guardian. As you handle both our estates, there can really be no impropriety in keeping up appearances. For Miss Twinning's sake.'

Mr Whitney bowed again. 'I foresee no problems, Your Grace.'

CHAPTER TWO

AFTER Mr Whitney left, Max issued a set of rapid and comprehensive orders to his major-domo Wilson. In response, his servants flew to various corners of London, some to Twyford House, others to certain agencies specialising in the hire of household staff to the élite of the *ton*. One footman was despatched with a note from the Duke to an address in Half Moon Street, requesting the favour of a private interview with his paternal aunt, Lady Benborough.

As Max had intended, his politely worded missive intrigued his aunt. Wondering what had prompted such a strange request from her reprehensible nephew, she immediately granted it and settled down to await his coming with an air of pleasurable anticipation.

Max arrived at the small house shortly after noon. He found his aunt attired in a very becoming gown of purple sarsenet with a new and unquestionably modish wig perched atop her commanding visage. Max, bowing elegantly before her, eyed the wig askance.

Augusta Benborough sighed. 'Well, I suppose I'll have to send it back, if that's the way you feel about it!'

Max grinned and bent to kiss the proffered cheek. 'Definitely not one of your better efforts, Aunt.'

She snorted. 'Unfortunately, I can hardly claim you know nothing about it. It's the very latest fashion, I'll have you know.' Max raised one laconic brow. 'Yes, well,' continued his aunt, 'I dare say you're right. Not quite my style.'

As she waited while he disposed his long limbs in a

chair opposite the corner of the chaise where she sat, propped up by a pile of colourful cushions, she passed a critical glance over her nephew's elegant figure. How he contrived to look so precise when she knew he cared very little how he appeared was more than she could tell. She had heard it said that his man was a genius. Personally, she was of the opinion it was Max's magnificent physique and dark good looks that carried the day.

'I hope you're going to satisfy my curiosity without a great deal of roundaboutation.'

'My dear aunt, when have I ever been other than direct?'

She looked at him shrewdly. 'Want a favour, do you? Can't imagine what it is but you'd better be quick about asking. Miriam will be back by one and I gather you'd rather not have her listening.' Miriam Alford was a faded spinster cousin of Lady Benborough's who lived with her, filling the post of companion to the fashionable old lady. 'I sent her to Hatchard's when I got your note,' she added in explanation.

Max smiled. Of all his numerous relatives, his Aunt Benborough, his father's youngest sister, was his favourite. While the rest of them, his mother included, constantly tried to reform him by ringing peals over him, appealing to his sense of what was acceptable, something he steadfastly denied any knowledge of, Augusta Benborough rarely made any comment on his lifestyle or the numerous scandals this provoked. When he had first come on the town, it had rapidly been made plain to his startled family that in Max they beheld a reincarnation of the second Viscount Delmere. If even half the tales were true, Max's great-grandfather had been a thoroughly unprincipled character, entirely devoid of morals. Lady Benborough, recently widowed, had asked Max to tea and had taken the opportunity to inform him in no uncertain terms of her opinion of his behaviour. She had then proceeded to outline all his faults, in detail. However, as she had concluded by saying that she fully expected her tirade to have no effect whatsoever on his subsequent conduct, nor could she imagine how anyone in their right mind could think it would, Max had borne the ordeal with an equanimity which would have stunned his friends. She had eventually dismissed him with the words, 'Having at least had the politeness to hear me out, you may now depart and continue to go to hell in your own fashion with my good will.'

Now a widow of many years' standing, she was still a force to be reckoned with. She remained fully absorbed in the affairs of the *ton* and continued to be seen at all the crushes and every gala event. Max knew she was as shrewd as she could hold together and, above all, had an excellent sense of humour. All in all, she was just what he needed.

'I've come to inform you that, along with all the other encumbrances I inherited from Uncle Henry, I seem to have acquired four wards.'

'*You*?' Lady Benborough's rendering of the word was rather more forceful than Miss Twinning's had been.

Max nodded. 'Me. Four young ladies, one, the only one I've so far set eyes on, as lovely a creature as any other likely to be presented this Season.'

'Good God! Who was so besotted as to leave four young girls in your care?' If anything, her ladyship was outraged at the very idea. Then, the full impact of the situation struck her. Her eyes widened. 'Oh, good lord!' She collapsed against her cushions, laughing uncontrollably.

Knowing this was an attitude he was going to meet

increasingly in the next few weeks, Max sighed. In an even tone suggestive of long suffering, he pointed out the obvious. 'They weren't left to me but to my esteemed and now departed uncle's care. Mind you, I can't see that he'd have been much use to 'em either.'

Wiping the tears from her eyes, Lady Benborough considered this view. 'Can't see it myself,' she admitted. 'Henry always was a slow-top. Who are they?'

'The Misses Twinning. From Hertfordshire.' Max proceeded to give her a brief résumé of the life history of the Twinnings, ending with the information that it transpired all four girls were heiresses.

Augusta Benborough was taken aback. 'And you say they're beautiful to boot?'

'The one I've seen, Caroline, the eldest, most definitely is.'

'Well, if anyone should know it's you!' replied her ladyship testily. Max acknowledged the comment with the slightest inclination of his head.

Lady Benborough's mind was racing. 'So, what do you want with me?'

'What I would *like*, dearest Aunt,' said Max, with his sweetest smile, 'is for you to act as chaperon to the girls and present them to the *ton*.' Max paused. His aunt said nothing, sitting quite still with her sharp blue eyes, very like his own, fixed firmly on his face. He continued, 'I'm opening up Twyford House. It'll be ready for them tomorrow. I'll stand the nonsense—all of it.' Still she said nothing. 'Will you do it?'

Augusta Benborough thought she would like nothing better than to be part of the hurly-burly of the marriage game again. But four? All at once? Still, there was Max's backing, and that would count for a good deal. Despite his giving the distinct impression of total uninterest in anything other than his own pleasure, she knew from experience that, should he feel inclined, Max could and would perform feats impossible for those with lesser clout in the fashionable world. Years after the event, she had learned that, when her youngest son had embroiled himself in a scrape so hideous that even now she shuddered to think of it, it had been Max who had rescued him. And apparently for no better reason than that it had been bothering her. She still owed him for that.

But there were problems. Her own small jointure was not particularly large and, while she had never asked Max for relief, turning herself out in the style he would expect of his wards' chaperon was presently beyond her slender means. Hesitantly, she said, 'My own wardrobe. . .'

'Naturally you'll charge all costs you incur in this business to me,' drawled Max, his voice bored as he examined through his quizzing glass a china cat presently residing on his aunt's mantelpiece. He knew perfectly well his aunt managed on a very slim purse but was too wise to offer direct assistance which would, he knew, be resented, not only by the lady herself but also by her pompous elder son.

'Can I take Miriam with me to Twyford House?'

With a shrug, Max assented. 'Aside from anything else, she might come in handy with four charges.'

'When can I meet them?'

'They're staying at Grillon's. I'm taking Miss Twinning for a drive this afternoon to tell her what I've decided. I'll arrange for them to move to Twyford House tomorrow afternoon. I'll send Wilson to help you and Mrs Alford in transferring to Mount Street. It would be best, I suppose, if you could make the move in the morning. You'll want to familiarise yourself with the staff and so on.' Bethinking himself that it would be wise to have one of his own well trained staff on hand, he added, 'I suppose I can let you have

Wilson for a week or two, until you settle in. I suggest you and I meet the Misses Twinning when they arrive—shall we say at three?'

Lady Benborough was entranced by the way her nephew seemed to dismiss complications like opening and staffing a mansion overnight. Still, with the efficient and reliable Wilson on the job, presumably it would be done. Feeling a sudden and unexpected surge of excitement at the prospect of embarking on the Season with a definite purpose in life, she drew a deep breath. 'Very well. I'll do it!'

'Good!' Max stood. 'I'll send Wilson to call on you this afternoon.'

His aunt, already engrossed in the matter of finding husbands for the Twinning chits, looked up. 'Have you seen the other three girls?'

Max shook his head. Imagining the likely scene should they be on hand this afternoon when he called for Miss Twinning, he closed his eyes in horror. He could just hear the *on-dits*. 'And I hope to God I don't see them in Grillon's foyer either!'

Augusta Benborough laughed.

When he called at Grillon's promptly at two, Max was relieved to find Miss Twinning alone in the foyer, seated on a chaise opposite the door, her bonnet beside her. He was not to know that Caroline had had to exert every last particle of persuasion to achieve this end. And she had been quite unable to prevent her three sisters from keeping watch from the windows of their bedchambers.

As she had expected, she had had to describe His Grace of Twyford in detail for her sisters. Looking up at the figure striding across the foyer towards her, she did not think she had done too badly. What had been hardest to convey was the indefinable air that hung about him—compelling, exciting, it immediately brought to mind a whole range of emotions well bred young ladies were not supposed to comprehend, let alone feel. As he took her hand for an instant in his own, and smiled down at her in an oddly lazy way, she decided she had altogether underestimated the attractiveness of that sleepy smile. It was really quite devastating.

Within a minute, Caroline found herself on the box seat of a fashionable curricle drawn by a pair of beautiful but restive bays. She resisted the temptation to glance up at the first-floor windows where she knew the other three would be stationed. Max mounted to the driving seat and the diminutive tiger, who had been holding the horses' heads, swung up behind. Then they were off, tacking through the traffic towards Hyde Park.

Caroline resigned herself to silence until the safer precincts of the Park were reached. However, it seemed the Duke was quite capable of conversing intelligently while negotiating the chaos of the London streets.

'I trust Grillon's has met with your approval thus far?'

'Oh, yes. They've been most helpful,' returned Caroline. 'Were you able to clarify the matter of our guardianship?'

Max was unable to suppress a smile at her directness. He nodded, his attention temporarily claimed by the off-side horse which had decided to take exception to a monkey dancing on the pavement, accompanied by an accordion player.

'Mr Whitney has assured me that, as I am the Duke of Twyford, I must therefore be your guardian.' He had allowed his reluctance to find expression in his tone. As the words left his lips, he realised that the unconventional woman beside him might well ask why he found the role of protector to herself and her sisters so distasteful. He immediately went on the attack. 'And, in that capacity, I should like to know how you have endeavoured to come by Parisian fashions?'

His sharp eyes missed little and his considerable knowledge of feminine attire told him Miss Twinning's elegant pelisse owed much to the French. But France was at war with England and Paris no longer the playground of the rich.

Initially stunned that he should know enough to come so close to the truth, Caroline quickly realised the source of his knowledge. A spark of amusement danced in her eyes. She smiled and answered readily, 'I assure you we did not run away to Brussels instead of New York.'

'Oh, I wasn't afraid of that!' retorted Max, perfectly willing to indulge in plain speaking. 'If you'd been in Brussels, I'd have heard of it.'

'Oh?' Caroline turned a fascinated gaze on him.

Max smiled down at her.

Praying she was not blushing, Caroline strove to get the conversation back on a more conventional course. 'Actually, you're quite right about the clothes, they are Parisian. But not from the Continent. There were two *couturières* from Paris on the boat going to New York. They asked if they could dress us, needing the business to become known in America. It was really most fortunate. We took the opportunity to get quite a lot made up before we returned—we'd been in greys for so long that none of us had anything suitable to wear.'

'How did you find American society?'

Caroline reminded herself to watch her tongue. She did not delude herself that just because the Duke was engaged in handling a team of high-couraged cattle through the busy streets of London he was likely to miss any slip she made. She was rapidly learning to respect the intelligence of this fashionable rake. 'Quite frankly, we found much to entertain us. Of course, our relatives were pleased to see us and organised a great many outings and entertainments.' No need to tell him they had had a riotous time.

'Did the tone of the society meet with your approval?'

He had already told her he would have known if they had been in Europe. Did he have connections in New York? How much could he know of their junketing? Caroline gave herself a mental shake. How absurd! He had not known of their existence until this morning. 'Well, to be sure, it wasn't the same as here. Many more cits and half-pay officers about. And, of course, nothing like the *ton*.'

Unknowingly, her answer brought some measure of relief to Max. Far from imagining his new-found wards had been indulging in high living abroad, he had been wondering whether they had any social experience at all. Miss Twinning's reply told him that she, at least, knew enough to distinguish the less acceptable among society's hordes.

They had reached the gates of the Park and turned into the carriage drive. Soon, the curricle was bowling along at a steady pace under the trees, still devoid of any but the earliest leaves. A light breeze lifted the ends of the ribbons on Caroline's hat and playfully danced along the horses' dark manes.

Max watched as Caroline gazed about her with interest. 'I'm afraid you'll not see many notables at this hour. Mostly nursemaids and their charges. Later, between three and five, it'll be crowded. The Season's not yet begun in earnest, but by now most people will have returned to town. And the Park is the place to be seen. All the old biddies come here to exchange the latest *on-dits* and all the young ladies promenade along the walks with their beaux.'

'I see.' Caroline smiled to herself, a secret smile as she imagined how she and her sisters would fit into this scene.

Max saw the smile and was puzzled. Caroline Twinning was decidedly more intelligent than the women with whom he normally consorted. He could not guess her thoughts and was secretly surprised at wanting to know them. Then, he remembered one piece of vital information he had yet to discover. 'Apropos of my uncle's plan to marry you all off, satisfy my curiosity, Miss Twinning. What do your sisters look like?'

This was the question she had been dreading. Caroline hesitated, searching for precisely the right words with which to get over the difficult ground. 'Well, they've always been commonly held to be well to pass.'

Max noted the hesitation. He interpreted her careful phrasing to mean that the other three girls were no more than average. He nodded, having suspected as much, and allowed the subject to drop.

They rounded the lake and he slowed his team to a gentle trot. 'As your guardian, I've made certain arrangements for your immediate future.' He noticed the grey eyes had flown to his face. 'Firstly, I've opened Twyford House. Secondly, I've arranged for my aunt, Lady Benborough, to act as your chaperon for the Season. She's very well connected and will know exactly how everything should be managed. You may place complete confidence in her advice. You will remove from Grillon's tomorrow. I'll send my man, Wilson, to assist you in the move to Twyford House.

He'll call for you at two tomorrow. I presume that gives you enough time to pack?'

Caroline assumed the question to be rhetorical. She was stunned. He had not known they existed at nine this morning. How could he have organised all that since ten?

Thinking he may as well clear all the looming fences while he was about it, Max added, 'As for funds, I presume your earlier arrangements still apply. However, should you need any further advances, as I now hold the purse-strings of your patrimonies, you may apply directly to me.'

His last statement succeeded in convincing Caroline that it would not be wise to underestimate this Duke. Despite having had only since this morning to think about it, he had missed very little. And, as he held the purse-strings, he could call the tune. As she had foreseen, life as the wards of a man as masterful and domineering as the present Duke of Twyford was rapidly proving to be was definitely not going to be as unfettered as they had imagined would be the case with his vague and easily led uncle. There were, however, certain advantages in the changed circumstances and she, for one, could not find it in her to repine.

More people were appearing in the Park, strolling about the lawns sloping down to the river and gathering in small groups by the carriageway, laughing and chatting.

A man of slight stature, mincing along beside the carriage drive, looked up in startled recognition as they passed. He was attired in a bottle-green coat with the most amazing amount of frogging Caroline had ever seen. In place of a cravat, he seemed to be wearing a very large floppy bow around his neck. 'Who on earth was that quiz?' she asked.

'That quiz, my dear ward, is none other than Walter Millington, one of the fops. In spite of his absurd clothes, he's unexceptionable enough but he has a sharp tongue so it's wise for young ladies to stay on his right side. Don't laugh at him.'

Two old ladies in an ancient landau were staring at them with an intensity which in lesser persons would be considered rude.

Max did not wait to be asked. 'And those are the Misses Berry. They're as old as bedamned and know absolutely everyone. Kind souls. One's entirely vague and the other's sharp as needles.'

Caroline smiled. His potted histories were entertaining.

A few minutes later, the gates came into view and Max headed his team in that direction. Caroline saw a horseman pulled up by the carriage drive a little way ahead. His face clearly registered recognition of the Duke's curricle and the figure driving it. Then his eyes passed to her and stopped. At five and twenty, Caroline had long grown used to the effect she had on men, particularly certain sorts of men. As they drew nearer, she saw that the gentleman was impeccably attired and had the same rakish air as the Duke. The rider held up a hand in greeting and she expected to feel the curricle slow. Instead, it flashed on, the Duke merely raising a hand in an answering salute.

Amused, Caroline asked, 'And who, pray tell, was that?'

Max was thinking that keeping his friends in ignorance of Miss Twinning was going to prove impossible. Clearly, he would be well advised to spend some time planning the details of this curious seduction, or he might find himself with rather more competition than he would wish. 'That was Lord Ramsleigh.'

'A friend of yours?'

'Precisely.'

Caroline laughed at the repressive tone. The husky sound ran tingling along Max's nerves. It flashed into his mind that Caroline Twinning seemed to understand a great deal more than one might expect from a woman with such a decidedly restricted past. He was prevented from studying her face by the demands of successfully negotiating their exit from the Park.

They were just swinging out into the traffic when an elegant barouche pulled up momentarily beside them, heading into the Park. The thin, middle-aged woman, with a severe, almost horsy countenance, who had been languidly lying against the silken cushions, took one look at the curricle and sat bolt upright. In her face, astonishment mingled freely with rampant curiosity. 'Twyford!'

Max glanced down as both carriages started to move again. 'My lady.' He nodded and then they were swallowed up in the traffic.

Glancing back, Caroline saw the elegant lady remonstrating with her coachman. She giggled. 'Who was she?'

'That, my ward, was Sally, Lady Jersey. A name to remember. She is the most inveterate gossip in London. Hence her nickname of Silence. Despite that, she's kind-hearted enough. She's one of the seven patronesses of Almack's. You'll have to get vouchers to attend but I doubt that will be a problem.'

They continued in companionable silence, threading their way through the busy streets. Max was occupied with imagining the consternation Lady Jersey's sighting of them was going to cause. And there was Ramsleigh, too. A wicked smile hovered on his lips. He rather thought he was going to spend a decidedly amusing evening. It would be some days before news of his guardianship got around. Until then, he would enjoy the speculation. He was certain he would not enjoy the mirth of his friends when they discovered the truth.

'Oooh, Caro! Isn't he magnificent?' Arabella's round eyes, brilliant and bright, greeted Caroline as she entered their parlour.

'Did he agree to be our guardian?' asked the phlegmatic Sarah.

And, 'Is he nice?' from the youngest, Lizzie.

All the important questions, thought Caroline with an affectionate smile, as she threw her bonnet aside and subsided into an armchair with a whisper of her stylish skirts. Her three half-sisters gathered around eagerly. She eyed them fondly. It would be hard to find three more attractive young ladies, even though she did say so herself. Twenty-year-old Sarah, with her dark brown hair and dramatically pale face, settling herself on one arm of her chair, Arabella on her other side, chestnut curls rioting around her heart-shaped and decidedly mischievous countenance, and Lizzie, the youngest and quietest of them all, curling up at her feet, her grey-brown eyes shining with the intentness of youth, the light dusting of freckles on the bridge of her nose persisting despite the ruthless application of Denmark lotion, crushed strawberries and every other remedy ever invented.

'*Commonly held to be well to pass*'. Caroline's own words echoed in her ears. Her smile grew. 'Well, my loves, it seems we are, incontrovertibly and without doubt, the Duke of Twyford's wards.'

'When does he want to meet us?' asked Sarah, ever practical.

'Tomorrow afternoon. He's opening up Twyford House and we're to move in then. He resides at Delmere House, where I went this morning, so the proprieties will thus be preserved. His aunt, Lady Benborough, is to act as our chaperon—she's apparently well connected and willing to sponsor us. She'll be there tomorrow.'

A stunned silence greeted her news. Then Arabella voiced the awe of all three. 'Since ten this morning?'

Caroline's eyes danced. She nodded.

Arabella drew a deep breath. 'Is he. . .masterful?'

'Very!' replied Caroline. 'But you'll be caught out, my love, if you think to sharpen your claws on our guardian. He's a deal too shrewd, and experienced besides.' Studying the pensive faces around her, she added, 'Any flirtation between any of us and Max Rotherbridge would be doomed to failure. As his wards, we're out of court, and he won't stand any nonsense, I warn you.'

'Hmm.' Sarah stood and wandered to the windows before turning to face her. 'So it's as you suspected? He won't be easy to manage?'

Caroline smiled at the thought and shook her head decisively. 'I'm afraid, my dears, that any notions we may have had of setting the town alight while in the care of a complaisant guardian have died along with the last Duke.' One slim forefinger tapped her full lower lip thoughtfully. 'However,' she continued, 'provided we adhere to society's rules and cause him no trouble, I doubt our new guardian will throw any rub in our way. We did come to London to find husbands, after all. And that,' she said forcefully, gazing at the three faces fixed on hers, 'is, unless I miss my guess, precisely what His Grace intends us to do.'

'So he's agreed to present us so we can find husbands?' asked Lizzie.

Again Caroline nodded. 'I think it bothers him, to have four wards.' She smiled in reminiscence, then added, 'And from what I've seen of the *ton* thus far, I suspect the present Duke as our protector may well be a distinct improvement over the previous incumbent. I doubt we'll have to fight off the fortune-hunters.'

Some minutes ticked by in silence as they considered their new guardian. Then Caroline stood and shook out her skirts. She took a few steps into the room before turning to address her sisters.

'Tomorrow we'll be collected at two and conveyed to Twyford House, which is in Mount Street.' She paused to let the implication of her phrasing sink in. 'As you love me, you'll dress demurely and behave with all due reticence. No playing off your tricks on the Duke.' She looked pointedly at Arabella, who grinned roguishly back. 'Exactly so! I think, in the circumstances, we should make life as easy as possible for our new guardian. I feel sure he could have broken the guardianship if he had wished and can only be thankful he chose instead to honour his uncle's obligations. But we shouldn't try him too far.' She ended her motherly admonitions with a stern air, deceiving her sisters not at all.

As the other three heads came together, Caroline turned to gaze unseeingly out of the window. A bewitching smile curved her generous lips and a twinkle lit her grey-green eyes. Softly, she murmured to herself, 'For I've a definite suspicion he's going to find us very trying indeed!'

Thup, thup, thup. The tip of Lady Benborough's thin cane beat a slow tattoo, muffled by the pile of the Aubusson carpet. She was pleasantly impatient, waiting with definite anticipation to see her new charges. Her sharp blue gaze had already taken in the state of the room, the perfectly organised furniture, everything tidy and in readiness. If she had not known it for fact, she would never have believed that, yesterday morn, Twyford House had been shut up, the knocker off the door, every piece of furniture shrouded in Holland covers. Wilson was priceless. There was even a bowl of early crocus on the side-table between the long windows. These stood open, giving access to the neat courtyard, flanked by flowerbeds bursting into colourful life. A marble fountain stood at its centre, a Grecian maiden pouring water never-endingly from an urn.

Her contemplation of the scene was interrupted by a peremptory knock on the street door. A moment later, she heard the deep tones of men's voices and relaxed. Max. She would never get used to thinking of him as Twyford—she had barely become accustomed to him being Viscount Delmere. Max was essentially Max—he needed no title to distinguish him.

The object of her vagaries strode into the room. As always, his garments were faultless, his boots beyond compare. He bowed with effortless grace over her hand, his blue eyes, deeper in shade than her own but alive with the same intelligence, quizzing her. 'A vast improvement, Aunt.'

It took a moment to realise he was referring to her latest wig, a newer version of the same style she had favoured for the past ten years. She was not sure whether she was pleased or insulted. She compromised and snorted. 'Trying to turn me up pretty, heh?'

'I would never insult your intelligence so, ma'am,' he drawled, eyes wickedly laughing.

Lady Benborough suppressed an involuntary smile in response. The trouble with Max was that he was such a thorough-going rake that the techniques had flowed into all spheres of his life. He would undoubtedly flirt outrageously with his old nurse! Augusta Benborough snorted again. 'Wilson's left to get the girls. He should be back any minute. Provided they're ready, that is.'

She watched as her nephew ran a cursory eye over the room before selecting a Hepplewhite chair and elegantly disposing his long length in it.

'I trust everything meets with your approval?'

She waved her hand to indicate the room. 'Wilson's been marvellous. I don't know how he does it.'

'Neither do I,' admitted Wilson's employer. 'And the rest of the house?'

'The same,' she assured him, then continued, 'I've been considering the matter of husbands for the chits. With that sort of money, I doubt we'll have trouble even if they have spots and squint.'

Max merely inclined his head. 'You may leave the fortune-hunters to me.'

Augusta nodded. It was one of the things she particularly appreciated about Max—one never needed to spell things out. The fact that the Twinning girls were his wards would certainly see them safe from the attentions of the less desirable elements. The new Duke of Twyford was a noted Corinthian and a crack shot.

'Provided they're immediately presentable, I thought I might give a small party next week, to start the ball rolling. But if their wardrobes need attention, or they can't dance, we'll have to postpone it.'

Remembering Caroline Twinning's stylish dress and her words on the matter, Max reassured her. 'And I'd bet a monkey they can dance, too.' For some reason, he felt quite sure Caroline Twinning waltzed. It was the only dance he ever indulged in; he was firmly convinced that she waltzed.

Augusta was quite prepared to take Max's word on such matters. If nothing else, his notorious career through the bedrooms and bordellos of England had left him with an unerring eye for all things feminine. 'Next week, then,' she said. 'Just a few of the more useful people and a smattering of the younger crowd.'

She looked up to find Max's eye on her.

'I sincerely hope you don't expect to see *me* at this event?'

'Good lord, no! I want all attention on your wards, not on their guardian!'

Max smiled his lazy smile.

'If the girls are at all attractive, I see no problems at all in getting them settled. Who knows? One of them might snare Wolverton's boy.'

'That milksop?' Max's mind rebelled at the vision of the engaging Miss Twinning on the arm of the future Earl of Wolverton. Then he shrugged. After all, he had yet to meet the three younger girls. 'Who knows?'

'Do you want me to keep a firm hand on the reins, give them a push if necessary or let them wander where they will?'

Max pondered the question, searching for the right words to frame his reply. 'Keep your eye on the three younger girls. They're likely to need some guidance. I haven't sighted them yet, so they may need more than that. But, despite her advanced years, I doubt Miss Twinning will need any help at all.'

His aunt interpreted this reply to mean that Miss Twinning's beauty, together with her sizeable fortune, would be sufficient to overcome the stigma of her years. The assessment was reassuring, coming as it did from her reprehensible nephew, whose knowledge was extensive in such matters. As her gaze rested on the powerful figure, negligently at ease in his chair, she reflected that it really was unfair he had inherited only the best from both his parents. The combination of virility, good looks and power of both mind and body was overwhelming; throw the titles in for good measure and it was no wonder Max Rotherbridge had been the target of so many matchmaking mamas throughout his adult life. But he had shown no sign whatever of succumbing to the demure attractions of any débutante. His preference was, always had been, for women of far more voluptuous charms. The litany of his past mistresses attested to his devotion to his ideal. They had all, every last one, been well endowed. Hardly surprising, she mused. Max was tall, powerful and vigorous. She could not readily imagine any of the delicate debs satisfying his appetites. Her wandering mind dwelt on the subject of his latest *affaire*, aside, of course, from his current *chère amie*, an opera singer, so she had been told. Emma, Lady Mortland was a widow of barely a year's standing but she had returned to town determined, it seemed, to make up for time lost through her marriage to an ageing peer. If the *on-dits* were true, she had fallen rather heavily in Max's lap. Looking at the strikingly handsome face of her nephew, Augusta grinned. Undoubtedly, Lady Mortland had set her cap at a Duchess's tiara. Deluded woman! Max, for all his air of unconcern, was born to his position. There was no chance he would offer marriage to Emma or any of her ilk. He would certainly avail himself of their proffered charms. Then, when he tired of them, he would dismiss them, generously rewarding those who had the sense to play the game with suitable grace, callously ignoring those who did not.

The sounds of arrival gradually filtered into the drawing-room. Max raised his head. A spurt of feminine chatter drifted clearly to their ears. Almost immediately, silence was restored. Then, the door opened and Millwade, the new butler, entered to announce, 'Miss Twinning.'

Caroline walked through the door and advanced into the room, her sunny confidence cloaking her like bright sunshine. Max, who had risen, blinked and then strolled forward to take her hand. He bowed over it, smiling with conscious charm into her large eyes.

Caroline returned the smile, thoroughly conversant with its promise. While he was their guardian, she could afford to play his games. His strong fingers retained their clasp on her hand as he drew her forward to meet his aunt.

Augusta Benborough's mouth had fallen open at first sight of her eldest charge. But by the time Caroline faced her, she had recovered her composure. No wonder Max had said she would need no help. Great heavens! The girl was. . .well, no sense in beating about the bush—she was devilishly attractive. Sensually so. Responding automatically to the introduction, Augusta recognised the amused comprehension in the large and friendly grey eyes. Imperceptibly, she relaxed.

'Your sisters?' asked Max.

'I left them in the hall. I thought perhaps. . .' Caroline's words died on her lips as Max moved to the bell pull. Before she could gather her wits, Millwade was in the room, receiving his instructions. Bowing to the inevitable, Caroline closed her lips on her unspoken excuses. As she turned to Lady Benborough, her ladyship's brows rose in mute question. Caroline smiled and, with a swish of her delicate skirts, sat beside Lady Benborough. 'Just watch,' she whispered, her eyes dancing.

Augusta Benborough regarded her thoughtfully, then turned her attention to the door. As she did so, it opened again. First Sarah, then Arabella, then Lizzie Twinning entered the room.

A curious hiatus ensued as both Max Rotherbridge

and his aunt, with more than fifty years of town bronze between them, stared in patent disbelief at their charges. The three girls stood unselfconsciously, poised and confident, and then swept curtsies, first to Max, then to her ladyship.

Caroline beckoned and they moved forward to be presented, to a speechless Max, who had not moved from his position beside his chair, and then to a flabbergasted Lady Benborough.

As they moved past him to make their curtsy to his aunt, Max recovered the use of his faculties. He closed his eyes. But when he opened them again, they were still there. He was not hallucinating. There they were: three of the loveliest lovelies he had ever set eyes on—four if you counted Miss Twinning. They were scene-stealers, every one—the sort of young women whose appearance suspended conversations, whose passage engendered rampant curiosity, aside from other, less nameable emotions, and whose departure left onlookers wondering what on earth they had been talking about before. All from the same stable, all under one roof. Nominally his. Incredible. And then the enormity, the mind-numbing, all-encompassing reality of his inheritance struck him. One glance into Miss Twinning's grey eyes, brimming with mirth, told him she understood more than enough. His voice, lacking its customary strength and in a very odd register, came to his ears. 'Impossible!'

His aunt Augusta collapsed laughing.

CHAPTER THREE

'NO!' MAX shook his head stubbornly, a frown of quite dramatic proportions darkening his handsome face.

Lady Benborough sighed mightily and frowned back. On recovering her wits, she had sternly repressed her mirth and sent the three younger Twinnings into the courtyard. But after ten minutes of carefully reasoned argument, Max remained adamant. However, she was quite determined her scapegrace nephew would not succeed in dodging his responsibilities. Aside from anything else, the situation seemed set to afford her hours of entertainment and, at her age, such opportunities could not be lightly passed by. Her lips compressed into a thin line and a martial light appeared in her blue eyes.

Max, recognising the signs, got in first. 'It's impossible! Just *think* of the talk!'

Augusta's eyes widened to their fullest extent. 'Why should you care?' she asked. 'Your career to date would hardly lead one to suppose you fought shy of scandal.' She fixed Max with a penetrating stare. 'Besides, while there'll no doubt be talk, none of it will harm anyone. Quite the opposite. It'll get these girls into the limelight!'

The black frown on Max's face did not lighten.

Caroline wisely refrained from interfering between the two principal protagonists, but sat beside Augusta, looking as innocent as she could. Max's gaze swept over her and stopped on her face. His eyes narrowed. Caroline calmly returned his scrutiny.

There was little doubt in Max's mind that Caroline Twinning had deliberately concealed from him the truth about her sisters until he had gone too far in establishing himself as their guardian to pull back. He felt sure some retribution was owing to one who had so manipulated him but, staring into her large grey-green eyes, was unable to decide which of the numerous and varied punishments his fertile imagination supplied would be the most suitable. Instead, he said, in the tones of one goaded beyond endurance, '"Commonly held to be well to pass", indeed!'

Caroline smiled.

Augusta intervened. 'Whatever you're thinking of, Max, it won't do! You're the girls' guardian—you told me so yourself. You cannot simply wash your hands of them. I can see it'll be a trifle awkward for you,' her eyes glazed as she thought of Lady Mortland, 'but if you don't concern yourself with them, who will?'

Despite his violent response to his first sight of all four Twinning sisters, perfectly understandable in the circumstances, Max had not seriously considered giving up his guardianship of them. His behaviour over the past ten minutes had been more in the nature of an emotional rearguard action in an attempt, which his rational brain acknowledged as futile, to resist the tide of change he could see rising up to swamp his hitherto well ordered existence. He fired his last shot. 'Do you seriously imagine that someone with my reputation will be considered a suitable guardian for four. . . ?' He paused, his eyes on Caroline, any number of highly apt descriptions revolving in his head. 'Excessively attractive virgins?' he concluded savagely.

Caroline's eyes widened and her dimple appeared.

'On the contrary!' Augusta answered. 'Who better than you to act as their guardian? Odds are you know every ploy ever invented and a few more besides. And if you can't keep the wolves at bay, then no one can. I really don't know why you're creating all this fuss.'

Max did not know either. After a moment of silence, he turned abruptly and crossed to the windows giving on to the courtyard. He had known from the outset that this was one battle he was destined to lose. Yet some part of his mind kept suggesting in panic-stricken accents that there must be some other way. He watched as the three younger girls—his wards, heaven forbid!—examined the fountain, prodding and poking in an effort to find the lever to turn it on. They were a breathtaking sight, the varied hues of their shining hair vying with the flowers, their husky laughter and the unconsciously seductive way their supple figures swayed this way and that causing him to groan inwardly. Up to the point when he had first sighted them, the three younger Twinnings had figured in his plans as largely irrelevant entities, easily swept into the background and of no possible consequence to his plans for their elder sister. One glimpse had been enough to scuttle that scenario. He was trapped—a guardian in very truth. And with what the Twinning girls had to offer he would have no choice but to play the role to the hilt. Every man in London with eyes would be after them!

Lady Benborough eyed Max's unyielding back with a frown. Then she turned to the woman beside her. She had already formed a high opinion of Miss Twinning. What was even more to the point, being considerably more than seven, Augusta had also perceived that her reprehensible nephew was far from indifferent to the luscious beauty. Meeting the grey-green eyes, her ladyship raised her brows. Caroline nodded and rose.

Max turned as Caroline laid her hand on his arm. She was watching her sisters, not him. Her voice, when she spoke, was tactfully low. 'If it would truly bother you to stand as our guardian, I'm sure we could make some other arrangement.' As she finished speaking, she raised her eyes to his.

Accustomed to every feminine wile known to woman, Max nevertheless could see nothing in the lucent grey eyes to tell him whether the offer was a bluff or not. But it only took a moment to realise that if he won this particular argument, if he succeeded in withdrawing as guardian to the Twinning sisters, Caroline Twinning would be largely removed from his orbit. Which would certainly make his seduction of her more difficult, if not impossible. Faced with those large grey-green eyes, Max did what none of the *habitués* of Gentleman Jackson's boxing salon had yet seen him do. He threw in the towel.

Having resigned himself to the inevitable, Max departed, leaving the ladies to become better acquainted. As the street door closed behind him, Lady Benborough turned a speculative glance on Caroline. Her lips twitched. 'Very well done, my dear. Clearly you need no lessons in how to manage a man.'

Caroline's smile widened. 'I've had some experience, I'll admit.'

'Well, you'll need it all if you're going to tackle my nephew.' Augusta grinned in anticipation. From where she sat, her world looked rosy indeed. Not only did she have four rich beauties to fire off, and unlimited funds to do it with, but, glory of glories, for the first time since he had emerged from short coats her reprehensible nephew was behaving in a less than predictable fashion. She allowed herself a full minute to revel in the wildest of imaginings, before settling down to extract all the pertinent details of their backgrounds and personalities from the Twinning sisters.

The younger girls returned when the teatray arrived. By the time it was removed, Lady Benborough had satisfied herself on all points of interest and the conversation moved on to their introduction to the *ton*.

'I wonder whether news of your existence has leaked out yet,' mused her ladyship. 'Someone may have seen you at Grillon's.'

'Lady Jersey saw me yesterday with Max in his curricle,' said Caroline.

'Did she?' Augusta sat up straighter. 'In that case, there's no benefit in dragging our heels. If Silence already has the story, the sooner you make your appearance, the better. We'll go for a drive in the Park tomorrow.' She ran a knowledgeable eye over the sisters' dresses. 'I must say, your dresses are very attractive. Are they all like that?'

Reassured on their wardrobes, she nodded. 'So there's nothing to stop us wading into the fray immediately. Good!' She let her eyes wander over the four faces in front of her, all beautiful yet each with its own allure. Her gaze rested on Lizzie. 'You—Lizzie, isn't it? You're eighteen?'

Lizzie nodded. 'Yes, ma'am.'

'If that's so, then there's no reason for us to be missish,' returned her ladyship. 'I assume you all wish to find husbands?'

They all nodded decisively.

'Good! At least we're all in agreement over the objective. Now for the strategy. Although your sudden appearance all together is going to cause a riot. I rather think that's going to be the best way to begin. At the very least, we'll be noticed.'

'Oh, we're *always* noticed!' returned Arabella, hazel eyes twinkling.

Augusta laughed. 'I dare say.' From any other young lady, the comment would have earned a reproof. However, it was impossible to deny the Twinning sisters were rather more than just beautiful, and as they were all more than green girls it was pointless to pretend they did not fully comprehend the effect they had on the opposite sex. To her ladyship's mind, it was a relief not to have to hedge around the subject.

'Aside from anything else,' she continued thoughtfully, 'your public appearance as the Duke of Twyford's wards will make it impossible for Max to renege on his decision.' Quite why she was so very firmly set on Max fulfilling his obligations she could not have said. But his guardianship would keep him in contact with Miss Twinning. And that, she had a shrewd suspicion, would be a very good thing.

Their drive in the Park the next afternoon was engineered by the experienced Lady Benborough to be tantalisingly brief. As predicted, the sight of four ravishing females in the Twyford barouche caused an immediate impact. As the carriage sedately bowled along the avenues, heads rapidly came together in the carriages they passed. Conversations between knots of elegant gentlemen and the more dashing of the ladies who had descended from their carriages to stroll about the well tended lawns halted in mid-sentence as all eyes turned to follow the Twyford barouche.

Augusta, happily aware of the stir they were causing, sat on the maroon leather seat and struggled to keep the grin from her face. Her charges were attired in a spectrum of delicate colours, for all the world like a posy of gorgeous blooms. The subtle peach of Caroline's round gown gave way to the soft turquoise tints of Sarah's. Arabella had favoured a gown of the most delicate rose muslin while Lizzie sat, like a quiet bluebell, nodding happily amid her sisters. In the soft spring sunshine, they looked like refugees from the fairy kingdom, too exquisite to be flesh and blood. Augusta lost her struggle and grinned widely at her fanciful thoughts. Then her eyes alighted on a landau drawn up to the side of the carriageway. She raised her parasol and tapped her coachman on the shoulder. 'Pull up over there.'

Thus it happened that Emily, Lady Cowper and Maria, Lady Sefton, enjoying a comfortable cose in the afternoon sunshine, were the first to meet the Twinning sisters. As the Twyford carriage drew up, the eyes of both experienced matrons grew round.

Augusta noted their response with satisfaction. She seized the opportunity to perform the introductions, ending with, 'Twyford's wards, you know.'

That information, so casually dropped, clearly stunned both ladies. '*Twyford's*?' echoed Lady Sefton. Her mild eyes, up to now transfixed by the spectacle that was the Twinning sisters, shifted in bewilderment to Lady Benborough's face. 'How on *earth*. . .?'

In a few well chosen sentences, Augusta told her. Once their ladyships had recovered from their amusement, both at once promised vouchers for the girls to attend Almack's.

'My dear, if your girls attend, we'll have to lay on more refreshments. The gentlemen will be there in droves,' said Lady Cowper, smiling in genuine amusement.

'Who knows? We might even prevail on Twyford himself to attend,' mused Lady Sefton.

While Augusta thought that might be stretching things a bit far, she was thankful for the immediate backing her two old friends had given her crusade to find four fashionable husbands for the Twinnings. The carriages remained together for some time as the two patronesses of Almack's learned more of His Grace of Twyford's wards. Augusta was relieved to find that all four girls could converse with ease. The two younger sisters prettily deferred to the elder two, allowing the more experienced Caroline, ably seconded by Sarah, to dominate the responses.

When they finally parted, Augusta gave the order to return to Mount Street. 'Don't want to rush it,' she explained to four enquiring glances. 'Much better to let them come to us.'

Two days later, the *ton* was still reeling from the discovery of the Duke of Twyford's wards. Amusement, from the wry to the ribald, had been the general reaction. Max had gritted his teeth and borne it, but the persistent demands of his friends to be introduced to his wards sorely tried his temper. He continued to refuse all such requests. He could not stop their eventual acquaintance but at least he did not need directly to foster it. Thus, it was in a far from benign mood that he prepared to depart Delmere House on that fine April morning, in the company of two of his particular cronies, Lord Darcy Hamilton and George, Viscount Pilborough.

As they left the parlour at the rear of the house and entered the front hallway, their conversation was interrupted by a knock on the street door. They paused in the rear of the hall as Hillshaw moved majestically past to answer it.

'I'm not at home, Hillshaw,' said Max.

Hillshaw regally inclined his head. 'Very good, Your Grace.'

But Max had forgotten that Hillshaw had yet to experience the Misses Twinning *en masse*. Resistance was impossible and they came swarming over the threshold, in a frothing of lace and cambrics, bright smiles, laughing eyes and dancing curls.

The girls immediately spotted the three men, standing rooted by the stairs. Arabella reached Max first. 'Dear guardian,' she sighed languishingly, eyes dancing, 'are you well?' She placed her small hand on his arm.

Sarah, immediately behind, came to his other side. 'We hope you are because we want to ask your permission for something.' She smiled matter-of-factly up at him.

Lizzie simply stood directly in front of him, her huge eyes trained on his face, a smile she clearly knew to be winning suffusing her countenance. 'Please?'

Max raised his eyes to Hillshaw, still standing dumb by the door. The sight of his redoubtable henchman rolled up by a parcel of young misses caused his lips to twitch. He firmly denied the impulse to laugh. The Misses Twinning were outrageous already and needed no further encouragement. Then his eyes met Caroline's.

She had hung back, watching her sisters go through their paces, but as his eyes touched her, she moved forward, her hand outstretched. Max, quite forgetting the presence of all the others, took it in his.

'Don't pay any attention to them, Your Grace; I'm afraid they're sad romps.'

'Not *romps*, Caro,' protested Arabella, eyes fluttering over the other two men, standing mesmerised just behind Max.

'It's just that we heard it was possible to go riding in the Park but Lady Benborough said we had to have your permission,' explained Sarah.

'So, here we are and can we?' asked Lizzie, big eyes beseeching.

'No,' said Max, without further ado. As his aunt had observed, he knew every ploy. And the opportunities afforded by rides in the Park, where chaperons could be present but sufficiently remote, were endless. The first rule in a seduction was to find the opportunity to speak alone to the lady in question. And a ride in the Park provided the perfect setting.

Caroline's fine brows rose at his refusal. Max noticed that the other three girls turned to check their elder sister's response before returning to the attack.

'Oh, you can't mean that! How shabby!'

'Why on earth not?'

'We all ride well. I haven't been out since we were at home.'

Both Arabella and Sarah turned to the two gentlemen still standing behind Max, silent auditors to the extraordinary scene. Arabella fixed Viscount Pilborough with pleading eyes. 'Surely there's nothing unreasonable in such a request?' Under the Viscount's besotted gaze, her lashes fluttered almost imperceptibly, before her lids decorously dropped, veiling those dancing eyes, the long lashes brushing her cheeks, delicately stained with a most becoming blush.

The Viscount swallowed. 'Why on earth not, Max? Not an unreasonable request at all. Your wards would look very lovely on horseback.'

Max, who was only too ready to agree on how lovely his wards would look in riding habits, bit back an oath. Ignoring Miss Twinning's laughing eyes, he glowered at the hapless Viscount.

Sarah meanwhile had turned to meet the blatantly admiring gaze of Lord Darcy. Not as accomplished a flirt as Arabella, she could nevertheless hold her own, and she returned his warm gaze with a serene smile. 'Is there any real reason why we shouldn't ride?'

Her low voice, cool and strangely musical, made Darcy Hamilton wish there were far fewer people in Max's hall. In fact, his fantasies would be more complete if they were not in Max's hall at all. He moved towards Sarah and expertly captured her hand.

Raising it to his lips, he smiled in a way that had thoroughly seduced more damsels than he cared to recall. He could well understand why Max did not wish his wards to ride. But, having met this Twinning sister, there was no way in the world he was going to further his friend's ambition.

His lazy drawl reached Max's ears. 'I'm very much afraid, Max, dear boy, that you're going to have to concede. The opposition is quite overwhelming.'

Max glared at him. Seeing the determination in his lordship's grey eyes and understanding his reasons only too well, he knew he was outnumbered on all fronts. His eyes returned to Caroline's face to find her regarding him quizzically. 'Oh, very well!'

Her smile warmed him and at the prompting lift of her brows he introduced his friends, first to her, and then to her sisters in turn. The chattering voices washed over him, his friends' deeper tones running like a counterpoint in the cacophony. Caroline moved to his side.

'You're not seriously annoyed by us riding, are you?'

He glanced down at her. The stern set of his lips reluctantly relaxed. 'I would very much rather you did not. However,' he continued, his eyes roving to the group of her three sisters and his two friends, busy with noisy plans for their first ride that afternoon, 'I can see that's impossible.'

Caroline smiled. 'We won't come to any harm, I assure you.'

'Allow me to observe, Miss Twinning, that gallivanting about the London *ton* is fraught with rather more difficulty than you would have encountered in American society, nor yet within the circle to which you were accustomed in Hertfordshire.'

A rich chuckle greeted this warning. 'Fear not, dear

guardian,' she said, raising laughing eyes to his. Max noticed the dimple, peeking irrepressibly from beside her soft mouth. 'We'll manage.'

Naturally, Max felt obliged to join the riding party that afternoon. Between both his and Darcy Hamilton's extensive stables, they had managed to assemble suitable mounts for the four girls. Caroline had assured him that, like all country misses, they could ride very well. By the time they gained the Park, he had satisfied himself on that score. At least he need not worry over them losing control of the frisky horses and being thrown. But, as they were all as stunning as he had feared they would be, elegantly gowned in perfectly cut riding habits, his worries had not noticeably decreased.

As they ambled further into the Park, by dint of the simple expedient of reining in his dappled grey, he dropped to the rear of the group, the better to keep the three younger girls in view. Caroline, riding by his side, stayed with him. She threw him a laughing glance but made no comment.

As he had expected, they had not gone more than two hundred yards before their numbers were swelled by the appearance of Lord Tulloch and young Mr Mitchell. But neither of these gentlemen seemed able to interrupt the rapport which, to Max's experienced eye, was developing with alarming rapidity between Sarah Twinning and Darcy Hamilton. Despite his fears, he grudgingly admitted the Twinning sisters knew a trick or two. Arabella flirted outrageously but did so with all gentlemen, none being able to claim any special consideration. Lizzie attracted the quieter men and was happy to converse on the matters currently holding the interest of the *ton*. Her natural shyness and understated youth, combined with her undeniable beauty, was a heady tonic for these more sober gentlemen. As they ventured deeper into the Park, Max was relieved to find Sarah giving Darcy no opportunity to lead her apart. Gradually, his watchfulness relaxed. He turned to Caroline.

'Have you enjoyed your first taste of life in London?'

'Yes, thank you,' she replied, grey eyes smiling. 'Your aunt has been wonderful. I can't thank you enough for all you've done.'

Max's brow clouded. As it happened, the last thing he wanted was her gratitude. Here he was, thinking along lines not grossly dissimilar from Darcy's present preoccupation, and the woman chose to thank him. He glanced down at her as she rode beside him, her face free of any worry, thoroughly enjoying the moment. Her presence was oddly calming.

'What plans do you have for the rest of the week?' he asked.

Caroline was slightly surprised by his interest but replied readily. 'We've been driving in the Park every afternoon except today. I expect we'll continue to appear, although I rather think, from now on, it will be on horseback.' She shot him a measuring glance to see how he would take that. His face was slightly grim but he nodded in acceptance. 'Last evening, we went to a small party given by Lady Malling. Your aunt said there are a few more such gatherings in the next week which we should attend, to give ourselves confidence in society.'

Max nodded again. From the corner of his eye, he saw Sarah avoid yet another of Darcy's invitations to separate from the group. He saw the quick frown which showed fleetingly in his friend's eyes. Serve him right if the woman drove him mad. But, he knew, Darcy was made of sterner stuff. The business of keeping his wards out of the arms of his friends was going to be deucedly tricky. Returning to contemplation of Miss Twinning's delightful countenance, he asked, 'Has Aunt Augusta got you vouchers for Almack's yet?'

'Yes. We met Lady Sefton and Lady Cowper on our first drive in the Park.'

Appreciating his aunt's strategy, Max grinned. 'Trust Aunt Augusta.'

Caroline returned his smile. 'She's been very good to us.'

Thinking that the unexpected company of four lively young women must have been a shock to his aunt's system, Max made a mental note to do anything in his power to please his aunt Benborough.

They had taken a circuitous route through the Park and only now approached the fashionable precincts. The small group almost immediately swelled to what, to Max, were alarming proportions, with every available gentleman clamouring for an introduction to his beautiful wards. But, to his surprise, at a nod from Caroline, the girls obediently brought their mounts closer and refused every attempt to draw them further from his protective presence. To his astonishment, they all behaved with the utmost decorum, lightened, of course, by their natural liveliness but nevertheless repressively cool to any who imagined them easy targets. Despite his qualms, he was impressed. They continued in this way until they reached the gates of the Park, by which time the group had dwindled to its original size and he could relax again.

He turned to Caroline, still by his side. 'Can you guarantee they'll always behave so circumspectly, or was that performance purely for my benefit?' As her laughing eyes met his, he tried to decide whether they were greeny-grey or greyish-green. An intriguing question.

'Oh, we're experienced enough to know which way to jump, I assure you,' she returned. After a pause, she continued, her voice lowered so only he could hear. 'In the circumstances, we would not willingly do anything to bring disrepute on ourselves. We are very much aware of what we owe to you and Lady Benborough.'

Max knew he should be pleased at this avowal of good intentions. Instead, he was aware of a curious irritation. He would certainly do everything in his power to reinforce her expressed sentiment with respect to the three younger girls, but to have Caroline Twinning espousing such ideals was not in keeping with his plans. Somehow, he was going to have to convince her that adherence to all the social strictures was not the repayment he, at least, would desire. The unwelcome thought that, whatever the case, she might now consider herself beholden to him, and would, therefore, grant him his wishes out of gratitude, very nearly made him swear aloud. His horse jibbed at the suddenly tightened rein and he pushed the disturbing thought aside while he dealt with the grey. Once the horse had settled again, he continued by Caroline's side as they headed back to Mount Street, a distracted frown at the back of his dark blue eyes.

Augusta Benborough flicked open her fan and plied it vigourously. Under cover of her voluminous skirts, she slipped her feet free of her evening slippers. She had forgotten how stifling the small parties, held in the run-up to the Season proper, could be. Every bit as bad as the crushes later in the Season. But there, at least, she would have plenty of her own friends to gossip with. The mothers and chaperons of the current batch of débutantes were a generation removed from her own and at these small parties they were generally the only older members present. Miriam Alford had elected to remain at Twyford House this evening, which left Augusta with little to do but watch her charges. And even that, she mused to herself, was not exactly riveting entertainment.

True, Max was naturally absent, which meant her primary interest in the entire business was in abeyance. Still, it was comforting to find Caroline treating all the gentlemen who came her way with the same unfailing courtesy and no hint of partiality. Arabella, too, seemed to be following that line, although, in her case, the courtesy was entirely cloaked in a lightly flirtatious manner. In any other young girl, Lady Benborough would have strongly argued for a more demure style. But she had watched Arabella carefully. The girl had quick wits and a ready tongue. She never stepped beyond what was acceptable, though she took delight in sailing close to the wind. Now, convinced that no harm would come of Arabella's artful play, Augusta nodded benignly as that young lady strolled by, accompanied by the inevitable gaggle of besotted gentlemen.

One of their number was declaiming,

'"My dearest flower,
More beautiful by the hour,
To you I give my heart."'

Arabella laughed delightedly and quickly said, 'My dear sir, I beg you spare my blushes! Truly, your verses do me more credit than I deserve. But surely, to do them justice, should you not set them down on parchment?' Anything was preferable to having them said out aloud.

The budding poet, young Mr Rawlson, beamed.

'*Nothing* would give me greater pleasure, Miss Arabella. I'll away and transcribe them immediately. And dedicate them to their inspiration!' With a flourishing bow, he departed precipitately, leaving behind a silence pregnant with suppressed laughter.

This was broken by a snigger from Lord Shannon. 'Silly puppy!'

As Mr Rawlson was a year or two older than Lord Shannon, who himself appeared very young despite his attempts to ape the Corinthians, this comment itself caused some good-natured laughter.

'Perhaps, Lord Shannon, you would be so good as to fetch me some refreshment?' Arabella smiled sweetly on the hapless youngster. With a mutter which all interpreted to mean he was delighted to be of service to one so fair, the young man escaped.

With a smile, Arabella turned to welcome Viscount Pilborough to her side.

Augusta's eyelids drooped. The temperature in the room seemed to rise another degree. The murmuring voices washed over her. Her head nodded. With a start, she shook herself awake. Determined to keep her mind active for the half-hour remaining, she sought out her charges. Lizzie was chattering animatedly with a group of débutantes much her own age. The youngest Twinning was surprisingly innocent, strangely unaware of her attractiveness to the opposite sex, still little more than a schoolgirl at heart. Lady Benborough smiled. Lizzie would learn soon enough; let her enjoy her girlish gossiping while she might.

A quick survey of the room brought Caroline to light, strolling easily on the arm of the most eligible Mr Willoughby.

'It's so good of you to escort your sister to these parties, sir. I'm sure Miss Charlotte must be very grateful.' Caroline found conversation with the reticent Mr Willoughby a particular strain.

A faint smile played at the corners of Mr Willoughby's thin lips. 'Indeed, I believe she is. But really, there is very little to it. As my mother is so delicate as to find these affairs quite beyond her, it would be churlish of me indeed to deny Charlotte the chance of becoming more easy in company before she is presented.'

With grave doubts over how much longer she could endure such ponderous conversation without running amok, Caroline seized the opportunity presented by passing a small group of young ladies, which included the grateful Charlotte, to stop. The introductions were quickly performed.

As she stood conversing with a Miss Denbright, an occupation which required no more than half her brain, Caroline allowed her eyes to drift over the company. Other than Viscount Pilborough, who was dangling after Arabella in an entirely innocuous fashion, and Darcy Hamilton, who was pursuing Sarah in a far more dangerous way, there was no gentleman in whom she felt the least interest. Even less than her sisters did she need the opportunity of the early parties to gain confidence. Nearly eighteen months of social consorting in the ballrooms and banquet halls in New York had given them all a solid base on which to face the London *ton*. And even more than her sisters, Caroline longed to get on with it. Time, she felt, was slipping inexorably by. Still, there were only four more days to go. And then, surely their guardian would reappear? She had already discovered that no other gentleman's eyes could make her feel quite the same breathless excitement as the Duke of Twyford's did. He had not called on them since that first ride in the Park, a fact which had left her with a wholly resented feeling of disappointment. Despite the common sense on which she prided herself, she had formed an irritating habit of comparing all the men she met with His domineering Grace and inevitably found them wanting. Such foolishness would have to stop. With a small suppressed sigh, she turned a charming smile on Mr Willoughby, wishing for the sixteenth time that his faded blue eyes were of a much darker hue.

Satisfied that Caroline, like Lizzie and Arabella, needed no help from her, Lady Benborough moved her gaze on, scanning the room for Sarah's dark head. When her first survey drew no result, she sat up straighter, a slight frown in her eyes. Darcy Hamilton was here, somewhere, drat him. He had attended every party they had been to this week, a fact which of itself had already drawn comment. His attentions to Sarah were becoming increasingly marked. Augusta knew all the Hamiltons. She had known Darcy's father and doubted not the truth of the 'like father, like son' adage. But surely Sarah was too sensible to. . . She wasted no time in completing that thought but started a careful, methodical and entirely well disguised visual search. From her present position, on a slightly raised dais to one side, she commanded a view of the whole room. Her gaze passed over the alcove set in the wall almost directly opposite her but then returned, caught by a flicker of movement within the shadowed recess.

There they were, Sarah and, without doubt, Darcy Hamilton. Augusta could just make out the blur of colour that was Sarah's green dress. How typical of Darcy. They were still in the room, still within sight, but, in the dim light of the alcove, almost private. As her eyes adjusted to the poor light, Augusta saw to her relief that, despite her fears and Darcy's reputation, they were merely talking, seated beside one another on a small settee. Still, to her experienced eye, there was a degree of familiarity in their pose, which, given that it must be unconscious, was all too revealing. With a sigh, she determined to have a word, if not several words, with Sarah, regarding the fascinations of men like Darcy Hamilton. She would have to do it, for Darcy's proclivities were too well known to doubt.

She watched as Darcy leant closer to Sarah.

'My dear,' drawled Darcy Hamilton, 'do you have any idea of the temptation you pose? Or the effect beauty such as yours has on mere men?'

His tone was lazy and warm, with a quality of velvety smoothness which fell like a warm cloak over Sarah's already hypersensitised nerves. He had flung one arm over the back of the settee and long fingers were even now twining in the soft curls at her nape. She knew she should move but could not. The sensations rippling down her spine were both novel and exhilarating. She was conscious of a ludicrous desire to snuggle into that warmth, to invite more soft words. But the desire which burned in his lordship's grey eyes was already frighteningly intense. She determinedly ignored the small reckless voice which urged her to encourage him and instead replied, 'Why, no. Of course not.'

Darcy just managed to repress a snort of disgust. Damn the woman! Her voice had held not the thread of a quaver. Calm and steady as a rock when his own pulses were well and truly racing. He simply did not believe it. He glanced down into her wide brown eyes, guileless as ever, knowing that his exasperation was showing. For a fleeting instant, he saw a glimmer of amusement and, yes, of triumph in the brown depths. But when he looked again, the pale face was once again devoid of emotion. His grey eyes narrowed.

Sarah saw his intent look and immediately dropped her eyes.

Her action confirmed Darcy's suspicions. By God, the chit was playing with him! The fact that Sarah could only be dimly aware of the reality of the danger she was flirting with was buried somewhere in the recesses of his mind. But, like all the Hamiltons, for him, desire could easily sweep aside all reason. In that instant, he determined he would have her, no matter what the cost. Not here, not now—neither place nor time was right. But some time, somewhere, Sarah Twinning would be his.

Augusta's attention was drawn by the sight of a mother gathering her two daughters and preparing to depart. As if all had been waiting for this signal, it suddenly seemed as if half the room was on their way. With relief, she turned to see Darcy lead Sarah from the alcove and head in her direction. As Caroline approached, closely followed by Lizzie and Arabella, Augusta Benborough wriggled her aching toes back into her slippers and rose. It was over. And in four days' time the Season would begin. As she smiled benignly upon the small army of gentlemen who had escorted her charges to her side, she reminded herself that, with the exception of Darcy Hamilton, there was none present tonight who would make a chaperon uneasy. Once in wider society, she would have no time to be bored. The Twinning sisters would certainly see to that.

CHAPTER FOUR

EMMA, LADY MORTLAND, thought Max savagely, had no right to the title. He would grant she was attractive, in a blowsy sort of way, but her conduct left much to be desired. She had hailed him almost as soon as he had entered the Park. He rarely drove there except when expediency demanded. Consequently, her ladyship had been surprised to see his curricle, drawn by his famous match bays, advancing along the avenue. He had been forced to pull up or run the silly woman down. The considerable difficulty in conversing at any length with someone perched six feet and more above you, particularly when that someone displayed the most blatant uninterest, had not discouraged Lady Mortland. She had done her best to prolong the exchange in the dim hope, Max knew, of gaining an invitation to ride beside him. She had finally admitted defeat and archly let him go, but not before issuing a thinly veiled invitation which he had had no compunction in declining. As she had been unwise enough to speak in the hearing of two gentlemen of her acquaintance, her resulting embarrassment was entirely her own fault. He knew she entertained hopes, totally unfounded, of becoming his Duchess. Why she should imagine he would consider taking a woman with the morals of an alley cat to wife was beyond him.

As he drove beneath the trees, he scanned the carriages that passed, hoping to find his wards. He had not seen them since that first ride in the Park, a feat of self-discipline before which any other he had ever accomplished in his life paled into insignificance.

Darcy Hamilton had put the idea into his head. His friend had returned with him to Delmere House after that first jaunt, vociferous in his complaints of the waywardness of Sarah Twinning. The fact that she was Max's ward had not subdued him in the least. Max had not been surprised; Darcy could be ruthlessly single-minded when hunting. It had been Darcy who had suggested that a short absence might make the lady more amenable and had departed with the firm resolve to give the Twinning girls the go-by for at least a week.

That had been six days ago. The Season was about to get under way and it was time to reacquaint himself with his wards. Having ascertained that their horses had not left his stable, he had had the bays put to and followed them to the Park. He finally spied the Twyford barouche drawn up to the side of the avenue. He pulled up alongside.

'Aunt Augusta,' he said as he nodded to her. She beamed at him, clearly delighted he had taken the trouble to find them. His gaze swept over the other occupants of the carriage in an appraising and approving manner, then came to rest on Miss Twinning. She smiled sunnily back at him. Suddenly alert, Max's mind returned from where it had wandered and again counted heads. There was a total of five in the carriage but Miriam Alford was there, smiling vaguely at him. Which meant one of his wards was missing. He quelled the urge to immediately question his aunt, telling himself there would doubtless be some perfectly reasonable explanation. Perhaps one was merely unwell. His mind reverted to its main preoccupation.

Responding automatically to his aunt's social chatter, he took the first opportunity to remark, 'But I can't keep my horses standing, ma'am. Perhaps Miss Twinning would like to come for a drive?'

He was immediately assured that Miss Twinning would and she descended from the carriage. He reached down to help her up beside him and they were off.

Caroline gloried in the brush of the breeze on her face as the curricle bowled along. Even reined in to the pace accepted in the Park, it was still infinitely more refreshing than the funereal plod favoured by Lady Benborough. That was undoubtedly the reason her spirits had suddenly soared. Even the sunshine seemed distinctly brighter.

'Not riding today?' asked Max.

'No. Lady Benborough felt we should not entirely desert the matrons.'

Max smiled. 'True enough. It don't do to put people's backs up unnecessarily.'

Caroline turned to stare at him. 'Your philosophy?' Augusta had told her enough of their guardian's past to realise this was unlikely.

Max frowned. Miss Caroline Twinning was a great deal too knowing. Unprepared to answer her query, he changed the subject. 'Where's Sarah?'

'Lord Darcy took her up some time ago. Maybe we'll see them as we go around?'

Max suppressed the curse which rose to his lips. How many friends was he going to have left by the end of this Season? Another thought occurred. 'Has she been seeing much of him?'

A deep chuckle answered this and his uneasiness grew. 'If you mean has he taken to haunting us, no. On the other hand, he seems to have the entrée to all the salons we've attended this week.'

He should, he supposed, have anticipated his friend's duplicity. Darcy was, after all, every bit as experienced as he. Still, it rankled. He would have a few harsh words to say to his lordship when next they met. 'Has he been. . .particularly attentive towards her?'

'No,' she replied in a careful tone, 'not in any unacceptable way.'

He looked his question and she continued, 'It's just that she's the only lady he pays any attention to at all. If he's not with Sarah, he either leaves or retires to the card tables or simply watches her from a distance.'

The description was so unlike the Darcy Hamilton he knew that it was on the tip of his tongue to verify they were talking about the same man. A sneaking suspicion that Darcy might, just might, be seriously smitten awoke in his mind. One black brow rose.

They paused briefly to exchange greetings with Lady Jersey, then headed back towards the barouche. Coming to a decision, Max asked, 'What's your next major engagement?'

'Well, we go to the first of Almack's balls tomorrow, then it's the Billingtons' ball the next night.'

The start of the Season proper. But there was no way he was going to cross the threshold of Almack's. He had not been near the place for years. Tender young virgins were definitely not on his menu these days. He did not equate that description with Miss Twinning. Nor, if it came to that, to her sisters. Uncertain what to do for the best, he made no response to the information, merely inclining his head to show he had heard.

Caroline was silent as the curricle retraced its journey. Max's questions had made her uneasy. Lord Darcy was a particular friend of his—surely Sarah was in no real danger with him? She stifled a small sigh. Clearly, their guardian's attention was wholly concentrated on their social performance. Which, of course, was precisely what a guardian should be concerned with. Why, then, did she feel such a keen sense of disappointment?

They reached the barouche to find Sarah already returned. One glance at her stormy countenance was sufficient to answer Max's questions. It seemed Darcy's plans had not prospered. Yet.

As he handed Caroline to the ground and acknowledged her smiling thanks, it occurred to him she had not expressed any opinion or interest in his week-long absence. So much for that tactic. As he watched her climb into the barouche, shapely ankles temporarily exposed, he realised he had made no headway during their interlude. Her sister's affair with his friend had dominated his thoughts. Giving his horses the office, he grimaced to himself. Seducing a woman while acting as guardian to her three younger sisters was clearly going to be harder going than he had imagined.

Climbing the steps to Twyford House the next evening, Max was still in two minds over whether he was doing the right thing. He was far too wise to be overly attentive to Caroline, yet, if he did not make a push to engage her interest, she would shortly be the object of the attentions of a far larger circle of gentlemen, few of whom would hesitate to attend Almack's purely because they disliked being mooned over by very young women. He hoped, in his capacity as their guardian, to confine his attentions to the Twinning sisters and so escape the usual jostle of matchmaking mamas. They should have learned by now that he was not likely to succumb to their daughters' vapid charms. Still, he was not looking forward to the evening.

If truth were told, he had been hearing about his wards on all sides for the past week. They had caught the fancy of the *ton*, starved as it was of novelty. And their brand of beauty always had attraction. But what he had not heard was worrying him more. There had been more than one incident when, entering a room, he had been aware of at least one conversation abruptly halted, then smoothly resumed. Another reason to identify himself more closely with his wards. He reminded himself that three of them were truly his responsibility and, in the circumstances, the polite world would hold him responsible for Miss Twinning as well. His duty was clear.

Admitted to Twyford House, Max paused to exchange a few words with Millwade. Satisfied that all was running smoothly, he turned and stopped, all thought deserting him. Transfixed, he watched the Twinning sisters descend the grand staircase. Seen together, gorgeously garbed for the ball, they were quite the most heart-stopping sight he had beheld in many a year. His eyes rested with acclaim on each in turn, but stopped when they reached Caroline. The rest of the company seemed to dissolve in a haze as his eyes roamed appreciatively over the clean lines of her eau-de-Nil silk gown. It clung suggestively to her ripe figure, the neckline scooped low over her generous breasts. His hands burned with the desire to caress those tantalising curves. Then his eyes locked with hers as she crossed the room to his side, her hand extended to him. Automatically, he took it in his. Then she was speaking, smiling up at him in her usual confiding way.

'Thank you for coming. I do hope you'll not be too bored by such tame entertainment.' Lady Benborough, on receiving Max's curt note informing them of his intention to accompany them to Almack's, had crowed with delight. When she had calmed, she had explained his aversion to the place. So it was with an unexpected feeling of guilt that Caroline had come forward to welcome him. But, gazing into his intensely blue eyes, she could find no trace of annoyance or irritation. Instead, she recognised the same emotion she had detected the very first time they had met. To add to her confusion, he raised her hand to his lips, his eyes warm and entirely too knowing.

'Do you know, I very much doubt that I'll be bored at all?' her guardian murmured wickedly.

Caroline blushed vividly. Luckily, this was missed by all but Max in the relatively poor light of the hall and the bustle as they donned their cloaks. Both Lady Benborough and Miriam Alford were to go, cutting the odds between chaperons and charges. Before Max's intervention, the coach would have had to do two trips to King Street. Now, Caroline found that Augusta and Mrs Alford, together with Sarah and Arabella, were to go in the Twyford coach while she and Lizzie were to travel with Max. Suddenly suspicious of her guardian's intentions, she was forced to accept the arrangement with suitable grace. As Max handed her into the carriage and saw her settled comfortably, she told herself she was a fool to read into his behaviour anything other than an attempt to trip her up. He was only amusing himself.

As if to confirm her supposition, the journey was unremarkable and soon they were entering the hallowed precincts of the Assembly Rooms. The sparsely furnished halls were already well filled with the usual mix of débutantes and unmarried young ladies, carefully chaperoned by their mamas in the hope of finding a suitable connection among the unattached gentlemen strolling through the throng. It was a social club to which it was necessary to belong. And it was clear from their reception that, at least as far as the gentlemen were concerned, the Twinning sisters definitely belonged. To Max's horror, they were almost mobbed.

He stood back and watched as the sisters artfully managed their admirers. Arabella had the largest court with all the most rackety and dangerous blades. A more discerning crowd of eminently eligible gentlemen had formed around Sarah while the youthful Lizzie had gathered all the more earnest of the younger men to her. But the group around Caroline drew his deepest consideration. There were more than a few highly dangerous roués in the throng gathered about her but all were experienced and none was likely to attempt anything scandalous without encouragement. As he watched, it became clear that all four girls had an innate ability to choose the more acceptable among their potential partners. They also had the happy knack of dismissing the less favoured with real charm, a not inconsiderable feat. The more he watched, the more intrigued Max became. He was about to seek clarification from his aunt, standing beside him, when that lady very kindly answered his unspoken query.

'You needn't worry, y'know. Those girls have got their heads firmly on their shoulders. Ever since they started going about, I've been bombarded with questions on who's eligible and who's not. Even Arabella, minx that she is, takes good care to know who she's flirting with.'

Max looked his puzzlement.

'Well,' explained her ladyship, surprised by his obtuseness, 'they're all set on finding husbands, of course!' She glanced up at him, eyes suddenly sharp, and added, 'I should think you'd be thrilled—it means they'll be off your hands all the sooner.'

'Yes. Of course,' Max answered absently.

He stayed by his wards until they were claimed for

the first dance. His sharp eyes had seen a number of less than desirable gentlemen approach the sisters, only to veer away as they saw him. If nothing else, his presence had achieved that much.

Searching through the crowd, he finally spotted Darcy Hamilton disappearing into one of the salons where refreshments were laid out.

'Going to give them the go-by for at least a week, huh?' he growled as he came up behind Lord Darcy.

Darcy choked on the lemonade he had just drunk.

Max gazed in horror at the glass in his friend's hand. 'No! Bless me, Darcy! You turned temperate?'

Darcy grimaced. 'Have to drink something and seemed like the best of a bad lot.' His wave indicated the unexciting range of beverages available. 'Thirsty work, getting a dance with one of your wards.'

'Incidentally——' intoned Max in the manner of one about to pass judgement.

But Darcy held up his hand. 'No. Don't start. I don't need any lectures from you on the subject. And you don't need to bother, anyway. Sarah Twinning has her mind firmly set on marriage and there's not a damned thing I can do about it.'

Despite himself, Max could not resist a grin. 'No luck?'

'None!' replied Darcy, goaded. 'I'm almost at the stage of considering offering for her but I can't be sure she wouldn't reject me, and *that* I couldn't take.'

Max, picking up a glass of lemonade himself, became thoughtful.

Suddenly, Darcy roused himself. 'Do you know what she told me yesterday? Said I spent too much time on horses and not enough on matters of importance. *Can* you believe it?'

He gestured wildly and Max nearly hooted with laughter. Lord Darcy's stables were known the length and breath of England as among the biggest and best producers of quality horseflesh.

'I very much doubt that she appreciates your interest in the field,' Max said placatingly.

'Humph,' was all his friend vouchsafed.

After a pause, Darcy laid aside his glass. 'Going to find Maria Sefton and talk her into giving Sarah permission to waltz with me. One thing she won't be able to refuse.' With a nod to Max, he returned to the main hall.

For some minutes, Max remained as he was, his abstracted gaze fixed on the far wall. Then, abruptly, he replaced his glass and followed his friend.

'You want me to give *your ward* permission to waltz with you?' Lady Jersey repeated Max's request, clearly unable to decide whether it was as innocuous as he represented or whether it had an ulterior motive concealed within and if so, what.

'It's really not such an odd request,' returned Max, unperturbed. 'She's somewhat older than the rest and, as I'm here, it seems appropriate.'

'Hmm.' Sally Jersey simply did not believe there was nothing more to it. She had been hard-pressed to swallow her astonishment when she had seen His Grace of Twyford enter the room. And she was even more amazed that he had not left as soon as he had seen his wards settled. But he was, after all, Twyford. And Delmere and Rotherbridge, what was more. So, if he wanted to waltz with his ward. . . She shrugged. 'Very well. Bring her to me. If you can separate her from her court, that is.'

Max smiled in a way that reminded Lady Jersey of the causes of his reputation. 'I think I'll manage,' he drawled, bowing over her hand.

* * *

Caroline was also surprised that Max had remained at the Assembly Rooms for so long. She lost sight of him for a while, and worked hard at forcing herself to pay attention to her suitors, for it was only to be expected their guardian would seek less tame entertainment elsewhere. But then his tall figure reappeared at the side of the room. He seemed to be scanning the multitude, then, over a sea of heads, his eyes met hers. Caroline fervently hoped the peculiar shock which went through her was not reflected in her countenance. After a moment, unobtrusively, he made his way to her side.

Under cover of the light flirtation she was engaged in with an ageing baronet, Caroline was conscious of the sudden acceleration of her heartbeat and the constriction that seemed to be affecting her breathing. Horrendously aware of her guardian's blue eyes, she felt her nervousness grow as he approached despite her efforts to remain calm.

But, when he gained her side and bowed over her hand in an almost bored way, uttering the most commonplace civilities and engaging her partner in a discussion of some sporting event, the anticlimax quickly righted her mind for her.

Quite how it was accomplished she could not have said, but Max succeeded in excusing them to her court, on the grounds that he had something to discuss with his ward. Finding herself on his arm, strolling apparently randomly down the room, she turned to him and asked, 'What was it you wished to say to me?'

He glanced down at her and she caught her breath. That devilish look was back in his eyes as they rested on her, warming her through and through. What on earth was he playing at?

'Good heavens, my ward. And I thought you up to all the rigs. Don't you know a ruse when you hear it?'

The tones of his voice washed languorously over Caroline, leaving a sense of relaxation in their wake. She made a grab for her fast-disappearing faculties. Interpreting his remark to mean that his previously bored attitude had also been false, Caroline was left wondering what the present reality meant. She made a desperate bid to get their interaction back on an acceptable footing. 'Where are we going?'

Max smiled. 'We're on our way to see Lady Jersey.'

'Why?'

'Patience, sweet Caroline,' came the reply, all the more outrageous for its tone. 'All will be revealed forthwith.'

They reached Lady Jersey's side where she stood just inside the main room.

'There you are, Twyford!'

The Duke of Twyford smoothly presented his ward. Her ladyship's prominent eyes rested on the curtsying Caroline, then, as the younger woman rose, widened with a suddenly arrested expression. She opened her mouth to ask the question burning the tip of her tongue but caught His Grace's eye and, reluctantly swallowing her curiosity, said, 'My dear Miss Twinning. Your guardian has requested you be given permission to waltz and I have no hesitation in granting it. And, as he is here, I present the Duke as a suitable partner.'

With considerable effort, Caroline managed to school her features to impassivity. Luckily, the musicians struck up at that moment, so that she barely had time to murmur her thanks to Lady Jersey before Max swept her on to the floor, leaving her ladyship, intrigued, staring after them.

Caroline struggled to master the unnerving sensation of being in her guardian's arms. He was holding her closer than strictly necessary but, as they twirled down the room, she realised that to everyone else they presented a perfect picture of the Duke of Twyford doing the pretty by his eldest ward. Only she was close enough to see the disturbing glint in his blue eyes and hear the warmth in his tone as he said, 'My dear ward, what a very accomplished dancer you are. Tell me, what other talents do you have that I've yet to sample?'

For the life of her, Caroline could not tear her eyes from his. She heard his words and understood their meaning but her brain refused to react. No shock, no scandalised response came to her lips. Instead, her mind was completely absorbed with registering the unbelievable fact that, despite their relationship of guardian and ward, Max Rotherbridge had every intention of seducing her. His desire was clear in the heat of his blue, blue gaze, in the way his hand at her back seemed to burn through the fine silk of her gown, in the gentle caress of his long fingers across her knuckles as he twirled her about the room under the long noses of the biggest gossips in London.

Mesmerised, she had sufficient presence of mind to keep a gentle smile fixed firmly on her face but her thoughts were whirling even faster than her feet. With a superhuman effort, she forced her lids to drop, screening her eyes from his. 'Oh, we Twinnings have many accomplishments, dear guardian.' To her relief, her voice was clear and untroubled. 'But I'm desolated to have to admit that they're all hopelessly mundane.'

A rich chuckle greeted this. 'Permit me to tell you, my ward, that, for the skills I have in mind, your qualifications are more than adequate.' Caroline's eyes flew to his. She could hardly believe her ears. But Max continued before she could speak, his blue eyes holding hers, his voice a seductive murmur. 'And while you naturally lack experience, I assure you that can easily, and most enjoyably, be remedied.'

It was too much. Caroline gave up the struggle to divine his motives and made a determined bid to reinstitute sanity. She smiled into the dark face above hers and said, quite clearly, 'This isn't happening.'

For a moment, Max was taken aback. Then, his sense of humour surfaced. 'No?'

'Of course not,' Caroline calmly replied. 'You're my guardian and I'm your ward. Therefore, it is simply not possible for you to have said what you just did.'

Studying her serene countenance, Max recognised the strategy and reluctantly admired her courage in adopting it. As things stood, it was not an easy defence for him to overcome. Reading in the grey-green eyes a determination not to be further discomposed, Max, too wise to push further, gracefully yielded.

'So what do you think of Almack's?' he asked.

Relieved, Caroline took the proffered olive branch and their banter continued on an impersonal level.

At the end of the dance, Max suavely surrendered her to her admirers, but not without a glance which, if she had allowed herself to think about it, would have made Caroline blush. She did not see him again until it was time for them to quit the Assembly Rooms. In order to survive the evening, she had sternly refused to let her mind dwell on his behaviour. Consequently, it had not occurred to her to arrange to exchange her place in her guardian's carriage for one in the Twyford coach. When Lizzie came to tug at her sleeve with the information that the others had already left, she perceived her error. But the extent of her guardian's foresight did not become apparent until they were halfway home.

She and Max shared the forward facing seat with Lizzie curled up in a corner opposite them. On departing King Street, they preserved a comfortable silence—due to tiredness in Lizzie's case, from being too absorbed with her thoughts in her case and, as she suddenly realised, from sheer experience in the case of her guardian.

They were still some distance from Mount Street when, without warning, Max took her hand in his. Surprised, she turned to look up at him, conscious of his fingers moving gently over hers. Despite the darkness of the carriage, his eyes caught hers. Deliberately, he raised her hand and kissed her fingertips. A delicious tingle raced along Caroline's nerves, followed by a second of increased vigour as he turned her hand over and placed a lingering kiss on her wrist. But they were nothing compared to the galvanising shock that hit her when, without giving any intimation of his intent, he bent his head and his lips found hers.

From Max's point of view, he was behaving with admirable restraint. He knew Lizzie was sound asleep and that his manipulative and normally composed eldest ward was well out of her depth. Yet he reined in his desires and kept the kiss light, his lips moving gently over hers, gradually increasing the pressure until she parted her lips. He savoured the warm sweetness of her mouth, then, inwardly smiling at the response she had been unable to hide, he withdrew and watched as her eyes slowly refocused.

Caroline, eyes round, looked at him in consternation. Then her shocked gaze flew to Lizzie, still curled in her corner.

'Don't worry. She's sound asleep.' His voice was deep and husky in the dark carriage.

Caroline, stunned, felt oddly reassured by the sound. Then she felt the carriage slow.

'And you're safe home,' came the gently mocking voice.

In a daze, Caroline helped him wake Lizzie and

then Max very correctly escorted them indoors, a smile of wicked contentment on his face.

Arabella stifled a wistful sigh and smiled brightly at the earnest young man who was guiding her around the floor in yet another interminable waltz. It had taken only a few days of the Season proper for her to sort through her prospective suitors. And come to the unhappy conclusion that none matched her requirements. The lads were too young, the men too old. There seemed to be no one in between. Presumably many were away with Wellington's forces, but surely there were those who could not leave the important business of keeping England running? And surely not all of them were old? She could not describe her ideal man, yet was sure she would instantly know when she met him. She was convinced she would feel it, like a thunderbolt from the blue. Yet no male of her acquaintance increased her heartbeat one iota.

Keeping up a steady and inconsequential conversation with her partner, something she could do half asleep, Arabella sighted her eldest sister, elegantly waltzing with their guardian. Now there was a coil. There was little doubt in Arabella's mind of the cause of Caroline's bright eyes and slightly flushed countenance. She looked radiant. But could a guardian marry his ward? Or, more to the point, was their guardian intent on marriage or had he some other arrangement in mind? Still, she had complete faith in Caroline. There had been many who had worshipped at her feet with something other than matrimony in view, yet her eldest sister had always had their measure. True, none had affected her as Max Rotherbridge clearly did. But Caroline knew the ropes, few better.

'I'll escort you back to Lady Benborough.'

The light voice of her partner drew her thoughts

back to the present. With a quick smile, Arabella declined. 'I think I've torn my flounce. I'll just go and pin it up. Perhaps you could inform Lady Benborough that I'll return immediately?' She smiled dazzlingly upon the young man. Bemused, he bowed and moved away into the crowd. Her flounce was perfectly intact but she needed some fresh air and in no circumstances could she have borne another half-hour of that particular young gentleman's serious discourse.

She started towards the door, then glanced back to see Augusta receive her message without apparent perturbation. Arabella turned back to the door and immediately collided with a chest of quite amazing proportions.

'Oh!'

For a moment, she thought the impact had winded her. Then, looking up into the face of the mountain she had met, she realised it wasn't that at all. It was the thunderbolt she had been waiting for.

Unfortunately, the gentleman seemed unaware of this momentous happening. 'My apologies, m'dear. Didn't see you there.'

The lazy drawl washed over Arabella. He was tall, very tall, and seemed almost as broad, with curling blond hair and laughing hazel eyes. He had quite the most devastating smile she had ever seen. Her knees felt far too weak to support her if she moved, so she stood still and stared, mouthing she knew not what platitudes.

The gentleman seemed to find her reaction amusing. But, with a polite nod and another melting smile, he was gone.

Stunned, Arabella found herself standing in the doorway staring at his retreating back. Sanity returned with a thump. Biting back a far from ladylike curse, she swept out in search of the withdrawing-room. The use of a borrowed fan and the consumption of a glass of cool water helped to restore her outward calm. Inside, her resentment grew.

No gentleman simply excused himself and walked away from her. That was her role. Men usually tried to stay by her side as long as possible. Yet this man had seemed disinclined to linger. Arabella was not vain but wondered what was more fascinating than herself that he needs must move on so abruptly. Surely he had felt that strange jolt just as she had? Maybe he wasn't a ladies' man? But no. The memory of the decided appreciation which had glowed so warmly in his hazel eyes put paid to that idea. And, now she came to think of it, the comprehensive glance which had roamed suggestively over most of her had been decidedly impertinent.

Arabella returned to the ballroom determined to bring her large gentleman to heel, if for no better reason than to assure herself she had been mistaken in him. But frustration awaited her. He was not there. For the rest of the evening, she searched the throng but caught no glimpse of her quarry. Then, just before the last dance, another waltz, he appeared in the doorway from the card-room.

Surrounded by her usual court, Arabella was at her effervescent best. Her smile was dazzling as she openly debated, laughingly teasing, over who to bestow her hand on for this last dance. Out of the corner of her eye, she watched the unknown gentleman approach. And walk past her to solicit the hand of a plain girl in an outrageously overdecorated pink gown.

Arabella bit her lip in vexation but managed to conceal it as severe concentration on her decision. As the musicians struck up, she accepted handsome Lord Tulloch as her partner and studiously paid him the most flattering attention for the rest of the evening.

CHAPTER FIVE

MAX was worried. Seriously worried. Since that first night at Almack's, the situation between Sarah Twinning and Darcy Hamilton had rapidly deteriorated to a state which, from experience, he knew was fraught with danger. As he watched Sarah across Lady Overton's ballroom, chatting with determined avidity to an eminently respectable and thoroughly boring young gentleman, his brows drew together in a considering frown. If, at the beginning of his guardianship, anyone had asked him where his sympathies would lie, with the Misses Twinning or the gentlemen of London, he would unhesitatingly have allied himself with his wards, on the grounds that four exquisite but relatively inexperienced country misses would need all the help they could get to defend their virtue successfully against the highly knowledgeable rakes extant within the *ton*. Now, a month later, having gained first-hand experience of the tenacious perversity of the Twinning sisters, he was not so sure.

His behaviour with Caroline on the night of their first visit to Almack's had been a mistake. How much of a mistake had been slowly made clear to him over the succeeding weeks. He was aware of the effect he had on her, had been aware of it from the first time he had seen her in his library at Delmere House. But in order to make any use of that weapon, he had to have her to himself. A fact, unfortunately, that she had worked out for herself. Consequently, whenever he approached her, he found her surrounded either by admirers who had been given too much encouragement for him to dismiss easily or one or more of her far too perceptive sisters. Lizzie, it was true, was not attuned to the situation between her eldest sister and their guardian. But he had unwisely made use of her innocence, to no avail as it transpired, and was now unhappily certain he would get no further opportunity by that route. Neither Arabella nor Sarah was the least bit perturbed by his increasingly blatant attempts to be rid of them. He was sure that, if he was ever goaded into ordering them to leave their sister alone with him, they would laugh and refuse. And tease him unmercifully about it, what was more. He had already had to withstand one episode of Arabella's artful play, sufficiently subtle, thank God, so that the others in the group had not understood her meaning.

His gaze wandered to where the third Twinning sister held court, seated on a chaise surrounded by ardent swains, her huge eyes wickedly dancing with mischief. As he watched, she tossed a comment to one of the circle and turned, her head playfully tilted, to throw a glance of open invitation into the handsome face of a blond giant standing before her. Max stiffened. Hell and the devil! He would have to put a stop to that game, and quickly. He had no difficulty in recognising the large frame of Hugo, Lord Denbigh. Although a few years younger than himself, in character and accomplishments there was little to choose between them. Under his horrified gaze, Hugo took advantage of a momentary distraction which had succeeded in removing attention temporarily from Arabella to lean forward to whisper something, Max could guess what, into her ear. The look she gave him in response made Max set his jaw grimly. Then, Hugo extended one large hand and Arabella, adroitly excusing herself to her other admirers, allowed him to lead her on to the floor. A waltz was just starting up.

Knowing there was only so much Hugo could do on a crowded ballroom floor, Max made a resolution to call on his aunt and wards on the morrow, firmly determined to acquaint them with his views on encouraging rakes. Even as the idea occurred, he groaned. How on earth could he tell Arabella to cease her flirtation with Hugo on the grounds he was a rake when he was himself trying his damnedest to seduce her sister and his best friend was similarly occupied with Sarah? He had known from the outset that this crazy situation would not work.

Reminded of what had originally prompted him to stand just inside the door between Lady Overton's ballroom and the salon set aside for cards and quietly study the company, Max returned his eyes to Sarah Twinning. Despite her assured manner, she was on edge, her hands betraying her nervousness as they played with the lace on her gown. Occasionally, her eyes would lift fleetingly to the door behind him. While to his experienced eyes she was not looking her best, Darcy, ensconced in the card-room, was looking even worse. He had been drinking steadily throughout the evening and, although far from drunk, was fast attaining a dangerous state. Suffering from Twinning-induced frustration himself, Max could readily sympathise. He sincerely hoped his pursuit of the eldest Miss Twinning would not bring him so low. His friendship with Darcy Hamilton stretched back over fifteen years. In all that time he had never seen his friend so affected by the desire for a particular woman. Like himself, Darcy was an experienced lover who liked to keep his affairs easy and uncomplicated. If a woman proved difficult, he was much more likely to shrug and, with a smile, pass on to greener fields. But with Sarah Twinning, he seemed unable to admit defeat.

The thought that he himself had no intention of

letting the elder Miss Twinning escape and was, even now, under the surface of his preoccupation with his other wards, plotting to get her into his arms, and, ultimately, into his bed, surfaced to shake his self-confidence. His black brows rose a little, in self-mockery. One could hardly blame the girls for keeping them at arm's length. The Twinning sisters had never encouraged them to believe they were of easy virtue, nor that they would accept anything less than marriage. Their interaction, thus far, had all been part of the game. By rights, it was they, the rakes of London, who should now acknowledge the evident truth that, despite their bountiful attractions, the Twinnings were virtuous females in search of husbands. And, having acknowledged that fact, to desist from their pursuit of the fair ladies. Without conscious thought on his part, his eyes strayed to where Caroline stood amid a group, mostly men, by the side of the dance-floor. She laughed and responded to some comment, her copper curls gleaming like rosy gold in the bright light thrown down by the chandeliers. As if feeling his gaze, she turned and, across the intervening heads, their eyes met. Both were still. Then, she smoothly turned back to her companions and Max, straightening his shoulders, moved further into the crowd. The trouble was, he did not think that he, any more than Darcy, could stop.

Max slowly passed through the throng, stopping here and there to chat with acquaintances, his intended goal his aunt, sitting in a blaze of glorious purple on a chaise by the side of the room. But before he had reached her, a hand on his arm drew him around to face the sharp features of Emma Mortland.

'Your Grace! It's been such an age since we've. . .talked.' Her ladyship's brown eyes quizzed him playfully.

Her arch tone irritated Max. It was on the tip of his tongue to recommend she took lessons in flirting from Arabella before she tried her tricks on him. Instead, he took her hand from his sleeve, bowed over it and pointedly returned it to her. 'As you're doubtless aware, Emma, I have other claims on my time.'

His careless use of her first name was calculated to annoy but Lady Mortland, having seen his absorption with his wards, particularly his eldest ward, over the past weeks, was fast coming to the conclusion that she should do everything in her power to bring Twyford to his knees or that tiara would slip through her fingers. As she was a female of little intelligence, she sincerely believed the attraction that had brought Max Rotherbridge to her bed would prove sufficient to induce him to propose. Consequently, she coyly glanced up at him through her long fair lashes and sighed sympathetically. 'Oh, my dear, *I know*. I do *feel* for you. This business of being guardian to four country girls must be such a bore to you. But surely, as a diversion, you could manage to spare us some few hours?'

Not for the first time, Max wondered where women such as Emma Mortland kept their intelligence. In their pockets? One truly had to wonder. As he looked down at her, his expression unreadable, he realised that she was a year or so younger than Caroline. Yet, from the single occasion on which he had shared her bed, he knew the frills and furbelows she favoured disguised a less than attractive figure, lacking the luscious curves that characterised his eldest ward. And Emma Mortland's energies, it seemed, were reserved for scheming. He had not been impressed. As he knew that a number of other gentlemen, including Darcy Hamilton, had likewise seen her sheets, he was at a loss to understand why she continued to single him out. A caustic dismissal was about to leave his lips when, amid a burst of hilarity from a group just behind them, he heard the rich tones of his eldest ward's laugh.

On the instant, a plan, fully formed, came into his head and, without further consideration, he acted. He allowed a slow, lazy smile to spread across his face. 'How well you read me, my sweet,' he drawled to the relieved Lady Mortland. Encouraged, she put her hand tentatively on his arm. He took it in his hand, intending to raise it to his lips, but to his surprise he could not quite bring himself to do so. Instead, he smiled meaningfully into her eyes. With an ease born of countless hours of practice, he instituted a conversation of the risqué variety certain to appeal to Lady Mortland. Soon, he had her gaily laughing and flirting freely with her eyes and her fan. Deliberately, he turned to lead her on to the floor for the waltz just commencing, catching, as he did, a look of innocent surprise on Caroline's face.

Grinning devilishly, Max encouraged Emma to the limits of acceptable flirtation. Then, satisfied with the scene he had created, as they circled the room, he raised his head to see the effect the sight of Lady Mortland in his arms was having on Caroline. To his chagrin, he discovered his eldest ward was no longer standing where he had last seen her. After a frantic visual search, during which he ignored Emma entirely, he located Caroline, also dancing, with the highly suitable Mr Willoughby. That same Mr Willoughby who, he knew, was becoming very particular in his attentions. Smothering a curse, Max half-heartedly returned his attention to Lady Mortland.

He had intended to divest himself of the encumbrance of her ladyship as soon as the dance ended but, as the music ceased, he realised they were next to

Caroline and her erstwhile partner. Again, Emma found herself the object of Max's undeniable, if strangely erratic charm. Under its influence, she blossomed and bloomed. Max, with one eye on Caroline's now unreadable countenance, leant closer to Emma to whisper an invitation to view the beauties of the moonlit garden. As he had hoped, she crooned her delight and, with an air of anticipated pleasure, allowed him to escort her through the long windows leading on to the terrace.

'Count me out.' Darcy Hamilton threw his cards on to the table and pushed back his chair. None of the other players was surprised to see him leave. Normally an excellent player, tonight his lordship had clearly had his mind elsewhere. And the brandy he had drunk was hardly calculated to improve matters, although his gait, as he headed for the ballroom, was perfectly steady.

In the ballroom, Darcy paused to glance about. He saw the musicians tuning up and then sighted his prey.

Almost as if she sensed his approach, Sarah turned as he came up to her. The look of sudden wariness that came into her large eyes pricked his conscience and, consequently, his temper. 'My dance, I think.'

It was not, as he well knew, but before she could do more than open her mouth to deny him Darcy had swept her on to the floor.

They were both excellent dancers and, despite their current difficulties, they moved naturally and easily together. Which was just as well, as their minds were each completely absorbed in trying to gauge the condition of the other. Luckily, they were both capable of putting on a display of calmness which succeeded in deflecting the interest of the curious.

Sarah, her heart, as usual, beating far too fast,

glanced up under her lashes at the handsome face above her, now drawn and slightly haggard. Her heart sank. She had no idea what the outcome of this strange relationship of theirs would be, but it seemed to be causing both of them endless pain. Darcy Hamilton filled her thoughts, day in, day out. But he had steadfastly refused to speak of marriage, despite the clear encouragement she had given him to do so. He had side-stepped her invitations, offering, instead, to introduce her to a vista of illicit delights whose temptation was steadily increasing with time. But she could not, would not accept. She would give anything in the world to be his wife but had no ambition to be his mistress. Lady Benborough had, with all kindness, dropped her a hint that he was very likely a confirmed bachelor, too wedded to his equestrian interests to be bothered with a wife and family, satisfied instead with mistresses and the occasional *affaire*. Surreptiously studying his rigid and unyielding face, she could find no reason to doubt Augusta's assessment. If that was so, then their association must end. And the sooner the better, for it was breaking her heart.

Seeing her unhappiness reflected in the brown pools of her eyes, Darcy inwardly cursed. There were times he longed to hurt her, in retribution for the agony she was putting him through, but any pain she felt seemed to rebound, ten times amplified, back on him. He was, as Lady Benborough had rightly surmised, well satisfied with his bachelor life. At least, he had been, until he had met Sarah Twinning. Since then, nothing seemed to be right any more. Regardless of the response he knew he awoke in her, she consistently denied any interest in the delightful pleasures he was only too willing to introduce her to. Or rather, held the prospect of said pleasures like a gun at his head, demanding matrimony. He would be damned if he would yield to such tactics. He had long ago considered matrimony, the state of, in a calm and reasoned way, and had come to the conclusion that it held few benefits for him. The idea of being driven, forced, pushed into taking such a step, essentially by the strength of his own raging desires, horrified him, leaving him annoyed beyond measure, principally with himself, but also, unreasonably he knew, with the object of said desires. As the music slowed and halted, he looked down at her lovely face and determined to give her one last chance to capitulate. If she remained adamant, he would have to leave London until the end of the Season. He was quite sure he could not bear the agony any longer.

As Sarah drew away from him and turned towards the room, Darcy drew her hand through his arm and deftly steered her towards the long windows leading on to the terrace. As she realised his intention, she hung back. With a few quick words, he reassured her. 'I just want to talk to you. Come into the garden.'

Thus far, Sarah had managed to avoid being totally private with him, too aware of her inexperience to chance such an interview. But now, looking into his pale grey eyes and seeing her own unhappiness mirrored there, she consented with a nod and they left the ballroom.

A stone terrace extended along the side of the house, the balustrade broken here and there by steps leading down to the gardens. Flambeaux placed in brackets along the walls threw flickering light down into the avenues and any number of couples could be seen, walking and talking quietly amid the greenery.

Unhurriedly, Darcy led her to the end of the terrace and then down the steps into a deserted walk. They both breathed in the heady freshness of the night air, calming their disordered senses and, without the need to exchange words, each drew some measure of comfort from the other's presence. At the end of the path, a secluded summer-house stood, white paintwork showing clearly against the black shadows of the shrubbery behind it.

As Darcy had hoped, the summer-house was deserted. The path leading to it was winding and heavily screened. Only those who knew of its existence would be likely to find it. He ushered Sarah through the narrow door and let it fall quietly shut behind them. The moonlight slanted through the windows, bathing the room in silvery tints. Sarah stopped in the middle of the circular floor and turned to face him. Darcy paused, trying to decide where to start, then crossed to stand before her, taking her hands in his. For some moments, they stood thus, the rake and the maid, gazing silently into each other's eyes. Then, Darcy bent his head and his lips found hers.

Sarah, seduced by the setting, the moonlight and the man before her, allowed him to gather her, unresisting, into his arms. The magic of his lips on hers was a more potent persuasion than any she had previously encountered. Caught by a rising tide of passion, she was drawn, helpless and uncaring, beyond the bounds of thought. Her lips parted and gradually the kiss deepened until, with the moonlight washing in waves over them, he stole her soul.

It was an unintentionally intimate caress which abruptly shook the stars from her eyes and brought her back to earth with an unsteady bump. Holding her tightly within one arm, Darcy had let his other hand slide, gently caressing, over her hip, intending to draw her more firmly against him. But the feel of his hand, scorching through her thin evening dress, sent shock waves of such magnitude through Sarah's pliant body that she pulled back with a gasp. Then, as horrified realisation fell like cold water over her heated flesh, she tore herself from his arms and ran.

For an instant, Darcy, stunned both by her response and by her subsequent reaction, stood frozen in the middle of the floor. A knot of jonquil ribbon from Sarah's dress had caught on the button of his cuff and impatiently he shook it free, then watched, fascinated, as it floated to the ground. The banging of the wooden door against its frame had stilled. Swiftly, he crossed the floor and, opening the door, stood in the aperture, listening to her footsteps dying in the spring night. Then, smothering a curse, he followed.

Sarah instinctively ran away from the main house, towards the shrubbery which lay behind the summer-house. She did not stop to think or reason, but just ran. Finally, deep within the tall clipped hedges and the looming bushes, her breath coming in gasps, she came to a clearing, a small garden at the centre of the shrubbery. She saw a marble bench set in an arbour. Thankfully, she sank on to it and buried her face in her hands.

Darcy, following, made for the shrubbery, her hurrying footsteps echoing hollowly on the gravel walks giving him the lead. But once she reached the grassed avenues between the high hedges, her feet made no sound. Penetrating the dark alleys, he was forced to go slowly, checking this way and that to make sure he did not pass her by. So quite fifteen minutes had passed before he reached the central garden and saw the dejected figure huddled on the bench.

In that time, sanity of a sort had returned to Sarah's mind. Her initial horror at her weakness had been replaced by the inevitable reaction. She was angry. Angry at herself, for being so weak that one kiss could overcome all her defences; angry at Darcy, for having engineered that little scene. She was busy whipping up the necessary fury to face the prospect of not seeing him ever again, when he materialised at her side. With a gasp, she came to her feet.

Relieved to find she was not crying, as he had thought, Darcy immediately caught her hand to prevent her flying from him again.

Stung by the shock his touch always gave her, intensified now, she was annoyed to discover, Sarah tried to pull her hand away. When he refused to let go, she said, her voice infused with an iciness designed to freeze, 'Kindly release me, Lord Darcy.'

On hearing her voice, Darcy placed the emotion that was holding her so rigid. The knowledge that she was angry, nay, furious, did nothing to improve his own temper, stirred to life by her abrupt flight. Forcing his voice to a reasonableness he was far from feeling, he said, 'If you'll give me your word you'll not run away from me, I'll release you.'

Sarah opened her mouth to inform him she would not so demean herself as to run from him when the knowledge that she just had, and might have reason to do so again, hit her. She remained silent. Darcy, accurately reading her mind, held on to her hand.

After a moment's consideration, he spoke. 'I had intended, my dear, to speak to you of our. . .curious relationship.'

Sarah, breathing rapidly and anxious to end the interview, immediately countered, 'I really don't think there's anything to discuss.'

A difficult pause ensued, then, 'So you would deny there's anything between us?'

The bleakness in his voice shook her, but she determinedly put up her chin, turning away from him as far as their locked hands would allow. 'Whatever's between us is neither here nor there,' she said, satisfied with the lightness she had managed to bring to her tone.

Her satisfaction was short-lived. Taking advantage of her movement, Darcy stepped quickly behind her, the hand still holding hers reaching across her, his arm wrapping about her waist and drawing her hard against him. His other hand came to rest on her shoulder, holding her still. He knew the shock it would give her, to feel his body against hers, and heard with grim satisfaction the hiss of her indrawn breath.

Sarah froze, too stunned to struggle, the sensation of his hard body against her back, his arm wound like steel about her waist, holding her fast, driving all rational thought from her brain. Then his breath wafted the curls around her ear. His words came in a deep and husky tone, sending tingling shivers up and down her spine.

'Well, sweetheart, there's very little between us now. So, perhaps we can turn our attention to our relationship?'

Sarah, all too well aware of how little there was between them, wondered in a moment of startling lucidity how he imagined that would improve her concentration. But Darcy's attention had already wandered. His lips were very gently trailing down her neck, creating all sorts of marvellous sensations which she tried very hard to ignore.

Then, he gave a deep chuckle. 'As I've been saying these weeks past, my dear, you're wasted as a virgin. Now, if you were to become my mistress, just think of all the delightful avenues we could explore.'

'I don't want to become your mistress!' Sarah almost wailed, testing the arm at her waist and finding it immovable.

'No?' came Darcy's voice in her ear. She had the impression he considered her answer for a full minute before he continued, 'Perhaps we should extend your education a trifle, my dear. So you fully appreciate what you're turning down. We wouldn't want you to make the wrong decision for lack of a few minutes' instruction, would we?'

Sarah had only a hazy idea of what he could mean but his lips had returned to her throat, giving rise to those strangely heady swirls of pleasure that washed through her, sapping her will. 'Darcy, stop! You know you shouldn't be doing this!'

He stilled. 'Do I?'

Into the silence, a nightingale warbled. Sarah held her breath.

But, when Darcy spoke again, the steel threading his voice, so often sensed yet only now recognised, warned her of the futility of missish pleas.

'Yes. You're right. I know I shouldn't.' His lips moved against her throat, a subtle caress. 'But what I want to do is to make love to you. As you won't allow that, then this will have to do for now.'

Sarah, incapable of further words, simply shook her head, powerless to halt the spreading fires he was so skilfully igniting.

Afterwards, Darcy could not understand how it had happened. He was as experienced with women as Max and had never previously lost control as he did that night. He had intended to do no more than reveal to the perverse woman her own desires and give her some inkling of the pleasures they could enjoy together. Instead, her responses were more than he had bargained for and his own desires stronger than he had been prepared to admit. Fairly early in the engagement, he had turned her once more into his arms, so he could capture her lips and take the lesson further. And further it had certainly gone, until the moon sank behind the high hedges and left them in darkness.

How the hell was he to get rid of her? Max, Lady Mortland on his arm, had twice traversed the terrace. He had no intention of descending to the shadowy avenues. He had no intention of paying any further attention to Lady Mortland at all. Lady Mortland, on the other hand, was waiting for his attentions to begin and was rather surprised at his lack of ardour in keeping to the terrace.

They were turning at the end of the terrace, when Max, glancing along, saw Caroline come out of the ballroom, alone, and walk quickly to the balustrade and peer over. She was clearly seeking someone. Emma Mortland, prattling on at his side, had not seen her. With the reflexes necessary for being one of the more successful rakes in the *ton*, Max whisked her ladyship back into the ballroom via the door they were about to pass.

Finding herself in the ballroom once more, with the Duke of Twyford bowing over her hand in farewell, Lady Mortland put a hand to her spinning head. 'Oh! But surely. . .'

'A guardian is never off duty for long, my dear,' drawled Max, about to move off.

'Perhaps I'll see you in the Park, tomorrow?' asked Emma, convinced his departure had nothing to do with inclination.

Max smiled. 'Anything's possible.'

He took a circuitous route around the ballroom and exited through the same door he had seen his ward use. Gaining the terrace, he almost knocked her over as she returned to the ballroom, looking back over her shoulder towards the gardens.

'Oh!' Finding herself unexpectedly in her guardian's arms temporarily suspended Caroline's faculties.

From her face, Max knew she had not been looking for him. He drew her further into the shadows of the terrace, placing her hand on his arm and covering it comfortingly with his. 'What is it?'

Caroline could not see any way of avoiding telling him. She fell into step beside him, unconsciously following his lead. 'Sarah. Lizzie saw her leave the ballroom with Lord Darcy. More than twenty minutes ago. They haven't returned.'

In the dim light, Max's face took on a grim look. He had suspected there would be trouble. He continued strolling towards the end of the terrace. 'I know where they'll be. There's a summer-house deeper in the gardens. I think you had better come with me.'

Caroline nodded and, unobtrusively, they made their way to the summer-house.

Max pushed open the door, then frowned at the empty room. He moved further in and Caroline followed. 'Not here?'

Max shook his head, then bent to pick up a knot of ribbon from the floor.

Caroline came to see and took it from him. She crossed to the windows, turning the small cluster this way and that to gauge the colour.

'Is it hers?' asked Max as he strolled to her side.

'Yes. I can't see the colour well but I know the knot. It's a peculiar one. I made it myself.'

'So they were here.'

'But where are they now?'

'Almost certainly on their way back to the house,' answered Max. 'There's nowhere else in this garden suitable for the purpose Darcy would have in mind. Presumably, your sister convinced him to return to more populated surroundings.' He spoke lightly, but, in truth, was puzzled. He could not readily imagine Sarah turning Darcy from his purpose, not in his present mood, not in this setting. But he was sure there was nowhere else they could go.

'Well, then,' said Caroline, dusting the ribbon, 'we'd better go back, too.'

'In a moment,' said Max.

His tone gave Caroline an instant's warning. She put out a hand to fend him off. 'No! This is *absurd*—you know it is.'

Despite her hand, Max succeeded in drawing her into his arms, holding her lightly. 'Absurd, is it? Well, you just keep on thinking how absurd it is, while I enjoy your very sweet lips.' And he proceeded to do just that.

As his lips settled over hers, Caroline told herself she should struggle. But, for some mystical reason, her body remained still, her senses turned inward by his kiss. Under gentle persuasion, her lips parted and, with a thrill, she felt his gentle exploration teasing her senses, somehow drawing her deeper. Time seemed suspended and she felt her will weakening as she melted into his arms and they locked around her.

Max's mind was ticking in double time, evaluating the amenities of the summer-house and estimating how long they could remain absent from the ballroom. He decided neither answer was appropriate. Seduction was an art and should not be hurried. Besides, he doubted his eldest ward was quite ready to submit yet. Reluctantly, he raised his head and grinned wolfishly at her. 'Still absurd?'

Caroline's wits were definitely not connected. She simply stared at him uncomprehendingly.

In face of this response, Max laughed and, drawing

her arm through his, steered her to the door. 'I think you're right. We'd better return.'

Sanity returned to Sarah's mind like water in a bucket, slowly filling from a dripping tap, bit by bit, until it was full. For one long moment, she allowed her mind to remain blank, savouring the pleasure of being held so gently against him. Then, the world returned and demanded her response. She struggled to sit up and was promptly helped to her feet. She checked her gown and found it perfectly tidy, bar one knot of ribbon on her sleeve which seemed to have gone missing.

Darcy, who had returned to earth long before, had been engaged in some furious thinking. But, try as he might, he could not imagine how she would react. Like Max, it had been a long time since young virgins had been his prey. As she stood, he tried to catch a glimpse of her face in the dim light but she perversely kept it averted. In the end, he caught her hands and drew her to stand before him. 'Sweetheart, are you all right?'

Strangely enough, it was the note of sincerity in his voice which snapped Sarah's control. Her head came up and, even in the darkness, her eyes flashed fire. 'Of course I'm not all right! How *dare* you take advantage of me?'

She saw Darcy's face harden at her words and, in fury at his lack of comprehension, she slapped him.

For a minute, absolute silence reigned. Then a sob broke from Sarah as she turned away, her head bent to escape the look on Darcy's face.

Darcy, slamming a door on his emotions, so turbulent that even he had no idea what he felt, moved to rescue them both. In a voice totally devoid of all feeling, he said, 'We had better get back to the house.'

In truth, neither had any idea how long they had been absent. In silence, they walked side by side, careful not to touch each other, until, eventually, the terrace was reached. Sarah, crying but determined not to let the tears fall, blinked hard, then mounted the terrace steps by Darcy's side. At the top, he turned to her. 'It would be better, I think, if you went in first.'

Sarah, head bowed, nodded and went.

Caroline and Max regained the ballroom and both glanced around for their party. Almost immediately, Lizzie appeared by her sister's side on the arm of one of her youthful swains. She prettily thanked him and dismissed him before turning to her sister and their guardian. 'Sarah came back just after you left to look for her. She and Lady Benborough and Mrs Alford have gone home.'

'Oh?' It was Max's voice which answered her. 'Why?'

Lizzie cast a questioning look at Caroline and received a nod in reply. 'Sarah was upset about something.'

Max was already scanning the room when Lizzie's voice reached him. 'Lord Darcy came in a little while after Sarah. He's left now, too.'

With a sigh, Max realised there was nothing more to be done that night. They collected Arabella and departed Overton House, Caroline silently considering Sarah's problem and Max wondering if he was going to have to wait until his friend solved his dilemma before he would be free to settle his own affairs.

CHAPTER SIX

MAX took a long sip of his brandy and savoured the smooth warmth as it slid down his throat. He stretched his legs to the fire. The book he had been trying to read rested, open, on his thighs, one strong hand holding it still. He moved his shoulders slightly, settling them into the comfort of well padded leather and let his head fall back against the chair.

It was the first night since the beginning of the Season that he had had a quiet evening at home. And he needed it. Who would have thought his four wards would make such a drastic change in a hitherto well ordered existence? Then he remembered. He had. But he had not really believed his own dire predictions. And the only reason he was at home tonight was because Sarah, still affected by her brush with Darcy the night before, had elected to remain at home and Caroline had stayed with her. He deemed his aunt Augusta and Miriam Alford capable of chaperoning the two younger girls between them. After the previous night, it was unlikely they would allow any liberties.

Even now, no one had had an accounting of what had actually taken place between Darcy and Sarah. But, knowing Darcy, his imagination had supplied a quantity of detail. He had left Delmere House at noon that day with the fell intention of running his lordship to earth and demanding an explanation. He had finally found him at Manton's Shooting Gallery, culping wafer after wafer with grim precision. One look at his friend's face had been enough to cool his temper. He had patiently waited until Darcy, having dispatched all the wafers currently in place, had thrown the pistol down with an oath and turned to him.

'Don't ask!'

So he had preserved a discreet silence on the subject and together they had rolled about town, eventually ending in Cribb's back parlour, drinking Blue Ruin. Only then had Darcy reverted to the topic occupying both their minds. 'I'm leaving town.'

'Oh?'

His lordship had run a hand through his perfectly cut golden locks, disarranging them completely, in a gesture Max had never, in all their years together, seen him use. 'Going to Leicestershire. I need a holiday.'

Max had nodded enigmatically. Lord Darcy's principal estates lay in Leicestershire and always, due to the large number of horses he raised, demanded attention. But in general, his lordship managed to run his business affairs quite comfortably from town.

'No, by God! I've a better idea. I'll go to Ireland. It's further away.'

As Max knew, Lord Darcy's brother resided on the family estates in Ireland. Still, he had said nothing, patiently waiting for what he had known would come.

Darcy had rolled his glass between his hands, studying the swirling liquid with apparent interest. 'About Sarah.'

'Mmm?' Max had kept his own eyes firmly fixed on his glass.

'I didn't.'

'Oh?'

'No. But I'm not entirely sure she knows what happened.' Darcy had drained his glass, using the opportunity to watch Max work this out.

Finally, comprehension had dawned. A glimmer of

a smile had tugged at the corners of His Grace of Twyford's mouth. 'Oh.'

'Precisely. I thought I'd leave it in your capable hands.'

'Thank you!' Max had replied. Then he had groaned and dropped his head into his hands. 'How the hell do you imagine I'm to find out what she believes and then explain it to her if she's wrong?' His mind had boggled at the awful idea.

'I thought you might work through Miss Twinning,' Darcy had returned, grinning for the first time that day.

Relieved to see his friend smile, even at his expense, Max had grinned back. 'I've not been pushing the pace quite as hard as you. Miss Twinning and I have some way to go before we reach the point where such intimate discussions would be permissible.'

'Oh, well,' Darcy had sighed. 'I only hope you have better luck than I.'

'Throwing in the towel?'

Darcy had shrugged. 'I wish I knew.' A silence had ensued which Darcy eventually broke. 'I've got to get away.'

'How long will you be gone?'

Another shrug. 'Who knows? As long as it takes, I suppose.'

He had left Darcy packing at Hamilton House and returned to the comfort of his own home to spend a quiet evening in contemplation of his wards. Their problems should really not cause surprise. At first sight, he had known what sort of men the Twinning girls would attract. And there was no denying they responded to such men. Even Arabella seemed hell-bent on tangling with rakes. Thankfully, Lizzie seemed too quiet and gentle to take the same road—three rakes in any family should certainly be enough.

Family? The thought sobered him. He sat, eyes on the flames leaping in the grate, and pondered the odd notion.

His reverie was interrupted by sounds of an arrival. He glanced at the clock and frowned. Too late for callers. What now? He reached the hall in time to see Hillshaw and a footman fussing about the door.

'Yes, it's all right, Hillshaw, I'm not an invalid, you know!'

The voice brought Max forward. 'Martin!'

The tousled brown head of Captain Martin Rotherbridge turned to greet his older brother. A winning grin spread across features essentially a more boyish version of Max's own. 'Hello, Max. I'm back, as you see. Curst Frogs put a hole in my shoulder.'

Max's gaze fell to the bulk of bandaging distorting the set of his brother's coat. He clasped the hand held out to him warmly, his eyes raking the other's face. 'Come into the library. Hillshaw?'

'Yes, Your Grace. I'll see to some food.'

When they were comfortably ensconced by the fire, Martin with a tray of cold meat by his side and a large balloon of his brother's best brandy in his hand, Max asked his questions.

'No, you're right,' Martin answered to one of these. 'It wasn't just the wound, though that was bad enough. They tell me that with rest it'll come good in time.' Max waited patiently. His brother fortified himself before continuing. 'No. I sold out simply because, now the action's over, it's deuced boring over there. We sit about and play cards half the day. And the other half, we just sit and reminisce about all the females we've ever had.' He grinned at his brother in a way Caroline, for one, would have recognised. 'Seemed to me I was running out of anecdotes. So I decided to come home and lay in a fresh stock.'

Max returned his brother's smile. Other than the shoulder wound, Martin was looking well. The difficult wound and slow convalescence had not succeeded in erasing the healthy glow from outdoor living which burnished his skin and, although there were lines present which had not been there before, these merely served to emphasise the fact that Martin Rotherbridge had seen more than twenty-five summers and was an old hand in many spheres. Max was delighted to hear he had returned to civilian life. Aside from his genuine concern for a much loved sibling, Martin was now the heir to the Dukedom of Twyford. While inheriting the Delmere holdings, with which he was well acquainted, would have proved no difficulty to Martin, the Twyford estates were a different matter. Max eyed the long, lean frame stretched out in the chair before him and wondered where to begin. Before he had decided, Martin asked, 'So how do you like being "Your Grace"?'

In a few pithy sentences, Max told him. He then embarked on the saga of horrors examination of his uncle's estate had revealed, followed by a brief description of their present circumstances. Seeing the shadow of tiredness pass across Martin's face, he curtailed his report, saying instead, 'Time for bed, stripling. You're tired.'

Martin started, then grinned sleepily at Max's use of his childhood tag. 'What? Oh, yes. I'm afraid I'm not up to full strength yet. And we've been travelling since first light.'

Max's hand at his elbow assisted him to rise from the depths of the armchair. On his feet, Martin stretched and yawned. Seen side by side, the similarity between the brothers was marked. Max was still a few inches taller and his nine years seniority showed in the heavier musculature of his chest and shoulders. Other than that, the differences were few—Martin's hair was a shade lighter than Max's dark mane and his features retained a softness Max's lacked, but the intensely blue eyes of the Rotherbridges shone in both dark faces.

Martin turned to smile at his brother. 'It's good to be home.'

'Good morning. Hillshaw, isn't it? I'm Lizzie Twinning. I've come to return a book to His Grace.'

Although he had only set eyes on her once before, Hillshaw remembered his master's youngest ward perfectly. As she stepped daintily over the threshold of Delmere House, a picture in a confection of lilac muslin, he gathered his wits to murmur, 'His Grace is not presently at home, miss. Perhaps his secretary, Mr Cummings, could assist you.' Hillshaw rolled one majestic eye towards a hovering footman who immediately, if reluctantly, disappeared in the direction of the back office frequented by the Duke's secretary.

Lizzie, allowing Hillshaw to remove her half-cape, looked doubtful. But all she said was, 'Wait here for me, Hennessy. I shan't be long.' Her maid, who had dutifully followed her in, sat primly on the edge of a chair by the wall and, under the unnerving stare of Hillshaw, lowered her round-eyed gaze to her hands.

Immediately, Mr Joshua Cummings came hurrying forward from the dimness at the rear of the hall. 'Miss Lizzie? I'm afraid His Grace has already left the house, but perhaps I may be of assistance?' Mr Cummings was not what one might expect of a nobleman's secretary. He was of middle age and small and round and pale, and, as Lizzie later informed her sisters, looked as if he spent his days locked away perusing dusty papers. In a sense, he did. He was a single man and, until taking his present post, had lived with his mother on the Rotherbridge estate in Surrey. His family had long been associated with the Rotherbridges and he was sincerely devoted to that family's interests. Catching sight of the book in Lizzie's small hand, he smiled. 'Ah, I see you have brought back Lord Byron's verses. Perhaps you'd like to read his next book? Or maybe one of Mrs Linfield's works would be more to your taste?'

Lizzie smiled back. On taking up residence at Twyford House, the sisters had been disappointed to find that, although extensive, the library there did not hold any of the more recent fictional works so much discussed among the *ton*. Hearing of their complaint, Max had revealed that his own library did not suffer from this deficiency and had promised to lend them any books they desired. But, rather than permit the sisters free rein in a library that also contained a number of works less suitable for their eyes, he had delegated the task of looking out the books they wanted to his secretary. Consequently, Mr Cummings felt quite competent to deal with the matter at hand.

'If you'd care to wait in the drawing-room, miss?' Hillshaw moved past her to open the door. With another dazzling smile, Lizzie handed the volume she carried to Mr Cummings, informing him in a low voice that one of Mrs Linfield's novels would be quite acceptable, then turned to follow Hillshaw. As she did so, her gaze travelled past the stately butler to rest on the figure emerging from the shadow of the library door. She remained where she was, her grey-brown eyes growing rounder and rounder, as Martin Rotherbridge strolled elegantly forward.

After the best night's sleep he had had in months, Martin had felt ready to resume normal activities but, on descending to the breakfast parlour, had discovered his brother had already left the house to call in at Tattersall's. Suppressing the desire to pull on his coat and follow, Martin had resigned himself to awaiting Max's return, deeming it wise to inform his brother in person that he was setting out to pick up the reins of his civilian existence before he actually did so. Knowing his friends, and their likely reaction to his reappearance among them, he was reasonably certain he would not be returning to Delmere House until the following morning. And he knew Max would worry unless he saw for himself that his younger brother was up to it. So, with a grin for his older brother's affection, he had settled in the library to read the morning's news sheets. But, after months of semi-invalidism, his returning health naturally gave rise to returning spirits. Waiting patiently was not easy. He had been irritably pacing the library when his sharp ears had caught the sound of a distinctly feminine voice in the hall. Intrigued, he had gone to investigate.

Setting eyes on the vision gracing his brother's hall, Martin's immediate thought was that Max had taken to allowing his ladybirds to call at his house. But the attitudes of Hillshaw and Cummings put paid to that idea. The sight of a maid sitting by the door confirmed his startled perception that the vision was indeed a young lady. His boredom vanishing like a cloud on a spring day, he advanced.

Martin allowed his eyes to travel, gently, so as not to startle her, over the delicious figure before him. Very nice. His smile grew. The silence around him penetrated his mind, entirely otherwise occupied. 'Hillshaw, I think you'd better introduce us.'

Hillshaw almost allowed a frown to mar his impassive countenance. But he knew better than to try to avoid the unavoidable. Exchanging a glance of fellow feeling with Mr Cummings, he obliged in sternly disapproving tones. 'Captain Martin Rotherbridge, Miss

Lizzie Twinning. The young lady is His Grace's youngest ward, sir.'

With a start, Martin's gaze, which had been locked with Lizzie's, flew to Hillshaw's face. 'Ward?' He had not been listening too well last night when Max had been telling him of the estates, but he was sure his brother had not mentioned any wards.

With a thin smile, Hillshaw inclined his head in assent.

Lizzie, released from that mesmerising gaze, spoke up, her soft tones a dramatic contrast to the masculine voices. 'Yes. My sisters and I are the Duke's wards, you know.' She held out her hand. 'How do you do? I didn't know the Duke had a brother. I've only dropped by to exchange some books His Grace lent us. Mr Cummings was going to take care of it.'

Martin took the small gloved hand held out to him and automatically bowed over it. Straightening, he moved to her side, placing her hand on his arm and holding it there. 'In that case, Hillshaw's quite right. You should wait in the drawing-room.' The relief on Hillshaw's and Mr Cummings' faces evaporated at his next words. 'And I'll keep you company.'

As Martin ushered Lizzie into the drawing-room and pointedly shut the door in Hillshaw's face, the Duke's butler and secretary looked at each other helplessly. Then Mr Cummings scurried away to find the required books, leaving Hillshaw to look with misgiving at the closed door of the drawing-room.

Inside, blissfully unaware of the concern she was engendering in her guardian's servants, Lizzie smiled trustingly up at the source of that concern.

'Have you been my brother's ward for long?' Martin asked.

'Oh, no!' said Lizzie. Then, 'That is, I suppose, yes.' She looked delightfully befuddled and Martin could not suppress a smile. He guided her to the chaise and, once she had settled, took the chair opposite her so that he could keep her bewitching face in full view.

'It depends, I suppose,' said Lizzie, frowning in her effort to gather her wits, which had unaccountably scattered, 'on what you'd call long. Our father died eighteen months ago, but then the other Duke—your uncle, was he not?—was our guardian. But when we came back from America, your brother had assumed the title. So then he was our guardian.'

Out of this jumbled explanation, Martin gleaned enough to guess the truth. 'Did you enjoy America? Were you there long?'

Little by little his questions succeeded in their aim and in short order, Lizzie had relaxed completely and was conversing in a normal fashion with her guardian's brother.

Listening to her description of her home, Martin shifted, trying to settle his shoulder more comfortably. Lizzie's sharp eyes caught the awkward movement and descried the wad of bandaging cunningly concealed beneath his coat.

'You're injured!' She leant forward in concern. 'Does it pain you dreadfully?'

'No, no. The Frogs just got lucky, that's all. Soon be right as rain, I give you my word.'

'You were in the army?' Lizzie's eyes had grown round. 'Oh, please tell me all about it. It must have been so exciting!'

To Martin's considerable astonishment, he found himself recounting for Lizzie's benefit the horrors of the campaign and the occasional funny incident which had enlivened their days. She did not recoil but listened avidly. He had always thought he was a dab hand at interrogation but her persistent questioning left him reeling. She even succeeded in dragging from him the reason he had yet to leave the house. Her ready sympathy, which he had fully expected to send him running, enveloped him instead in a warm glow, a sort of prideful care which went rapidly to his head.

Then Mr Cummings arrived with the desired books. Lizzie took them and laid them on a side-table beside her, patently ignoring the Duke's secretary who was clearly waiting to escort her to the front door. With an ill-concealed grin, Martin dismissed him. 'It's all right, Cummings. Miss Twinning has taken pity on me and decided to keep me entertained until my brother returns.'

Lizzie, entirely at home, turned a blissful smile on Mr Cummings, leaving that gentleman with no option but to retire.

An hour later, Max crossed his threshold to be met by Hillshaw, displaying, quite remarkably, an emotion very near agitation. This was instantly explained. 'Miss Lizzie's here. In the drawing-room. With Mr Martin.'

Max froze. Then nodded to his butler. 'Very good, Hillshaw.' His sharp eyes had already taken in the bored face of the maid sitting in the shadows. Presumably, Lizzie had been here for some time. His face was set in grim lines as his hand closed on the handle of the drawing-room door.

The sight which met his eyes was not at all what he had expected. As he shut the door behind him, Martin's eyes lifted to his, amused understanding in the blue depths. He was seated in an armchair and Lizzie occupied the nearest corner of the chaise. She was presently hunched forward, pondering what lay before her on a small table drawn up between them. As Max rounded the chaise, he saw to his stupefication that they were playing chequers.

Lizzie looked up and saw him. 'Oh! You're back. I

was just entertaining your brother until you returned.' Max blinked but Lizzie showed no consciousness of the implication of her words and he discarded the notion of enlightening her.

Then Lizzie's eyes fell on the clock on the mantelshelf. 'Oh, dear! I didn't realise it was so late. I must go. Where are those books Mr Cummings brought?'

Martin fetched them for her and, under the highly sceptical gaze of his brother, very correctly took leave of her. Max, seeing the expression in his brother's eyes as they rested on his youngest ward, almost groaned aloud. This was really too much.

Max saw Lizzie out, then returned to the library. But before he could launch into his inquisition, Martin got in first. 'You didn't tell me you had inherited four wards.'

'Well, I have,' said Max, flinging himself into an armchair opposite the one his brother had resumed.

'Are they all like that?' asked Martin in awe.

Max needed no explanation of what 'that' meant. He answered with a groan, 'Worse!'

Eyes round, Martin did not make the mistake of imagining the other Twinning sisters were antidotes. His gaze rested on his brother for a moment, then his face creased into a wide smile. 'Good lord!'

Max brought his blue gaze back from the ceiling and fixed it firmly on his brother. 'Precisely. That being so, I suggest you revise the plans you've been making for Lizzie Twinning.'

Martin's grin, if anything, became even broader. 'Why so? It's you who's their guardian, not I. Besides, you don't seriously expect me to believe that, if our situations were reversed, you'd pay any attention to such restrictions?' When Max frowned, Martin continued, 'Anyway, good heavens, you must have seen it for yourself. They're like ripe plums, ready for the picking.' He stopped at Max's raised hand.

'Permit me to fill you in,' drawled his older brother. 'For a start, I've nine years on you and there's nothing about the business you know that I don't. However, quite aside from that, I can assure you the Twinning sisters, ripe though they may be, are highly unlikely to fall into anyone's palms without a prior proposal of marriage.'

A slight frown settled over Martin's eyes. Not for a moment did he doubt the accuracy of Max's assessment. But he had been strongly attracted to Lizzie Twinning and was disinclined to give up the idea of converting her to his way of thinking. He looked up and blue eyes met blue. 'Really?'

Max gestured airily. 'Consider the case of Lord Darcy Hamilton.' Martin looked his question. Max obliged. 'Being much taken with Sarah, the second of the four, Darcy's been engaged in storming her citadel for the past five weeks and more. No holds barred, I might add. And the outcome, you ask? As of yesterday, he's retired to his estates, to lick his wounds and, unless I miss my guess, to consider whether he can stomach the idea of marriage.'

'Good lord!' Although only peripherally acquainted with Darcy Hamilton, Martin knew he was one of Max's particular friends and that his reputation in matters involving the fairer sex was second only to Max's own.

'Exactly,' nodded Max. 'Brought low by a chit of a girl. So, brother dear, if it's your wish to tangle with any Twinnings, I suggest you first decide how much you're willing to stake on the throw.'

As he pondered his brother's words, Martin noticed that Max's gaze had become abstracted. He only just caught the last words his brother said, musing, almost to himself. 'For, brother mine, it's my belief the Twinnings eat rakes for breakfast.'

The coach swayed as it turned a corner and Arabella clutched the strap swinging by her head. As equilibrium returned, she settled her skirts once more and glanced at the other two occupants of the carriage. The glow from a street lamp momentarily lit the interior of the coach, then faded as the four horses hurried on. Arabella grinned into the darkness.

Caroline had insisted that she and not Lizzie share their guardian's coach. One had to wonder why. Too often these days, her eldest sister had the look of the cat caught just after it had tasted the cream. Tonight, that look of guilty pleasure, or, more specifically, the anticipation of guilty pleasure, was marked.

She had gone up to Caroline's room to hurry her sister along. Caroline had been sitting, staring at her reflection in the mirror, idly twisting one copper curl to sit more attractively about her left ear.

'Caro? Are you ready? Max is here.'

'Oh!' Caroline had stood abruptly, then paused to cast one last critical glance over her pale sea-green dress, severely styled as most suited her ample charms, the neckline daringly *décolleté*. She had frowned, her fingers straying to the ivory swell of her breasts. 'What do you think, Bella? Is it too revealing? Perhaps a piece of lace might make it a little less. . .?'

'Attractive?' Arabella had brazenly supplied. 'To be perfectly frank, I doubt our guardian would approve a fichu.'

The delicate blush that had appeared on Caroline's cheeks had been most informative. But, 'Too true,' was all her sister had replied.

Arabella looked across the carriage once more and caught the gleam of warm approval that shone in their guardian's eyes as they rested on Caroline. It was highly unlikely that the conservative Mr Willoughby was the cause of her sister's blushes. That being so, what game was the Duke of Twyford playing? And, even more to the point, was Caro thinking of joining in?

Heaven knew, they had had a close enough call with Sarah and Lord Darcy. Nothing had been said of Sarah's strange affliction, yet they were all close enough for even the innocent Lizzie to have some inkling of the root cause. And while Max had been the soul of discretion in speaking privately to Caroline and Sarah in the hall before they had left, it was as plain as a pikestaff the information he had imparted had not included news of a proposal. Sarah's pale face had paled further. But the Twinnings were made of stern stuff and Sarah had shaken her head at Caro's look of concern.

The deep murmur of their guardian's voice came to her ears, followed by her sister's soft tones. Arabella's big eyes danced. She could not make out their words but those tones were oh, so revealing. But if Sarah was in deep waters and Caro was hovering on the brink, she, to her chagrin, had not even got her toes wet yet.

Arabella frowned at the moon, showing fleetingly between the branches of a tall tree. Hugo, Lord Denbigh. The most exasperating man she had ever met. She would give anything to be able to say she didn't care a button for him. Unfortunately, he was the only man who could make her tingle just by looking at her.

Unaware that she was falling far short of Caroline's expectations, Arabella continued to gaze out of the window, absorbed in contemplation of the means available for bringing one large gentleman to heel.

* * *

The heavy Twyford coach lumbered along in the wake of the sleek Delmere carriage. Lady Benborough put up a hand to right her wig, swaying perilously as they rounded a particularly sharp corner. For the first time since embarking on her nephew's crusade to find the Twinning girls suitable husbands, she felt a twinge of nervousness. She was playing with fire and she knew it. Still, she could not regret it. The sight of Max and Caroline together in the hall at Twyford House had sent a definite thrill through her old bones. As for Sarah, she doubted not that Darcy Hamilton was too far gone to desist, resist and retire. True, he might not know it yet, but time would certainly bring home to him the penalty he would have to pay to walk away from the snare. Her shrewd blue eyes studied the pale face opposite her. Even in the dim light, the strain of the past few days was evident. Thankfully, no one outside their party had been aware of that contretemps. So, regardless of what Sarah herself believed, Augusta had no qualms. Sarah was home safe; she could turn her attention elsewhere.

Arabella, the minx, had picked a particularly difficult nut to crack. Still, she could hardly fault the girl's taste. Hugo Denbigh was a positive Adonis, well born, well heeled and easy enough in his ways. Unfortunately, he was so easy to please that he seemed to find just as much pleasure in the presence of drab little girls as he derived from Arabella's rather more scintillating company. Gammon, of course, but how to alert Arabella to that fact? Or would it be more to the point to keep quiet and allow Hugo a small degree of success? As her mind drifted down that particular path, Augusta suddenly caught herself up and had the grace to look sheepish. What appalling thoughts for a chaperon!

Her gaze fell on Lizzie, sweet but far from demure

in a gown of delicate silver gauze touched with colour in the form of embroidered lilacs. A soft, introspective smile hovered over her classically moulded lips. Almost a smile of anticipation. Augusta frowned. Had she missed something?

Mentally reviewing Lizzie's conquests, Lady Benborough was at a loss to account for the suppressed excitement evident, now she came to look more closely, in the way the younger girl's fingers beat an impatient if silent tattoo on the beads of her reticule. Clearly, whoever he was would be at the ball. She would have to watch her youngest charge like a hawk. Lizzie was too young, in all conscience, to be allowed the licence her more worldly sisters took for granted.

Relaxing back against the velvet squabs, Augusta smiled. Doubtless she was worrying over nothing. Lizzie might have the Twinning looks but surely she was too serious an innocent to attract the attention of a rake? Three rakes she might land, the Twinnings being the perfect bait, but a fourth was bound to be wishful thinking.

CHAPTER SEVEN

MARTIN puzzled over Max's last words on the Twinnings but it was not until he met the sisters that evening, at Lady Montacute's drum, that he divined what had prompted his brother to utter them. He had spent the afternoon dropping in on certain old friends, only to be, almost immediately, bombarded with requests for introductions to the Twinnings. He had come away with the definite impression that the best place to be that evening would be wherever the Misses Twinning were destined. His batman and valet, Jiggins, had turned up the staggering information that Max himself usually escorted his wards to their evening engagements. Martin had found this hard to credit, but when, keeping an unobtrusive eye on the stream of arrivals from a vantage-point beside a potted palm in Lady Montacute's ballroom, he had seen Max arrive surrounded by Twinning sisters, he had been forced to accept the crazy notion as truth. When the observation that the fabulous creature on his brother's arm was, in fact, his eldest ward finally penetrated his brain all became clear.

Moving rapidly to secure a dance with Lizzie, who smiled up at him with flattering welcome, Martin was close enough to see the expression in his brother's eyes as he bent to whisper something in Miss Twinning's ear, prior to relinquishing her to the attention of the circle forming about her. His brows flew and he pursed his lips in surprise. As his brother's words of that morning returned to him, he grinned. How much was Max prepared to stake?

For the rest of the evening, Martin watched and plotted and planned. He used his wound as an excuse not to dance, which enabled him to spend his entire time studying Lizzie Twinning. It was an agreeable pastime. Her silvery dress floated about her as she danced and the candlelight glowed on her sheening brown curls. With her natural grace, she reminded him of a fairy sprite, except that he rather thought such mythical creatures lacked the fulsome charms with which the Twinning sisters were so well endowed. Due to his experienced foresight, Lizzie accommodatingly returned to his side after every dance, convinced by his chatter of the morning that he was in dire need of cheering up. Lady Benborough, to whom he had dutifully made his bow, had snorted in disbelief at his die-away airs but had apparently been unable to dissuade Lizzie's soft heart from bringing him continual succour. By subtle degrees, he sounded her out on each of her hopeful suitors and was surprised at his own relief in finding she had no special leaning towards any.

He started his campaign in earnest when the musicians struck up for the dance for which he *had* engaged her. By careful manoeuvring, they were seated in a sheltered alcove, free for the moment of her swains. Schooling his features to grave disappointment, he said, 'Dear Lizzie. I'm so sorry to disappoint you, but. . .' He let his voice fade away weakly.

Lizzie's sweet face showed her concern. 'Oh! Do you not feel the thing? Perhaps I can get Mrs Alford's smelling salts for you?'

Martin quelled the instinctive response to react to her suggestion in too forceful a manner. Instead, he waved aside her words with one limp hand. 'No! No! Don't worry about me. I'll come about shortly.' He smiled forlornly at her, allowing his blue gaze to rest, with calculated effect, on her grey-brown eyes. 'But maybe you'd like to get one of your other beaux to dance with you? I'm sure Mr Mallard would be only too thrilled.' He made a move as if to summon this gentleman, the most assiduous of her suitors.

'Heavens, no!' exclaimed Lizzie, catching his hand in hers to prevent the action. 'I'll do no such thing. If you're feeling poorly then of course I'll stay with you.' She continued to hold his hand and, for his part, Martin made no effort to remove it from her warm clasp.

Martin closed his eyes momentarily, as if fighting off a sudden faintness. Opening them again, he said, 'Actually, I do believe it's all the heat and noise in here that's doing it. Perhaps if I went out on to the terrace for a while, it might clear my head.'

'The very thing!' said Lizzie, jumping up.

Martin, rising more slowly, smiled down at her in a brotherly fashion. 'Actually, I'd better go alone. Someone might get the wrong idea if we both left.'

'Nonsense!' said Lizzie, slightly annoyed by his implication that such a conclusion could, of course, have no basis in fact. 'Why should anyone worry? We'll only be a few minutes and anyway, I'm your brother's ward, after all.'

Martin made some small show of dissuading her, which, as he intended, only increased her resolution to accompany him. Finally, he allowed himself to be bullied on to the terrace, Lizzie's small hand on his arm, guiding him.

As suppertime was not far distant, there were only two other couples on the shallow terrace, and within minutes both had returned to the ballroom. Martin, food very far from his mind, strolled down the terrace, apparently content to go where Lizzie led. But his sharp soldier's eyes had very quickly adjusted to the moonlight. After a cursory inspection of the surroundings, he allowed himself to pause dramatically as they neared the end of the terrace. 'I really think...' He waited a moment, as if gathering strength, then continued, 'I really think I should sit down.'

Lizzie looked around in consternation. There were no benches on the terrace, not even a balustrade.

'There's a seat under that willow, I think,' said Martin, gesturing across the lawn.

A quick glance from Lizzie confirmed this observation. 'Here, lean on me,' she said. Martin obligingly draped one arm lightly about her shoulders. As he felt her small hands gripping him about his waist, a pang of guilt shook him. She really was so trusting. A pity to destroy it.

They reached the willow and brushed through the long strands which conveniently fell back to form a curtain around the white wooden seat. Inside the chamber so formed, the moonbeams danced, sprinkling sufficient light to lift the gloom and allow them to see. Martin sank on to the seat with a convincing show of weakness. Lizzie subsided in a susurration of silks beside him, retaining her clasp on his hand and half turning the better to look into his face.

The moon was behind the willow and one bright beam shone through over Martin's shoulder to fall gently on Lizzie's face. Martin's face was in shadow, so Lizzie, smiling confidingly up at him, could only see that he was smiling in return. She could not see the expression which lit his blue eyes as they devoured her delicate face, then dropped boldly to caress the round swell of her breasts where they rose and fell invitingly below the demurely scooped neckline of her gown. Carefully, Martin turned his hand so that now he was holding her hand, not she his. Then he was still.

After some moments, Lizzie put her head on one side and softly asked, 'Are you all right?'

It was on the tip of Martin's tongue to answer truthfully. No, he was not all right. He had brought her out here to commence her seduction and now some magical power was holding him back. What was the matter with him? He cleared his throat and answered huskily, 'Give me a minute.'

A light breeze wafted the willow leaves and the light shifted. Lizzie saw the distracted frown which had settled over his eyes. Drawing her hand from his, she reached up and gently ran her fingers over his brow, as if to smooth the frown away. Then, to Martin's intense surprise, she leaned forward and, very gently, touched her lips to his.

As she drew away, Lizzie saw to her dismay that, if Martin had been frowning before, he was positively scowling now. 'Why did you do that?' he asked, his tone sharp.

Even in the dim light he could see her confusion. 'Oh, dear! I'm s. . .so sorry. Please excuse me! I shouldn't have done that.'

'Damn right, you shouldn't have,' Martin growled. His hand, which had fallen to the bench, was clenched hard with the effort to remain still and not pull the damn woman into his arms and devour her. He realised she had not answered his question. 'But why did you?'

Lizzie hung her head in contrition. 'It's just that you looked. . .well, so troubled. I just wanted to help.' Her voice was a small whisper in the night.

Martin sighed in frustration. That sort of help he could do without.

'I suppose you'll think me very forward, but. . .' This time, her voice died away altogether.

What Martin did think was that she was adorable

and he hurt with the effort to keep his hands off her. Now he came to think of it, while he had not had a headache when they came out to the garden, he certainly had one now. Repressing the desire to groan aloud, he straightened. 'We'd better get back to the ballroom. We'll just forget the incident.' As he drew her to her feet and placed her hand on his arm, an unwelcome thought struck him. 'You don't go around kissing other men who look troubled, do you?'

The surprise in her face was quite genuine. 'No! Of course not!'

'Well,' said Martin, wondering why the information so thrilled him, 'just subdue any of these sudden impulses of yours. Except around me, of course. I dare say it's perfectly all right with me, in the circumstances. You are my brother's ward, after all.'

Lizzie, still stunned by her forward behaviour, and the sudden impulse that had driven her to it, smiled trustingly up at him.

Caroline smiled her practised smile and wished, for at lest the hundredth time, that Max Rotherbridge were not their guardian. At least, she amended, not *her* guardian. He was proving a tower of strength in all other respects and she could only be grateful, both for his continuing support and protection, as well as his experienced counsel over the affair of Sarah and Lord Darcy. But there was no doubt in her mind that her own confusion would be immeasurably eased by dissolution of the guardianship clause which tied her so irrevocably to His Grace of Twyford.

While she circled the floor in the respectful arms of Mr Willoughby who, she knew, was daily moving closer to a declaration despite her attempts to dampen his confidence, she was conscious of a wish that it was her guardian's far less gentle clasp she was in. Mr

Willoughby, she had discovered, was worthy. Which was almost as bad as righteous. She sighed and covered the lapse with a brilliant smile into his mild eyes, slightly below her own. It was not that she despised short men, just that they lacked the ability to make her feel delicate and vulnerable, womanly, as Max Rotherbridge certainly could. In fact, the feeling of utter helplessness that seemed to overcome her every time she found herself in his powerful arms was an increasing concern.

As she and her partner turned with the music, she sighted Sarah, dancing with one of her numerous court, trying, not entirely successfully, to look as if she was enjoying it. Her heart went out to her sister. They had stayed at home the previous night and, in unusual privacy, thrashed out the happenings of the night before. While Sarah had skated somewhat thinly over certain aspects, it had been clear that she, at least, knew her heart. But Max had taken the opportunity of a few minutes' wait in the hall at Twyford House to let both herself and Sarah know, in the most subtle way, that Lord Darcy had left town for his estates. She swallowed another sigh and smiled absently at Mr Willoughby.

As the eldest, she had, in recent years, adopted the role of surrogate mother to her sisters. One unfortunate aspect of that situation was that she had no one to turn to herself. If the gentleman involved had been anyone other than her guardian, she would have sought advice from Lady Benborough. In the circumstances, that avenue, too, was closed to her. But, after that interlude in the Overtons' summer-house, she was abysmally aware that she needed advice. All he had to do was to take her into his arms and her well ordered defences fell flat. And his kiss! The effect of that seemed totally to disorder her mind, let alone her senses. She had not yet fathomed what, exactly, he was about, yet it seemed inconceivable that he would seduce his own ward. Which fact, she ruefully admitted, but only to herself when at her most candid, was at the seat of her desire to no longer be his ward.

It was not that she had any wish to join the *demimonde*. But face facts she must. She was nearly twenty-six and she knew what she wanted. She wanted Max Rotherbridge. She knew he was a rake and, if she had not instantly divined his standing as soon as she had laid eyes on him, Lady Benborough's forthright remarks on the subject had left no room for doubt. But every tiny particle of her screamed that he was the one. Which was why she was calmly dancing with each of her most ardent suitors, careful not to give any one of them the slightest encouragement, while waiting for her guardian to claim her for the dance before supper. On their arrival in the overheated ballroom, he had, in a sensual murmur that had wafted the curls over her ear and sent shivery tingles all the way down her spine, asked her to hold that waltz for him. She looked into Mr Willoughby's pale eyes. And sighed.

'Sir Malcolm, I do declare you're flirting with me!' Desperation lent Arabella's bell-like voice a definite edge. Using her delicate feather fan to great purpose, she flashed her large eyes at the horrendously rich but essentially dim-witted Scottish baronet, managing meanwhile to keep Hugo, Lord Denbigh, in view. Her true prey was standing only feet away, conversing amiably with a plain matron with an even plainer daughter. What was the matter with him? She had tried every trick she knew to bring the great oaf to her tiny feet, yet he persistently drifted away. He would be politely attentive but seemed incapable of settling long enough even to be considered one of her court. She had kept the supper waltz free, declaring it to be taken to all her other suitors, convinced he would ask her for that most favoured dance. But now, with suppertime fast approaching, she suddenly found herself facing the prospect of having no partner at all. Her eyes flashing, she turned in welcome to Mr Pritchard and Viscount Molesworth.

She readily captivated both gentlemen, skilfully steering clear of any lapse from her own rigidly imposed standards. She was an outrageous flirt, she knew, but a discerning flirt, and she had long made it her policy never to hurt anyone with her artless chatter. She enjoyed the occupation but it had never involved her heart. Normally, her suitors happily fell at her feet without the slightest assistance from her. But, now that she had at last found someone she wished to attract, she had, to her horror, found she had less idea of how to draw a man to her side than plainer girls who had had to learn the art.

To her chagrin, she saw the musicians take their places on the rostrum. There was only one thing to do. She smiled sweetly at the three gentlemen around her. 'My dear sirs,' she murmured, her voice mysteriously low, 'I'm afraid I must leave you. No! Truly. Don't argue.' Another playful smile went around. 'Until later, Sir Malcolm. Mr Pritchard, my lord.' With a nod and a mysterious smile she moved away, leaving the three gentlemen wandering who the lucky man was.

Slipping through the crowd, Arabella headed for the exit to the ballroom. Doubtless there would be an antechamber somewhere where she could hide. She was not hungry anyway. She timed her exit to coincide with the movement of a group of people across the door, making it unlikely that anyone would see her retreat. Once in the passage, she glanced about. The main stairs lay directly in front of her. She glanced to her left in time to see two ladies enter one of the rooms. The last thing she needed was the endless chatter of a withdrawing-room. She turned purposefully to her right. At the end of the dimly lit corridor, a door stood open, light from the flames of a hidden fire flickering on its panels. She hurried down the corridor and, looking in, saw a small study. It was empty. A carafe and glasses set in readiness on a small table suggested it was yet another room set aside for the use of guests who found the heat of the ballroom too trying. With a sigh of relief, Arabella entered. After some consideration, she left the door open.

She went to the table and poured herself a glass of water. As she was replacing the glass, she heard voices approaching. Her eyes scanned the room and lit on the deep window alcove; the curtain across it, if fully drawn, would make it a small room. On the thought, she was through, drawing the heavy curtain tightly shut.

In silence, her heart beating in her ears, she listened as the voices came nearer and entered the room, going towards the fire. She waited a moment, breathless, but no one came to the curtain. Relaxing, she turned. And almost fell over the large pair of feet belonging to the gentleman stretched at his ease in the armchair behind the curtain.

'Oh!' Her hand flew to her lips in her effort to smother the sound. 'What are you doing here?' she whispered furiously.

Slowly, the man turned his head towards her. He smiled. 'Waiting for you, my dear.'

Arabella closed her eyes tightly, then opened them again but he was still there. As she watched, Lord Denbigh unfurled his long length and stood, magnificent and, suddenly, to Arabella at least, oddly intimidating, before her. In the light of the full moon spilling through the large windows, his tawny eyes roved appreciatively over her. He caught her small hand in his and raised it to his lips. 'I didn't think you'd be long.'

His lazy tones, pitched very low, washed languidly over Arabella. With a conscious effort, she tried to break free of their hypnotic hold. 'How could you know I was coming here? *I* didn't.'

'Well,' he answered reasonably, 'I couldn't think where else you would go, if you didn't have a partner for the supper waltz.'

He *knew*! In the moonlight, Arabella's fiery blush faded into more delicate tints but the effect on her temper was the same. 'You oaf!' she said in a fierce whisper, aiming a stinging slap at the grin on his large face. But the grin grew into a smile as he easily caught her hand and drew it down and then behind her, drawing her towards him. He captured her other hand as well and imprisoned that in the same large hand behind her back.

'Lord Denbigh! Let me go!' Arabella pleaded, keeping her voice low for fear the others beyond the curtain would hear. How hideously embarrassing to be found in such a situation. And now she had another problem. What was Hugo up to? As her anger drained, all sorts of other emotions came to the fore. She looked up, her eyes huge and shining in the moonlight, her lips slightly parted in surprise.

Hugo lifted his free hand and one long finger traced the curve of her full lower lip.

Even with only the moon to light his face, Arabella saw the glimmer of desire in his eyes. 'Hugo, let me go. Please?'

He smiled lazily down at her. 'In a moment, sweetheart. After I've rendered you incapable of scratching my eyes out.'

His fingers had taken hold of her chin and he waited to see the fury in her eyes before he chuckled and bent his head until his lips met hers.

Arabella had every intention of remaining aloof from his kisses. Damn him—he'd tricked her! She tried to whip up her anger, but all she could think of was how wonderfully warm his lips felt against hers. And what delicious sensations were running along her nerves. Everywhere. Her body, entirely of its own volition, melted into his arms.

She felt, rather than heard, his deep chuckle as his arms shifted and tightened about her. Finding her hands free and resting on his shoulders, she did not quite know what to do with them. Box his ears? In the end, she twined them about his neck, holding him close.

When Hugo finally lifted his head, it was to see the stars reflected in her eyes. He smiled lazily down at her. 'Now you have to admit that's more fun than waltzing.'

Arabella could think of nothing to say.

'No quips?' he prompted.

She blushed slightly. 'We should be getting back.' She tried to ease herself from his embrace but his arms moved not at all.

Still smiling in that sleepy way, he shook his head. 'Not yet. That was just the waltz. We've supper to go yet.' His lips lightly brushed hers. 'And I'm ravenously hungry.'

Despite the situation, Arabella nearly giggled at the boyish tone. But she became much more serious when his lips returned fully to hers, driving her into far deeper waters than she had ever sailed before.

But he was experienced enough correctly to gauge

her limits, to stop just short and retreat, until they were sane again. Later, both more serious than was their wont, they returned separately to the ballroom.

Despite her strategies, Arabella was seen as she slipped from the ballroom. Max, returning from the card-room where he had been idly passing his time until he could, with reasonable excuse, gravitate to the side of his eldest ward, saw the bright chestnut curls dip through the doorway and for an instant had thought that Caroline was deserting him. But his sharp ears had almost immediately caught the husky tone of her laughter from a knot of gentlemen near by and he realised it must have been Arabella, most like Caroline in colouring, whom he had seen.

But he had more serious problems on his mind than whether Arabella had torn her flounce. His pursuit of the luscious Miss Twinning, or, rather, the difficulties which now lay in his path to her, were a matter for concern. The odd fact that he actually bothered to dance with his eldest ward had already been noted. As there were more than a few ladies among the *ton* who could give a fairly accurate description of his preferences in women, the fact that Miss Twinning's endowments brought her very close to his ideal had doubtless not been missed. However, he cared very little for the opinions of others and foresaw no real problem in placating the *ton* after the deed was done. What was troubling him was the unexpected behaviour of the two principals in the affair, Miss Twinning and himself.

With respect to his prey, he had miscalculated on two counts. Firstly, he had imagined it would take a concerted effort to seduce a twenty-five-year-old woman who had lived until recently a very retired life. Instead, from the first, she had responded so freely that he had almost lost his head. He was too experienced not to know that it would take very little of his persuasion to convince her to overthrow the tenets of her class and come to him. It irritated him beyond measure that the knowledge, far from spurring him on to take immediate advantage of her vulnerability, had made him pause and consider, in a most disturbing way, just what he was about. His other mistake had been in thinking that, with his intensive knowledge of the ways of the *ton*, he would have no difficulty in using his position as her guardian to create opportunities to be alone with Caroline. Despite—or was it because of?—her susceptibility towards him, she seemed able to avoid his planned tête-à-têtes with ease and, with the exception of a few occasions associated with some concern over one or other of her sisters, had singularly failed to give him the opportunities he sought. And seducing a woman whose mind was filled with worry over one of her sisters was a task he had discovered to be beyond him.

He had, of course, revised his original concept of what role Caroline was to play in his life. However, he was fast coming to the conclusion that he would have to in some way settle her sisters' affairs before either he or Caroline would have time to pursue their own destinies. But life, he was fast learning, was not all that simple. In the circumstances, the *ton* would expect Miss Twinning's betrothal to be announced before that of her sisters. And he was well aware he had no intention of giving his permission for any gentleman to pay his addresses to Miss Twinning. As he had made no move to clarify for her the impression of his intentions he had originally given her, he did not delude himself that she might not accept some man like Willoughby, simply to remove herself from the temptation of her guardian. Yet if he told her she was not his ward, she would undoubtedly be even more vigilant with respect to himself and, in all probability, even more successful in eluding him.

There was, of course, a simple solution. But he had a perverse dislike of behaving as society dictated. Consequently, he had formed no immediate intention of informing Caroline of his change of plans. There was a challenge, he felt, in attempting to handle their relationship his way. Darcy had pushed too hard and too fast and, consequently, had fallen at the last fence. He, on the other hand, had no intention of rushing things. Timing was everything in such a delicate matter as seducation.

The congestion of male forms about his eldest ward brought a slight frown to his face. But the musicians obligingly placed bow to string, allowing him to extricate her from their midst and sweep her on to the floor.

He glanced down into her grey-green eyes and saw his own pleasure in dancing with her reflected there. His arm tightened slightly and her attention focused. 'I do hope your sisters are behaving themselves?'

Caroline returned his weary question with a smile. 'Assuming your friends are doing likewise, I doubt there'll be a problem.'

Max raised his brows. So she knew at least a little of what had happened. After negotiating a difficult turn to avoid old Major Brumidge and his similarly ancient partner, he jettisoned the idea of trying to learn more of Sarah's thoughts in favour of spiking a more specific gun. 'Incidentally, apropos of your sisters' and your own fell intent, what do you wish me to say to the numerous beaux who seem poised to troop up the steps of Delmere House?'

He watched her consternation grow as she grappled with the sticky question. He saw no reason to tell her that, on his wards' behalf, he had already turned down a number of offers, none of which could be considered remotely suitable. He doubted they were even aware of the interest of the gentlemen involved.

Caroline, meanwhile, was considering her options. If she was unwise enough to tell him to permit any acceptable gentlemen to address them, they could shortly be bored to distraction with the task of convincing said gentlemen that their feelings were not reciprocated. On the other hand, giving Max Rotherbridge a free hand to choose their husbands seemed equally unwise. She temporised. 'Perhaps it would be best if we were to let you know if we anticipated receiving an offer from any particular gentleman that we would wish to seriously consider.'

Max would have applauded if his hands had not been so agreeably occupied. 'A most sensible suggestion, my ward. Tell me, how long does it take to pin up a flounce?'

Caroline blinked at this startling question.

'The reason I ask,' said Max as they glided to a halt, 'is that Arabella deserted the room some minutes before the music started and, as far as I can see, has yet to return.'

A frown appeared in Caroline's fine eyes but, in deference to the eyes of others, she kept her face free of care and her voice light. 'Can you see if Lord Denbigh is in the room?'

Max did not need to look. 'Not since I entered it.' After a pause, he asked, 'Is she seriously pursuing that line? If so, I fear she'll all too soon reach point non plus.'

Caroline followed his lead as he offered her his arm and calmly strolled towards the supper-room. A slight smile curled her lips as, in the increasing crowd, she leant closer to him to answer. 'With Arabella, it's hard to tell. She seems so obvious, with her flirting. But that's really all superficial. In reality, she's rather reticent about such things.'

Max smiled in reply. Her words merely confirmed his own reading of Arabella. But his knowledge of the relationship between Caroline and her sisters prompted him to add, 'Nevertheless, you'd be well advised to sound her out on that score. Hugo Denbigh, when all is said and done, is every bit as dangerous as. . .' He paused to capture her eyes with his own before, smiling in a devilish way, he continued, 'I am.'

Conscious of the eyes upon them, Caroline strove to maintain her composure. 'How very. . .reassuring, to be sure,' she managed.

The smile on Max's face broadened. They had reached the entrance of the supper-room and he paused in the doorway to scan the emptying ballroom. 'If she hasn't returned in ten minutes, we'll have to go looking. But come, sweet ward, the lobster patties await.'

With a flourish, Max led her to a small table where they were joined, much to his delight, by Mr Willoughby and a plain young lady, a Miss Spence. Mr Willoughby's transparent intention of engaging the delightful Miss Twinning in close converse, ignoring the undemanding Miss Spence and Miss Twinning's guardian, proved to be rather more complicated than Mr Willoughby, for one, had imagined. Under the subtle hand of His Grace of Twyford, Mr Willoughby found himself the centre of a general discussion on philosophy. Caroline listened in ill-concealed delight as Max blocked every move poor Mr Willoughby made to polarise the conversation. It became apparent that her guardian understood only too well Mr Willoughby's state and she found herself caught somewhere between embarrassment and relief. In the end, relief won the day.

Eventually, routed, Mr Willoughby rose, ostensibly to return Miss Spence to her parent. Watching his retreat with laughing eyes, Caroline returned her gaze to her guardian, only to see him look pointedly at the door from the ballroom. She glanced across and saw Arabella enter, slightly flushed and with a too-bright smile on her lips. She made straight for the table where Sarah was sitting with a number of others and, with her usual facility, merged with the group, laughing up at the young man who leapt to his feet to offer her his chair.

Caroline turned to Max, a slight frown in her eyes, to find his attention had returned to the door. She followed his gaze and saw Lord Denbigh enter.

To any casual observer, Hugo was merely coming late to the supper-room, his languid gaze and sleepy-smile giving no hint of any more pressing emotion than to discover whether there were any lobster patties left. Max Rotherbridge, however, was a far from casual observer. As he saw the expression in his lordship's heavy-lidded eyes as they flicked across the room to where Arabella sat, teasing her company unmercifully, His Grace of Twyford's black brows rose in genuine astonishment. Oh, God! Another one?

Resigned to yet another evening spent with no progress in the matter of his eldest ward, Max calmly escorted her back to the ballroom and, releasing her to the attentions of her admirers, not without a particularly penetrating stare at two gentlemen of dubious standing who had had the temerity to attempt to join her circle, he prepared to quit the ballroom. He had hoped to have persuaded Miss Twinning to view the moonlight from the terrace. There was a useful bench he knew of, under a concealing willow, which would have come in quite handy. However, he had no illusions concerning his ability to make love to a woman who was on tenterhooks over the happiness of not one but two sisters. So he headed for the card-room.

On his way, he passed Arabella, holding court once again in something close to her usual style. His blue gaze searched her face. As if sensing his regard, she turned and saw him. For a moment, she looked lost. He smiled encouragingly. After a fractional pause, she flashed her brilliant smile back and, putting up her chin, turned back to her companions, laughing at some comment.

Max moved on. Clearly, Caroline did have another problem on her hands. He paused at the entrance to the card-room and, automatically, scanned the packed ballroom. Turning, he was about to cross the threshold when a disturbing thought struck him. He turned back to the ballroom.

'Make up your mind! Make up your mind! Oh, it's you, Twyford. What are you doing at such an occasion? Hardly your style these days, what?'

Excusing himself to Colonel Weatherspoon, Max moved out of the doorway and checked the room again. Where was Lizzie? He had not seen her at supper, but then again he had not looked. He had mentally dubbed her the baby of the family but his rational mind informed him that she was far from too young. He was about the cross the room to where his aunt Augusta sat, resplendent in bronze bombazine, when a movement by the windows drew his eyes.

Lizzie entered from the terrace, a shy and entirely guileless smile on her lips. Her small hand rested with easy assurance on his brother's arm. As he watched, she turned and smiled up at Martin, a look so full of trust that a newborn lamb could not have bettered it. And Martin, wolf that he was, returned the smile readily.

Abruptly, Max turned on his heel and strode into the card-room. He needed a drink.

CHAPTER EIGHT

ARABELLA swatted at the bumble-bee blundering noisily by her head. She was lying on her stomach on the stone surround of the pond in the courtyard of Twyford House, idly trailing her fingers in the cool green water. Her delicate mull muslin, petal-pink in hue, clung revealingly to her curvaceous form while a straw hat protected her delicate complexion from the afternoon sun. Most other young ladies in a similar pose would have looked childish. Arabella, with her strangely wistful air, contrived to look mysteriously enchanting.

Her sisters were similarly at their ease. Sarah was propped by the base of the sundial, her *bergère* hat shading her face as she threaded daisies into a chain. The dark green cambric gown she wore emphasised her arrestingly pale face, dominated by huge brown eyes, darkened now by the hint of misery. Lizzie sat beside the rockery, poking at a piece of embroidery with a noticeable lack of enthusiasm. Her sprigged mauve muslin proclaimed her youth yet its effect was ameliorated by her far from youthful figure.

Caroline watched her sisters from her perch in a cushioned hammock strung between two cherry trees. If her guardian could have seen her, he would undoubtedly have approved the simple round gown of particularly fine amber muslin she had donned for the warm day. The fabric clung tantalisingly to her mature figure while the neckline revealed an expanse of soft ivory breasts.

The sisters had gradually drifted here, one by one,

drawn by the warm spring afternoon and the heady scents rising from the rioting flowers which crammed the beds and overflowed on to the stone flags. The period between luncheon and the obligatory afternoon appearance in the Park was a quiet time they were coming increasingly to appreciate as the Season wore on. Whenever possible, they tended to spend it together, a last vestige, Caroline thought, of the days when they had only had each other for company.

Sarah sighed. She laid aside her hat and looped the completed daisy chain around her neck. Cramming her headgear back over her dark curls, she said, 'Well, what are we going to do?'

Three pairs of eyes turned her way. When no answer was forthcoming, she continued, explaining her case with all reasonableness, 'Well, we can't go on as we are, can we? None of us is getting anywhere.'

Arabella turned on her side better to view her sisters. 'But what can we do? In your case, Lord Darcy's not even in London.'

'True,' returned the practical Sarah. 'But it's just occurred to me that he must have friends still in London. Ones who would write to him, I mean. Other than our guardian.'

Caroline grinned. 'Whatever you do, my love, kindly explain all to me before you set the *ton* ablaze. I don't think I could stomach our guardian demanding an explanation and not having one to give him.'

Sarah chuckled. 'Has he been difficult?'

But Caroline would only smile, a secret smile of which both Sarah and Arabella took due note.

'He hasn't said anything about me, has he?' came Lizzie's slightly breathless voice. Under her sisters' gaze, she blushed. 'About me and Martin,' she mumbled, suddenly becoming engrossed in her *petit point*.

Arabella laughed. 'Artful puss. As things stand, you're the only one with all sails hoisted and a clear wind blowing. The rest of us are becalmed, for one reason or another.'

Caroline's brow had furrowed. 'Why do you ask? Has Max given you any reason to suppose he disapproves?'

'Well,' temporised Lizzie, 'he doesn't seem entirely. . .happy, about us seeing so much of each other.'

Her attachment to Martin Rotherbridge had progressed in leaps and bounds. Despite Max's warning and his own innate sense of danger, Martin had not been able to resist the temptation posed by Lizzie Twinning. From that first, undeniably innocent kiss he had, by subtle degrees, led her to the point where, finding herself in his arms in the gazebo in Lady Malling's garden, she had permitted him to kiss her again. Only this time, it had been Martin leading the way. Lizzie, all innocence, had been thoroughly enthralled by the experience and stunned by her own response to the delightful sensations it had engendered. Unbeknownst to her, Martin Rotherbridge had been stunned, too.

Belatedly, he had tried to dampen his own increasing desires, only to find, as his brother could have told him, that that was easier imagined than accomplished. Abstinence had only led to intemperance. In the end, he had capitulated and returned to spend every moment possible at Lizzie's side, if not her feet.

Lizzie was right in her assessment that Max disapproved of their association but wrong in her idea of the cause. Only too well acquainted with his brother's character, their guardian entertained a grave concern that the frustrations involved in behaving with decorum in the face of Lizzie Twinning's bounteous temptations would prove overwhelming long before Martin was brought to admit he was in love with the chit. His worst fears had seemed well on the way to being realised when he had, entirely unintentionally, surprised them on their way back to the ballroom. His sharp blue eyes had not missed the glow in Lizzie's face. Consequently, the look he had directed at his brother, which Lizzie had intercepted, had not been particularly encouraging. She had missed Martin's carefree response.

Caroline, reasonably certain of Max's thoughts on the matter, realised these might not be entirely clear to Lizzie. But how to explain Max's doubts of his own brother to the still innocent Lizzie? Despite the fact that only a year separated her from Arabella, the disparity in their understandings, particularly with respect to the male of the species, was enormous. All three elder Twinnings had inherited both looks and dispositions from their father's family, which in part explained his aversion to women. Thomas Twinning had witnessed first hand the dance his sisters had led all the men of their acquaintance before finally settling in happily wedded bliss. The strain on his father and himself had been considerable. Consequently, the discovery that his daughters were entirely from the same mould had prompted him to immure them in rural seclusion. Lizzie, however, had only inherited the Twinning looks, her gentle and often quite stubborn innocence deriving from the placid Eleanor. Viewing the troubled face of her youngest half-sister, Caroline decided the time had come to at least try to suggest to Lizzie's mind that there was often more to life than the strictly obvious. Aside from anything else, this time, she had both Sarah and Arabella beside her to help explain.

'I rather think, my love,' commenced Caroline, 'that

it's not that Max would disapprove of the connection. His concern is more for your good name.'

Lizzie's puzzled frown gave no indication of lightening. 'But why should my being with his brother endanger my good name?'

Sarah gave an unladylike snort of laughter. 'Oh, Lizzie, love! You're going to have to grow up, my dear. Our guardian's concerned because he knows what his brother's like and that, generally speaking, young ladies are not safe with him.'

The effect of this forthright speech on Lizzie was galvanising. Her eyes blazed in defence of her absent love. 'Martin's not like that at all!'

'Oh, sweetheart, you're going to have to open your eyes!' Arabella bought into the discussion, sitting up the better to do so. 'He's not only "like that", Martin Rotherbridge has made a career specialising in being "like that". He's a rake. The same as Hugo and Darcy Hamilton, too. And, of course, the greatest rake of them all is our dear guardian, who has his eye firmly set on Caro here. Rakes and Twinnings go together, I'm afraid. We attract them and they—' she put her head on one side, considering her words '—well, they attract us. It's no earthly good disputing the evidence.'

Seeing the perturbation in Lizzie's face, Caroline sought to reassure her. 'That doesn't mean that the end result is not just the same as if they were more conservative. It's just that, well, it very likely takes longer for such men to accept the. . .the desirability of marriage.' Her eyes flicked to Sarah who, head bent and eyes intent on her fingers, was plaiting more daisies. 'Time will, I suspect, eventually bring them around. The danger is in the waiting.'

Lizzie was following her sister's discourse with difficulty. 'But Martin's never. . .well, you know, tried to make love to me.'

'Do you mean to say he's never kissed you?' asked Arabella in clear disbelief.

Lizzie blushed. 'Yes. But I kissed him first.'

'Lizzie!' The startled exclamation was drawn from all three sisters who promptly thereafter fell about laughing. Arabella was the last to recover. 'Oh, my dear, you're more a Twinning than we'd thought!'

'Well, it was nice, I thought,' said Lizzie, fast losing her reticence in the face of her sisters' teasing. 'Anyway, what am I supposed to do? Avoid him? That wouldn't be much fun. And I don't think I could stop him kissing me, somehow. I rather like being kissed.'

'It's not the kissing itself that's the problem,' stated Sarah. 'It's what comes next. And that's even more difficult to stop.'

'Very true,' confirmed Arabella, studying her slippered toes. 'But if you want lessons in how to hold a rake at arm's length you shouldn't look to me. Nor to Sarah either. It's only Caro who's managed to hold her own so far.' Arabella's eyes started to dance as they rested on her eldest sister's calm face. 'But, I suspect, that's only because our dear guardian is playing a deep game.'

Caroline blushed slightly, then reluctantly smiled. 'Unfortunately, I'm forced to agree with you.'

A silence fell as all four sisters pondered their rakes. Eventually, Caroline spoke. 'Sarah, what are you planning?'

Sarah wriggled her shoulders against the sundial's pedestal. 'Well, it occurred to me that perhaps I should make some effort to bring things to a head. But if I did the obvious, and started wildly flirting with a whole bevy of gentlemen, then most likely I'd only land myself in the suds. For a start, Darcy would very likely not believe it and I'd probably end with a very odd reputation. I'm not good at it, like Bella.'

Arabella put her head on one side, the better to observe her sister. 'I could give you lessons,' she offered.

'No,' said Caroline. 'Sarah's right. It wouldn't wash.' She turned to Lizzie to say, 'Another problem, my love, is that rakes know all the tricks, so bamming them is very much harder.'

'Too true,' echoed Arabella. She turned again to Sarah. 'But if not that, what, then?'

A wry smile touched Sarah's lips. 'I rather thought the pose of the maiden forlorn might better suit me. Nothing too obvious, just a subtle withdrawing. I'd still go to all the parties and balls, but I'd just become quieter and ever so gradually, let my. . .what's the word, Caro? My despair? My broken heart? Well, whatever it is, show through.'

Her sisters considered her plan and found nothing to criticise. Caroline summed up their verdict. 'In truth, my dear, there's precious little else you could do.'

Sarah's eyes turned to Arabella. 'But what are you going to do about Lord Denbigh?'

Arabella's attention had returned to her toes. She wrinkled her pert nose. 'I really don't know. I can't make him jealous; as Caro said, he knows all those tricks. And the forlorn act would not do for me.'

Arabella had tried by every means possible to tie down the elusive Hugo but that large gentleman seemed to view her attempts with sleepy humour, only bestirring himself to take advantage of any tactical error she made. At such times, as Arabella had found to her confusion and consternation, he could move with ruthless efficiency. She was now very careful not to leave any opening he could exploit to be private with her.

'Why not try. . . ?' Caroline broke off, suddenly

assailed by a twinge of guilt at encouraging her sisters in their scheming. But, under the enquiring gaze of Sarah and Arabella, not to mention Lizzie, drinking it all in, she mentally shrugged and continued. 'As you cannot convince him of your real interest in any other gentleman, you'd be best not to try, I agree. But you could let him understand that, as he refused to offer marriage, and you, as a virtuous young lady, are prevented from accepting any other sort of offer, then, with the utmost reluctance and the deepest regret, you have been forced to turn aside and consider accepting the attentions of some other gentleman.'

Arabella stared at her sister. Then, her eyes started to dance. 'Oh, Caro!' she breathed. 'What a perfectly marvellous plan!'

'Shouldn't be too hard for you to manage,' said Sarah. 'Who are the best of your court for the purpose? You don't want to raise any overly high expectations on their parts but you've loads of experience in playing that game.'

Arabella was already deep in thought. 'Sir Humphrey Bullard, I think. And Mr Stone. They're both sober enough and in no danger of falling in love with me. They're quite coldly calculating in their approach to matrimony; I doubt they have hearts to lose. They both want an attractive wife, preferably with money, who would not expect too much attention from them. To their minds, I'm close to perfect but to scramble for my favours would be beneath them. They should be perfect for my charade.'

Caroline nodded. 'They sound just the thing.'

'Good! I'll start tonight,' said Arabella, decision burning in her huge eyes.

'But what about you, Caro?' asked Sarah with a grin. 'We've discussed how the rest of us should go on, but you've yet to tell us how you plan to bring our dear guardian to his knees.'

Caroline smiled, the same gently wistful smile that frequently played upon her lips these days. 'If I knew that, my dears, I'd certainly tell you.' The last weeks had seen a continuation of the unsatisfactory relationship between His Grace of Twyford and his eldest ward. Wary of his ability to take possession of her senses should she give him the opportunity, Caroline had consistently avoided his invitations to dally alone with him. Indeed, too often in recent times her mind had been engaged in keeping a watchful eye over her sisters, something their perceptive guardian seemed to understand. She could not fault him for his support and was truly grateful for the understated manner in which he frequently set aside his own inclinations to assist her in her concern for her siblings. In fact, it had occurred to her that, far from being a lazy guardian, His Grace of Twyford was very much *au fait* with the activities of each of his wards. Lately, it had seemed to her that her sisters' problems were deflecting a considerable amount of his energies from his pursuit of herself. So, with a twinkle in her eye, she said, 'If truth be told, the best plan I can think of to further my own ends is to assist you all in achieving your goals as soon as may be. Once free of you three, perhaps our dear guardian will be able to concentrate on me.'

It was Lizzie who initiated the Twinning sisters' friendship with the two Crowbridge girls, also being presented that year. The Misses Crowbridge, Alice and Amanda, were very pretty young ladies in the manner which had been all the rage until the Twinnings came to town. They were pale and fair, as ethereal as the Twinnings were earthy, as fragile as the Twinnings were robust, and, unfortunately for them, as penniless as the Twinnings were rich. Consequently, the push to find well heeled husband for the Misses Crowbridge had not prospered.

Strolling down yet another ballroom, Lady Mott's as it happened, on the arm of Martin, of course, Lizzie had caught the sharp words uttered by a large woman of horsey mien to a young lady, presumably her daughter, sitting passively at her side. 'Why can't you two be like that? Those girls simply walk off with any man they fancy. All it needs is a bit of push. But you and Alice. . .' The rest of the tirade had been swallowed up by the hubbub around them. But the words returned to Lizzie later, when, retiring to the withdrawing-room to mend her hem which Martin very carelessly had stood upon, she found the room empty except for the same young lady, huddled in a pathetic bundle, trying to stifle her sobs.

As a kind heart went hand in hand with Lizzie's innocence, it was not long before she had befriended Amanda Crowbridge and learned of the difficulty facing both Amanda and Alice. Lacking the Twinning sisters' confidence and abilities, the two girls, thrown without any preparation into the heady world of the *ton*, found it impossible to converse with the elegant gentlemen, becoming tongue-tied and shy, quite unable to attach the desired suitors. To Lizzie, the solution was obvious.

Both Arabella and Sarah, despite having other fish to fry, were perfectly willing to act as tutors to the Crowbridge girls. Initially, they agreed to this more as a favour to Lizzie than from any more magnanimous motive, but as the week progressed they became quite absorbed with their protégées. For the Crowbridge girls, being taken under the collective wing of the three younger Twinnings brought a cataclysmic change to their social standing. Instead of being left to decorate the wall, they now spent their time firmly embedded amid groups of chattering young people. Drawn ruthlessly into conversations by the artful Arabella or Sarah at her most prosaic, they discovered that talking to the swells of the *ton* was not, after all, so very different from conversing with the far less daunting lads at home. Under the steady encouragement provided by the Twinnings, the Crowbridge sisters slowly unfurled their petals.

Caroline and His Grace of Twyford watched the growing friendship from a distance and were pleased to approve, though for very different reasons. Having ascertained that the Crowbridges were perfectly acceptable acquaintances, although their mother, for all her breeding, was, as Lady Benborough succinctly put it, rather too pushy, Caroline was merely pleased that her sisters had found some less than scandalous distraction from their romantic difficulties. Max, on the other hand, was quick to realise that with the three younger girls busily engaged in this latest exploit, which kept them safely in the ballrooms and salons, he stood a much better chance of successfully spending some time, in less populated surroundings, with his eldest ward.

In fact, as the days flew past, his success in his chosen endeavour became so marked that Caroline was forced openly to refuse any attempt to detach her from her circle. She had learned that their relationship had become the subject of rampant speculation and was now seriously concerned at the possible repercussions, for herself, for her sisters and for him. Max, reading her mind with consummate ease, paid her protestations not the slightest heed. Finding herself once more in His Grace's arms and, as usual, utterly helpless, Caroline was moved to remonstrate. 'What on earth do you expect to accomplish by all this? I'm your *ward*, for heaven's sake!'

A deep chuckle answered her. Engaged in tracing her left brow, first with one long finger, then with his lips, Max had replied, 'Consider your time spent with me as an educational experience, sweet Caro. As Aunt Augusta was so eager to point out,' he continued, transferring his attention to her other brow, 'who better than your guardian to demonstrate the manifold dangers to be met with among the *ton*?'

She was prevented from telling him what she thought of his reasoning, in fact, was prevented from thinking at all, when his lips moved to claim hers and she was swept away on a tide of sensation she was coming to appreciate all too well. Emerging, much later, pleasantly witless, she found herself the object of His Grace's heavy-lidded blue gaze. 'Tell me, my dear, if you were not my ward, would you consent to be private with me?'

Mentally adrift, Caroline blinked in an effort to focus her mind. For the life of her she could not understand his question, although the answer seemed clear enough. 'Of course not!' she lied, trying unsuccessfully to ease herself from his shockingly close embrace.

A slow smile spread across Max's face. As the steel bands about her tightened, Caroline was sure he was laughing at her.

Another deep chuckle, sending shivers up and down her spine, confirmed her suspicion. Max bent his head until his lips brushed hers. Then, he drew back slightly and blue eyes locked with grey. 'In that case, sweet ward, you have some lessons yet to learn.'

Bewildered, Caroline would have asked for enlightenment but, reading her intent in her eyes, Max avoided her question by the simple expedient of kissing her again. Irritated by his cat-and-mouse tactics, Caroline tried to withdraw from participation in this strange game whose rules were incomprehensible to her. But she quickly learned that His Grace of Twyford had no intention of letting her backslide. Driven, in the end, to surrender to the greater force, Caroline relaxed, melting into his arms, yielding body, mind and soul to his experienced conquest.

It was at Lady Richardson's ball that Sir Ralph Keighly first appeared as a cloud on the Twinnings' horizon. Or, more correctly, on the Misses Crowbridge's horizon, although, by that stage, it was much the same thing. Sir Ralph, with a tidy estate in Gloucestershire, was in London to look for a wife. His taste, it appeared, ran to sweet young things of the type personified by the Crowbridge sisters, Amanda Crowbridge in particular. Unfortunately for him, Sir Ralph was possessed of an overwhelming self-conceit combined with an unprepossessing appearance. He was thus vetoed on sight as beneath consideration by the Misses Crowbridge and their mentors.

However, Sir Ralph was rather more wily than he appeared. Finding his attentions to Amanda Crowbridge compromised by the competing attractions of the large number of more personable young men who formed the combined Twinning-Crowbridge court, he retired from the lists and devoted his energies to cultivating Mr and Mrs Crowbridge. In this, he achieved such notable success that he was invited to attend Lady Richardson's ball with the Crowbridges. Despite the tearful protestations of both Amanda and Alice at his inclusion in their party, when they crossed the threshold of Lady Richardson's ballroom, Amanda, looking distinctly seedy, had her hand on Sir Ralph's arm.

At her parents' stern instruction, she was forced to endure two waltzes with Sir Ralph. As Arabella acidly observed, if it had been at all permissible, doubtless Amanda would have been forced to remain at his side for the entire ball. As it was, she dared not join her friends for supper but, drooping with dejection, joined Sir Ralph and her parents.

To the three Twinnings, the success of Sir Ralph was like waving a red rag to a bull. Without exception, they took it as interference in their, up until then, successful development of their protégées. Even Lizzie was, metaphorically speaking, hopping mad. But the amenities offered by a ball were hardly conducive to a council of war, so, with admirable restraint, the three younger Twinnings devoted themselves assiduously to their own pursuits and left the problem of Sir Ralph until they had leisure to deal with it appropriately.

Sarah was now well down the road to being acknowledged as having suffered an unrequited love. She bore up nobly under the strain but it was somehow common knowledge that she held little hope of recovery. Her brave face, it was understood, was on account of her sisters, as she did not wish to ruin their Season by retiring into seclusion, despite this being her most ardent wish. Her large brown eyes, always fathomless, and her naturally pale and serious face were welcome aids in the projection of her new persona. She danced and chatted, yet the vitality that had burned with her earlier in the Season had been dampened. That, at least, was no more than the truth.

Arabella, all were agreed, was settling down to the sensible prospect of choosing a suitable connection. As Huge Denbigh had contrived to be considerably more careful in his attentions to Arabella than Darcy Hamilton had been with Sarah, the gossips had never connected the two. Consequently, the fact that Lord Denbigh's name was clearly absent from Arabella's list did not in itself cause comment. But, as the Twinning sisters had been such a hit, the question of who precisely Arabella would choose was a popular topic for discussion. Speculation was rife and, as was often the case in such matters, a number of wagers had already been entered into the betting books held by the gentlemen's clubs. According to rumour, both Mr Stone and Sir Humphrey Bullard featured as possible candidates. Yet not the most avid watcher could discern which of these gentlemen Miss Arabella favoured.

Amid all this drama, Lizzie Twinning continued as she always had, accepting the respectful attentions of the sober young men who sought her out while reserving her most brilliant smiles for Martin Rotherbridge. As she was so young and as Martin wisely refrained from any overtly amorous or possessive act in public, most observers assumed he was merely helping his brother with what must, all were agreed, constitute a definite handful. Martin, finding her increasingly difficult to lead astray, was forced to live with his growing frustrations and their steadily diminishing prospects for release.

The change in Amanda Crowbridge's fortunes brought a frown to Caroline's face. She would not have liked the connection for any of her sisters. Still, Amanda Crowbridge was not her concern. As her sisters appeared to have taken the event philosophically enough, she felt justified in giving it no further thought, reserving her energies, mental and otherwise, for her increasingly frequent interludes with her guardian.

Despite her efforts to minimise his opportunities, she found herself sharing his carriage on their return journey to Mount Street. Miriam Alford sat beside her and Max, suavely elegant and exuding a subtle aura of powerful sensuality, had taken the seat opposite her. Lady Benborough and her three sisters were following in the Twyford coach. As Caroline had suspected, their chaperon fell into a sound sleep before the carriage had cleared the Richardson House drive.

Gazing calmly at the moonlit fields, she calculated they had at least a forty-minute drive ahead of them. She waited patiently for the move she was sure would come and tried to marshal her resolve to deflect it. As the minutes ticked by, the damning knowledge slowly seeped into her consciousness that, if her guardian was to suddenly become afflicted with propriety and the journey was accomplished without incident, far from being relieved, she would feel let down, cheated of an eagerly anticipated treat. She frowned, recognising her already racing pulse and the tense knot in her stomach that restricted her breathing for the symptoms they were. On the thought, she raised her eyes to the dark face before her.

He was watching the countryside slip by, the silvery light etching the planes of his face. As if feeling her gaze, he turned and his eyes met hers. For a moment, he read her thoughts and Caroline was visited by the dreadful certainty that he knew the truth she was struggling to hide. Then, a slow, infinitely wicked smile spread across his face. Caroline stopped breathing. He leant forward. She expected him to take her hand and draw her to sit beside him. Instead, his strong hands slipped about her waist and, to her utter astonishment, he lifted her across and deposited her in a swirl of silks on his lap.

'Max!' she gasped.

'Sssh. You don't want to wake Mrs Alford. She'd have palpitations.'

Horrified, Caroline tried to get her feet to the ground, wriggling against the firm clasp about her waist. Almost immediately, Max's voice sounded in her ear, in a tone quite different from any she had previously heard. 'Sweetheart, unless you cease wriggling your delightful *derrière* in such an enticing fashion, this lesson is likely to go rather further than I had intended.'

Caroline froze. She held her breath, not daring to so much as twitch. Then Max's voice, the raw tones of an instant before no longer in evidence, washed over her in warm approval. 'Much better.'

She turned to face him, carefully keeping her hips still. She placed her hands on his chest in an effort, futile, she knew, to fend him off. 'Max, this is madness. You must stop doing this!'

'Why? Don't you like it?' His hands were moving gently on her back, his touch scorching through the thin silk of her gown.

Caroline ignored the sardonic lift of his black brows and the clear evidence in his eyes that he was laughing at her. She found it much harder to ignore the sensations his hands were drawing forth. Forcing her face into strongly disapproving lines, she answered his first question, deeming it prudent to conveniently forget the second. 'I'm your *ward*, remember? You know I am. You told me so yourself.'

'A fact you should strive to bear in mind, my dear.'

Caroline wondered what he meant by that. But Max's mind, and hands, had shifted their focus of attention. As his hands closed over her breasts, Caroline nearly leapt to her feet. '*Max!*'

But, 'Sssh,' was all her guardian said as his lips settled on hers.

CHAPTER NINE

THE Twyford coach was also the scene of considerable activity, though of a different sort. Augusta, in sympathy with Mrs Alford, quickly settled into a comfortable doze which the whisperings of the other occupants of the carriage did nothing to disturb. Lizzie, Sarah and Arabella, incensed by Amanda's misfortune, spent some minutes giving vent to their feelings.

'It's not as if Sir Ralph's such a good catch, even,' Sarah commented.

'Certainly not,' agreed Lizzie with uncharacteristic sharpness. 'It's really too bad! Why, Mr Minchbury is almost at the point of offering for her and he has a much bigger estate, besides being much more attractive. And Amanda *likes* him, what's more.'

'Ah,' said Arabella, wagging her head sagely, 'but he's not been making up to Mrs Crowbridge, has he? That woman must be all about in her head, to think of giving little Amanda to Keighly.'

'Well,' said Sarah decisively, 'what are we going to do about it?'

Silence reigned for more than a mile as the sisters considered the possibilities. Arabella eventually spoke into the darkness. 'I doubt we'd get far discussing matters with the Crowbridges.'

'Very true,' nodded Sarah. 'And working on Amanda's equally pointless. She's too timid.'

'Which leaves Sir Ralph,' concluded Lizzie. After a pause, she went on: 'I know we're not precisely to his taste, but do you think you could do it, Bella?'

Arabella's eyes narrowed as she considered Sir Ralph. Thanks to Hugo, she now had a fairly extensive understanding of the basic attraction between men and women. Sir Ralph was, after all, still a man. She shrugged. 'Well, it's worth a try. I really can't see what else we can do.'

For the remainder of the journey, the sisters' heads were together, hatching their plan.

Arabella started her campaign to steal Sir Ralph from Amanda the next evening, much to the delight of Amanda. When she was informed in a whispered aside of the Twinnings' plan for her relief, Amanda's eyes had grown round. Swearing to abide most faithfully by any instructions they might give her, she had managed to survive her obligatory two waltzes with Sir Ralph in high spirits, which Sarah later informed her was not at all helpful. Chastised, she begged pardon and remained by Sarah's side as Arabella took to the floor with her intended.

As Sir Ralph had no real affection for Amanda, it took very little of Arabella's practised flattery to make him increasingly turn his eyes her way. But, to the Twinnings' consternation, their plan almost immediately developed a hitch.

Their guardian was not at all pleased to see Sir Ralph squiring Arabella. A message from him, relayed by both Caroline and Lady Benborough, to the effect that Arabella should watch her step, pulled Arabella up short. A hasty conference, convened in the withdrawing-room, agreed there was no possibility of gaining His Grace's approval for their plan. Likewise, none of the three sisters had breathed a word of their scheme to Caroline, knowing that, despite her affection for them, there were limits to her forbearance.

'But we can't just give up!' declared Lizzie in trenchant tones.

Arabella was nibbling the end of one finger. 'No. We won't give up. But we'll have to reorganise. You two,' she said, looking at Sarah and Lizzie, quite ignoring Amanda and Alice who were also present, 'are going to have to cover for me. That way, I won't be obviously spending so much time with Sir Ralph, but he'll still be thinking about me. You must tell Sir Ralph that our guardian disapproves but that, as I'm head over heels in love with him, I'm willing to go against the Duke's wishes and continue to see him.' She frowned, pondering her scenario. 'We'll have to be careful not to paint our dear guardian in too strict colours. The story is that we're sure he'll eventually come around, when he sees how attached I am to Sir Ralph. Max knows I'm a flighty, flirtatious creature and so doubts the strength of my affections. That should be believable enough.'

'All right,' Sarah nodded. 'We'll do the groundwork and you administer the *coup de grâce*.'

And so the plan progressed.

For Arabella, the distraction of Sir Ralph came at an opportune time in her juggling of Sir Humphrey and Mr Stone. It formed no part of her plans for either of these gentlemen to become too particular. And while her sober and earnest consideration of their suits had, she knew, stunned and puzzled Lord Denbigh, who watched with a still sceptical eye, her flirtation with Sir Ralph had brought a strange glint to his hazel orbs.

In truth, Hugo had been expecting Arabella to flirt outrageously with her court in an attempt to make him jealous and force a declaration. He had been fully prepared to sit idly by, watching her antics from the sidelines with his usual sleepily amused air, waiting for the right moment to further her seduction. But her apparent intention to settle for a loveless marriage had thrown him. It was not a reaction he had expected. Knowing what he did of Arabella, he could not stop himself from thinking of what a waste it would be. True, as the wife of a much older man, she was likely to be even more receptive to his own suggestions of a discreet if illicit relationship. But the idea of her well endowed charms being brutishly enjoyed by either of her ageing suitors set his teeth on edge. Her sudden pursuit of Sir Ralph Keighly, in what he was perceptive enough to know was not her normal style, seriously troubled him, suggesting as it did some deeper intent. He wondered whether she knew what she was about. The fact that she continued to encourage Keighly despite Twyford's clear disapproval further increased his unease.

Arabella, sensing his perturbation, continued to tread the difficult path she had charted, one eye on him, the other on her guardian, encouraging Sir Ralph with one hand while using the other to hold back Sir Humphrey and Mr Stone. As she confessed to her sisters one morning, it was exhausting work.

Little by little, she gained ground with Sir Ralph, their association camouflaged by her sisters' ploys. On the way back to the knot of their friends, having satisfactorily twirled around Lady Summerhill's ballroom, Arabella and Sir Ralph were approached by a little lady, all in brown.

Sir Ralph stiffened.

The unknown lady blushed. 'How do you do?' she said, taking in both Arabella and Sir Ralph in her glance. 'I'm Harriet Jenkins,' she explained helpfully to Arabella, then, turning to Sir Ralph, said, 'Hello, Ralph,' in quite the most wistful tone Arabella had ever heard.

Under Arabella's interested gaze, Sir Ralph became tongue-tied. He perforce bowed over the small hand held out to him and managed to say, 'Mr Jenkins' estates border mine.'

Arabella's eyes switched to Harriet Jenkins. 'My father,' she supplied.

Sir Ralph suddenly discovered someone he had to exchange a few words with and precipitately left them. Arabella looked down into Miss Jenkins' large eyes, brown, of course, and wondered. 'Have you lately come to town, Miss Jenkins?'

Harriet Jenkins drew her eyes from Sir Ralph's departing figure and dispassionately viewed the beauty before her. What she saw in the frank hazel eyes prompted her to reply, 'Yes. I was. . .bored, at home. So my father suggested I come to London for a few weeks. I'm staying with my aunt, Lady Cottesloe.'

Arabella was only partly satisfied with this explanation. Candid to a fault, she put the question in her mind. 'Pardon me, Miss Jenkins, but are you and Sir Ralph. . .?'

Miss Jenkins' wistfulness returned. 'No. Oh, you're right in thinking I want him. But Ralph has other ideas. I've known him from the cradle, you see. And I suppose familiarity breeds contempt.' Suddenly realising to whom she was speaking, she blushed and continued, 'Not that I could hope to hold a candle to the London beauties, of course.'

Her suspicions confirmed, Arabella merely laughed and slipped an arm through Miss Jenkins'. 'Oh, I shouldn't let that bother you, my dear.' As she said the words, it occurred to her that, if anything, Sir Ralph was uncomfortable and awkward when faced with beautiful women, as evidenced by his behaviour with either herself or Amanda. It was perfectly possible that some of his apparent conceit would drop away when he felt less threatened; for instance, in the presence of Miss Jenkins.

Miss Jenkins had stiffened at Arabella's touch and her words. Then, realising the kindly intent behind them, she relaxed. 'Well, there's no sense in deceiving myself. I suppose I shouldn't say so, but Ralph and I were in a fair way to being settled before he took this latest notion of looking about him before he made up his mind irrevocably. I sometimes think it was simply fear of tying the knot that did it.'

'Very likely,' Arabella laughingly agreed as she steered Miss Jenkins in the direction of her sisters.

'My papa was furious and said I should give him up. But I convinced him to let me come to London, to see how things stood. Now, I suppose, I may as well go home.'

'Oh, on no account should you go home yet awhile, Miss Jenkins!' said Arabella, a decided twinkle in her eye. 'May I call you Harriet? Harriet, I'd like you to meet my sisters.'

The advent of Harriet Jenkins caused a certain amount of reworking of the Twinnings' plan for Sir Ralph. After due consideration, she was taken into their confidence and willingly joined the small circle of conspirators. In truth, her appearance relieved Arabella's mind of a nagging worry over how she was to let Sir Ralph down after Amanda accepted Mr Minchbury, who, under the specific guidance of Lizzie, was close to popping the question. Now, all she had to do was to play the hardened flirt and turn Sir Ralph's bruised ego into Harriet's tender care. All in all, things were shaping up nicely.

However, to their dismay, the Twinnings found that Mrs Crowbridge was not yet vanquished. The news of her latest ploy was communicated to them two days later, at Beckenham, where they had gone to watch a balloon ascent. The intrepid aviators had yet to arrive at the field, so the three Twinnings had descended from their carriage and, together with the Misses Crowbridge and Miss Jenkins, were strolling elegantly about the field, enjoying the afternoon sunshine and a not inconsiderable amount of male attention. It transpired that Mrs Crowbridge had invited Sir Ralph to pay a morning call and then, on the slightest of pretexts, had left him alone with Amanda for quite twenty minutes. Such brazen tactics left them speechless. Sir Ralph, to do him justice, had not taken undue advantage.

'He probably didn't have time to work out the odds against getting Arabella versus the benefits of Amanda,' said Sarah with a grin. 'Poor man! I can almost pity him, what with Mrs Crowbridge after him as well.'

All the girls grinned but their thoughts quickly returned to their primary preoccupation. 'Yes, but,' said Lizzie, voicing a fear already in both Sarah's and Arabella's minds, 'if Mrs Crowbridge keeps behaving like this, she might force Sir Ralph to offer for Amanda by tricking him into compromising her.'

'I'm afraid that's only too possible,' agreed Harriet. 'Ralph's very gullible.' She shook her head in such a deploring way that Arabella and Sarah were hard put to it to smother their giggles.

'Yes, but it won't do,' said Amanda, suddenly. 'I know my mother. She'll keep on and on until she succeeds. You've got to think of some way of. . .of removing Sir Ralph quickly.'

'For his sake as well as your own,' agreed Harriet. 'The only question is, how?'

Silence descended while this conundrum revolved in their minds. Further conversation on the topic was necessarily suspended when they were joined by a number of gentlemen disinclined to let the opportunity of paying court to such a gaggle of very lovely young ladies pass by. As His Grace of Twyford's curricle was conspicuously placed among the carriages drawn up to the edge of the field, the behaviour of said gentlemen remained every bit as deferential as within the confines of Almack's, despite the sylvan setting.

Mr Mallard was the first to reach Lizzie's side, closely followed by Mr Swanston and Lord Brookfell. Three other fashionable exquisites joined the band around Lizzie, Amanda, Alice and Harriet, and within minutes an unexceptionable though thoroughly merry party had formed. Hearing one young gentleman allude to the delicate and complementary tints of the dresses of the four younger girls as 'pretty as a posy', Sarah could not resist a grimace, purely for Arabella's benefit. Arabella bit hard on her lip to stifle her answering giggle. Both fell back a step or two from the younger crowd, only to fall victim to their own admirers.

Sir Humphrey Bullard, a large man of distinctly florid countenance, attempted to capture Arabella's undivided attention but was frustrated by the simultaneous arrival of Mr Stone, sleekly saturnine, on her other side. Both offered their arms, leaving Arabella, with a sunshade to juggle, in a quandry. She laughed and shook her head at them both. 'Indeed, gentlemen, you put me to the blush. What can a lady do under such circumstances?'

'Why, make your choice, m'dear,' drawled Mr Stone, a strangely determined glint in his eye.

Arabella's eyes widened at this hint that Mr Stone, at least, was not entirely happy with being played on a string. She was rescued by Mr Humphrey, irritatingly aware that he did not cut such a fine figure as Mr Stone. 'I see the balloonists have arrived. Perhaps you'd care to stroll to the enclosure and watch the inflation, Miss Arabella?'

'We'll need to get closer if we're to see anything at all,' said Sarah, coming up on the arm of Lord Tulloch.

By the time they reached the area cordoned off in the centre of the large field, a crowd had gathered. The balloon was already filling slowly. As they watched, it lifted from the ground and slowly rose to hover above the cradle slung beneath, anchored to the ground by thick ropes.

'It looks such a flimsy contraption,' said Arabella, eyeing the gaily striped silk balloon. 'I wonder that anyone could trust themselves to it.'

'They don't always come off unscathed, I'm sorry to say,' answered Mr Stone, his schoolmasterish tones evincing strong disapproval of such reckless behaviour.

'Humph!' said Sir Humphrey Bullard.

Arabella's eyes met Sarah's in mute supplication. Sarah grinned.

It was not until the balloon had taken off, successfully, to Arabella's relief, and the crowd had started to disperse that the Twinnings once more had leisure to contemplate the problem of Sir Ralph Keighly. Predictably, it was Sarah and Arabella who conceived the plot. In a few whispered sentences, they developed its outline sufficiently to see that it would require great attention to detail to make it work. As they would have no further chance that day to talk with the others in private, they made plans to meet the next morning at Twyford House. Caroline had mentioned her intention of visiting her old nurse, who had left the Twinnings' employ after her mother had died and hence was unknown to the younger Twinnings.

Thus, ensconced in the back parlour of Twyford House, they would be able to give free rein to their thoughts. Clearly, the removal of Sir Ralph was becoming a matter of urgency.

Returning to their carriage, drawn up beside the elegant equipage bearing the Delmere crest, the three youngest Twinnings smiled serenely at their guardian, who watched them from the box seat of his curricle, a far from complaisant look in his eyes.

Max was, in fact, convinced that something was in the wind but had no idea what. His highly developed social antennae had picked up the undercurrents of his wards' plotting and their innocent smiles merely confirmed his suspicions. He was well aware that Caroline, seated beside him in a fetching gown of figured muslin, was not privy to their schemes. As he headed his team from the field, he smiled. His eldest ward had had far too much on her mind recently to have had any time free for scheming.

Beside him, Caroline remained in blissful ignorance of her sisters' aims. She had spent a thoroughly enjoyable day in the company of her guardian and was in charity with the world. They had had an excellent view of the ascent itself from the height of the box seat of the curricle. And when she had evinced the desire to stroll among the crowds, Max had readily escorted her, staying attentively by her side, his acerbic comments forever entertaining and, for once, totally unexceptionable. She looked forward to the drive back to Mount Street with unimpaired calm, knowing that in the curricle, she ran no risk of being subjected to another of His Grace's 'lessons'. In fact, she was beginning to wonder how many more lessons there could possibly be before the graduation ceremony. The thought brought a sleepy smile to her face. She turned to study her guardian.

His attention was wholly on his horses, the bays, as sweet a pair as she had ever seen. Her eyes fell to his hands as they tooled the reins, strong and sure. Remembering the sensations those hands had drawn forth as they had knowledgeably explored her body, she caught her breath and rapidly looked away. Keeping her eyes fixed on the passing landscape, she forced her thoughts into safer fields.

The trouble with Max Rotherbridge was that he invaded her thoughts, too, and, as in other respects, was well nigh impossible to deny. She was fast coming to the conclusion that she should simply forget all else and give herself up to the exquisite excitement she found in his arms. All the social and moral strictures ever intoned, all her inhibitions seemed to be consumed to ashes in the fire of her desire. She was beginning to feel it was purely a matter of time before she succumbed. The fact that the idea did not fill her with trepidation but rather with a pleasant sense of anticipation was in itself, she felt, telling.

As the wheels hit the cobbles and the noise that was London closed in around them, her thoughts flew ahead to Lady Benborough, who had stayed at home recruiting her energies for the ball that night. It was only this morning, when, with Max, she had bid her ladyship goodbye, that the oddity in Augusta's behaviour had struck her. While the old lady had been assiduous in steering the girls through the shoals of the acceptable gentlemen of the *ton*, she had said nothing about her eldest charge's association with her nephew. No matter how Caroline viewed it, invoke what reason she might, there was something definitely odd about that. As she herself had heard the rumours about His Grace of Twyford's very strange relationship with his eldest ward, it was inconceivable that Lady Benborough had not been edified with their tales. However, far from urging her to behave with greater discretion towards Max, impossible task though that might be, Augusta continued to behave as if there was nothing at all surprising in Max Rotherbridge escorting his wards to a balloon ascent. Caroline wondered what it was that Augusta knew that she did not.

The Twinning sisters attended the opera later that week. It was the first time they had been inside the ornate structure that was the Opera House; their progress to the box organised for them by their guardian was perforce slow as they gazed about them with interest. Once inside the box itself, in a perfect position in the first tier, their attention was quickly claimed by their fellow opera-goers. The pit below was a teeming sea of heads; the stylish crops of the fashionable young men who took a perverse delight in rubbing shoulders with the masses bobbed amid the unkempt locks of the hoi polloi. But it was upon the occupants of the other boxes that the Twinnings' principal interest focused. These quickly filled as the time for the curtain to rise approached. All four girls were absorbed in nodding and waving to friends and acquaintances as the lights went out.

The first act consisted of a short piece by a little-known Italian composer, as the prelude to the opera itself, which would fill the second and third acts, before another short piece ended the performance. Caroline sat, happily absorbed in the spectacle, beside and slightly in front of her guardian. She was blissfully content. She had merely made a comment to Max a week before that she would like to visit the opera. Two days later, he had arranged it all. Now she sat, superbly elegant in a silver satin slip overlaid with bronzed lace, and revelled in the music, conscious, despite her preoccupation, of the warmth of the Duke of Twyford's blue gaze on her bare shoulders.

Max watched her delight with satisfaction. He had long ago ceased to try to analyse his reactions to Caroline Twinning; he was besotted and knew it. Her happiness had somehow become his happiness; in his view, nothing else mattered. As he watched, she turned and smiled, a smile of genuine joy. It was, he felt, all the thanks he required for the effort organising such a large box at short notice had entailed. He returned her smile, his own lazily sensual. For a moment, their eyes locked. Then, blushing, Caroline turned back to the stage.

Max had little real interest in the performance, his past experiences having had more to do with the singer than the song. He allowed his gaze to move past Caroline to dwell on her eldest half-sister. He had not yet fathomed exactly what Sarah's ambition was, yet felt sure it was not as simple as it appeared. The notion that any Twinning would meekly accept unwedded solitude as her lot was hard to swallow. As Sarah sat by Caroline's side, dramatic as ever in a gown of deepest green, the light from the stage lit her face. Her troubles had left no mark on the classical lines of brow and cheek but the peculiar light revealed more clearly than daylight the underlying determination in the set of the delicate mouth and chin. Max's lips curved in a wry grin. He doubted that Darcy had heard the last of Sarah Twinning, whatever the outcome of his self-imposed exile.

Behind Sarah sat Lord Tulloch and Mr Swanston, invited by Max to act as squires for Sarah and Arabella respectively. Neither was particularly interested in the opera, yet both had accepted the invitations with alacrity. Now, they sat, yawning politely behind their hands, waiting for the moment when the curtain would fall and they could be seen by the other attending members of the *ton*, escorting their exquisite charges through the corridors.

Arabella, too, was fidgety, settling and resettling her pink silk skirts and dropping her fan. She appeared to be trying to scan the boxes on the tier above. Max smiled. He could have told her that Hugo Denbigh hated opera and had yet to be seen within the portals of Covent Garden.

Lady Benborough, dragon-like in puce velvet, sat determinedly following the aria. Distracted by Arabella's antics, she turned to speak in a sharp whisper, whereat Arabella grudgingly subsided, a dissatisfied frown marring her delightful visage.

At the opposite end of the box sat Martin, with Lizzie by the parapet beside him. She was enthralled by the performance, hanging on every note that escaped the throat of the soprano performing the lead. Martin, most improperly holding her hand, evinced not the slightest interest in the buxom singer but gazed solely at Lizzie, a peculiar smile hovering about his lips. Inwardly, Max sighed. He just hoped his brother knew what he was about.

The aria ended and the curtain came down. As the applause died, the large flambeaux which lit the pit were brought forth and re-installed in their brackets. Noise erupted around them as everyone talked at once.

Max leant forward to speak by Caroline's ear. 'Come. Let's stroll.'

She turned to him in surprise and he smiled. 'That's what going to the opera is about, my dear. To see and be seen. Despite appearances, the most important performances take place in the corridors of Covent Garden, not on the stage.'

'Of course,' she returned, standing and shaking out

her skirts. 'How very provincial of me not to realise.' Her eyes twinkled. 'How kind of you, dear guardian, to attend so assiduously to our education.'

Max took her hand and tucked it into his arm. As they paused to allow the others to precede them, he bent to whisper in her ear, 'On the contrary, sweet Caro. While I'm determined to see your education completed, my interest is entirely selfish.'

The wicked look which danced in his dark blue eyes made Caroline blush. But she was becoming used to the highly improper conversations she seemed to have with her guardian. 'Oh?' she replied, attempting to look innocent and not entirely succeeding. 'Won't I derive any benefit from my new-found knowledge?'

They were alone in the box, hidden from view of the other boxes by shadows. For a long moment, they were both still, blue eyes locked with green-grey, the rest of the world far distant. Caroline could not breathe; the intensity of that blue gaze and the depth of the passion which smouldered within it held her mesmerised. Then, his eyes still on hers, Max lifted her hand and dropped a kiss on her fingers. 'My dear, once you find the key, beyond that particular door lies paradise. Soon, sweet Caro, very soon, you'll see.'

Once in the corridor, Caroline's cheeks cooled. They were quickly surrounded by her usual court and Max, behaving more circumspectly than he ever had before, relinquished her to the throng. Idly, he strolled along the corridors, taking the opportunity to stretch his long legs. He paused here and there to exchange a word with friends but did not stop for long. His preoccupation was not with extending his acquaintance of the *ton*. His ramblings brought him to the corridor serving the opposite arm of the horseshoe of boxes. The bell summoning the audience to their seats for the next act rang shrilly. Max was turning to make his way back to his box when a voice hailed him through the crush.

'Your Grace!'

Max closed his eyes in exasperation, then opened them and turned to face Lady Mortland. He nodded curtly. 'Emma.'

She was on the arm of a young man whom she introduced and immediately dismissed, before turning to Max. 'I think perhaps we should have a serious talk, Your Grace.'

The hard note in her voice and the equally rock-like glitter in her eyes were not lost on the Duke of Twyford. Max had played the part of fashionable rake for fifteen years and knew well the occupational hazards. He lifted his eyes from an uncannily thorough contemplation of Lady Mortland and sighted a small alcove, temporarily deserted. 'I think perhaps you're right, my dear. But I suggest we improve our surroundings.'

His hand under her elbow steered Emma towards the alcove. The grip of his fingers through her silk sleeve and the steely quality in his voice were a surprise to her ladyship, but she was determined that Max Rotherbridge should pay, one way or another, for her lost dreams.

They reached the relative privacy of the alcove. 'Well, Emma, what's this all about?'

Suddenly, Lady Mortland was rather less certain of her strategy. Faced with a pair of very cold blue eyes and an iron will she had never previously glimpsed, she vacillated. 'Actually, Your Grace,' she cooed, 'I had rather hoped you would call on me and we could discuss the matter in. . .greater privacy.'

'Cut line, Emma,' drawled His Grace. 'You know perfectly well I have no wish whatever to be private with you.'

The bald statement ignited Lady Mortland's temper. 'Yes!' she hissed, fingers curling into claws. 'Ever since you set eyes on that little harpy you call your ward, you've had no time for me!'

'I wouldn't, if I were you, make scandalous statements about a young lady to her guardian,' said Max, unmoved by her spleen.

'Guardian, ha! Lover, more like!'

One black brow rose haughtily.

'Do you deny it? No, of course not! Oh, there are whispers aplenty, let me tell you. But they're as nothing to the storm there'll be when I get through with you. I'll tell—Ow!'

Emma broke off and looked down at her wrist, imprisoned in Max's right hand. 'L. . .let me go. Max, you're hurting me.'

'Emma, you'll say nothing.'

Lady Mortland looked up and was suddenly frightened. Max nodded, a gentle smile, which was quite terrifyingly cold, on his lips. 'Listen carefully, Emma, for I'll say this once only. You'll not, verbally or otherwise, malign my ward—any of my wards—in any way whatever. Because, if you do, rest assured I'll hear about it. Should that happen, I'll ensure your stepson learns of the honours you do his father's memory by your retired lifestyle. Your income derives from the family estates, does it not?'

Emma had paled. 'You. . .you wouldn't.'

Max released her. 'No. You're quite right. I wouldn't,' he said. 'Not unless you do first. Then, you may be certain that I would.' He viewed the woman before him, with understanding if not compassion. 'Leave be, Emma. What Caroline has was never yours and you know it. I suggest you look to other fields.'

With a nod, Max left Lady Mortland and returned through the empty corridors to his box.

Caroline turned as he resumed his seat. She studied his face for a moment, then leant back to whisper, 'Is anything wrong?'

Max's gaze rested on her sweet face, concern for his peace of mind the only emotion visible. He smiled reassuringly and shook his head. 'A minor matter of no moment.' In the darkness, he reached for her hand and raised it to his lips. With a smile, Caroline returned her attention to the stage. When she made no move to withdraw her hand, Max continued to hold it, mimicking Martin, placating his conscience with the observation that, in the dark, no one could see the Duke of Twyford holding hands with his eldest ward.

CHAPTER TEN

EXECUTION of the first phase of the Twinnings' master plot to rescue Amanda and Sir Ralph from the machinations of Mrs Crowbridge fell to Sarah. An evening concert was selected as the venue most conducive to success. As Sir Ralph was tone deaf, enticing him from the real pleasure of listening to the dramatic voice of *Señorita Muscariña*, the Spanish soprano engaged for the event, proved easier than Sarah had feared.

Sir Ralph was quite content to escort Miss Sarah for a stroll on the balcony, ostensibly to relieve the stuffiness in Miss Twinning's head. In company with the rest of the *ton*, he knew Sarah was pining away and thus, he reasoned, he was safe in her company. That she was one of the more outstandingly opulent beauties he had ever set eyes on simply made life more complete. It was rare that he felt at ease with such women and his time in London had made him, more than once, wish he was back in the less demanding backwoods of Gloucestershire. Even now, despite his successful courtship of the beautiful, the effervescent, the gorgeous Arabella Twinning, there were times Harriet Jenkins's face reminded him of how much more comfortable their almost finalised relationship had been. In fact, although he tried his best to ignore them, doubts kept appearing in his mind, of whether he would be able to live up to Arabella's expectations once they were wed. He was beginning to understand that girls like Arabella—well, she was a woman, really—were used to receiving the most specific advances from the more hardened of the male population. Sir Ralph swallowed nervously, woefully aware that he lacked the abilities to compete with such gentlemen. He glanced at the pale face of the beauty beside him. A frown marred her smooth brow. He relaxed. Clearly, Miss Sarah's mind was not bent on illicit dalliance.

In thinking this, Sir Ralph could not have been further from the truth. Sarah's frown was engendered by her futile attempts to repress the surge of longing that had swept through her—a relic of that fateful evening in Lady Overton's shrubbery, she felt sure—when she had seen Darcy Hamilton's tall figure negligently propped by the door. She had felt the weight of his gaze upon her and, turning to seek its source, had met his eyes across the room. Fool that she was! She had had to fight to keep herself in her seat and not run across the room and throw herself into his arms. Then, an arch look from Arabella, unaware of Lord Darcy's return, had reminded her of her duty. She had put her hand to her head and Lizzie had promptly asked if she was feeling the thing. It had been easy enough to claim Sir Ralph's escort and leave the music-room. But the thunderous look in Darcy's eyes as she did so had tied her stomach in knots.

Pushing her own concerns abruptly aside, she transferred her attention to the man beside her. 'Sir Ralph, I hope you won't mind if I speak to you on a matter of some delicacy?'

Taken aback, Sir Ralph goggled.

Sarah ignored his startled expression. Harriet had warned her how he would react. It was her job to lead him by the nose. 'I'm afraid things have reached a head with Arabella. I know it's not obvious; she's so reticent about such things. But I feel it's my duty to try to explain it to you. She's in such low spirits.

Something must be done or she may even go into a decline.'

It was on the tip of Sir Ralph's tongue to say that he had thought it was Sarah who was going into the decline. And the suggestion that Arabella, last seen with an enchanting sparkle in her big eyes, was in low spirits confused him utterly. But Sarah's next comment succeeded in riveting his mind. 'You're the only one who can save her.'

The practical tone in which Sarah brought out her statement lent it far greater weight than a more dramatic declaration. In the event, Sir Ralph's attention was all hers. 'You see, although she would flay me alive for telling you, you should know that she was very seriously taken with a gentleman earlier in the Season, before you arrived. He played on her sensibilities and she was so vulnerable. Unfortunately, he was not interested in marriage. I'm sure I can rely on your discretion. Luckily, she learned of his true intentions before he had time to achieve them. But her heart was sorely bruised, of course. Now that she's found such solace in your company, we had hoped, my sisters and I, that you would not let her down.'

Sir Ralph was heard to mumble that he had no intention of letting Miss Arabella down.

'Ah, but you see,' said Sarah, warming to her task, 'what she needs is to be taken out of herself. Some excitement that would divert her from the present round of balls and parties and let her forget her past hurts in her enjoyment of a new love.'

Sir Ralph, quite carried away by her eloquence, muttered that yes, he could quite see the point in that.

'So you see, Sir Ralph, it's imperative that she be swept off her feet. She's very romantically inclined, you know.'

Sir Ralph, obediently responding to his cue,

declared he was only too ready to do whatever was necessary to ensure Arabella's happiness.

Sarah smiled warmly. 'In that case, I can tell you exactly what you must do.'

It took Sarah nearly half an hour to conclude her instructions to Sir Ralph. Initially, he had been more than a little reluctant even to discuss such an enterprise. But, by dwelling on the depth of Arabella's need, appealing quite brazenly to poor Sir Ralph's chivalrous instincts, she had finally wrung from him his sworn agreement to the entire plan.

In a mood of definite self-congratulation, she led the way back to the music-room and, stepping over the door sill, all but walked into Darcy Hamilton. His hand at her elbow steadied her, but, stung by his touch, she abruptly pulled away. Sir Ralph, who had not previously met Lord Darcy, stopped in bewilderment, his eyes going from Sarah's burning face to his lordship's pale one. Then, Darcy Hamilton became aware of his presence. 'I'll return Miss Twinning to her seat.'

Responding to the commanding tone, Sir Ralph bowed and departed.

Sarah drew a deep breath. 'How *dare* you?' she uttered furiously as she made to follow Sir Ralph.

But Darcy's hand on her arm detained her. 'What's that. . .country bumpkin to you?' The insulting drawl in his voice drew a blaze of fire from Sarah's eyes.

But before she could wither him where he stood, several heads turned their way. 'Sssh!'

Without a word, Darcy turned her and propelled her back out of the door.

'Disgraceful!' said Lady Malling to Mrs Benn, nodding by her side.

On the balcony, Sarah stood very still, quivering

with rage and a number of other more interesting emotions, directly attributable to the fact that Darcy was standing immediately behind her.

'Perhaps you'd like to explain what you were doing with that gentleman on the balcony for half an hour and more?'

Sarah almost turned, then remembered how close he was. She lifted her chin and kept her temper with an effort. 'That's hardly any affair of yours, my lord.'

Darcy frowned. 'As a friend of your guardian——'

At that Sarah did turn, uncaring of the consequences, her eyes flashing, her voice taut. 'As a friend of my guardian, you've been trying to seduce me ever since you first set eyes on me!'

'True,' countered Darcy, his face like granite. 'But not even Max has blamed me for that. Besides, it's what you Twinning girls expect, isn't it? Tell me, my dear, how many other lovestruck puppies have you had at your feet since I left?'

It was on the tip of Sarah's tongue to retort that she had had no lack of suitors since his lordship had quit the scene. But, just in time, she saw the crevasse yawning at her feet. In desperation, she willed herself to calm, and coolly met his blue eyes, her own perfectly candid. 'Actually, I find the entertainments of the *ton* have palled. Since you ask, I've formed the intention of entering a convent. There's a particularly suitable one, the Ursulines, not far from our old home.'

For undoubtedly the first time in his adult life, Darcy Hamilton was completely nonplussed. A whole range of totally unutterable responses sprang to his lips. He swallowed them all and said, 'You wouldn't be such a fool.'

Sarah's brows rose coldly. For a moment she held his gaze, then turned haughtily to move past him.

'Sarah!' The word was wrung from him and then she was in his arms, her lips crushed under his, her head spinning as he gathered her more fully to him.

For Sarah, it was a repeat of their interlude in the shrubbery. As the kiss deepened, then deepened again, she allowed herself a few minutes' grace, to savour the paradise of being once more in his arms. Then, she gathered her strength and tore herself from his hold. For an instant, they remained frozen, silently staring at each other, their breathing tumultuous, their eyes liquid fire. Abruptly, Sarah turned and walked quickly back into the music-room.

With a long-drawn-out sigh, Darcy Hamilton leant upon the balustrade, gazing unseeingly at the well-manicured lawns.

His Grace of Twyford carefully scrutinised Sarah Twinning's face as she returned to the music-room and joined her younger sisters in time to applaud the singer's operatic feats. Caroline, seated beside him, had not noticed her sister's departure from the room, nor her short-lived return. As his gaze slid gently over Caroline's face and noted the real pleasure the music had brought her, he decided that he had no intention of informing her of her sister's strange behaviour. That there was something behind the younger Twinnings' interest in Sir Ralph Keighly he did not doubt. But whatever it was, he would much prefer that Caroline was not caught up in it. He was becoming accustomed to having her complete attention and found himself reluctant to share it with anyone.

He kept a watchful eye on the door to the balcony and, some minutes later, when the singer was once more in full flight, saw Darcy Hamilton enter and, unobtrusively, leave the room. His eyes turning once more to the bowed dark head of Sarah Twinning, Max sighed. Darcy Hamilton had been one of the coolest hands in the business. But in the case of Sarah Twinning his touch seemed to have deserted him entirely. His friend's disintegration was painful to watch. He had not yet had time to do more than nod a greeting to Darcy when he had seen him enter the room. Max wondered what conclusions he had derived from his sojourn in Ireland. Whatever they were, he wryly suspected that Darcy would be seeking him out soon enough.

Which, of course, was likely to put a time limit on his own affair. His gaze returned to Caroline and, as if in response, she turned to smile up at him, her eyes unconsciously warm, her lips curving invitingly. Regretfully dismissing the appealing notion of creating a riot by kissing her in the midst of the cream of the *ton*, Max merely returned the smile and watched as she once more directed her attention to the singer. No, he did not need to worry. She would be his long before her sisters' affairs became pressing.

The masked ball given by Lady Penbright was set to be one of the highlights of an already glittering Season. Her ladyship had spared no expense. Her ballroom was draped in white satin and the terraces and trellised walks with which Penbright House was lavishly endowed were lit by thousands of Greek lanterns. The music of a small orchestra drifted down from the minstrels' gallery, the notes falling like petals on the gloriously covered heads of the *ton*. By decree, all the guests wore long dominos, concealing their evening dress, hoods secured over the ladies' curls to remove even that hint of identity. Fixed masks concealing the upper face were the order, far harder to penetrate than the smaller and often more bizarre hand-held masks, still popular in certain circles for flirtation. By eleven, the Penbright ball had been accorded the ultimate accolade of being declared a sad crush and her ladyship retired from her position by the door to join in the revels with her guests.

Max, wary of the occasion and having yet to divine the younger Twinnings' secret aim, had taken special note of his wards' dresses when he had arrived at Twyford House to escort them to the ball. Caroline he would have had no difficulty in detecting; even if her domino in a subtle shade of aqua had not been virtually unique, the effect her presence had on him, he had long ago noticed, would be sufficient to enable him to unerringly find her in a crowded room blindfold. Sarah, looking slightly peaked but carrying herself with the grace he expected of a Twinning, had flicked a moss-green domino over her satin dress which was in a paler shade of the same colour. Arabella had been struggling to settle the hood of a delicate rose-pink domino over her bright curls while Lizzie's huge grey eyes had watched from the depths of her lavender hood. Satisfied he had fixed the particular tints in his mind, Max had ushered them forth.

On entering the Penbright ballroom, the three younger Twinnings melted into the crowd but Caroline remained beside Max, anchored by his hand under her elbow. To her confusion, she found that one of the major purposes of a masked ball seemed to be to allow those couples who wished to spend an entire evening together without creating a scandal to do so. Certainly, her guardian appeared to have no intention of quitting her side.

While the musicians were tuning up, she was approached in a purposeful manner by a grey domino, under which she had no difficulty in recognising the slight frame of Mr Willoughby. The poor man was not entirely sure of her identity and Caroline gave him no hint. He glared at the tall figure by her side, which resulted in a slow, infuriating grin spreading across that gentleman's face. Then, as Mr Willoughby cleared his throat preparatory to asking the lady in the aqua domino for the pleasure of the first waltz, Max got in before him.

After her second waltz with her guardian, who was otherwise behaving impeccably, Caroline consented to a stroll about the rooms. The main ballroom was full and salons on either side took up the overflow. A series of interconnecting rooms made Caroline's head spin. Then, Max embarked on a long and involved anecdote which focused her attention on his masked face and his wickedly dancing eyes.

She should, of course, have been on her guard, but Caroline's defences against her dangerous guardian had long since fallen. Only when she had passed through the door he held open for her, and discovered it led into a bedroom, clearly set aside for the use of any guests overcome by the revels downstairs, did the penny drop. As she turned to him, she heard the click of the lock falling into its setting. And then Max stood before her, his eyes alight with an emotion she dared not define. That slow grin of his, which by itself turned her bones to jelly, showed in the shifting light from the open windows.

She put her hands on his shoulders, intending to hold him off, yet there was no strength behind the gesture and instead, as he drew her against him, her arms of their own accord slipped around his neck. She yielded in that first instant, as his lips touched hers, and Max knew it. But he saw no reason for undue haste. Savouring the feel of her, the taste of her, he spun out their time, giving her the opportunity to learn of each pleasure as it came, gently guiding her to the chaise by the windows, never letting her leave his arms or that state of helpless surrender she was in.

Caroline Twinning was heady stuff, but Max remembered he had a question for her. He drew back to gaze at her as she lay, reclining against the colourful cushions, her eyes unfocused as his long fingers caressed the satin smoothness of her breasts as they had once before in the carriage on the way back from the Richardsons' ball, with Miriam Alford snoring quietly in the corner. 'Caro?'

Caroline struggled to make sense of his voice through the haze of sensation clouding her mind. 'Mmm?'

'Sweet Caro,' he murmured wickedly, watching her efforts. 'If you recall, I once asked you if, were I not your guardian, you would permit me to be alone with you. Do you still think, if that was the case, you'd resist?'

To Caroline, the question was so ridiculous that it broke through to her consciousness, submerged beneath layers of pleasurable sensation. A slight frown came to her eyes as she wondered why on earth he kept asking such a hypothetical question. But his hands had stilled so it clearly behoved her to answer it. 'I've always resisted you,' she declared. 'It's just that I've never succeeded in impressing that fact upon you. Even if you weren't my guardian, I'd still try to resist you.' Her eyes closed and she gave up the attempt at conversation as his hands resumed where they had left off. But all too soon they stilled again.

'What do you mean, *even* if I weren't your guardian?'

Caroline groaned. 'Max!' But his face clearly showed that he wanted her answer, so she explained with what patience she could muster. 'This, you and me, together, would be scandalous enough if you weren't my guardian, but you are, so it's ten times worse.' She closed her eyes again. 'You must know that.'

Max did, but it had never occurred to him that she would have readily accepted his advances even had he not had her guardianship to tie her to him. His slow smile appeared. He should have known. Twinnings and rakes, after all. Caroline, her eyes still closed, all senses focused on the movement of his hands upon her breasts, did not see the smile, nor the glint in her guardian's very blue eyes that went with it. But her eyes flew wide open when Max bent his head and took one rosy nipple into his mouth.

'Oh!' She tensed and Max lifted his head to grin wolfishly at her. He cocked one eyebrow at her but she was incapable of speech. Then, deliberately, his eyes holding hers, he lowered his head to her other breast, feeling her tense in his arms against the anticipated shock. Gradually, she relaxed, accepting that sensation too. Slowly, he pushed her further, knowing he would meet no resistance. She responded freely, so much so that he was constantly drawing back, trying to keep a firm hold on his much tried control. Experienced though he was, Caroline Twinning was something quite outside his previous knowledge.

Soon, they had reached that subtle point beyond which there would be no turning back. He knew it, though he doubted she did. And, to his amazement, he paused, then gently disengaged, drawing her around to lean against his chest so that he could place kisses in the warm hollow of her neck and fondle her breasts, ensuring she would stay blissfully unaware while he did some rapid thinking.

The pros were clear enough, but she would obviously come to him whenever he wished, now or at any time in the future. Such as tomorrow. The cons were rather more substantial. Chief among these was that tonight they would have to return to the ball afterwards, usually a blessing if one merely wanted to bed a woman, not spend the entire night with her. But, if given the choice, he would prefer to spend at least twenty-four hours in bed with Caroline, a reasonable compensation for his forbearance to date. Then, too, there was the very real problem of her sisters. Despite the preoccupation of his hands, he knew that a part of his mind was taken up with the question of what they were doing while he and his love were otherwise engaged. He would infinitely prefer to be able to devote his entire attention to the luscious person in his arms. He sighed. His body did not like what his mind was telling it. Before he could change his decision, he pulled Caroline closer and bent to whisper on her ear. 'Caro?'

She murmured his name and put her hand up to his face. Max smiled. 'Sweetheart, much as I'd like to complete your education here and now, I have a dreadful premonition of what hideous scandals your sisters might be concocting with both of us absent from the ballroom.'

He knew it was the right excuse to offer, for her mind immediately reasserted itself. 'Oh, dear,' she sighed, disappointment ringing clearly in her tone, deepening Max's smile. 'I suspect you're right.'

'I know I'm right,' he said, straightening and sitting her upright. 'Come, let's get you respectable again.'

As soon as she felt sufficiently camouflaged from her guardian's eye by the gorgeously coloured throng, Lizzie Twinning made her way to the ballroom window further from the door. It was the meeting place Sarah had stipulated where Sir Ralph was to await further instructions. He was there, in a dark green domino and a black mask.

Lizzie gave him her hand. 'Good!' The hand holding hers trembled. She peered into the black mask. 'You're not going to let Arabella down, are you?'

To her relief, Sir Ralph swallowed and shook his head. 'No. Of course not. I've got my carriage waiting, as Miss Sarah suggested. I wouldn't dream of deserting Miss Arabella.'

Despite the weakness of his voice, Lizzie was satisfied. 'It's all right,' she assured him. 'Arabella is wearing a rose-pink domino. It's her favourite colour so you should recognise it. We'll bring her to you, as we said we would. Don't worry,' she said, giving his hand a squeeze, 'it'll all work out for the best, you'll see.' She patted his hand and, returning it to him, left him. As she moved down the ballroom, she scanned the crowd and picked out Caroline in her aqua domino waltzing with a black domino who could only be their guardian. She grinned to herself and the next instant, walked smack into a dark blue domino directly in her path.

'Oh!' She fell back and put up a hand to her mask, which had slipped.

'Lizzie,' said the blue domino in perfectly recognisable accents, 'what were you doing talking to Keighly?'

'Martin! What a start you gave me. My mask nearly fell. Wh. . .what do you mean?'

'I mean, Miss Innocence,' said Martin sternly, taking her arm and compelling her to walk beside him on to the terrace, 'that I saw you come into the ballroom and then, as soon as you were out of Max's sight, make a bee-line for Keighly. Now, out with it! What's going on?'

Lizzie was in shock. What was she to do? Not for a

moment did she imagine that Martin would agree to turn a blind eye to their scheme. But she was not a very good liar. Still, she would have to try. Luckily, the mask hid most of her face and her shock had kept her immobile, gazing silently up at him in what could be taken for her usual innocent manner. 'But I don't know what you mean, Martin. I know I talked to Sir Ralph, but that was because he was the only one I recognised.'

The explanation was so reasonable that Martin felt his sudden suspicion was as ridiculous as it had seemed. He felt decidedly foolish. 'Oh.'

'But now you're here,' said Lizzie, putting her hand on his arm. 'So I can talk to you.'

Martin's usual grin returned. 'So you can.' He raised his eyes to the secluded walks, still empty as the dancing had only just begun. 'Why don't we explore while we chat?'

Lately, Lizzie had been in the habit of refusing such invitations but tonight she was thankful for any suggestion that would distract Martin from their enterprise. So she nodded and they stepped off the terrace on to the gravel. They followed a path into the shrubbery. It wended this way and that until the house was a glimmer of light and noise beyond the screening bushes. They found an ornamental stream and followed it to a lake. There was a small island in the middle with a tiny summer-house, reached by a rustic bridge. They crossed over and found the door of the summer-house open.

'Isn't this lovely?' said Lizzie, quite enchanted by the scene. Moonbeams danced in a tracery of light created by the carved wooden shutters. The soft swish of the water running past the reed-covered banks was the only sound to reach their ears.

'Mmm, yes, quite lovely,' murmured Martin,

enchanted by something quite different. Even Lizzie in her innocence heard the warning in his tone but she turned only in time to find herself in his arms. Martin tilted her face up and smiled gently down at her. 'Lizzie, sweet Lizzie. Do you have any idea how beautiful you are?'

Lizzie's eyes grew round. Martin's arms closed around her, gentle yet quite firm. It seemed unbelievable that their tightness could be restricting her breathing, yet she found herself quite unable to draw breath. And the strange light in Martin's eyes was making her dizzy. She had meant to ask her sisters for guidance on how best to handle such situations but, due to her absorption with their schemes, it had slipped her mind. She suspected this was one of those points where using one's wits came into it. But, as her tongue seemed incapable of forming any words, she could only shake her head and hope that was acceptable.

'Ah,' said Martin, his grin broadening. 'Well, you're so very beautiful, sweetheart, that I'm afraid I can't resist. I'm going to kiss you again, Lizzie. And it's going to be thoroughly enjoyable for both of us.' Without further words, he dipped his head and, very gently, kissed her. When she did not draw back, he continued the caress, prolonging the sensation until he felt her response. Gradually, with the moonlight washing over them, he deepened the kiss, then, as she continued to respond easily, gently drew her further into his arms. She came willingly and Martin was suddenly unsure of the ground rules. He had no wish to frighten her, innocent as she was, yet he longed to take their dalliance further, much further. He gently increased the pressure of his lips on hers until they parted for him. Slowly, continually reminding himself of her youth, he taught her how pleasurable a kiss could be. Her responses drove him to seek more.

Kisses were something Lizzie felt she could handle. Being held securely in Martin's arms was a delight. But when his hand closed gently over her breast she gasped and pulled away. The reality of her feelings hit her. She burst into tears.

'Lizzie?' Martin, cursing himself for a fool, for pushing her too hard, gathered her into his arms, ignoring her half-hearted resistance. 'I'm sorry, Lizzie. It was too soon, I know. Lizzie? Sweetheart?'

Lizzie gulped and stifled her sobs. 'It's true!' she said, her voice a tear-choked whisper. 'They said you were a rake and you'd want to take me to bed and I didn't believe them but it's *true*.' She ended this astonishing speech on a hiccup.

Martin, finding much of her accusation difficult to deny, fastened on the one aspect that was not clear. 'They—who?'

'Sarah and Bella and Caro. They said you're *all* rakes. You and Max and Lord Darcy and Lord Denbigh. They said there's something about us that means we attract rakes.'

Finding nothing in all this that he wished to dispute, Martin kept silent. He continued to hold Lizzie, his face half buried in her hair. 'What did they suggest you should do about it?' he eventually asked, unsure if he would get an answer.

The answer he got was unsettling. 'Wait.'

Wait. Martin did not need to ask what for. He knew.

Very much later in the evening, when Martin had escorted Lizzie back to the ballroom, Max caught sight of them from the other side of the room. He had been forced to reassess his original opinion of the youngest Twinning's sobriety. Quite how such a youthful innocent had managed to get Martin into her toils he could not comprehend, but one look at his brother's face, even with his mask in place, was enough to tell him she had succeeded to admiration. Well, he had warned him.

Arabella's role in the great plan was to flirt so outrageously that everyone in the entire room would be certain that it was indeed the vivacious Miss Twinning under the rose-pink domino. None of the conspirators had imagined this would prove at all difficult and, true to form, within half an hour Arabella had convinced the better part of the company of her identity. She left one group of revellers, laughing gaily, and was moving around the room, when she found she had walked into the arms of a large, black-domino-clad figure. The shock she received from the contact immediately informed her of the identity of the gentleman.

'Oh, sir! You quite overwhelm me!'

'In such a crowd as this, my dear? Surely you jest?'

'Would you contradict a lady, sir? Then you're no gentleman, in truth.'

'In truth, you're quite right, sweet lady. Gentlemen lead such boring lives.'

The distinctly seductive tone brought Arabella up short. He could not know who she was, could he? As if in answer to her unspoken question, he asked, 'And who might you be, my lovely?'

Arabella's chin went up and she playfully retorted, 'Why, that's not for you to know, sir. My reputation might be at stake, simply for talking to so unconventional a gentleman as you.'

To her unease, Hugo responded with a deep and attractive chuckle. Their light banter continued, Arabella making all the customary responses, her quick ear for repartee saving her from floundering when his returns made her cheeks burn. She flirted with Hugo to the top of her bent. And hated every minute of it. He did not know who she was, yet was prepared to push an unknown lady to make an assignation with him for later in the evening. She was tempted to do so and then confront him with her identity. But her heart failed her. Instead, when she could bear it no longer, she made a weak excuse and escaped.

They had timed their plan carefully, to avoid any possible mishap. The unmasking was scheduled for one o'clock. At precisely half-past twelve, Sarah and Sir Ralph left the ballroom and strolled in a convincingly relaxed manner down a secluded walk which led to a little gazebo. The gazebo was placed across the path and, beyond it, the path continued to a gate giving access to the carriage drive.

Within sight of the gazebo, Sarah halted. 'Arabella's inside. I'll wait here and ensure no one interrupts.'

Sir Ralph swallowed, nodded once and left her. He climbed the few steps and entered the gazebo. In the dimness, he beheld the rose-pink domino, her mask still in place, waiting nervously for him to approach. Reverently, he went forward and then went down on one knee.

Sarah, watching from the shadows outside, grinned in delight. The dim figures exchanged a few words, then Sir Ralph rose and kissed the lady. Sarah held her breath, but all went well. Hand in hand, the pink domino and her escort descended by the opposite door of the gazebo and headed for the gate. To make absolutely sure of their success, Sarah entered the gazebo and stood watching the couple disappear through the gate. She waited, silently, then the click of horses' hoofs came distantly on the breeze. With a quick smile, she turned to leave. And froze.

Just inside the door to the gazebo stood a tall, black-domino-clad figure, his shoulders propped negligently against the frame in an attitude so characteristic Sarah would have known him anywhere. 'Are you perchance waiting for an assignation, my dear?'

Sarah made a grab for her fast-disappearing wits. She drew herself up but, before she could speak, his voice came again. 'Don't run away. A chase through the bushes would be undignified at best and I would catch you all the same.'

Sarah's brows rose haughtily. She had removed her mask which had been irritating her and it hung by its strings from her fingers. She swung it back and forth nervously. 'Run? Why should I run?' Her voice, she was pleased to find, was calm.

Darcy did not answer. Instead, he pushed away from the door and crossed the floor to stand in front of her. He reached up and undid his mask. Then his eyes caught hers. 'Are you still set on fleeing to a convent?'

Sarah held his gaze steadily. 'I am.'

A wry smile, self-mocking, she thought, twisted his mobile mouth. 'That won't do, you know. You're not cut out to be a bride of Christ.'

'Better a bride of Christ than the mistress of any man.' She watched the muscles in his jaw tighten.

'You think so?'

Despite the fact that she had known it would happen, had steeled herself to withstand it, her defences crumbled at his touch and she was swept headlong into abandonment, freed from restraint, knowing where the road led and no longer caring.

But when Darcy stooped and lifted her, to carry her to the wide cushioned seats at the side of the room, she shook her head violently. 'Darcy, no!' Her voice caught on a sob. 'Please, Darcy, let me go.'

Her tears sobered him as nothing else could have. Slowly, he let her down until her feet touched the floor. She was openly crying, as if her heart would break. 'Sarah?' Darcy put out a hand to smooth her brown hair.

Sarah had found her handkerchief and was mopping her streaming eyes, her face averted. 'Please go, Darcy.'

Darcy stiffened. For the first time in his adult life, he wanted to take a woman into his arms purely to comfort her. All inclination to make love to her had vanished at the first hint of her distress. But, sensing behind her whispered words a confusion she had yet to resolve, he sighed and, with a curt bow, did as she asked.

Sarah listened to his footsteps die away. She remained in the gazebo until she had cried herself out. Then, thankful for the at least temporary protection of her mask, she returned to the ballroom to tell her sisters and their protégées of their success.

Hugo scanned the room again, searching through the sea of people for Arabella. But the pink domino was nowhere in sight. He was as thoroughly disgruntled as only someone of a generally placid nature could become. Arabella had flirted outrageously with an unknown man. Admittedly him, but she had not known that. Here he had been worrying himself into a state over her getting herself stuck in a loveless marriage for no reason and underneath she was just a heartless flirt. A jade. Where the hell was she?

A small hand on his arm made him jump. But, contrary to the conviction of his senses, it was not Arabella but a lady in a brown domino with a brown mask fixed firmly in place. ' 'Ello, kind sir. You seem strangely lonely.'

Hugo blinked. The lady's accent was heavily middle European, her tone seductively low.

'I'm all alone,' sighed the lady in brown. 'And as you seemed also alone, I thought that maybe we could cheer one another up, no?'

In spite of himself, Hugo's glance flickered over the lady. Her voice suggested a wealth of experience yet her skin, what he could see of it, was as delicate as a young girl's. The heavy mask she wore covered most of her face, even shading her lips, though he could see these were full and ripe. The domino, as dominos did, concealed her figure. Exasperated, Hugo sent another searching glance about the room in vain. Then, he looked down and smiled into the lady's hazel eyes. 'What a very interesting idea, my dear. Shall we find somewhere to further develop our mutual acquaintance?'

He slipped an arm around the lady's waist and found that it was indeed very neat. She seemed for one instant to stiffen under his arm but immediately relaxed. Damn Arabella! She had driven him mad. He would forget her existence and let this lovely lady restore his sanity. 'What did you say your name was, my dear?'

The lady smiled up at him, a wickedly inviting smile. 'Maria Pavlovska,' she said as she allowed him to lead her out of the ballroom.

They found a deserted ante-room without difficulty and, without waiting time in further, clearly unnecessary talk, Hugo drew Maria Pavlovska into his arms. She allowed him to kiss her and, to his surprise, raised no demur when he deepened the kiss. His senses were racing and her responses drove him wild. He let his hand wander and she merely chuckled softly, the sound suggesting that he had yet to reach her limit. He found a convenient armchair and pulled her on to his lap and let her drive him demented. She was the most satisfyingly responsive woman he had ever found. Bewildered by his good fortune, he smiled understandingly when she whispered she would leave him for a moment.

He sighed in anticipation and stretched his long legs in front of him as the door clicked shut.

As the minutes ticked by and Maria Pavlovska did not return, sanity slowly settled back into Hugo's fevered brain. Where the hell was she? She'd deserted him. Just like Arabella. The thought hit him with the force of a sledgehammer. *Just like Arabella*? No, he was imagining things. True, Maria Pavlovska had aroused him in a way he had begun to think only Arabella could. *Hell*! She had even *tasted* like Arabella. But Arabella's domino was pink. Maria Pavlovska's domino was brown. And, now he came to think of it, it had been a few inches too short; he had been able to see her pink slippers and the pink hem of her dress. Arabella's favourite colour was pink but pink was, after all, a very popular colour. Damn, where was she? Where were they? With a long-suffering sigh, Hugo rose and, forswearing all women, left to seek the comparative safety of White's for the rest of the night.

CHAPTER ELEVEN

AFTER returning to the ballroom with Caroline, Max found his temper unconducive to remaining at the ball. In short, he had a headache. His wards seemed to be behaving themselves, despite his premonitions, so there was little reason to remain at Penbright House. But the night was young and his interlude with Caroline had made it unlikely that sleep would come easily, so he excused himself to his eldest ward and his aunt, and left to seek entertainment of a different sort.

He had never got around to replacing Carmelita. There hardly seemed much point now. He doubted he would have much use for such women in future. He grinned to himself, then winced. Just at that moment, he regretted not having a replacement available. He would try his clubs—perhaps a little hazard might distract him.

The carriage had almost reached Delmere House when, on the spur of the moment, he redirected his coachman to a discreet house in Bolsover Street. Sending the carriage back to Penbright House, he entered the newest gaming hell in London. Naturally, the door was opened to His Grace of Twyford with an alacrity that brought a sardonic grin to His Grace's face. But the play was entertaining enough and the beverages varied and of a quality he could not fault. The hell claimed to be at the forefront of fashion and consequently there were a number of women present, playing the green baize tables or, in some instances, merely accompanying their lovers. To his amusement,

Max found a number of pairs of feminine eyes turned his way, but was too wise to evince an interest he did not, in truth, feel. Among the patrons he found more than a few refugees from the Penbright ball, among them Darcy Hamilton.

Darcy was leaning against the wall, watching the play at the hazard table. He glowered as Max approached. 'I noticed both you and your eldest ward were absent from the festivities for an inordinately long time this evening. Examining etchings upstairs, I suppose?'

Max grinned. 'We were upstairs, as it happens. But it wasn't etchings I was examining.'

Darcy nearly choked on his laughter. 'Damn you, Max,' he said when he could speak. 'So you've won through, have you?'

A shrug answered him. 'Virtually. But I decided the ball was not the right venue.' The comment stunned Darcy but before he could phrase his next question Max continued, 'Her sisters seem to be hatching some plot, though I'm dashed if I can see what it is. But when I left all seemed peaceful enough.' Max's blue eyes went to his friend's face. 'What are you doing here?'

'Trying to avoid thinking,' said Darcy succinctly.

Max grinned. 'Oh. In that case, come and play a hand of piquet.'

The two were old adversaries who only occasionally found the time to play against each other. Their skills were well matched and before long their game had resolved into an exciting tussle which drew an increasing crowd of spectators. The owners of the hell, finding their patrons leaving the tables to view the contest, from their point an unprofitable exercise, held an urgent conference. They concluded that the cachet associated with having hosted a contest between two such well known players was worth the expense. Consequently, the two combatants found their glasses continually refilled with the finest brandy and new decks of cards made readily available.

Both Max and Darcy enjoyed the battle, and as both were able to stand the nonsense, whatever the outcome, they were perfectly willing to continue the play for however long their interest lasted. In truth, both found the exercise a welcome outlet for their frustrations of the past weeks.

The brandy they both consumed made absolutely no impression on their play or their demeanour. Egged on by a throng of spectators, all considerably more drunk than the principals, the game was still underway at the small table in the first parlour when Lord McCubbin, an ageing but rich Scottish peer, entered with Emma Mortland on his arm.

Drawn to investigate the cause of the excitement, Emma's bright eyes fell on the elegant figure of the Duke of Twyford. An unpleasant smile crossed her sharp features. She hung on Lord McCubbin's arm, pressing close to whisper to him.

'Eh? What? Oh, yes,' said his lordship, somewhat incoherently. He turned to address the occupants of the table in the middle of the crowd. 'Twyford! There you are! Think you've lost rather more than money tonight, what?'

Max, his hand poised to select his discard, let his eyes rise to Lord McCubbin's face. He frowned, an unwelcome premonition filling him as his lordship's words sank in. 'What, exactly, do you mean by that, my lord?' The words were even and precise and distinctly deadly.

But Lord McCubbin seemed not to notice. 'Why, dear boy, you've lost one of your wards. Saw her, clear as daylight. The flighty one in that damned pink domino. Getting into a carriage with that chap Keighly outside the Penbright place. Well, if you don't know, it's probably too late anyway, don't you know?'

Max's eyes had gone to Emma Mortland's face and seen the malicious triumph there. But he had no time to waste on her. He turned back to Lord McCubbin. 'Which way did they go?'

The silence in the room had finally penetrated his lordship's foggy brain. 'Er—didn't see. I went back to the ballroom.'

Martin Rotherbridge paused, his hand on the handle of his bedroom door. It was past seven in the morning. He had sat up all night since returning from the ball, with his brother's brandy decanter to keep him company, going over his relationship with Lizzie Twinning. And still he could find only one solution. He shook his head and opened the door. The sounds of a commotion in the hall drifted up the stairwell. He heard his brother's voice, uplifted in a series of orders to Hillshaw, and then to Wilson. The tone of voice was one he had rarely heard from Max. It brought him instantly alert. Sleep forgotten, he strode back to the stairs.

In the library, Max was pacing back and forth before the hearth, a savage look on his face. Darcy Hamilton stood silently by the window, his face showing the effects of the past weeks, overlaid by the stress of the moment. Max paused to glance at the clock on the mantelshelf. 'Seven-thirty,' he muttered. 'If my people haven't traced Keighly's carriage by eight-thirty, I'll have to send around to Twyford House.' He stopped as a thought struck him. Why hadn't they sent for him anyway? It could only mean that, somehow or other, Arabella had managed to conceal her disappearance. He resumed his pacing. The idea of his aunt in hysterics, not to mention Miriam Alford, was a sobering thought. His own scandalous career would be as nothing when compared to the repercussions from this little episode. He would wring Arabella's neck when he caught her.

The door opened. Max looked up to see Martin enter. 'What's up?' asked Martin.

'Arabella!' said his brother, venom in his voice. 'The stupid chit's done a bunk with Keighly.'

'*Eloped*?' said Martin, his disbelief patent.

Max stopped pacing. 'Well, I presume he means to marry her. Considering how they all insist on the proposal first, I can't believe she'd change her spots quite so dramatically. But if I have anything to say about it, she won't be marrying Keighly. I've a good mind to shove her into a convent until she comes to her senses!'

Darcy started, then smiled wryly. 'I'm told there's a particularly good one near their old home.'

Max turned to stare at him as if he had gone mad.

'But think of the waste,' said Martin, grinning.

'Precisely my thoughts,' nodded Darcy, sinking into an armchair. 'Max, unless you plan to ruin your carpet, for God's sake sit down.'

With something very like a growl, Max threw himself into the other armchair. Martin drew up a straight-backed chair from the side of the room and sat astride it, his arms folded over its back. 'So what now?' he asked. 'I've never been party to an elopement before.'

His brother's intense blue gaze, filled with silent warning, only made him grin more broadly. 'Well, how the hell should I know?' Max eventually exploded.

Both brothers turned to Darcy. He shook his head, his voice unsteady as he replied, 'Don't look at me. Not in my line. Come to think of it, none of us has had much experience in trying to get women to marry us.'

'Too true,' murmured Martin. A short silence fell, filled with uncomfortable thoughts. Martin broke it. 'So, what's your next move?'

'Wilson's sent runners out to all the posting houses. I can't do a thing until I know which road they've taken.'

At that moment, the door silently opened and shut again, revealing the efficient Wilson, a small and self-effacing man, Max's most trusted servitor. 'I thought you'd wish to know, Your Grace. There's been no sightings of such a vehicle on any of the roads leading north, north-east or south. The man covering the Dover road has yet to report back, as has the man investigating the road to the south-west.'

Max nodded. 'Thank you, Wilson. Keep me informed as the reports come in.'

Wilson bowed and left as silently as he had entered.

The frown on Max's face deepened. 'Where would they go? Gretna Green? Dover? I know Keighly's got estates somewhere, but I never asked where.' After a moment, he glanced at Martin. 'Did Lizzie ever mention it?'

Martin shook his head. Then, he frowned. 'Not but what I found her talking to Keighly as soon as ever they got to the ball this evening. I asked her what it was about but she denied there was anything in it.' His face had become grim. 'She must have known.'

'I think Sarah knew too,' said Darcy, his voice quite unemotional. 'I saw her go out with Keighly, then found her alone in a gazebo not far from the carriage gate.'

'Hell and the devil!' said Max. 'They can't all simultaneously have got a screw loose. What I can't understand is what's so attractive about *Keighly*?'

A knock on the door answered this imponderable question. At Max's command, Hillshaw entered. 'Lord Denbigh desires a word with you, Your Grace.'

For a moment, Max's face was blank. Then, he sighed. 'Show him in, Hillshaw. He's going to have to know sooner or later.'

As it transpired, Hugo already knew. As he strode into the library, he was scowling furiously. He barely waited to shake Max's hand and exchange nods with the other two men before asking, 'Have you discovered which road they've taken?'

Max blinked and waved him to the armchair he had vacated, moving to take the chair behind the desk. 'How did you know?'

'It's all over town,' said Hugo, easing his large frame into the chair. 'I was at White's when I heard it. And if it's reached that far, by later this morning your ward is going to be featuring in the very latest *on-dit* all over London. I'm going to wring her neck!'

This last statement brought a tired smile to Max's face. But, 'You'll have to wait in line for the privilege,' was all he said.

The brandy decanter, replenished after Martin's inroads, had twice made the rounds before Wilson again slipped noiselessly into the room. He cleared his throat to attract Max's attention. 'A coach carrying a gentleman and a young lady wearing a rose-pink domino put in at the Crown at Acton at two this morning, Your Grace.'

The air of despondency which had settled over the room abruptly lifted. 'Two,' said Max, his eyes going to the clock. 'And it's well after eight now. So they must be past Uxbridge. Unless they made a long stop?'

Wilson shook his head. 'No, Your Grace. They only stopped long enough to change horses.' If anything, the little man's impassive face became even more devoid of emotion. 'It seems the young lady was most anxious to put as much distance as possible behind them.'

'As well she might,' said Max, his eyes glittering. 'Have my curricle put to. And good work, Wilson.'

'Thank you, Your Grace.' Wilson bowed and left. Max tossed off the brandy in his glass and rose.

'I'll come with you,' said Hugo, putting his own glass down. For a moment, his eyes met Max's, then Max nodded.

'Very well.' His gaze turned to his brother and Darcy Hamilton. 'Perhaps you two could break the news to the ladies at Twyford House?'

Martin nodded.

Darcy grimaced at Max over the rim of his glass. 'I thought you'd say that.' After a moment, he continued, 'As I said before, I'm not much of a hand at elopements and I don't know Keighly at all. But it occurs to me, Max, dear boy, that it's perfectly possible he might not see reason all that easily. He might even do something rash. So, aside from Hugo here, don't you think you'd better take those along with you?'

Darcy pointed at a slim wooden case that rested on top of the dresser standing against the wall at the side of the room. Inside, as he knew, reposed a pair of Mr Joseph Manton's duelling pistols, with which Max was considered a master.

Max hesitated, then shrugged. 'I suppose you're right.' He lifted the case to his desk-top and, opening it, quickly checked the pistols. They looked quite lethal, the long black barrels gleaming, the silver mountings glinting wickedly. He had just picked up the second, when the knocker on the front door was plied with a ruthlessness which brought a definite wince to all four faces in the library. The night had been a long one. A moment later, they heard Hillshaw's sonorous tones, remonstrating with the caller. Then, an unmistakably feminine voice reached their ears. With an oath, Max strode to the door.

Caroline fixed Hillshaw with a look which brooked no argument. 'I wish to see His Grace *immediately*, Hillshaw.'

Accepting defeat, Hillshaw turned to usher her to the drawing-room, only to be halted by his master's voice.

'Caro! What are you doing here?'

From the library door, Max strolled forward to take the hand Caroline held out to him. Her eyes widened as she took in the pistol he still held in his other hand. 'Thank God I'm in time!' she said, in such heartfelt accents that Max frowned.

'It's all right. We've found out which road they took. Denbigh and I were about to set out after them. Don't worry, we'll bring her back.'

Far from reassuring her as he had intended, his matter-of-fact tone seemed to set her more on edge. Caroline clasped both her small hands on his arm. 'No! You don't understand.'

Max's frown deepened. He decided she was right. He could not fathom why she wished him to let Arabella ruin herself. 'Come into the library.'

Caroline allowed him to usher her into the apartment where they had first met. As her eyes took in the other occupants, she coloured slightly. 'Oh, I didn't realise,' she said.

Max waved her hesitation aside. 'It's all right. They already know.' He settled her in the armchair Hugo had vacated. 'Caro, do you know where Keighly's estates are?'

Caroline was struggling with his last revelation.

They already knew? How? 'Gloucestershire, I think,' she replied automatically. Then, her mind registered the fact that Max had laid the wicked-looking pistol he had been carrying on his desk, with its mate, no less, and was putting the box which she thought ought to contain them back, empty, on the dresser. A cold fear clutched at her stomach. Her voice seemed thin and ready. 'Max, what are you going to do with those?'

Max, still standing behind the desk, glanced down at the pistols. But it was Hugo's deep voice which answered her. 'Have to make sure Keighly sees reason, ma'am,' he explained gently. 'Need to impress on him the wisdom of keeping his mouth shut over this.'

Her mind spinning, Caroline looked at him blankly. 'But why? I mean, what can he say? Well, it's all so ridiculous.'

'Ridiculous?' echoed Max, a grim set to his mouth.

'I'm afraid you don't quite understand, Miss Twinning,' broke in Darcy. 'The story's already all over town. But if Max can get her back and Keighly keeps his mouth shut, then it's just possible it'll all blow over, you see.'

'But. . .but why should Max interfere?' Caroline put a hand to her head, as if to still her whirling thoughts.

This question was greeted by stunned silence. It was Martin who broke it. 'But, dash it all! He's her *guardian*!'

For an instant, Caroline looked perfectly blank. 'Is he?' she whispered, weakly.

This was too much for Max. 'You know perfectly well I am.' It appeared to him that his Caro had all but lost her wits with shock. He reined in his temper, sorely tried by the events of the entire night, and said, 'Hugo and I are about to leave to get Arabella back——'

'No!' The syllable was uttered with considerable force by Caroline as she leapt to her feet. It had the desired effect of stopping her guardian in his tracks. One black brow rose threateningly, but before he could voice his anger she was speaking again. 'You *don't* understand! I didn't *think* you did, but you kept telling me you *knew*.'

Caroline's eyes grew round as she watched Max move around the desk and advance upon her. She waved one hand as if to keep him back and enunciated clearly, 'Arabella did not go with Sir Ralph.'

Max stopped. Then his eyes narrowed. 'She was seen getting into a carriage with him in the Penbrights' drive.'

Caroline shook her head as she tried to work this out. Then she saw the light. 'A rose-pink domino was seen getting into Sir Ralph's carriage?'

At her questioning look, Max thought back to Lord McCubbin's words. Slowly, he nodded his head. 'And you're sure it wasn't Arabella?'

'When I left Twyford House, Arabella was at the breakfast table.'

'So who. . .?'

'Sarah?' came the strangled voice of Darcy Hamilton.

Caroline looked puzzled. 'No. She's at home, too.'

'*Lizzie*?'

Martin's horrified exclamation startled Caroline. She regarded him in increasing bewilderment. 'Of course not. She's at Twyford House.'

By now, Max could see the glimmer of reason for what seemed like the first time in hours. 'So who went with Sir Ralph?'

'Miss Harriet Jenkins,' said Caroline.

'*Who*?' The sound of four male voices in puzzled unison was very nearly too much for Caroline. She sank back into her chair and waved them back to their seats. 'Sit down and I'll explain.'

With wary frowns, they did as she bid them.

After a pause to marshal her thoughts, Caroline began. 'It's really all Mrs Crowbridge's fault. She decided she wanted Sir Ralph for a son-in-law. Sir Ralph had come to town because he took fright at the thought of the marriage he had almost contracted with Miss Jenkins in Gloucestershire.' She glanced up, but none of her audience seemed to have difficulty understanding events thus far. 'Mrs Crowbridge kept throwing Amanda in Sir Ralph's way. Amanda did not like Sir Ralph and so, to help out, and especially because Mr Minchbury had almost come to the point with Amanda and she favoured his suit, Arabella started flirting with Sir Ralph, to draw him away from Amanda.' She paused, but no questions came. 'Well, you, Max, made that a bit difficult when you told Arabella to behave herself with respect to Sir Ralph. But they got around that by sharing the work, as it were. It was still Arabella drawing Sir Ralph off, but the other two helped to cover her absences. Then, Miss Jenkins came to town, following Sir Ralph. She joined in the...the plot. I gather Arabella was to hold Sir Ralph off until Mr Minchbury proposed and then turn him over to Miss Jenkins.'

Max groaned and Caroline watched as he put his head in his hand. 'Sir Ralph has my heart-felt sympathy,' he said. He gestured to her. 'Go on.'

'Well, then Mrs Crowbridge tried to trap Sir Ralph by trying to put him in a compromising situation with Amanda. After that, they all decided something drastic needed to be done, to save both Sir Ralph and Amanda. At the afternoon concert, Sarah wheedled a declaration of sorts from Sir Ralph over Arabella and got him to promise to go along with their plan. He thought Arabella was about to go into a decline and had to be swept off her feet by an elopement.'

'My sympathy for Sir Ralph has just died,' said Max. 'What a slow-top if he believed that twaddle!'

'So that's what she was doing on the balcony with him,' said Darcy. 'She was there for at least half an hour.'

Caroline nodded. 'She said she had had to work on him. But Harriet Jenkins has known Sir Ralph from the cradle and had told her how best to go about it.'

When no further comment came, Caroline resumed her story. 'At the Penbrights' ball last night, Lizzie had the job of making sure Sir Ralph had brought his carriage and would be waiting for Sarah when she came to take him to the rendezvous later.'

'And that's why she went to talk to Keighly as soon as you got in the ballroom,' said Martin, putting his piece of the puzzle into place.

'All Arabella had to do was to flirt outrageously as usual, so that everyone, but particularly Sir Ralph, would be convinced it was her in the rose-pink domino. At twelve-twenty, Arabella swapped dominos with Harriet Jenkins and Harriet went down to a gazebo by the carriage gate.'

'Oh, God!' groaned Hugo Denbigh. The horror in his voice brought all eyes to him. He had paled. 'What was the colour? Of the second domino?'

Caroline stared at him. 'Brown.'

'Oh, no! I should have guessed. But her *accent.*' Hugo dropped his head into his large hands.

For a moment, his companions looked on in total bewilderment. Then Caroline chuckled, her eyes dancing. 'Oh. Did you meet Maria Pavlovska?'

'Yes, I did!' said Hugo, emerging from his depression. 'Allow me to inform you, Miss Twinning, that your sister is a minx!'

'I know that,' said Caroline. 'Though I must say, it's rather trying of her.' In answer to Max's look of patent enquiry, she explained, 'Maria Pavlovska was a character Arabella acted in a play on board ship. A Polish countess of – er——' Caroline broke off, blushing.

'Dubious virtue,' supplied Hugo, hard pressed.

'Well, she was really very good at it,' said Caroline.

Looking at Hugo's flushed countenance, none of the others doubted it.

'Where was I?' asked Caroline, trying to appear unconscious. 'Oh, yes. Well, all that was left to do was to get Sir Ralph to the gazebo. Sarah apparently did that.'

Darcy nodded. 'Yes. I saw her.'

Max waited for more. His friend's silence brought a considering look to his eyes.

'So, you see, it's all perfectly all right. It's Harriet Jenkins who has gone with Sir Ralph. I gather he proposed before they left and Miss Jenkins's family approve the match, and as they are headed straight back to Gloucestershire, I don't think there's anything to worry about. Oh, and Mr Minchbury proposed last night and the Crowbridges accepted him, so all's ended well after all and everyone's happy.'

'Except for the four of us, who've all aged years in one evening,' retorted Max acerbically.

She had the grace to blush. 'I came as soon as I found out.'

Hugo interrupted. 'But they've forgotten one thing. It's all over town that Arabella eloped with Keighly.'

'Oh, no. I don't think that can be right,' said Caroline, shaking her head. 'Anyone who was at the unmasking at the Penbrights' ball would know Arabella was there until the end.' Seeing the questioning looks, she explained, 'The unmasking was held at one o'clock. And someone suggested there should be

a. . .a competition to see who was best disguised. People weren't allowed to unmask until someone correctly guessed who they were. Well, no one guessed who Maria Pavlovska was, so Arabella was the toast of the ball.'

Max sat back in his chair and grinned tiredly. 'So anyone putting about the tale of my ward's elopement will only have the story rebound on them. I'm almost inclined to forgive your sisters their transgression for that one fact.'

Caroline looked hopeful, but he did not elaborate. Max stood and the others followed suit. Hugo, still shaking his head in disbelief, took himself off, and Darcy left immediately after. Martin retired for a much needed rest and Caroline found herself alone with her guardian.

Max crossed to where she sat and drew her to her feet and into his arms. His lips found hers in a reassuring kiss. Then, he held her, her head on his shoulder, and laughed wearily. 'Sweetheart, if I thought your sisters would be on my hands for much longer, I'd have Whitney around here this morning to instruct him to break that guardianship clause.'

'I'm sorry,' mumbled Caroline, her hands engrossed in smoothing the folds of his cravat. 'I did come as soon as I found out.'

'I know you did,' acknowledged Max. 'And I'm very thankful you did, what's more! Can you imagine how Hugo and I would have looked if we *had* succeeded in overtaking Keighly's carriage and demanded he return the lady to us? God!' He shuddered. 'It doesn't bear thinking about.' He hugged her, then released her. 'Now you should go home and rest. And I'm going to get some sleep.'

'One moment,' she said, staying within his slackened hold, her eyes still on his cravat. 'Remember I said I'd tell you whether there were any gentlemen who we'd like to consider seriously, should they apply to you for permission to address us?'

Max nodded. 'Yes. I remember.' Surely she was not going to mention Willoughby? What had gone on last night, after he had left? He suddenly felt cold.

But she was speaking again. 'Well, if Lord Darcy should happen to ask, then you know about that, don't you?'

Max nodded. 'Yes. Darcy would make Sarah a fine husband. One who would keep her sufficiently occupied so she wouldn't have time for scheming.' He grinned at Caroline's blush. 'And you're right. I'm expecting him to ask at any time. So that's Sarah dealt with.'

'And I'd rather thought Lord Denbigh for Arabella, though I didn't know then about Maria Pavlovska.'

'Oh, I wouldn't deal Hugo short. Maria Pavlovska might be a bit hard to bear but I'm sure he'll come about. And, as I'm sure Aunt Augusta has told you, he's perfectly acceptable as long as he can be brought to pop the question.'

'And,' said Caroline, keeping her eyes down, 'I'm not perfectly sure, but. . .'

'You think Martin might ask for Lizzie,' supplied Max, conscious of his own tiredness. It was sapping his will. All sorts of fantasies were surfacing in his brain and the devil of it was they were all perfectly achievable. But he had already made other plans, better plans. 'I foresee no problems there. Martin's got more money than is good for him. I'm sure Lizzie will keep him on his toes, hauling her out of the scrapes her innocence will doubtless land her in. And I'd much rather it was him than me.' He tried to look into Caroline's face but she kept her eyes—were they greyish-green or greenish-grey? He had never decided—firmly fixed on his cravat.

'I'm thrilled that you approve of my cravat, sweetheart, but is there anything more? I'm dead on my feet,' he acknowledged with a rueful grin, praying that she did not have anything more to tell him.

Caroline's eyes flew to his, an expression he could not read in their depths. 'Oh, of course you are! No. There's nothing more.'

Max caught the odd wistfulness in her tone and correctly divined its cause. His grin widened. As he walked her to the door, he said, 'Once I'm myself again, and have recovered from your sisters' exploits, I'll call on you—say at three this afternoon? I'll take you for a drive. There are some matters I wish to discuss with you.' He guided her through the library door and into the hall. In answer to her questioning look, he added, 'About your ball.'

'Oh. I'd virtually forgotten all about it,' Caroline said as Max took her cloak from Hillshaw and placed it about her shoulders. They had organised to hold a ball in the Twinnings' honour at Twyford House the following week.

'We'll discuss it at three this afternoon,' said Max as he kissed her hand and led her down the steps to her carriage.

CHAPTER TWELVE

SARAH wrinkled her nose at the piece of cold toast lying on her plate. Pushing it away, she leant back in her chair and surveyed her elder sister. With her copper curls framing her expressive face, Caroline sat at the other end of the small table in the breakfast-room, a vision of palest cerulean blue. A clearly distracted vision. A slight frown had settled in the greeny eyes, banishing the lively twinkle normally lurking there. She sighed, apparently unconsciously, as she stared at her piece of toast, as cold and untouched as Sarah's, as if concealed in its surface were the answers to all unfathomable questions. Sarah was aware of a guilty twinge. Had Max cut up stiff and Caroline not told them?

They had all risen early, being robust creatures and never having got into the habit of lying abed, and had gathered in the breakfast parlour to examine their success of the night before. That it had been a complete and unqualified success could not have been divined from their faces; all of them had looked drawn and peaked. While Sarah knew the cause of her own unhappiness, and had subsequently learned of her younger sisters' reasons for despondency, she had been and still was at a loss to explain Caroline's similar mood. She had been in high feather at the ball. Then Max had left early, an unusual occurrence which had made Sarah wonder if they had had a falling-out. But her last sight of them together, when he had taken leave of Caroline in the ballroom, had not supported such a fancy. They had looked. . .well, intimate. Happily so. Thoroughly immersed in each other. Which, thought the knowledgeable Sarah, was not especially like either of them. She sent a sharp glance to the other end of the table.

Caroline's bloom had gradually faded and she had been as silent as the rest of them during the drive home. This morning, on the stairs, she had shared their quiet mood. And then, unfortunately, they had had to make things much worse. They had always agreed that Caroline would have to be told immediately after the event. That had always been their way, ever since they were small children. No matter the outcome, Caroline could be relied on to predict unerringly the potential ramifications and to protect her sisters from any unexpected repercussions. This morning, as they had recounted to her their plan and its execution, she had paled. When they had come to a faltering halt, she had, uncharacteristically, told them in a quiet voice to wait as they were while she communicated their deeds to their guardian forthwith. She had explained nothing. Rising from the table without so much as a sip of her coffee, she had immediately called for the carriage and departed for Delmere House.

She had returned an hour and a half later. They had not left the room; Caroline's orders, spoken in that particular tone, were not to be dismissed lightly. In truth, each sunk in gloomy contemplation of her state, they had not noticed the passage of time. Caroline had re-entered the room, calmly resumed her seat and accepted the cup of coffee Arabella had hastily poured for her. She had fortified herself from this before explaining to them, in quite unequivocal terms, just how close they had come to creating a hellish tangle. It had never occurred to them that someone might see Harriet departing and, drawing the obvious conclusion, inform Max of the fact, especially in such a public manner. They had been aghast at the realisation of how close to the edge of scandal they had come and were only too ready to behave as contritely as Caroline wished. However, all she had said was, 'I don't really think there's much we should do. Thankfully, Arabella, your gadding about as Maria Pavlovska ensured that everyone knows you did not elope from the ball. I suppose we could go riding.' She had paused, then added, 'But I really don't feel like it this morning.'

They had not disputed this, merely shaken their heads to convey their agreement. After a moment of silence, Caroline had added, 'I think Max would expect us to behave as if nothing had happened, other than there being some ridiculous tale about that Bella had eloped. You'll have to admit, I suppose, that you swapped dominos with Harriet Jenkins, but that could have been done in all innocence. And remember to show due interest in the surprising tale that Harriet left the ball with Sir Ralph.' An unwelcome thought reared its head. 'Will the Crowbridge girls have the sense to keep their mouths shut?'

They had hastened to assure her on this point. 'Why, it was all for Amanda's sake, after all,' Lizzie had pointed out.

Caroline had not been entirely convinced but had been distracted by Arabella. Surmising from Caroline's use of her shortened name that the worse was over, she had asked, 'Is Max very annoyed with us?'

Caroline had considered the question while they had all hung, unexpectedly nervous, on her answer. 'I think he's resigned, now that it's all over and no real harm done, to turn a blind eye to your misdemeanours. However, if I were you, I would not be going out of my way to bring myself to his notice just at present.'

Their relief had been quite real. Despite his reputation, their acquaintance with the Duke of Twyford had left his younger wards with the definite impression that he would not condone any breach of conduct and was perfectly capable of implementing sufficiently draconian measures in response to any transgression. In years past, they would have ignored the potential threat and relied on Caroline to make all right in the event of any trouble. But, given that the man in question was Max Rotherbridge, none was sure how successful Caroline would be in turning him up sweet. Reassured that their guardian was not intending to descend, in ire, upon them, Lizzie and Arabella, after hugging Caroline and avowing their deepest thanks for her endeavours on their behalf, had left the room. Sarah suspected they would both be found in some particular nook, puzzling out the uncomfortable feeling in their hearts.

Strangely enough, she no longer felt the need to emulate them. In the long watches of a sleepless night, she had finally faced the fact that she could not live without Darcy Hamilton. In the gazebo the previous evening, it had been on the tip of her tongue to beg him to take her from the ball, to some isolated spot where they could pursue their lovemaking in greater privacy. She had had to fight her own nearly overwhelming desire to keep from speaking the words. If she had uttered them, he would have arranged it all in an instant, she knew; his desire for her was every bit as strong as her desire for him. Only her involvement in their scheme and the consternation her sudden disappearance would have caused had tipped the scales. Her desire for marriage, for a home and family, was still as strong as ever. But, if he refused to consider such an arrangement, she was now prepared to listen to whatever alternative suggestions he had to offer. There was Max's opposition to be overcome, but presumably Darcy was aware of that. She felt sure he would seek her company soon enough and then she would make her acquiescence plain. That, at least, she thought with a small, introspective smile, would be very easy to do.

Caroline finally pushed the unhelpful piece of toast aside. She rose and shook her skirts in an unconsciously flustered gesture. In a flash of unaccustomed insight, Sarah wondered if her elder sister was in a similar state to the rest of them. After all, they were all Twinnings. Although their problems were superficially quite different, in reality, they were simply variations on the same theme. They were all in love with rakes, all of whom seemed highly resistant to matrimony. In her case, the rake had won. But surely Max wouldn't win, too? For a moment, Sarah's mind boggled at the thought of the two elder Twinnings falling by the wayside. Then, she gave herself a mental shake. No, of course not. He was their guardian, after all. Which, Sarah thought, presumably meant Caroline would even the score. Caroline was undoubtedly the most capable of them all. So why, then, did she look so troubled?

Caroline was indeed racked by the most uncomfortable thoughts. Leaving Sarah to her contemplation of the breakfast table, she drifted without purpose into the drawing-room and thence to the small courtyard beyond. Ambling about, her delicate fingers examining some of the bountiful blooms, she eventually came to the hammock, slung under the cherry trees, protected from the morning sun by their leafy foliage. Climbing into it, she rested her aching head against the cushions with relief and prepared to allow the conflicting emotions inside her to do battle.

Lately, it seemed to her that there were two Caroline Twinnings. One knew the ropes, was thoroughly acquainted with society's expectations and had no hesitation in laughing at the idea of a gentlewoman such as herself sharing a man's bed outside the bounds of marriage. She had been acquainted with this Caroline Twinning for as long as she could remember. The other woman, for some mysterious reason, had only surfaced in recent times, since her exposure to the temptations of Max Rotherbridge. There was no denying the increasing control this second persona exerted over her. In truth, it had come to the point where she was seriously considering which Caroline Twinning she preferred.

She was no green girl and could hardly pretend she had not been perfectly aware of Max's intentions when she had heard the lock fall on that bedroom door. Nor could she comfort herself that the situation had been beyond her control—at least, not then. If she had made any real effort to bring the illicit encounter to a halt, as she most certainly should have done, Max would have instantly acquiesced. She could hardly claim he had forced her to remain. But it had been that other Caroline Twinning who had welcomed him into her arms and had proceeded to enjoy, all too wantonly, the delights to be found in his.

She had never succeeded in introducing marriage as an aspect of their relationship. She had always been aware that what Max intended was an illicit affair. What she had underestimated was her own interest in such a scandalous proceeding. But there was no denying the pleasure she had found in his arms, nor the disappointment she had felt when he had cut short their interlude. She knew she could rely on him to ensure that next time there would be no possible impediment to the completion of her education. And she would go to his arms with neither resistance nor regrets. Which, to the original Caroline Twinning, was a very lowering thought.

Swinging gently in the hammock, the itinerant breeze wafting her curls, she tried to drum up all the old arguments against allowing herself to become involved in such an improper relationship. She had been over them all before; they held no power to sway her. Instead, the unbidden memory of Max's mouth on her breast sent a thrill of warm desire through her veins. 'Fool!' she said, without heat, to the cherry tree overhead.

Martin Rotherbridge kicked a stone out of his path. He had been walking for nearly twenty minutes in an effort to rid himself of a lingering nervousness over the act he was about to perform. He would rather have raced a charge of Chasseurs than do what he must that day. But there was nothing else for it—the events of the morning had convinced him of that. That dreadful instant when he had thought, for one incredulous and heart-stopping moment, that Lizzie had gone with Keighly was never to be repeated. And the only way of ensuring that was to marry the chit.

It had certainly not been his intention, and doubtless Max would laugh himself into hysterics, but there it was. Facts had to be faced. Despite his being at her side for much of the time, Lizzie had managed to embroil herself very thoroughly in a madcap plan which, even now, if it ever became known, would see her ostracised by those who mattered in the *ton*. She was a damned sight too innocent to see the outcome of her actions; either that, or too naïve in her belief in her abilities to come about. She needed a husband to keep a firm hand on her reins, to steer her clear of the perils her beauty and innocence would unquestionably lead her into. And, as he desperately wanted the foolish woman, and had every intention of fulfilling the role anyway, he might as well officially be it.

He squared his shoulders. No sense in putting off the evil moment any longer. He might as well speak to Max.

He turned his steps towards Delmere House. Rounding a corner, some blocks from his destination, he saw the impressive form of Lord Denbigh striding along on the opposite side of the street, headed in the same direction. On impulse, Martin crossed the street.

'Hugo!'

Lord Denbigh halted in his purposeful stride and turned to see who had hailed him. Although a few years separated them, he and Martin Rotherbridge had many interests in common and had been acquainted even before the advent of the Twinnings. His lordship's usual sleepy grin surfaced. 'Hello, Martin. On your way home?'

Martin nodded and fell into step beside him. At sight of Hugo, his curiosity over Maria Pavlovska had returned. He experimented in his head with a number of suitable openings before settling for, 'Dashed nuisances, the Twinning girls!'

'Very!' The curt tone in Hugo's deep voice was not encouraging.

Nothing loath, Martin plunged on. 'Waltz around, tying us all in knots. What exactly happened when Arabella masqueraded as that Polish countess?'

To his amazement, Hugo coloured. 'Never you mind,' he said, then, at the hopeful look in Martin's eyes, relented. 'If you must know, she behaved in a manner which. . .well, in short, it was difficult to tell who was seducing whom.'

Martin gave a burst of laughter, which he quickly controlled at Hugo's scowl. By way of returning the confidence, he said, 'Well, I suppose I may as well tell you, as it's bound to be all over town all too soon. I'm on my way to beg Max's permission to pay my addresses to Lizzie Twinning.'

Hugo's mild eyes went to Martin's face in surprise. He murmured all the usual condolences, adding, 'Didn't really think you'd be wanting to get leg-shackled just yet.'

Martin shrugged. 'Nothing else for it. Aside from making all else blessedly easy, it's only as her husband I'd have the authority to make certain she didn't get herself involved in any more hare-brained schemes.'

'There is that,' agreed Hugo ruminatively. They continued for a space in silence before Martin realised they were nearing Delmere House.

'Where are you headed?' he enquired of the giant by his side.

For the second time, Hugo coloured. Looking distinctly annoyed by this fact, he stopped. Martin, puzzled, stopped by his side, but before he could frame any question, Hugo spoke. 'I may as well confess, I suppose. I'm on my way to see Max, too.'

Martin howled with laughter and this time made no effort to subdue it. When he could speak again, he clapped Hugo on the back. 'Welcome to the family!' As they turned and fell into step once more, Martin's eyes lifted. 'And lord, what a family it's going to be! Unless I miss my guess, that's Darcy Hamilton's curricle.'

Hugo looked up and saw, ahead of them, Lord Darcy's curricle drawn up outside Delmere House. Hamilton himself, elegantly attired, descended and turned to give instructions to his groom, before strolling towards the steps leading up to the door. He was joined by Martin and Hugo.

Martin grinned. 'Do you want to see Max, too?'

Darcy Hamilton's face remained inscrutable. 'As it happens, I do,' he answered equably. As his glance flickered over the unusually precise picture both Martin and Hugo presented, he added, 'Am I to take it there's a queue?'

'Afraid so,' confirmed Hugo, grinning in spite of himself. 'Maybe we should draw lots?'

'Just a moment,' said Martin, studying the carriage waiting by the pavement in front of Darcy's curricle. 'That's Max's travelling chaise. Is he going somewhere?'

This question was addressed to Darcy Hamilton, who shook his head. 'He's said nothing to me.'

'Maybe the Twinnings have proved too much for him and he's going on a repairing lease?' suggested Hugo.

'Entirely understandable, but I don't somehow think that's it,' mused Darcy. Uncertain, they stood on the pavement, and gazed at the carriage. Behind them, the door of Delmere House opened. Masterton hurried down the steps and climbed into the chaise. As soon as the door had shut, the coachman flicked his whip and the carriage pulled away. Almost immediately, the vacated position was filled with Max's curricle, the bays stamping and tossing their heads.

Martin's brows had risen. 'Masterton and baggage,' he said. 'Now why?'

'Whatever the reason,' said Darcy succinctly, 'I suspect we'd better catch your brother now or he'll merrily leave us to our frustrations for a week or more.'

The looks of horror which passed over the two faces before him brought a gleam of amusement to his eyes.

'Lord, yes!' said Hugo.

Without further discussion, they turned *en masse* and started up the steps. At that moment, the door at the top opened and their prey emerged. They stopped.

Max, eyeing them as he paused to draw on his driving gloves, grinned. The breeze lifted the capes of his greatcoat as he descended the steps.

'Max, we need to talk to you.'

'Where are you going?'

'You can't leave yet.'

With a laugh, Max held up his hand to stem the tide. When silence had fallen, he said, 'I'm so glad to see you all.' His hand once more quelled the surge of explanation his drawling comment drew forth. 'No! I find I have neither the time nor the inclination to discuss the matters. My answers to your questions are yes, yes and yes. All right?'

Darcy Hamilton laughed. 'Fine by me.'

Hugo nodded bemusedly.

'Are you going away?' asked Martin.

Max nodded. 'I need a rest. Somewhere tranquil.'

His exhausted tone brought a grin to his brother's face. 'With or without company?'

Max's wide grin showed fleetingly. 'Never you mind, brother dear. Just channel your energies into keeping Lizzie from engaging in any further crusades to help the needy and I'll be satisfied.' His gaze took in the two curricles beside the pavement, the horses fretting impatiently. 'In fact, I'll make life easy for you. For all of you. I suggest we repair to Twyford House. I'll engage to remove Miss Twinning. Aunt Augusta and Mrs Alford rest all afternoon. And the house is a large one. If you can't manage to wrest agreement to your proposals from the Misses Twinning under such circumstances, I wash my hands of you.'

They all agreed very readily. Together, they set off immediately, Max and his brother in his curricle, Lord Darcy and Hugo Denbigh following in Darcy's carriage.

The sound of male voices in the front hall drifted to Caroline's ears as she sat with her sisters in the back parlour. With a sigh, she picked up her bonnet and bade the three despondent figures scattered through the room goodbye. They all looked distracted. She felt much the same. Worn out by her difficult morning and from tossing and turning half the night, tormented by a longing she had tried valiantly to ignore, she had fallen asleep in the hammock under the cherry trees. Her sisters had found her but had left her to recover, only waking her for a late lunch before her scheduled drive with their guardian.

As she walked down the corridor to the front hall, she was aware of the leaping excitement the prospect of seeing Max Rotherbridge always brought her. At the mere thought of being alone with him, albeit on the box seat of a curricle in broad daylight in the middle of fashionable London, she could feel that other Caroline Twinning taking over.

Her sisters had taken her words of the morning to heart and had wisely refrained from joining her in greeting their guardian. Alone, she emerged into the hallway. In astonishment, she beheld, not one elegantly turned out gentleman, but four.

Max, his eyes immediately drawn as if by some magic to her, smiled and came forward to take her hand. His comprehensive glance swept her face, then dropped to her bonnet, dangling loosely by its ribbons from one hand. His smile broadened, bringing a delicate colour to her cheeks. 'I'm glad you're ready, my dear. But where are your sisters?'

Caroline blinked. 'They're in the back parlour,' she answered, turning to greet Darcy Hamilton.

Max turned. 'Millwade, escort these gentlemen to the back parlour.'

Millwade, not in Hillshaw's class, looked slightly scandalised. But an order from his employer was not to be disobeyed. Caroline, engaged in exchanging courtesies with the gentlemen involved, was staggered. But before she could remonstrate, her cloak appeared about her shoulders and she was firmly propelled out of the door. She was constrained to hold her fire until Max had dismissed the urchin holding the bays and climbed up beside her.

'You're supposed to be our guardian! Don't you think it's a little unconventional to leave three gentlemen with your wards unchaperoned?'

Giving his horses the office, Max chuckled. 'I don't think any of them need chaperoning at present. They'd hardly welcome company when trying to propose.'

'Oh! You mean they've asked?'

Max nodded, then glanced down. 'I take it you're still happy with their suits?'

'Oh, yes! It's just that. . .well, the others didn't seem to hold out much hope.' After a pause, she asked, 'Weren't you surprised?'

He shook his head. 'Darcy I've been expecting for weeks. After this morning, Hugo was a certainty. And Martin's been more sternly silent than I've ever seen him before. So, no, I can't say I was surprised.' He turned to grin at her. 'Still, I hope your sisters have suffered as much as their swains—it's only fair.'

She was unable to repress her answering grin, the dimple by her mouth coming delightfully into being.

A subtle comment of Max's had the effect of turning the conversation into general fields. They laughed and discussed, occasionally with mock seriousness, a number of tonnish topics, then settled to determined consideration of the Twyford House ball.

This event had been fixed for the following Tuesday, five days distant. More than four hundred guests were expected. Thankfully, the ballroom was huge and the house would easily cater for this number. Under Lady Benborough's guidance, the Twinning sisters had coped with all the arrangements, a fact known to Max. He had a bewildering array of questions for Caroline. Absorbed with answering these, she paid little attention to her surroundings.

'You don't think,' she said, airing a point she and her sisters had spent much time pondering, 'that, as it's not really a proper come-out, in that we've been about for the entire Season and none of us is truly a débutante, the whole thing might fall a little flat?'

Max grinned. 'I think I can assure you that it will very definitely not be flat. In fact,' he continued, as if pondering a new thought, 'I should think it'll be one of the highlights of the Season.'

Caroline looked her question but he declined to explain.

As usual when with her guardian, time flew and it was only when a chill in the breeze penetrated her thin cloak that Caroline glanced up and found the afternoon gone. The curricle was travelling smoothly down a well surfaced road, lined with low hedges set back a little from the carriageway. Beyond these, neat fields stretched sleepily under the waning sun, a few scattered sheep and cattle attesting to the fact that they were deep in the country. From the direction of the sun, they were travelling south, away from the capital. With a puzzled frown, she turned to the man beside her. 'Shouldn't we be heading back?'

Max glanced down at her, his devilish grin in evidence. 'We aren't going back.'

Caroline's brain flatly refused to accept the implications of that statement. Instead, after a pause, she asked conversationally, 'Where are we?'

'A little past Twickenham.'

'Oh.' If they were that far out of town, then it was difficult to see how they could return that evening even if he was only joking about not going back. But he had to be joking, surely?

The curricle slowed and Max checked his team for the turn into a beech-lined drive. As they whisked through the gateway, Caroline caught a glimpse of a coat of arms worked into the impressive iron gates. The Delmere arms, Max's own. She looked about her with interest, refusing to give credence to the suspicion growing in her mind. The drive led deep into the beechwood, then opened out to run along a ridge bordered by cleared land, close-clipped grass dropping away on one side to run down to a distant river. On the other side, the beechwood fell back as the curricle continued towards a rise. Cresting this, the road descended in a broad sweep to end in a gravel courtyard before an old stone house. It nestled into an unexpected curve of a small stream, presumably a tributary of the larger river which Caroline rather thought must be the Thames. The roof sported many gables. Almost as many chimneys, intricate pots capping them, soared high above the tiles. In the setting sun, the house glowed mellow and warm. Along one wall, a rambling white rose nodded its blooms and released its perfume to the freshening breeze. Caroline thought she had seen few more appealing houses.

They were expected, that much was clear. A groom

came running at the sound of the wheels on the gravel. Max lifted her down and led her to the door. It opened at his touch. He escorted her in and closed the door behind them.

Caroline found herself in a small hall, neatly panelled in oak, a small round table standing in the middle of the tiled floor. Max's hand at her elbow steered her to a corridor giving off the back of the hall. It terminated in a beautifully carved oak door. As Max reached around her to open it, Caroline asked, 'Where are the servants?'

'Oh, they're about. But they're too well trained to show themselves.'

Her suspicions developing in leaps and bounds, Caroline entered a large room, furnished in a fashion she had never before encountered.

The floor was covered in thick, silky rugs, executed in the most glorious hues. Low tables were scattered amid piles of cushions in silks and satins of every conceivable shade. There was a bureau against one wall, but the room was dominated by a dais covered with silks and piled with cushions, more silks draping down from above to swirl about it in semi-concealing mystery. Large glass doors gave on to a paved courtyard. The doors stood slightly ajar, admitting the comforting gurgle of the stream as it passed by on the other side of the courtyard wall. As she crossed to peer out, she noticed the ornate brass lamps which hung from the ceiling. The courtyard was empty and, surprisingly, entirely enclosed. A wooden gate was set in one side-wall and another in the wall opposite the house presumably gave on to the stream. As she turned back into the room, Caroline thought it had a strangely relaxing effect on the senses—the silks, the glowing but not overbright colours, the soothing murmur of the stream. Then, her eyes lit on the silk-covered dais. And grew round. Seen from this angle, it was clearly a bed, heavily disguised beneath the jumble of cushions and silks, but a bed nevertheless. Her suspicions confirmed, her gaze flew to her guardian's face.

What she saw there tied her stomach in knots. 'Max. . .' she began uncertainly, the conservative Miss Twinning hanging on grimly.

But then he was standing before her, his eyes glinting devilishly and that slow smile wreaking havoc with her good intentions. 'Mmm?' he asked.

'What are we doing here?' she managed, her pulse racing, her breath coming more and more shallowly, her nerves stretching in anticipation.

'Finishing your education,' the deep voice drawled.

Well, what had she expected? asked that other Miss Twinning, ousting her competitor and taking total possession as Max bent his head to kiss her. Her mouth opened welcomingly under his and he took what she offered, gradually drawing her into his embrace until she was crushed against his chest. Caroline did not mind; breathing seemed unimportant just at that moment.

When Max finally raised his head, his eyes were bright under their hooded lids and, she noticed with smug satisfaction, his breathing was almost as ragged as hers. His eyes searched her face, then his slow smile appeared. 'I notice you've ceased reminding me I'm your guardian.'

Caroline, finding her arms twined around his neck, ran her fingers through his dark hair. 'I've given up,' she said in resignation. 'You never paid the slightest attention, anyway.'

Max chuckled and bent to kiss her again, then pulled back and turned her about. 'Even if I were your guardian, I'd still have seduced you, sweetheart.'

Caroline obligingly stood still while his long fingers unlaced her gown. She dropped her head forward to move her curls, which he had loosed, out of his way. Then, the oddity in his words struck her. Her head came up abruptly. '*Even*? Max. . .' She tried to turn around but his hand pushed her back.

'Stand still,' he commanded. 'I have no intention of making love to you with your clothes on.'

Having no wish to argue that particular point, Caroline, seething with impatience, stood still until she felt the last ribbon freed. Then, she turned. 'What do you mean, *even* if you were my guardian? You are my guardian. You told me so yourself.' Her voice tapered away as one part of her mind tried to concentrate on her questions while the rest was more interested in the fact that Max had slipped her dress from her shoulders and it had slid, in a softly sensuous way, down to her feet. In seconds, her petticoats followed.

'Yes, I know I did,' Max agreed helpfully, his fingers busy with the laces of the light stays which restrained her ample charms. 'I lied. Most unwisely, as it turned out.'

'Wh. . .what?' Caroline was having a terrible time trying to focus her mind. It kept wandering. She supposed she really ought to feel shy about Max undressing her. The thought that there were not so many pieces of her clothing left for him to remove, spurred her to ask, 'What do you mean, you lied? And why unwisely?'

Max dispensed with her stays and turned his attention to the tiny buttons of her chemise. 'You were never my ward. You ceased to be a ward of the Duke of Twyford when you turned twenty-five. But I arranged to let you believe I was still your guardian, thinking that if you knew I wasn't you would never let me near you.' He grinned wolfishly at her as his hands slipped over her shoulders and her chemise joined the rest of her clothes at her feet. 'I didn't then know that the Twinnings are. . .susceptible to rakes.'

His smug grin drove Caroline to shake her head. 'We're not. . .susceptible.'

'Oh?' One dark brow rose.

Caroline closed her eyes and her head fell back as his hands closed over her breasts. She heard his deep chuckle and smiled to herself. Then, as his hands drifted, and his lips turned to hers, her mind went obligingly blank, allowing her senses free rein. As her bones turned to jelly and her knees buckled, Max's arm helpfully supported her. Then, her lips were free and she was swung up into his arms. A moment later, she was deposited in the midst of the cushions and silks on the dais.

Feeling excitement tingling along every nerve, Caroline stretched sensuously, smiling at the light that glowed in Max's eyes as they watched her while he dispensed with his clothes. But when he stretched out beside her, and her hands drifted across the hard muscles of his chest, she felt him hold back. In unconscious entreaty, she turned towards him, her body arching against his. His response was immediate and the next instant his lips had returned to hers, his arms gathering her to him. With a satisfied sigh, Caroline gave her full concentration to her last lesson.

CHAPTER THIRTEEN

'SARAH?' Darcy tried to squint down at the face under the dark hair covering his chest.

'Mmm,' Sarah replied sleepily, snuggling comfortably against him.

Darcy grinned and gave up trying to rouse her. His eyes drifted to the ceiling as he gently stroked her back. Serve her right if she was exhausted.

Together with Martin and Hugo, he had followed the strongly disapproving Millwade to the back parlour. He had announced them, to the obvious consternation of the three occupants. Darcy's grin broadened as he recalled the scene. Arabella had looked positively stricken with guilt, Lizzie had not known what to think and Sarah had simply stood, her back to the windows, and watched him. At his sign, she had come to his side and they had left the crowded room together.

At his murmured request to see her privately, she had led the way to the morning-room. He had intended to speak to her then, but she had stood so silently in the middle of the room, her face quite unreadable, that before he had known it he was kissing her. Accomplished rake though he was, her response had been staggering. He had always known her for a sensual woman but previously her reactions had been dragged unwillingly from her. Now that they came freely, their potency was enhanced a thousandfold. After five minutes, he had forcibly disengaged to return to the door and lock it. After that, neither of them had spared a thought for anything save the quenching of their raging desires.

Much later, when they had recovered somewhat, he had managed to find time, in between other occupations, to ask her to marry him. She had clearly been stunned and it was only then that he realised she had not expected his proposal. He had been oddly touched. Her answer, given without the benefit of speech, had been nevertheless comprehensive and had left him in no doubt of her desire to fill the position he was offering. His wife. The idea made him laugh. Would he survive?

The rumble in his chest disturbed Sarah but she merely burrowed her head into his shoulder and returned to her bliss-filled dreams. Darcy moved slightly, settling her more comfortably.

Her eagerness rang all sorts of warning bells in his mind. Used to taking advantage of the boredom of sensual married women, he made a resolution to ensure that his Sarah never came within arm's reach of any rakes. It would doubtless be wise to establish her as his wife as soon as possible, now he had whetted her appetite for hitherto unknown pleasures. Getting her settled in Hamilton House and introducing her to his country residences, and perhaps giving her a child or two, would no doubt keep her occupied. At least, he amended, sufficiently occupied to have no desire left over for any other than himself.

The light was fading. He glanced at the window to find the afternoon far advanced. With a sigh, he shook Sarah's white shoulder gently.

'Mmm,' she murmured protestingly, sleepily trying to shake off his hand.

Darcy chuckled. 'I'm afraid, my love, that you'll have to awaken. The day is spent and doubtless someone will shortly come looking for us. I rather think we should be dressed when they do.'

With a long-drawn-out sigh, Sarah struggled to lift her head, propping her elbows on his chest to look into his face. Then, her gaze wandered to take in the scene about them. They were lying on the accommodatingly large sofa before the empty fireplace, their clothes strewn about the room. She dropped her head into her hands. 'Oh, God. I suppose you're right.'

'Undoubtedly,' confirmed Darcy, smiling. 'And allow me to add, sweetheart, that, as your future husband, I'll always be right.'

'Oh?' Sarah enquired innocently. She sat up slightly, her hair in chaos around her face, straggling down her back to cover his hands where they lay, still gently stroking her satin skin.

Darcy viewed her serene face with misgiving. Thinking to distract her, he asked, 'Incidentally, when should we marry? I'm sure Max won't care what we decide.'

Sarah's attention was drawn from tracing her finger along the curve of his collarbone. She frowned in concentration. 'I rather think,' she eventually said, 'that it had better be soon.'

Having no wish to disagree with this eminently sensible conclusion, Darcy said, 'A wise decision. Do you want a big wedding? Or shall we leave that to Max and Caroline?'

Sarah grinned. 'A very good idea. I think our guardian should be forced to undergo that pleasure, don't you?'

As this sentiment exactly tallied with his own, Darcy merely grinned in reply. But Sarah's next question made him think a great deal harder.

'How soon is it possible to marry?'

It took a few minutes to check all the possible pros

and cons. Then he said, uncertain of her response, 'Well, theoretically speaking, it would be possible to get married tomorrow.'

'Truly? Well, let's do that,' replied his prospective bride, a decidedly wicked expression on her face.

Seeing it, Darcy grinned. And postponed their emergence from the morning-room for a further half-hour.

The first thought that sprang to Arabella's mind on seeing Hugo Denbigh enter the back parlour was how annoyed he must have been to learn of her deception. Caroline had told her of the circumstances; they would not have improved his temper. Oblivious to all else save the object of her thoughts, she did not see Sarah leave the room, nor Martin take Lizzie through the long windows into the garden. Consequently, she was a little perturbed to suddenly find herself alone with Hugo Denbigh.

'Maria Pavlovska, I presume?' His tone was perfectly equable but Arabella did not place any reliance on that. He came to stand before her, dwarfing her by his height and the breadth of his magnificent chest.

Arabella was conscious of a devastating desire to throw herself on that broad expanse and beg forgiveness for her sins. Then she remembered how he had responded to Maria Pavlovska. Her chin went up, enough to look his lordship in the eye. 'I'm so glad you found my little. . .charade entertaining.'

Despite having started the conversation, Hugo abruptly found himself at a loss for words. He had not intended to bring up the subject of Maria Pavlovska, at least not until Arabella had agreed to marry him. But seeing her standing there, obviously knowing he knew and how he had found out, memory of the desire Arabella-Maria so readily provoked had stirred disquietingly and he had temporarily lost his head. But now was not the time to indulge in a verbal brawl with a woman who, he had learnt to his cost, could match his quick tongue in repartee. So, he smiled lazily down at her, totally confusing her instead, and rapidly sought to bring the discussion to a field where he knew he possessed few defences. 'Mouthy baggage,' he drawled, taking her in his arms and preventing any riposte by the simple expedient of placing his mouth over hers.

Arabella was initially too stunned by this unexpected manoeuvre to protest. And by the time she realised what had happened, she did not want to protest. Instead, she twined her arms about Hugo's neck and kissed him back with all the fervour she possessed. Unbeknownst to her, this was a considerable amount, and Hugo suddenly found himself desperately searching for a control he had somehow misplaced.

Not being as hardened a rake as Max or Darcy, he struggled with himself until he won some small measure of rectitude; enough, at least, to draw back and sit in a large armchair, drawing Arabella on to his lap. She snuggled against his chest, drawing comfort from his warmth and solidity.

'Well, baggage, will you marry me?'

Arabella sat bolt upright, her hands braced against his chest, and stared at him. 'Marry you? Me?'

Hugo chuckled, delighted to have reduced her to dithering idiocy.

But Arabella was frowning. 'Why do you want to marry me?'

The frown transferred itself to Hugo's countenance. 'I should have thought the answer to that was a mite obvious, m'dear.'

Arabella brushed that answer aside. 'I mean, besides the obvious.'

Hugo sighed and, closing his eyes, let his head fall back against the chair. He had asked himself the same question and knew the answer perfectly well. But he had not shaped his arguments into any coherent form, not contemplating being called on to recite them. He opened his eyes and fixed his disobliging love with a grim look. 'I'm marrying you because the idea of you flirting with every Tom, Dick and Harry drives me insane. I'll tear anyone you flirt with limb from limb. So, unless you wish to be responsible for murder, you'd better stop flirting.' A giggle, quickly suppressed, greeted this threat. 'Incidentally,' Hugo continued, 'you don't go around kissing men like that all the time, do you?'

Arabella had no clear idea of what he meant by 'like that' but as she had never kissed any other man, except in a perfectly chaste manner, she could reply with perfect truthfulness, 'No, of course not. That was only you.'

'Thank God for that!' said a relieved Lord Denbigh. 'Kindly confine all such activities to your betrothed in future. Me,' he added, in case this was not yet plain.

Arabella lifted one fine brow but said nothing. She was conscious of his hands gently stroking her hips and wondered if it would be acceptable to simply blurt out 'yes'. Then, she felt Hugo's hands tighten about her waist.

'And one thing more,' he said, his eyes kindling. 'No more Maria Pavlovska. Ever.'

Arabella grinned. 'No?' she asked wistfully, her voice dropping into the huskily seductive Polish accent.

Hugo stopped and considered this plea. 'Well,' he temporised, inclined to be lenient, 'Only with me. I dare say I could handle closer acquaintance with Madame Pavlovska.'

Arabella giggled and Hugo took the opportunity to

kiss her again. This time, he let the kiss develop as he had on other occasions, keeping one eye on the door, the other on the windows and his mind solely on her responses. Eventually, he drew back and, retrieving his hands from where they had wandered, bringing a blush to his love's cheeks, he gripped her about her waist and gently shook her. 'You haven't given me your answer yet.'

'Yes, please,' said Arabella, her eyes alight. 'I couldn't bear not to be able to be Maria Pavlovska every now and again.'

Laughing, Hugo drew her back into his arms. 'When shall we wed?'

Tracing the strong line of his jaw with one small finger, Arabella thought for a minute, then replied, 'Need we wait very long?'

The undisguised longing in her tone brought her a swift response. 'Only as long as you wish.'

Arabella chuckled. 'Well, I doubt we could be married tomorrow.'

'Why not?' asked Hugo, his eyes dancing.

His love looked puzzled. 'Is it possible? I thought all those sorts of things took forever to arrange.'

'Only if you want a big wedding. If you do, I warn you it'll take months. My family's big and distributed all about. Just getting in touch with half of them will be bad enough.'

But the idea of waiting for months did not appeal to Arabella. 'If it can be done, can we really be married tomorrow? It would be a lovely surprise—stealing a march on the others.'

Hugo grinned. 'For a baggage, you do have some good ideas sometimes.'

'Really?' asked Maria Pavlovska.

* * *

For Martin Rotherbridge, the look on Lizzie's face as he walked into the back parlour was easy to read. Total confusion. On Lizzie, it was a particularly attractive attitude and one with which he was thoroughly conversant. With a grin, he went to her and took her hand, kissed it and tucked it into his arm. 'Let's go into the garden. I want to talk to you.'

As talking to Martin in gardens had become something of a habit, Lizzie went with him, curious to know what it was he wished to say and wondering why her heart was leaping about so uncomfortably.

Martin led her down the path that bordered the large main lawn until they reached an archway formed by a rambling rose. This gave access to the rose gardens. Here, they came to a stone bench bathed in softly dappled sunshine. At Martin's nod, Lizzie seated herself with a swish of her muslin skirts. After a moment's consideration, Martin sat beside her. Their view was filled with ancient rosebushes, the spaces beneath crammed with early summer flowers. Bees buzzed sleepily and the occasional dragonfly darted by, on its way from the shrubbery to the pond at the bottom of the main lawn. The sun shone warmly and all was peace and tranquillity.

All through the morning, Lizzie had been fighting the fear that in helping Amanda Crowbridge she had unwittingly earned Martin's disapproval. She had no idea why his approval mattered so much to her, but with the single-mindedness of youth, was only aware that it did. 'Wh. . .what did you wish to tell me?'

Martin schooled his face into stern lines, much as he would when bawling out a young lieutenant for some silly but understandable folly. He took Lizzie's hand in his, his strong fingers moving comfortingly over her slight ones. 'Lizzie, this scheme of yours, m'dear. It really was most unwise.' Martin kept his eyes on her slim fingers. 'I suppose Caroline told you how close-run the thing was. If she hadn't arrived in the nick of time, Max and Hugo would have been off and there would have been no way to catch them. And the devil to pay when they came up with Keighly.'

A stifled sob brought his eyes to her, but she had averted her face. 'Lizzie?' No lieutenant he had ever had to speak to had sobbed. Martin abruptly dropped his stance of stern mentor and gathered Lizzie into his arms. 'Oh, sweetheart. Don't cry. I didn't mean to upset you. Well, yes, I did. Just a bit. You upset me the devil of a lot when I thought you had run off with Keighly.'

Lizzie had muffled her face in his coat but she looked up at that. 'You thought... But whyever did you think such a silly thing?'

Martin flushed slightly. 'Well, yes. I know it was silly. But it was just the way it all came out. At one stage, we weren't sure who had gone in that blasted coach.' He paused for a moment, then continued in more serious vein, 'But really, sweetheart, you mustn't start up these schemes to help people. Not when they involve sailing so close to the wind. You'll set all sorts of people's backs up, if ever they knew.'

Rather better acquainted with Lizzie than his brother was, Martin had no doubt at all whose impulse had started the whole affair. It might have been Arabella who had carried out most of the actions and Sarah who had worked out the details, but it was his own sweet Lizzie who had set the ball rolling.

Lizzie was hanging her head in contrition, her fingers idly playing with his coat buttons. Martin tightened his arms about her until she looked up. 'Lizzie, I want you to promise me that if ever you get any more of these helpful ideas you'll immediately come and tell me about them, before you do anything at all. Promise?'

Lizzie's downcast face cleared and a smile like the sun lit her eyes. 'Oh, yes. That will be safer.' Then, a thought struck her and her face clouded again. 'But, you might not be about. You'll. . .well, now your wound is healed, you'll be getting about more. Meeting lots of l-ladies and. . .things.'

'Things?' said Martin, struggling to keep a straight face. 'What things?'

'Well, you know. The sort of things you do. With l-ladies.' At Martin's hoot of laughter, she set her lips firmly and doggedly went on. 'Besides, you might marry and your wife wouldn't like it if I was hanging on your sleeve.' There, she had said it. Her worst fear had been brought into the light.

But, instead of reassuring her that all would, somehow, be well, Martin was in stitches. She glared at him. When that had no effect, she thumped him hard on his chest.

Gasping for breath, Martin caught her small fists and then a slow grin, very like his brother's, broke across his face as he looked into her delightfully enraged countenance. He waited to see the confusion show in her fine eyes before drawing her hands up, pulling her hard against him and kissing her.

Lizzie had thought he had taught her all about kissing, but this was something quite different. She felt his arms lock like a vice about her waist, not that she had any intention of struggling. And the kiss went on and on. When she finally emerged, flushed, her eyes sparkling, all she could do was gasp and stare at him.

Martin uttered a laugh that was halfway to a groan. 'Oh, Lizzie! Sweet Lizzie. For God's sake, say you'll marry me and put me out of my misery.'

Her eyes grew round. 'Marry you?' The words came out as a squeak.

Martin's grin grew broader. 'Mmm. I thought it might be a good idea.' His eyes dropped from her face to the lace edging that lay over her breasts. 'Aside from ensuring I'll always be there for you to discuss your hare-brained schemes with,' he continued conversationally, 'I could also teach you about all the things I do with l-ladies.'

Lizzie's eyes widened as far as they possibly could.

Martin grinned devilishly. 'Would you like that Lizzie?'

Mutely, Lizzie nodded. Then, quite suddenly, she found her voice. 'Oh, yes!' She flung her arms about Martin's neck and kissed him ferociously. Emerging from her wild embrace, Martin threw back his head and laughed. Lizzie did not, however, confuse this with rejection. She waited patiently for him to recover.

But, 'Lizzie, oh, Lizzie. What a delight you are!' was all Martin Rotherbridge said, before gathering her more firmly into his arms to explore her delights more thoroughly.

A considerable time later, when Martin had called a halt to their mutual exploration on the grounds that there were probably gardeners about, Lizzie sat comfortably in the circle of his arms, blissfully happy, and turned her thought to the future. 'When shall we marry?' she asked.

Martin, adrift in another world, came back to earth and gave the matter due consideration. If he had been asked the same question two hours ago, he would have considered a few months sufficiently soon. Now, having spent those two hours with his Lizzie in unfortunately restrictive surroundings, he rather thought a few days would be too long to wait. But presumably she would want a big wedding, with all the trimmings.

However, when questioned, Lizzie disclaimed all interest in wedding breakfasts and the like. Hesitantly, not sure how he would take the suggestion, she toyed with the pin in his cravat and said, 'Actually, I wondered if it would be possible to be married quite soon. Tomorrow, even?'

Martin stared at her.

'I mean,' Lizzie went on, 'that there's bound to be quite a few weddings in the family—what with Arabella and Sarah.'

'And Caroline,' said Martin.

Lizzie looked her question.

'Max has taken Caroline off somewhere. I don't know where, but I'm quite sure why.'

'Oh.' Their recent occupation in mind, Lizzie could certainly see how he had come to that conclusion. It was on the tip of her tongue to ask for further clarification of the possibilities Caroline might encounter, but her tenacious disposition suggested she settle the question of her own wedding first. 'Yes, well, there you are. With all the fuss and bother, I suspect we'll be at the end of the list.'

Martin looked much struck by her argument.

'But,' Lizzie continued, sitting up as she warmed to her theme, 'if we get married tomorrow, without any of the others knowing, then it'll be done and we shan't have to wait.' In triumph, she turned to Martin.

Finding her eyes fixed on him enquiringly, Martin grinned. 'Sweetheart, you put together a very convincing argument. So let's agree to be married tomorrow. Now that's settled, it seems to me you're in far too composed a state. From what I've learnt, it would be safest for everyone if you were kept in a perpetual state of confusion. So come here, my sweet, and let me confuse you a little.'

Lizzie giggled and, quite happily, gave herself up to delighted confusion.

The clink of crockery woke Caroline. She stretched languorously amid the soft cushions, the sensuous drift of the silken covers over her still tingling skin bringing back clear memories of the past hours. She was alone in the bed. Peering through the concealing silk canopy, she spied Max, tastefully clad in a long silk robe, watching a small dapper servant laying out dishes on the low tables on the other side of the room. The light from the brass lamps suffused the scene with a soft glow. She wondered what the time was.

Lying back in the luxurious cushions, she pondered her state. Her final lesson had been in two parts. The first was concluded fairly soon after Max had joined her in the huge bed; the second, a much more lingering affair, had spun out the hours of the evening. In between, Max had, to her lasting shock, asked her to marry him. She had asked him to repeat his request three times, after which he had refused to do it again, saying she had no choice in the matter anyway as she was hopelessly compromised. He had then turned his attention to compromising her even further. As she had no wish to argue the point, she had meekly gone along with his evident desire to examine her responses to him in even greater depth than he had hitherto, a proceeding which had greatly contributed to their mutual content. She was, she feared, fast becoming addicted to Max's particular expertise; there were, she had discovered, certain benefits attached to going to bed with rakes.

She heard the door shut and Max's tread cross the floor. The silk curtains were drawn back and he stood by the bed. His eyes found her pale body, covered only by the diaphanous silks, and travelled slowly from her legs all the way up until, finally, they reached her face, and he saw she was awake and distinctly amused. He grinned and held out a hand. 'Come and eat. I'm ravenous.'

It was on the tip of Caroline's tongue to ask what his appetite craved, but the look in his eyes suggested that might not be wise if she wished for any dinner. She struggled to sit up and looked wildly around for her clothes. They had disappeared. She looked enquiringly at Max. He merely raised one black brow.

'I draw the line at sitting down to dinner with you clad only in silk gauze,' Caroline stated.

With a laugh, Max reached behind him and lifted a pale blue silk wrap from a chair and handed it to her. She struggled into it and accepted his hand to help her from the depths of the cushioned dais.

The meal was well cooked and delicious. Max contrived to turn eating into a sensual experience of a different sort and Caroline eagerly followed his lead. At the end of the repast, she was lying, relaxed and content, against his chest, surrounded by the inevitable cushions and sipping a glass of very fine chilled wine.

Max, equally content, settled one arm around her comfortably, then turned to a subject they had yet to broach. 'When shall we be married?'

Caroline raised her brows. 'I hadn't really thought that far ahead.'

'Well, I suggest you do, for there are certain cavils to be met.'

'Oh?'

'Yes,' said Max. 'Given that I left my brother, Darcy Hamilton and Hugo Denbigh about to pay their addresses to my three wards, I suspect we had better return to London tomorrow afternoon. Then, if you want a big wedding, I should warn you that the

Rotherbridge family is huge and, as I am its head, will all expect to be invited.'

Caroline was shaking her head. 'Oh, I don't think a big wedding would be at all wise. I mean, it looks as though the Twinning family will have a surfeit of weddings. But,' she paused, 'maybe your family will expect it?'

'I dare say they will, but they're quite used to me doing outrageous things. I should think they'll be happy enough that I'm marrying at all, let alone to someone as suitable as yourself, my love.'

Suddenly, Caroline sat bolt upright. 'Max! I just remembered. What's the time? They'll all be in a flurry because I haven't returned. . .'

But Max drew her back against his chest. 'Hush. It's all taken care of. I left a note for Aunt Augusta. She knows you're with me and will not be returning until tomorrow.'

'But. . .won't she be upset?'

'I should think she'll be dancing a jig.' He grinned as she turned a puzzled face to him. 'Haven't you worked out Aunt Augusta's grand plan yet?' Bemused, Caroline shook her head. 'I suspect she had it in mind that I should marry you from the moment she first met you. That was why she was so insistent that I keep my wards. Initially, I rather think she hoped that by her throwing us forever together I would notice you.' He chuckled. 'Mind you, a man would have to be blind not to notice your charms at first sight, m'dear. By that first night at Almack's, I think she realised she didn't need to do anything further, just give me plenty of opportunity. She knows me rather well, you see, and knew that, despite my reputation, you were in no danger of being offered a *carte blanche* by me.'

'I did wonder why she never warned me about you,' admitted Caroline.

'But to return to the question of our marriage. If you wish to fight shy of a full society occasion, then it still remains to fix the date.'

Caroline bent her mind to the task. Once they returned to London, she would doubtless be caught up in all the plans for her sisters' weddings, and, she supposed, her own would have to come first. But it would all take time. And meanwhile, she would be living in Twyford House, not Delmere House. The idea of returning to sleeping alone in her own bed did not appeal. The end of one slim finger tapping her lower lip, she asked, 'How soon could we be married?'

'Tomorrow, if you wish.' As she turned to stare at him again, Max continued, 'Somewhere about here,' he waved his arm to indicate the room, 'lies a special licence. And our neighbour happens to be a retired bishop, a long-time friend of my late father's, who will be only too thrilled to officiate at my wedding. If you truly wish it, I'll ride over tomorrow morning and we can be married before luncheon, after which we had better get back to London. Does that programme meet with your approval?'

Caroline leant forward and placed her glass on the table. Then she turned to Max, letting her hands slide under the edge of his robe. 'Oh, yes,' she purred. 'Most definitely.'

Max looked down at her, a glint in his eyes. 'You, madam, are proving to be every bit as much a houri as I suspected.'

Caroline smiled, slowly. 'And do you approve, my lord?'

'Most definitely,' drawled Max, as his lips found hers.

* * *

The Duke of Twyford returned to London the next afternoon, accompanied by his Duchess. They went directly to Twyford House, to find the entire household at sixes and sevens. They found Lady Benborough in the back parlour, reclining on the chaise, her wig askew, an expression of smug satisfaction on her face. At sight of them, she abruptly sat up, struggling to control the wig. 'There you are! And about time, too!' Her shrewd blue eyes scanned their faces, noting the inner glow that lit Caroline's features and the contented satisfaction in her nephew's dark face. 'What have you been up to?'

Max grinned wickedly and bent to kiss her cheek. 'Securing my Duchess, as you correctly imagined.'

'You've tied the knot already?' she asked in disbelief.

Caroline nodded. 'It seemed most appropriate. That way, our wedding won't get in the way of the others.'

'Humph!' snorted Augusta, disgruntled at missing the sight of her reprehensible nephew getting leg-shackled. She glared at Max.

His smile broadened. 'Strange, I had thought you would be pleased to see us wed. Particularly considering your odd behaviour. Why, even Caro had begun to wonder why you never warned her about me, despite the lengths to which I went to distract her mind from such concerns.'

Augusta blushed. 'Yes, well,' she began, slightly flustered, then saw the twinkle in Max's eye. 'You know very well I'm *aux anges* to see you married at last, but I would have given my best wig to have seen it!'

Caroline laughed. 'I do assure you we are truly married. But where are the others?'

'And that's another thing!' said Augusta, turning to Max. 'The next time you set about creating a bordello in a household I'm managing, at least have the goodness to warn me beforehand! I came down after my nap to find Arabella in Hugo Denbigh's lap. That was bad enough, but the door to the morning-room was locked. Sarah and Darcy Hamilton *eventually* emerged, but only much later.' She glared at Max but was obviously having difficulty keeping her face straight. 'Worst of all,' she continued in a voice of long suffering, 'Miriam went to look at the roses just before sunset. Martin had apparently chosen the rose garden to further his affair with Lizzie, don't ask me why. It was an hour before Miriam's palpitations had died down enough for her to go to bed. I've packed her off to her sister's to recuperate. Really, Max, you've had enough experience to have foreseen what would happen.'

Both Max and Caroline were convulsed with laughter.

'Oh, dear,' said Caroline when she could speak, 'I wonder what would have happened if she had woken up on the way back from the Richardsons' ball?'

Augusta looked interested but, before she could request further information, the door opened and Sarah entered, followed by Darcy Hamilton. From their faces it was clear that all their troubles were behind them—Sarah looked radiant, Darcy simply looked besotted. The sisters greeted each other affectionately, then Sarah drew back and surveyed the heavy gold ring on Caroline's left hand. 'Married already?'

'We thought to do you the favour of getting our marriage out of the way forthwith,' drawled Max, releasing Darcy's hand. 'So there's no impediment to your own nuptials.'

Darcy and Sarah exchanged an odd look, then burst

out laughing. 'I'm afraid, dear boy,' said Darcy, 'that we've jumped the gun, too.'

Sarah held out her left hand, on which glowed a slim gold band.

While the Duke and Duchess of Twyford and Lord and Lady Darcy exchanged congratulations all around, Lady Benborough looked on in disgust. 'What I want to know,' she said, when she could make herself heard once more, 'is if I'm to be entirely done out of weddings, even after all my efforts to see you all in parson's mouse-trap?'

'Oh, there are still two Twinnings to go, so I wouldn't give up hope,' returned her nephew, smiling down at her with transparent goodwill. 'Apropos of which, has anyone see the other two lately?'

No one had. When applied to, Millwade imparted the information that Lord Denbigh had called for Miss Arabella just before two. They had departed in Lord Denbigh's carriage. Mr Martin had dropped by for Miss Lizzie at closer to three. They had left in a hack.

'A hack?' queried Max.

Millwade merely nodded. Dismissed, he withdrew.

Max was puzzled. 'Where on earth could they have gone?'

As if in answer, voices were heard in the hall. But it was Arabella and Hugo who had returned. Arabella danced in, her curls bouncing, her big eyes alight with happiness. Hugo ambled in in her wake, his grin suggesting that he suspected his good fortune was merely a dream and he would doubtless wake soon enough. Meanwhile, he was perfectly content with the way this particular dream was developing. Arabella flew to embrace Caroline and Sarah, then turned to the company at large and announced, 'Guess what!'

A pregnant silence greeted her words, the Duke

and his Duchess, the Lord and his Lady, all struck dumb by a sneaking suspicion. Almost unwillingly, Max voiced it. 'You're married already?'

Arabella's face fell a little. 'How did you guess?' she demanded.

'No!' moaned Augusta. 'Max, see what happens when you leave town? I won't have it!'

But her words fell on deaf ears. Too blissfully happy themselves to deny their friends the same pleasures, the Duke and his Duchess were fully engaged in wishing the new Lady Denbigh and her Lord all manner of felicitations. And then, of course, there was their own news to hear, and that of the Hamiltons. The next ten minutes were filled with congratulations and good wishes.

Left much to herself, Lady Benborough sat in a corner of the chaise and watched the group with an indulgent eye. Truth to tell, she was not overly concerned with the absence of weddings. At her age, they constituted a definite trial. She smiled at the thought of the stories she would tell of the rapidity with which the three rakes before her had rushed their brides to the altar. Between them, they had nearly forty years of experience in evading parson's mouse-trap, yet, when the right lady had loomed on their horizon, they had found it expedient to wed her with all speed. She wondered whether that fact owed more to their frustrations or their experience.

Having been assured by Arabella that Martin had indeed proposed and been accepted, the Duke and Duchess allowed themselves to be distracted by the question of the immediate housing arrangements. Eventually, it was decided that, in the circumstances, it was perfectly appropriate that Sarah should move to Hamilton House immediately, and Arabella likewise to Denbigh House. Caroline, of course, would henceforth be found at Delmere House. Relieved to find their ex-guardian so accommodating, Sarah and Arabella were about to leave to attend to their necessary packing, when the door to the drawing-room opened.

Martin and Lizzie entered.

It was Max, his sharp eyes taking in the glow in Lizzie's face and the ridiculously proud look stamped across Martin's features, who correctly guessed their secret.

'Don't tell me!' he said, in a voice of long suffering. 'You've got married, too?'

Needless to say, the Twyford House ball four days later was hardly flat. In fact, with four blushing brides, sternly watched over by their four handsome husbands, it was, as Max had prophesied, one of the highlights of the Season.